SLEEPING THE CHURCHYARD SLEEP

RETT MACPHERSON

Word Posse

Dedication
For the real Blanche Lamont.

Acknowledgements
I wish to thank my writer's group: Tom Drennan, Laurell K. Hamilton,
Martha Kneib, Deborah Millitello, Sharon Shinn, and Mark Sumner for all of
their support and friendship over the years. And for Martha, in particular,
who figured out all of the difficult parts of self-publishing this novel. Also,
many thanks to my husband Joe and my children. And although this book was
inspired by events in my mother's real life, it is a work of fiction.

From Word Posse

The Naturalist, Mark Sumner
Sleeping the Churchyard Sleep, Rett MacPherson
Pandora's Mirror, Marella Sands

Visit us at www.wordposse.com

This book has been typeset in Fanwood. Titles and headers are in Alien League. Cover design by Word Posse. Cover image of the Beech Glen Boarding House, Beech Glen, West Virginia, ca. 1910.

ISBN-10: 0990839206
ISBN-13: 978-0-9908392-0-0

The Stranger
August 1958

Never underestimate the power of an old lady to manipulate you like warm taffy. *I* was the cripple. *I* was the girl with the gimpy legs. You'd think I'd be the one doing the manipulating. And yet, every time one of my great aunts approached me with those tender eyes and that flawless old-lady skin that somehow looked creamy and yet tissue paper thin at the same time, she ended up suckering me into doing her bidding. Correction, *their* bidding, because there was a whole horde of great aunts—the Aunties, we called them collectively—and rarely did any of them work alone. They did seem to be an organized lot, with at least two dozen non-related cohorts.

I, Olivia VanBibber, was not safe.

Take for instance, the business with the stranger.

Strangers were not welcome in Appalachia. Oh, we'd be perfectly polite, fatten you up on whatever goodies we had in the cellar and offer to help you in any way we could, but that was because we knew you were moving on. You were not staying. A stranger who came to town and stayed, well, that was a whole different story, because that just never happened.

And Jeb McDowell seemed to be staying.

He'd moved in well over a month ago and had only been seen at Arnie's store for supplies and Mumford's Diner for dinner. He hadn't spoken to anybody other than to place an order, hadn't posed any questions or even so much as asked for directions. He'd bought the old Renshaw place on Sassafras Mountain, a hundred-year-old farmhouse built right into the sloping hill that Henry Renshaw had spent his lifetime trying to farm. A few people had found an excuse to wander up there and noticed that the stranger had rebuilt and painted the front porch. This nearly made the front page news.

I supposed most people would have been all right with him moving in big as you please as if he was from here—because we all knew that only those of us whose ancestors had carved an existence out of this wilderness centuries ago were entitled to be from here—if a reasonable explanation could be deduced.

There were no jobs to be had here. He was not related to anybody who lived here, either, or somebody would have claimed him by now. So that meant he was either an axe murderer or a Communist and Uncle Pete said that between the two, the axe murderer would be the one we'd be more likely to reason with. So that's what the town was hoping for...an axe murderer. The Aunties decided to send me, the cripple, the most unassuming person in the county, up the mountain to see what his business was and to discover his agenda. For my protection, they sent me with my brother Clive and armed with Aunt Mildred's fried chicken and peach cobbler.

So I went.

I went because I, too, wanted to know what this man was doing here.

Clive and I piled into his father's battered and rusted, decade-old Chevy truck and headed down the road to see the stranger. The road forks just as it begins to swell again and you have your choice of climbing two different mountains. The paved road would eventually take you all the way to Charleston, but the gravel road would take you up Sassafras Mountain and to the Renshaw place. At this all-but-forgotten intersection, a hulking weeping willow tree stands guardian of the crossroad. Every time I saw it, I thought of Shakespeare's Ophelia, although there was no river nearby for her to throw herself into. But the long flowing branches reminded me of Ophelia's hair. Oh, the tragedy of a girl who was to live her life for everybody else. In a way it's every woman's story.

The community of Greenhaven had at its center a stereotypical small town that fanned out to many houses on small lots of land to fewer houses on bigger lots of land until you were just plain in the country and who knew what you'd run into. The houses hugged the roads because flat land was scarce and when you did find some, the trains, people and roads all had to share it. Sometimes the byways were so narrow and the mountains so close that you had to suck your breath in to make it around the curve. Mountain A and Mountain B might only have twenty feet separating them.

On Sunday mornings, passersby could hear music ringing from the white clapboard church with its gothic style windows and stone front porch. We sang so loud that it sounded as if we had a thousand parishioners. Every Sunday and every Tuesday and sometimes every Thursday if Brother Dixon was feeling himself a bit "close" to sin, he'd ring the bell and people would come even if it wasn't on the schedule. In Appalachia there was an unwritten law that there had to be a church every three to five miles, lest its inhabitants would all succumb to evil.

And there was the store run by Arnie Pickens, who was my cousin twice or three times removed, not that it mattered when you started getting into the "removeds." He was kin and that was easier.

Aside from that, Greenhaven boasted several creeks, a one-room school house which was now used as Winnie McClung's greenhouse, a forgotten Civil War battlefield, and a generous amount of inhabitants, descendants of the first pioneers, which meant most of us were related in some form or other and some more than others.

As the old truck begrudgingly fought its way up the mountain, we left dust and dirt and rocks in our wake. The old jalopy squeaked and lurched and for a moment, I was worried we were going to start losing parts. I kept watching the side mirror thinking I'd see a tire bounce down the mountain behind us at any moment. There was no point in complaining to Clive, it wasn't his fault. But if Aunt Mildred's fried chicken and cobbler ended up all squashed together, there'd be hell to pay.

Clive, seventeen and a year my junior, was going into his last year of high school. Mousy blond hair greased back into a duck's butt framed his otherwise ordinary face that was home to extraordinarily blue eyes. He wore his hair like his hero, Elvis, but he resembled Jerry Lee Lewis much more, but I would never tell him that. Clive was soft-hearted, had a particularly soft heart for me, and blood or not, he was my only real sibling.

As we climbed higher, we made a corkscrew turn, nearly coming back on ourselves. Within a quarter of a mile, the road rose and dipped and we pulled into the long drive that led to the Renshaw place. An extremely tall, angular, clean-shaven and dark-haired man stood with his feet planted firmly in the gravel, with a shotgun—open at the hilt—resting across his forearm. I wasn't sure who was more wary of us, the stranger or the two bloodhounds that sat at attention to the right and left of his feet.

I glanced at Clive and said, "You're going to have to get my wheelchair out of the back of the truck fast, or he's going to send us packing."

"My thoughts exactly," he said. Both of us just kept smiling at the man, his dogs, and his gun.

Clive opened the truck door and Jeb closed the shotgun and said, "What's your business here, son?" The hounds did not budge.

"Hello there, Mister," Clive said. "We've just come with some neighborly refreshments."

Jeb gave him a wary glance and then his gaze moved over to me. We were just two kids. What harm could we do? Still the shotgun stayed firmly in the crook of his arm, ready to go should we prove to be Bonnie and Clyde.

"What if I don't want any neighborly refreshments?" he asked.

Clive managed to wrestle the wheelchair out of the bed of the truck and pushed it around to my side of the vehicle. Jeb watched him like a hawk, narrowing his eyes. I opened my door and Clive helped me out, putting his hands under my arms and guiding me down into the wheelchair. Then he placed Aunt Mildred's food in my lap.

Clearing his throat, Clive pushed me toward the man and his dogs. I said, "Well, I suppose I'd get my feelings hurt just a bit."

It had been a coordinated effort, me looking as angelic as I could and Clive playing the neighborly country boy. I smiled up at Jeb with my eyes as big and innocent as I could make them. The shotgun lowered to point toward the ground, and, after he made the slightest movement of his left hand, the dogs ran up to the porch and resumed a leisurely posture that I imagined they spent the majority of their day perfecting.

"Oh, well," he said. "I didn't mean to be rude. I'm Jeb McDowell."

Oh, yes he had meant to be rude. He'd meant to be rude and intimidating. And he didn't need to tell me his name. The whole town knew his name because Aunt Runa's husband, who delivered the mail, had already told everybody. "I'm Olivia VanBibber," I said. "And this is my brother Clive Morrison."

The stranger seemed to be at a loss for words. Girls in wheelchairs do that to people. "Well, I uh..."

"We brought you some fried chicken and peach cobbler," I said.

"You don't say?"

I held the goodies up toward him. "Best in three counties."

"Well, won't you all come in the house?" he asked.

That was, of course, exactly what I had wanted, but looking at the condition of the home, I nearly changed my mind.

The house was a two-story farmhouse that was built right into the side of the mountain. If you looked at it at just the right angle, it seemed as though the steep slopes and the tin roof were just an extension of each other. Legend is that Old Henry Renshaw had one leg shorter than the other, the result of a lifetime of trying to plow his farm on such a steep countryside. I can't say as to whether or not that's the reason, but he had walked with a limp for the nine years or so that I'd known him. The condition of the house—or the incline of the land that seemed to defy the very laws of physics—didn't seem to bother Jeb McDowell one bit. Slats were missing and strewn across the lawn, and the brand new porch seemed crooked, but I soon realized that it was the house that was leaning. The sparkling white porch was actually straight. The rest of the paint on the sad building curled up and away from the wood as if even it didn't want to be anywhere near the house and was about to take flight into the hills.

Before I could answer yes or no, Clive had turned my wheelchair around, leaned me back onto the big rear wheels, and pulled me up each step until we were on the porch.

"The place is kind of a mess," Jeb said, with a very worried look on his face. There he was, caught halfway between being neighborly and just realizing that his house was in no condition for company. I sort of felt sorry for him, so I gave him an out.

"Well, it's such a hot and sticky day, why don't we just sit out here on the porch and catch the breeze?" He nodded and I handed him the food. An awkward silence stretched out in front of us as he and Clive pulled up chairs and sat down without either one knowing what to do or say next.

"So, Mr. McDowell," I began.

"Call me Jeb," he said. He kept glancing at my legs, which was not unusual. They were covered of course by the jeans I wore, but obviously he knew they didn't work.

It was at this point that I got a chance to really study him. If I had not already known that he wasn't from around here, his appearance would have confirmed it in a second. He wore black jeans, ankle boots and a black and white striped pullover shirt. The stripes had to be at least two inches wide. I estimated his age to be about thirty, although I was never good at guessing that sort of thing. His hair was dark, as were his lashes and brows, and his eyes were a vivid green that seemed to have their own source of light. His cheeks had a healthy glow as though somebody had just slapped him on both sides of his face. He was thin, but not undernourished. In general, he had the air of somebody who was healthy, well fed, well-educated and much more up on the fashion of the day than anybody in Greenhaven. Ankle boots? Only in Charleston had I seen ankle boots. He was a fish out of water all right. Even his dialect was not Appalachian. At least not West Virginian, anyway. "This chicken sure does smell good," he said. "I haven't eaten all day."

"Feel free to eat. We've had our share."

"Do you mind, terribly?" he asked, blushing. "It's just that it smells so good."

"Not at all," I said and smiled.

Jeb leaned the gun up against the house, resting it on the door frame. When he pulled the towel back, revealing the golden fried chicken—a whole chicken, I might add—one of the hounds raised his head and sniffed. "Lordy, there's a lot of chicken in here."

I waved a dismissive hand. Aunt Mildred had gone overboard. It was as if she thought I'd get information by the pound. Jeb tore into a leg and after the second bite, his eyes rolled around inside their sockets. Nodding he said, "You weren't kiddin', were ya? That's some mighty fine chicken."

"Thank you," I said, smiling and clearing my throat. "You live here all alone?"

He nodded and smacked his lips.

"It can get awfully lonely up here on these mountains. You should come down to the square dances and come to the church for box-social. There are all kinds of good food at those events," I said. "You know, since you don't have a wife or anybody to cook for you. No daughters?"

He stopped chewing then and examined me. "What happened to your legs?" he asked.

Clive immediately bristled at that question. He was fiercely protective and couldn't stand it when people even noticed my legs. He got much more upset than I did. Not only was I used to it, but I understood people's curious nature. And after seeing some of the children that I had shared a hospital with, I knew that my restrictions were mild by comparison, and so I didn't get my bowels in a kink over people's invasive and sometimes rude questions. I could still use my hands. I could feed myself, brush my own hair. I could breathe on my own without the help of an iron lung, and most importantly, I could handle my own hygiene issues. "Polio," I answered.

He nodded as if he'd expected as much. "When?"

"October of fifty-three."

He shook his head. "That's a shame."

Another silence wormed its way into our visit.

"So did you get a fair price for the house?" I asked.

"Fair enough."

So he wasn't an heir of Henry Renshaw's.

"You in school?" he asked.

"Finished," I said. "Clive here will be starting his last year come September."

"Is this your only brother?"

"Unfortunately no. I have an older sister and an older brother. I try not to claim them," I said. "And you? Any siblings?"

"Three sisters and two brothers. I claim all of them." He ate more chicken. I glanced at the gun.

After a moment he said, "Sorry about the gun." Then he added, almost as if he'd just realized it. "You've got panthers on these mountains."

"And some bears, on occasion," Clive added.

"Yes, but bears and panthers hardly drive pick-up trucks," I said, trying to bat my eyelashes without actually doing so.

He smiled at me and it was not an unpleasant event. His eyes seemed to pick up all the light reflecting off the mountain and turned a purer shade of green. He shrugged. "Heard some prowlers out a few nights in a row. You know, squatters and hobos get used to a place being vacant, get surprised when it's suddenly occupied. Just trying to be prepared."

Jeb looked at his hands with some unease. "I've got grease all over my fingers. Why don't you all come in while I wash up?" He stood then and held the door for me with his pinky. Apparently, we had passed some sort of test and he felt comfortable enough to let us see his house, no matter what shape it was in. Either that or this was the point that he'd murder us.

I wheeled myself through the door and was immediately taken by the fact that it was in much worse condition than I had imagined. Maneuvering by boxes piled in haphazard fashion all over the living room floor, I passed dirty socks and a few soiled shirts. Loose-leaf paper was tossed about as though somebody had turned a fan on just for fun. A plate of half-eaten...*stuff,* made my skin crawl because it was no longer recognizable. Animal, mineral, vegetable? Apparently, it was so far gone that not even the dogs had bothered to finish it. Two chairs and a table with a typewriter on it looked right at home with the stack of books on the coffee table, the mound of books on the floor, another stack on one of the chairs, and a pile on the kitchen counter. My breath nearly caught in my throat. I had died and gone to heaven. Once I saw the books, the unidentifiable half-eaten stuff no longer mattered.

The kitchen, which I could see from my position in the living room, had no table, only one chair. It was not lost on me that he had no refrigerator but had a typewriter, no curtains, but had three bottles of unopened whiskey next to the stack of books on the kitchen counter. I'd bet my last dollar that he slept on the floor.

"Oh, uh..." I said, at a loss for words. It was at times like these, that I was happy I had my own chair. What could I say? I could not possibly, with a straight face, say what a nice place he had. So, I zeroed in on the obvious and made it a compliment. "You have so many books!"

"Yes," he said. He wiped his hands on a towel. "I don't have any indoor plumbing yet. That's next on my list of things to do. Have a...a...seat."

Clive sat precariously on two boxes next to me. Jeb took the only open chair.

"So...you read a lot?" I asked. That was a stupid question, but it was all I could think of.

"All the time. What about you?"

"I absolutely love to read. I mean, I'm sort of limited to what I can do..."

"Olivia is really smart," Clive said. "She's like a genius. And she's an excellent shot!"

Jeb smiled at Clive, and his smile had just as much effect indoors as it did out. "What type of shooting do you do?"

"Archery. It was one of the recreations at the hospital."

"So, what about college?" he asked.

That statement sort of sealed the deal on him being foreign born. Nobody ever suggested a woman go to college. The word *college* was damn near on the list of offensive language. If a girl went away to college, it was against her family's wishes and with the threat of excommunication over her head. "Well, I have no way to go."

"How'd you get to high school?"

"Clive drove me."

"Did your school have steps?"

I nodded.

"Then how'd you get to your classrooms and such?"

"I have a friend, Louis McCutcheon."

"Big fella," Clive chimed in.

"Lou carried me to my classes. That way I could finish."

"That was nice of him. So what do you read?" he asked.

"Everything."

He smiled at me then, cocked his head to one side and a lone lock of dark hair fell across his forehead. He *whished* it back out of his face with one obviously habitual swipe of his left hand.

I glanced at the typewriter. "Are you a writer?"

"Yes, although not hugely successful. But writing is what makes you a writer. Selling is what makes you a good businessman. So, I do way more writing than selling," he said, with no trace of bitterness whatsoever. And the way he proclaimed it was so casual! A *real* writer?

"Olivia just finished reading *The Postman Always Rings Twice*," Clive said.

"Did you like it?" Jeb asked.

I shrugged. "It was predictable."

"How did it end?" Clive asked.

"He went to prison for the murder he didn't commit instead of the murder he did. Personally, I think any time a woman asks you to kill somebody, you should quietly walk away," I said. Jeb laughed. "And there wasn't a postman anywhere in the book. I even read it twice to make sure I didn't miss him."

"Well, that's dumb," Clive said.

"Were you born and raised here?" Jeb asked.

"Mostly," I said. But I was much more interested in what a writer was doing here in Greenhaven! "Except the few years I was in Morris Memorial Hospital in Milton."

"So all your family is from here?" he asked.

"Yes. My ancestors were the first whites here."

He inclined his head and watched me, as if sizing me up. I really wasn't all that interesting so I had no idea why he kept questioning me.

"You mentioned that your ancestors were the first whites. I've noticed that most Americans forget that there were native peoples here first. But not you."

"Most people like to forget."

"But not you," he repeated.

"I have no reason to rewrite history because I didn't participate in the genocide and demoralization of those people. I know what my ancestors did. I'm ashamed of it, but I wasn't alive then. Most of my ancestors were Scots-Irish. They were a displaced people themselves, so they thought nothing of displacing others. To them that was the way it was done. You had one culture who didn't believe in owning the land and another who thought you can own everything down to the blades of grass. Surely nobody thought that encounter was going to go well."

Jeb stared, open mouthed. And he stared at me for a very long time. In fact, Clive was starting to shift nervously on his box. I had to look away, finally, worried that I'd offended him in some way. He was probably thinking I shouldn't worry my pretty little head about such things, which I had been told before.

Finally, he said, "VanBibber is not Scots-Irish."

"No, they're Dutch."

"You don't look Dutch. You look..."

"Like what, exactly?" I said, raising my chin just a notch.

"You look like a gypsy."

"You take that back!" Clive said, nearly jumping off the box. I laid a hand on his arm. To most, being called a gypsy wasn't exactly a compliment. But it didn't bother me any. Besides, I didn't think Jeb meant it as an insult. And really, an insult is only an insult if the intent is so. Otherwise, it's just a harmless comment.

"It's possible one snuck in the woodpile somewhere. There used to be a gypsy camp about ten miles from here. They were there...gosh, up until about 1940. Most of my family has these dark eyes; we're not sure which branch of the family they came from."

Jeb just smiled at me and it made me uncomfortable. "You know a lot about your forefathers."

"In Appalachia most people know a thing or two about where they come from. It becomes part of your oral tradition. We wear all of those scalping and killings and Civil War battles on our sleeves as some sort of club membership. Aside from that, my great Aunt Stella fancies herself a historian. I do a lot of listening."

He was quiet a moment and I took my opportunity. "So what about you, Mr. McDowell? Where did you grow up?"

"Baltimore."

"So what brings you here?" It was a simple enough question. The question that the posse of Aunties had sent me here to ask and yet I'd seemed to have so much trouble getting around to.

He paused, for dramatic effect or to conjure up a memory, I couldn't be sure. He glanced out his window, back at his hands and finally he shocked me with a quote from a book. *"We had finally found the magic land at the end of the road and we never dreamed the extent of the magic."*

"You're quoting Kerouac?" I asked, wondering if it was going to be this difficult to get a straight answer from him all the time.

"You've read Kerouac?" he countered. He was clearly astonished. Surprised that a girl my age stuck in a holler in the middle of nowhere would have read Kerouac. It was understandable.

Clive leaned forward and said, "Is that the book you read out loud to me? The one about the guy who just goes from one place to another?" Clive did not like to read very much, so I often read to him. When I'd first taken ill with polio, of course, the first three weeks I barely even remembered. It was a blur of pain and thirst and sadness, but once the fever had subsided—leaving me only a few tufts of hair, but thankfully, it had all grown back within a year— one of the orderlies had brought in boxes upon boxes of comic books for us to read. I read all of those in a matter of days, and so he began bringing in pulp novels. I read those between therapy and treatments and swimming and drag racing down the halls with the other wheelchair-bound children. Then the head nurse, Roberta, had brought me a worn and much loved copy of *Sense and Sensibility* and my whole world changed.

"Yes," I said to Clive. "Same book."

Jeb finally said, "The truth is I came here to write. This is the magic land, Olivia. Away from everybody and everything. The end of the road. I want no interruptions."

"While you write your masterpiece?" I asked.

"Possibly."

"Does anybody know you're here?"

"Only a few business associates."

"How long do you plan to stay?" I asked.

"As long as I want. Because I can," he said.

"Oh, well..." I said. Apparently, there was one person in all of America who decided to move to central West Virginia for the fun of it. I wasn't sure how the Aunties would take it. No communist spy running from the FBI. No axe-murderer who craved blood. Just some guy wanting to disappear and write a masterpiece. "Well, it was certainly nice to meet you, Mr. McDowell."

"Jeb."

"Right, Jeb," I said. "Clive and I must get going. Don't forget about the dances and box socials. I know you want to be undisturbed, but a man has to eat and have some fun."

He walked us out and he told us to return any time we wanted and I believed him. We made it down the porch and into the truck, the whole time Jeb stared, watching Clive and me move. We had just turned the truck around to head down the mountain when, in the side mirror, I saw Jeb run into his house and then back out the door—the screen door *thawacking* as he did—and take the porch steps two at a time. "Wait!" he called out.

Clive stopped the truck abruptly, spewing rocks and dust into the trees that lined the road. "Here," Jeb said. Breathing heavily, he handed me a book.

That lock of hair had fallen astray again. "You might like this. Just bring it back when you're finished and I'll give you another one."

Glancing down, I read the title out loud. *"You Can't Go Home Again.* Thomas Wolfe."

"Have you read it?" he asked.

"No, I haven't," I managed to say. I was stupefied at his thoughtfulness.

"Good," was all he said.

I have read about fateful meetings. In a town where a person was born, raised, lived and died with the same cast of characters, it was nearly impossible to have an encounter with a stranger that would change your life. But I felt as though that had just happened to me. Roberta the head nurse had changed my life by placing *Sense and Sensibility* into my hands. An act so mundane had turned me into a voracious reader. She couldn't possibly have known. Or maybe she had. That's the beauty of it. And in the way of these things, I'd have to wait and see how this encounter would unfold in the days to come. I felt change coming.

Aunt Dotie, at least, would be happy to know that Jeb was not an axe-murderer or a communist, and I had decided that I wasn't all that upset about being manipulated by the posse this time. A writer! On Sassafras Mountain! That in and of itself was fascinating. My mind was already racing with all the questions I would ask him.

I waved at Jeb as the truck lurched forward, and Clive and I descended down the hill at full speed. My brother knew how much I loved to go fast. And he always did what he could to make me happy.

Deputy Gunnar Ryan
Colton County Sheriff's Department

Long before North America was occupied by humans, the mountains were here. They used to be tall, piercing mountains like the Alps and the Rockies, but time had eroded them away, until now all that was left were low, gentle ridges, covered in extensive, thick forests. They ran nearly in an unbroken line of heave and ho, almost the length of the eastern seaboard for fifteen hundred miles, a crested wave and a rushing descent of green-covered rock to the subterranean floor. The mountains had been there when Gunnar was born, and they had been there for every major—and minor—event of every human being's life who had resided within the self-enclosed communities of what is known as Appalachia. They had witnessed it all.

Even older, and this Gunnar found curious, was the New River. It snaked its way through the mountains until it dumped into the New River Gorge, and from there into the Kanawha River and from there into the Ohio and into the Mississippi and down through the delta. To think it was actually older than the mountains. It seemed as though nothing could be older than the mountains, and Gunnar, when he took time to think about it, was glad that he'd be long dead when those comforting hills eventually wore down to nothing. No ridges, no peaks, no valleys? The thought was more depressing than death itself.

Gunnar had been born on a farm just outside of Greenhaven, West Virginia, where the Cumberland Mountains met the Alleghany Mountains, just south of the Allegheny Plateau. That could be confusing to school kids, how one mountain range, the Appalachians, could have smaller ranges within it. When his grandpa used to take him into the woods hunting, they'd climb the tallest peak in the area and his Grandpa Ryan would say, "Right there, do you see it?"

And Gunnar would pretend that he didn't see it, so that his Grandpa would tell him. "Show me again," he'd say. And his Grandpa would lean down and run his finger through the air at an angle that Gunnar could follow.

"Right there, that dark line that cuts across that ridge. That's where the volcano erupted years ago."

"How many years ago?" Gunnar would ask.

"So many years ago that they ain't got no numbers that count that high."

"That's alotta years," Gunnar would say.

"Look at all that rock on top of it."

Gunnar would look and smile and be dutifully impressed and wonder at the vastness of time. And wonder how his grandpa knew this information, since he wasn't an educated man. Gunnar didn't want to ask his grandpa how he had come by this information because he didn't want him to think that he thought he was an uneducated man. So, Gunnar chalked it up, without honestly knowing, to his grandpa being friends with some of the Cherokees, because everybody knew that the Cherokees knew everything about the land.

That thin dark line of ash had fascinated Grandpa Ryan. And even though Gunnar had gone away to a big city college and had gotten his degree in anthropology with a minor in geology, when he'd returned to West Virginia, one of the first things he'd done was hike up this mountain and find the horizon of ash deep within the rock and stare at it as though he didn't understand how all of it worked. He preferred at that moment to be eight years old again, hanging on his grandfather's every word, discovering something he'd never known before, because once you'd learned it, you couldn't unlearn it and there was something almost spiritual about learning something for the first time.

And to this mountain, gazing out at that ridge, was still where he went when he needed to get away from the world, which seemed like a lot and not enough all at the same time. Like today, he'd traversed the steep incline, lunch in tow, needing to steal a few hours before he had to start his shift as deputy of Colton County. He had the evening shift this week, so his mornings were free. And that was fine with him. The mountains were the most majestic in the morning anyway.

His mother had made him a cheese sandwich and sent a peach and some zucchini bread along with it. He finished off the peach and the zucchini bread within minutes, but paused a moment to take in the scene of various shades of green that lay before him. Green was his favorite color. It was nature's neutral. Everything looked good with green and it was soothing and cool and represented life without shame. It looked particularly beautiful draped on the flowing hills below him and it played well with the early morning sunlight.

A chipmunk scurried in front of him and he decided to share his lunch. He tore off the crust and threw it in the direction the chipmunk had disappeared. He never liked the crust anyway, and what his mother didn't know wouldn't hurt her. He thought about the other secret that Grandpa Ryan had shared with him years ago. It was something that lent credence to his grandpa's educators being the natives. It was something Gunnar had never told or showed another living human. And as far as he could tell, nobody else knew about it, because Gunnar had never come across any mention of it in any history book or any anthropological studies in print. It was quite possible that even the native peoples had forgotten it was here.

He didn't have time to go by and see it today, but he would later this week. And sooner or later he would have to report it to somebody. Vandals were jack-asses who were always looking for something to destroy and it would only be a matter of time before they found it. But he wouldn't share it today. Not tomorrow either, probably not even this year. He'd report it someday soon. But he wanted to hold onto it for just a little bit longer before the whole world devoured it.

The chipmunk stuck its nose out from the undergrowth and sniffed tentatively at the crust. Before he could eat it, though, a blue jay swooped down out of the tree and snatched it. Gunnar laughed and said to the chipmunk. "You're too slow."

The chipmunk looked insulted, rubbed its face with its paw and scampered back into the forest.

Gunnar headed down the mountain and toward town to clock in and see what sort of trouble the good townsfolk of Wellston, Greenhaven and the rest of Colton County had gotten into while he was sleeping.

When he arrived at his office, Etta, the secretary, cornered him at the front door.

"There's a disturbance on Snake Bottom," she said. Her mousy brown hair was pulled so tight up into a bun that it made her eyelids all squinty.

Gunnar rolled his eyes because he'd already been out to Snake Bottom twice in the last three weeks and he didn't think showing up in his squad car with his pistol was going to change lifelong bad habits any time soon. He'd only been a deputy for Colton County a little over a year, and so far most of the locals didn't put too much stock into anything he said or requested of them. Most of them thought that he was now "above his raising" and no longer considered him one of them. Even though he'd spent his entire life, except his college years, right here in this same valley as everybody else. It was the strangest thing. He'd left Gunnar Ryan, or "Tadpole Ryan," and returned to an unspoken demotion. He was now an outsider. Untrustworthy. And if he was above his raising, what did that say about what they thought of themselves?

Not that any of it bothered him, too much, but he got tired of driving out to domestic disturbances and being shooed away like a mosquito. It wasn't like he was some yahoo who just happened to put a badge on a brown shirt. He was a bon-a-fide deputy and an educated man. Maybe his neighbors could tell that he was just biding his time until he could leave. He was on target to go back to school and work in his field of study, right about the same time his father sobered up and the messiah returned. In other words, not any time soon. But that was the plan, and everybody knew it.

"McKees called in a disturbance at the Cabbels' house," Etta said, as Gunnar found his time card and punched in.

"All right, I'm going," he said.

He pulled his squad car onto Bradford Street and drove it out of town. A few minutes later and a few miles of winding roads, he came to Greenhaven and Goosefoot Mountain. Passing Arnie's store and Pete's curve he passed two cars going way too fast, but he couldn't do anything about that right now. He had to get to the Cabbel's house. Just after Pete's curve the road bowed out and dragged bottom land for about a mile. Glancing over at the collection of tiny homes that belonged to various members of the Graham family, he thought of Olivia VanBibber. The girl had been stricken with polio years ago and she lived in the yellow-gold colored house that sat on stilts just where the road began to climb and turned to meet Sassafras Mountain. Even though Olivia was about eight years younger than he was, they had led similar lives as children. Hers just ended differently. His little sister Betty Jo was a friend of Olivia's and Gunnar liked that. He wasn't sure why. Maybe it was because Betty Jo's sunny disposition could bring sunlight to anybody's life, but also, he thought Olivia's pragmatic point of view was good for Betty Jo, who could be a big daydreamer. Daydreaming for young girls in this county, for the most part, would only lead to heartbreak.

Passing Sassafras Mountain, he made a mental note to go and meet the newcomer, Jeb McDowell. His arrival was a bit odd, considering there were virtually no jobs to be had in this part of the world, and it had set people to worrying. Gunnar just wanted to introduce himself and see if he got the feeling the stranger was up to no good. After the war, the mining dwindled because there were new gadgets to extract the coal from the hills. Not as many miners were needed to do the job. There were still those who had mining jobs, and coal trucks still rumbled up and down the roads, but those jobs were far fewer now. The landscape of West Virginia was now dotted with old abandoned mines, the tipples swooping down off rolling green hillsides like roller coasters, and coal towns with one identical building lined up after another. Not much imagination went into those towns, but then that wasn't important. What was important was for the government to squeeze as much out of this land as it could, be it coal or lumber, and the inhabitants be damned.

A few minutes later he came to Snake Bottom and made a left, passing by the Copper River, with its seven foot waterfalls and rapids causing frothy white foam to form on the surface. His stomach grumbled a little even though he'd just eaten. That wasn't unusual, he usually ate every two to three hours, and what his mother had packed him had really only been a snack. For a moment he considered what he would eat once he left the Cabbel place. Maybe he'd go to Mumford's and get some pie.

An old grist mill stood about two miles up the river from where he was. The McKee family lived there, and the mill had been the center of a land dispute well over a hundred years ago. Today, there was still a land dispute but it wasn't about the grist mill, and the players were all different, although still within the same family. There always seemed to be a feud among families, no matter who they were or where they lived. Being a deputy even for a short time had proven to him that human beings loved drama and couldn't stand to be happy. The McKees were a perfect example of that. But they weren't his problem today.

Without having any prior knowledge of today's events, he would bet his fossil collection that he was being summoned to old Noah Cabbel's house because he got drunk and tried to shoot his son-in-law. And Gunnar didn't make that bet lightly, because he had a great fossil collection. He had several ammonites, one was as big as his hand; an allosaur claw, a mosasaur tooth, trilobites, and about a hundred rocks with imprints of various plants and sea life. He wouldn't bet his collection unless he knew for sure. And besides, it was time for such an event. Every time Noah Cabbel made moonshine, he sampled it—all day—and then tried to shoot his son-in-law, although he always denied trying to actually kill him. "I'm just tryin' to teach him a lesson or two," he'd say. It was lost on Gunnar how shooting a man would teach him a lesson, but there were times he'd like to try it out on a few people. In a non-lethal sort of way, of course.

At any rate, Sheriff Boland had started writing down on a calendar the cycle in which Noah Cabbel made his moonshine. Not only did Noah try to shoot his son-in-law every time a batch got finished, but in the week following, drunk and disorderly conduct went up throughout the county. One would think, why not simply stop Noah from making his moonshine? To be blunt, the sheriff would sooner arrest a kindergartener for picking his nose. Noah Cabbel pretty much had no other income. And Sheriff Boland would not take that from him.

It was a warm day, humid as hell, and right on noon so the sun was directly overhead, casting harsh shadows on the dirt road as he travelled back into the hollow to Noah Cabbel's house. Gunnar's stomach gave another growl and he pondered, momentarily, of the possibility that he could have a case of the worms since he was always hungry. He dismissed the thought, though, as soon as he thought about the pie he would have at Mumford's. Rhubarb or peach?

Outside the windows of his squad car, framing his drive, were hills that nearly went straight up, eventually degrading into a clearing where Noah Cabbel lived in a sturdy but ancient building that was a hundred and twenty years old if it was a day.

Old Noah's property held some of the last of the old growth virgin forests there were in the county, and Gunnar trampled all over it during hunting season or when he went fishing. There were no logging roads, skidder trails or cut stumps in the acreage that belonged to Noah. There were only ancient trees, stretching toward the sky, each one vying for its share of the sunlight, and snags—the standing dead trees so essential to forest life. He knew for a fact that there was one scarlet oak up on the hill behind the Cabbel house that was two-hundred and twenty-five inches in circumference and one-hundred and thirty feet tall. Most of the land had been raped long ago, which made him sick to his stomach. Sometimes, he walked through the forest for no other reason than to hear it breathe.

As he pulled his car into the dirt driveway, chickens scattered in every direction. Noah's house was small and perfectly square, having been reinforced just in the past ten years so that it didn't resemble the lean-to shacks that dotted the landscape back up on top of some of the mountains. The white paint job was thin, exposing boards beneath, but not unkempt. Immediately, Lorna Cabbel, Noah's wife, came running out onto the porch.

"Now, Gunnar, you just go a gettin' back in that car of yours and head on back to town. We don't need you here." Lorna, a woman of about sixty years, was top heavy and her wispy fly-away white hair framed her perfectly round face like some sort of halo, although a saint she was not. She wore a big white apron over top of her blue cotton dress and traces of lye could be smelled on the air. It must be wash day.

"Lorna, where's Noah?"

"Ain't here," she said, raising her chin a notch and causing the sagging skin to jostle like a wattle.

Gunnar was about ready to tell her that he really didn't have the patience for her to be wasting his time today, when he heard a gunshot originating from somewhere behind the house. Instinctively, his right hand went to his pistol, his left hand raised up as if to tell her not to move. "Now, Lorna, I know he's here someplace on this property. May as well tell me before somebody gets hurt."

"Nobody's gonna get hurt unless *you* shoot them. He's just a drunken ol' fool, but he ain't no killer. And besides, there ain't nobody here but me and him."

"Lorna, am I going to have to arrest you for interfering with my job? Because I will."

Both hands landed on her hips. "You just go ahead and arrest me, Gunnar Sinclair Ryan, and I'll have your momma on the phone...just as soon as I get to one."

The Cabbels didn't have a phone, which wasn't all that uncommon. Most of the people out in the hollers and the hills didn't have phones. The McKees did. And they were the ones who had called this in, so apparently there had been more than just a few gunshots. Gunnar imagined seeing Noah's son-in-law, Andrew, running across the field with Noah chasing him and shooting at his feet. Yeah, it had been most likely an event like that to cause the McKees to phone the sheriff.

"Lorna, I don't care who you call, you tell me where Noah is right now this minute."

Her shoulders slumped, obviously defeated since the only leverage she'd had—his mother—had failed to intimidate him. Jerking her thumb over her shoulder, she said, "Out by the smokehouse."

"How many guns does he have?"

"He just got the one out there right now, I hid the others. But no tellin' how many bullets he got in his pockets, damn fool."

"Now, get back in the house, so you don't get shot."

"He's not gonna shoot me, Gunnar. What you think just 'cause he's drunk he done forgot who his wife is?" she said. But she opened the front door all the same and entered the house.

Gunnar made his way around the building, gun drawn and expecting the worst, only to find Noah lying on his back in a wheel barrow with his .22 rifle pointed toward the sky, and his feet dangling over the edge. He was shoeless and shirtless and wore only his grease-covered overalls. A bird flew in front of him and he shot at it and missed. He shot the corner off of the smoke house. Then he shot the birdhouse next, which sent what few birds that hadn't already scattered fluttering out of the little entrance holes all in a panic. Gunnar couldn't be sure if either the smokehouse or the birdhouse had been hit on purpose, but he'd seen enough.

Before he could say or do anything, Noah shot a hole clean through Gunnar's hat.

"Whoa, now you just hold it right there, Noah. Put down that gun," he said, raising his higher and cocking the hammer.

"I ain't puttin' down shit," Noah said. "You come take it outta my hands, you pansy city boy."

Gunnar let the insult go. It wasn't the first time he'd been referred to as "the city boy" even though his birth certificate said Greenhaven, Colton County, right on it in plain English, and he could hunt, fish and survive in the wilderness probably better than most. Yes, he let the insult go, but his heart was still hammering from the near miss of the rifle and it made him uneasy. "Now, Noah, I don't have any beef with you, but as a lawman, I have to ask you to stop brandishing that weapon when you're drunk. You damn near shot me."

Noah squinted his eyes at Gunnar and said, "I missed? I was aiming for yer head."

"Of course you missed, how else would I be talking to you?" Gunnar said.

"Oh." He laid his head back and stared up at the sky. "Hey, you ever wonder why you can't shoot the clouds? I mean, they're right there. You oughta be able to shoot 'em."

"Bullet won't travel that far up." Gunnar took a step closer.

"How far up you think it is? Can't be too much farther than the moon. If I got in the tree, you think I could hit a cloud?"

Gunnar snuck another step toward him.

"Maybe," Gunnar said. "But then you'd probably fall out of the tree."

"Ain't that the truth of it," Noah said, giggling and then immediately dissolved into a coughing fit. "Hooo, doggy."

Gunnar was about six feet from him now. Noah looked like he hadn't slept in weeks. His eyes were puffy, beard scruffy. And then the wind blew from behind him and Gunnar got a real good whiff of moonshine and sweat. Maybe even urine, it was difficult to tell when it was all mixed in together like that. "Noah, I need you to put that gun down for me, all right?"

"I am so sick of people telling me what I have to do. Next person tells me what I gotta do I'm gonna stick my fist right up their—"

"I never said you *had* to put it down, I said I *need* you to put it down. Does that sound like the same thing? Come on Noah. Let's do this civil like, all right?"

"Civil like?" he asked. Raising his head, he tried to stare Gunnar down, but he was too drunk. His gaze kept skittering all about. "Tell that to that no account husband of my ex-daughter."

"Noah..."

"I try, Gunnar. I really do. I give them feed for their chickens when they's low, and I give them all our table scraps, but it still ain't enough. I mean, I give them those scraps so much, that Lorna and I ain't had no leftovers in a year! Then Andrew, well, he just goes hanging with that no-good colored fella, stealin' and takin' what's not theirs. Well, I just can't abide by that, Gunnar. No, I can't. And what do you law folk do about it? Not a damn thing, far as I can tell. It's one thing to make a living at a dishonest act, because at least you're doin' somethin'. You're tryin', ya know? You're workin', just maybe not at anything honest. But thievin' from others...why that's just not even workin' at all. I need you to arrest him, Gunnar. That's what I need. Go on and arrest him and leave me the hell alone!"

"I have to have proof that there's been some wrong done," Gunnar stated.

"Proof! Oh, Gunnar," Noah said with a whimper. Then fast as quicksilver he was angry again. "He done got my baby girl in the family way. She's gonna have his baby! A baby! Can't feed himself, how he gonna feed a baby? And what kind a kin is that to have anyway? That poor baby gonna grow up knowin' his daddy's a good for nothin'. That scars them boys, yes it does. Girls, they forgive daddy, boys no. No, you gotta stop him. He needs to be put away somewheres that he can't cause no more babies!" With that he tried to jump up and lunge for Gunnar, but he lost his balance and the wheel barrow tipped over with him in it and just as he hit the ground the gun went off and shot a hole clean through the top of his foot and out the bottom.

"Oh, Jesus, shit! I been shot, Gunnar. *I done been shot!*" he screamed from under the wheel barrow.

Gunnar slid Noah's shotgun away from him and then kicked it over a couple of feet. Then he holstered his gun and threw the wheel barrow off of Noah in damn near one fluid motion. Lorna came running out of the house and jumped over the two steps on the back porch without even hesitating. "Good Lord, good Lord, what happened?"

"He shot himself in the foot," Gunnar said.

She started wailing and crying and making all sorts of sounds and noises that represented praying of some sort. Gunnar let it go for a few minutes to let the reality of the situation set in—yes, Noah had been shot, but he wasn't going to die—and let the shock wear off.

"Lorna, get some clean rags, an old pillow you don't need, and a bottle of whatever he's been drinking."

She glanced up at the deputy with a tear-stained face, all the while Noah was screaming his head off and cussing a mile a minute. "Go on!" he said. "I've got to drive him to the hospital and that's at least an hour and a half away if I speed."

Lorna just stood there, stricken with fear and not quite believing what she was seeing. Finally, Gunnar grabbed her around the waist with both hands, not an easy task since she was a fairly large woman, and dragged her up on the porch, opened the back door, slapped her on the shoulder and said, "Go to it, before he bleeds to death, woman!"

Finally, she came out of her hysterics and ran into the house to do as he said. Gunnar managed to get Noah up on one foot, then turned the wheel barrow over and shoved him into it. Sighing, Gunnar pushed Noah and his wounded foot all the way back to the squad car and dumped him by the tire, thanking nobody in particular that the only gun Noah had access to was an old tin can plinker. If he'd been wielding a shotgun, he wouldn't have any foot left! Opening the car door for him, Gunnar said, "Now sit there on the side of the seat. And don't touch anything."

Noah sat sideways toward the deputy. Gunnar stared at the hole in his foot and the trail of blood leading back toward the house. Scratching his head, he wondered just how this had happened. Definitely not what he'd expected when he left his office a short while ago and he was certainly glad he hadn't bet his fossil collection that nobody would get hurt. He would have lost that one. Lorna came running out then with rags, a pillow and a bottle of homemade liquor.

"Ya ain't gonna pour that on my foot, are ya?" Noah asked, wide eyed, gasping for breath and heaving every now and again. His dirty face was now streaked with tears, spittle collected in his beard, but his eyes, even though they were riddled with red streaks, were wild with fear, and that's what registered with Gunnar. "You don't understand! It'll burn it clean off!"

"No," Gunnar said. He wasn't going to argue with him that if his stomach could take the abuse of the moonshine, his foot sure could. "Take a big ol' swig."

Noah chugged down his home-made brew without so much as a second's hesitation, but gasping as the liquid slid past his throat and hit his stomach. Well, maybe his stomach couldn't take the abuse, either, Gunnar thought.

"Now, I'm going to have to wrap that foot, to get some pressure on it. And it's not gonna feel very good."

"Oh, no," he said. "You can't do that. Nope, nope, I won't allow it." Then he started screaming about what all he was going to do to the pansy-city-boy-deputy just as soon as he could stand up, and Gunnar took that opportunity to punch him, right in the jaw and knocked old Noah for a loop. He didn't quite pass out all the way, but slumped backward and while he tried to orient himself, Gunnar snatched the bottle of mash, doused Noah's foot in it, grabbed the rags and tied them as best as he could around his bleeding foot. Then he threw the pillow in the floor board, pulled Noah upright and placed the injured foot on the pillow. Noah was in such shock and pain that all he could do was gasp for air.

Gunnar nodded at Lorna, realized he was going to have to buy another hat, and got in the car to drive her husband to the hospital. As he pulled onto the road, he caught a glimpse of Lorna wringing her hands in his side mirror, and realized, a little too late, that he hadn't even asked if she wanted to ride along. But, that was okay, Lorna was pretty much in shock—she hadn't even reacted when Gunnar hit Noah. He also wanted time alone with Noah, unarmed, so he could ask him some more questions about his son-in-law and Mosie Gibbon, whom he knew without a doubt was the man Noah had referred to.

Just as he hit the blacktop, Noah finally found his voice and started screaming and cussing. A great deal of it was what all he was going to do to Gunnar once the world stopped spinning.

With a resounding clarity, Gunnar realized that he wouldn't be eating any pie any time soon, and that ticked him off more than losing the hat.

A Letter to Aunt Viola from Olivia

Mrs. Viola Reinhardt
Dayton, Ohio
14 August 1958

Dear Aunt Viola,

Clara says to tell you that the earrings you sent for her birthday are absolutely divine—even though she says that you should know perfectly well that she is not 65 this year, but only 62. Harry won't let her wear them out of the house because he says they make her look like a jezebel, which I think, secretly, makes her like them all the more. But, don't worry she wears them when gathering eggs from the hen house, so they're definitely getting use.

There's a newcomer to Greenhaven, West Virginia—well, Sassafras Mountain in particular. Somebody bought the Renshaw place. Since it's been vacant for close to eight years, you can imagine the hullabaloo. (You were aware that Henry Renshaw passed, right? In case you were unaware, Junior Renshaw died in a German P.O. camp and Mabel from some sort of lung disorder back in 1949. Not that I remember Mabel all that well, but she always shared her licorice with me. So there are no living descendants. Really, you are at such a disadvantage being away from all of us.) Everybody I've encountered for a week has done nothing but wonder who this stranger is and why he's here. Aunt Stella and Aunt Mildred made me agree to take Mr. McDowell some of Aunt Mildred's fried chicken, under the guise of pure neighborly benevolence, but of course I was to infiltrate and report back. Who better to spy than an invalid with scrawny legs and a certain bucolic charm, right? He spilled the beans in no time! He is a novelist—maybe you've heard of him? I'm under the impression that he's garnered great reviews, but lousy sales, so maybe you haven't. I'd never heard of him. Apparently he's just trying to find some out of the way place to write his masterpiece. I have to report my findings to the posse tomorrow, but figured since you wouldn't get this letter for a week it was okay to tell you. I cannot possibly express how excited I am about the prospects of a friendship with him. A writer. He must know everything! Although, I will say that he's not nearly as wealthy as I imagined a writer would be.

You asked about Uncle Pete's rheumatism, and the report, straight from Aunt Runa, is that he feels absolutely horrible and that his hips continually feel as though they are being torn apart. I believe he likened the feeling to being a lot like the wishbone on Thanksgiving, only not as greasy. He still delivers the mail. He plans to die in his mail truck, his words, not mine. My only hope is that it's parked at the time.

Everybody else is the same, Willie Gene is overworked, Mom is tired, Clive is saving his money to buy his own car—he's threatened to drive Aunt Mildred's tractor to work and back, but what he doesn't understand is that tractor is older than he is and he'd probably have to push it. Betsy is repulsively obsessed with the state of her unmarriedness—yes, I invented that word just for her—and Humpy is not worth my time to report to you, so I won't.

The aunties are all well, although Aunt Stella's knee hurts more with each ten- degree drop in temperature.

As for me, Mrs. Hollingberry sent me a letter protesting my stance on *Wuthering Heights*. She gave me an A on the paper at the end of school last year, simply because it was well written, logically stated and well researched— she could find nothing wrong with the paper other than the fact she whole heartedly disagreed with me at every turn on every point! Since I graduated last year, she won't see me this year and, I'm assuming, felt a burning desire— after having considered it ALL SUMMER long—to write to me and tell me how wrong I was on my assessment of the book. You most likely know my stance and can probably imagine the twenty-four-page paper that spewed from my fingers without much thought or effort. I'm afraid Mrs. Hollingberry is extremely upset that I challenged her long-held and dare I say, rather antiquated and Victorian views on *Wuthering Heights*. ALL SUMMER it took her to write a rebuttal. An "in defense" of great literature etc. And yes, imagine "literature" said with a quick jerk of the head so that her nose ends up pointing at the ceiling. The nerve! I simply can't stand people who have to convince you of their opinion. I swear they only do it because to allow another person his opinion would be detrimental to their existence. As if their opinion was not valid, simply because someone else's differed! And without validity of their opinion, well, there goes their whole existence right down the drain. Like they were never born...

Anyway, so I'm off to write a rebuttal to her rebuttal, which will most likely be simple and to the point. Five words to be exact: I'm entitled to my opinion! Or I suppose I could tell her five other words: *Wuthering Heights* stunk beyond compare! I wonder what Jeb McDowell thinks of it?

Take care, my wonderful auntie, thank you so much for the new typewriter. You spoil me, really, and try and visit soon!

Love, your niece,
Olivia VanBibber

The Posse
August 1958

If my father, Hiram VanBibber, hadn't walked out on all of us when I was six-years-old, I'm sure my opinion of the male race would be much higher, although having a suffragette great aunt, it would have only been by a smidge. As it was, there were only a few men who had managed to worm their way into my good graces, or at the very least, were on my list of not entirely wasteful oxygen-eaters. It was very difficult to get past being abandoned by one's own father. One minute you're his precious little Suzie Belle—a nickname which was nothing close to Olivia Anne—being bounced upon his knee, helping him change tires, skipping up the road to visit kinfolk together, and singing *On the Sea of Galilee* from the loft of the barn so the whole valley could hear it. The next minute, you're not even worth a loaf of bread. He was gone, without taking one item—except the car, the bastard—his only words of warning being, "I'm goin' to git a loaf of bread, Rosie." He breathed not one slightest hint of affection, showed not one twinge to betray the awful deed he was about to do. And then he ran into the arms of a woman damned near young enough to have been his daughter. At least that's the gossip we heard from his siblings who still lived in Greenhaven.

And he stayed gone. Eleven years and counting this November. May as well be dead, for all I cared. He'd been gone long enough to miss my brother Humpy's flash-in-the pan marriage in 1957. The whole thing, from day one to day forty-two, when Georgia said she couldn't live with Humpy one more minute. Hiram was gone long enough to miss the death of his mother, gone long enough to miss every single excruciatingly painful and lonely moment that his Suzie Belle spent in the Morris Memorial polio hospital. I wasn't sure if he was even aware that Suzie Belle's skipping legs no longer worked. I wasn't like my sister, Bessie; I didn't blame myself for him hightailing it out of here as though Lucifer himself was riding shotgun in his 1946 Desoto Deluxe. I wasn't narcissistic enough to think that his decision to leave everybody and everything he'd ever known rested on my shoulders alone. I believed firmly that it was all Hiram's fault. He was defective in some way. He was also a drunk. But it was his choice to become a drunk, not mine. And from the day he walked out leaving my mother with three mouths to feed and no way of doing so, I decided that all men had to *apply* for citizenship to the realm of Olivia VanBibber's Human Beings, and sometimes the acceptance process could take quite a long time. I required proof that a man was worthy before I trusted him.

It's not as if all women were given automatic membership to the realm of Human Beings either, because there were at least three nurses (Hilda, Tilda, and Myrtle) who inflicted enough pain and suffering on me in the autumn of 1953 that I believed they were the heirs to an evil empire that made Hitler's look tame. One had only to look at past examples, to see that I was right, though. Most men were born evil, and some were truly heinous. My only consolation was that sometimes if the stars were aligned just right, they got their comeuppance in the end. Adolph Hitler murdered millions, took his own life, and was set on fire. Attila the Hun spread nothing but death wherever he went, and drowned in his own blood on his wedding night. Robespierre, who sent so many to Madame Guillotine, was guillotined in turn without a trial. Vlad Tepes, whose head ended up on a stake in Constantinople. Caligula...assassinated. All in all, it gave me hope that Hiram VanBibber would get his due someday.

At any rate, this issue caused some tensions within the family. While I firmly believed that my step-father Willie Gene had entered the ranks of living breathing humans, and his son, Clive as well, I was sure that without an intervention of Biblical proportions, my brother, Humpy, would never gain entrance. Upon the failure of his ridiculous marriage—which I'd known would fail—he of course, moved back home. I'd known that would happen, too. My sister Bessie, four years my senior, and Humpy, two years my senior, did not get along, to say the least, and quite often I had to navigate my wheelchair to a screeching halt between the two of them, because if they dared continue a fight over top of the head of their "invalid" sister, there would be hell to pay. And it would not be Willie Gene who'd be wielding the belt, or frying pan, or whatever happened to be handy, it'd be my mother. To think that anybody would need to threaten a twenty-year-old with a frying pan!

I, however, was pretty much given free passage to do what I wanted. In an attempt to "make up" for my legs, my mother allowed me privileges that she'd never allow Bessie, but at the same time, she knew I was limited and couldn't take full advantage of that freedom. I couldn't drive a car, and unless I had a friend or a relative who happened to show up with one, I was pretty much confined to my house or the auntie's houses. I did have chores to do. I was in charge of the dishes and dusting and cleaning up my own messes. Beyond that, the days were mine to do with what I wanted. Most of the time, I read.

Today, however, I was expected to report to Aunt Mildred and give her the lowdown on Jeb McDowell. And so, Clive and I got up as usual, but instead of driving into Wellston to his job at the filling station, he took me down the mountain to see Aunt Mildred.

I felt sorry for Clive, because quite often people forget he's in the room. It happened yesterday when I was talking to Jeb. Bessie and Humpy often feel the same way. I was sort of like the war hero who had been captured by the enemy and spent years behind enemy lines in a work camp and then freed. People wanted to know everything about me and my experiences in the war, but they were also in a sort of awe that I'd survived and that I breathed and talked just like everybody else. Paying attention to me was also people's way of paying sympathy. I understood it; it was not always easy on my siblings. Bessie and Humpy could be pretty vocal about it, and once they started whining, I no longer felt as sorry for them. Clive took it on the chin. Which is why I tried to do nice things for him. Currently I was knitting him a scarf, but it looked more like a long blue fluffy corkscrew.

Clive took me to my Aunt Mildred's, meaning that he held on to my wheel chair so that I didn't lose control of it and end up plummeting to my death down the side of the mountain. We didn't have either of the vehicles today, so we went without one, which we did a lot. As a child, before the polio, I walked and climbed all over Greenhaven and would never have chosen a car over walking. The funny thing was, I could get down the mountain by myself in my wheelchair. It was my legs that were useless, not my arms. But allowing Clive to take me caused fewer confrontations with my mother, and I needed to save my confrontations for things that really mattered.

Getting back up the mountain was another thing altogether.

We came around the bend in the road and after a few minutes we could see Aunt Mildred's house in the distance. She was lucky enough to live on one of the few acres of flat bottomland in the whole county. The other flatland had been used to build the city of Wellston. That's an exaggeration, but only just. The road continued to curve to the west, and there in the valley to the east were two houses. One belonged to Aunt Mildred, the other, about five acres away, belonged to her sister Runa. Both were actually great aunts, having been the sisters of my grandmother Blanche, who died when my mother was a little girl. Mildred, a single woman until her forties, had never had any children, and was the natural choice of my great grandma's siblings, to continue raising Blanche's children. And so my Aunt Mildred was really more like a grandmother.

The mountains of central West Virginia were old and gentle mountains, although the weather contained within them could be brutal. But they weren't all jagged and pointy and snowy like the mountains out west. Rather they sloped gently, folding in on each other to create rounded, tree covered mounds. Living in central West Virginia was like being surrounded by green waves of trees, full of birds, butterflies, deer and panthers. That land never ceased to humble me.

We turned off of the road and followed the long driveway up to her house. Clive turned my wheelchair around backwards and took me up the steps like he's done a thousand times. The small white, clap-board sided house contained two bedrooms, a living room, a kitchen, and a dining area. While we waited for Aunt Mildred to answer the door, I began unbundling my legs. My mother insisted I wrap a blanket around them while we were going down the mountain. I wasn't exactly sure why, but I assumed she thought my legs would suddenly start flailing about on their own and Clive would roll over one of them. I was not ashamed or embarrassed to have had polio or be in a wheelchair, but I was embarrassed at one thing; since I was only eleven, almost twelve, when I took polio, it had left my legs visibly smaller than the rest of my body, the left even smaller than the right. My mother tells me it's not that noticeable, since I was a fairly small person in general. Still, to me, it was an enormous difference. So, most of the time I wore boy's jeans, because if I wore skirts like most women did everyone could see how uneven and small my legs were. My choice of pants annoyed Aunt Mildred to no end, having been a staunch wearer of dresses her whole life. She had never, not when working at the boarding house, or in the fields, donned a pair of pants. Only in Europe during World War I, as a Red Cross nurse behind enemy lines she'd been forced to wear pants because she'd used all her skirting to staunch the blood flow of young men. She'd plainly told me on many occasions that only a war and wounded would get her to wear them again.

So I knew as soon as she opened the door I would hear, "Olivia, Clive, so nice to see the two of you. It's such a shame, Olivia, that you don't have the sense of God to put on a dress. Come in, come in."

Aunt Mildred answered the door, and said exactly those words.

I was, after all, going to embarrass her in front of her friends and sisters with my lack of appropriate attire.

She invited us in and she gave Clive a pinch on his cheek. The house smelled of biscuits and bacon left over from breakfast, and something sweet that was currently baking in the oven. We went through the house and out the back door to the back porch where my great aunts Runa and Stella were sitting in big Adirondack chairs and Aunt Dotie in the porch swing. Molly Tennyson, Eloise Dille (pronounced deel) and Pearl Hargrave sat in the metal folding chairs. We received various greetings from everybody and I got a hug and a kiss from Aunt Dotie, and a squeeze of my hand from Aunt Stella. It did seem like a lot of little old ladies on one porch—they ranged from age sixty to eighty—but it was really only the tip of the iceberg. Mildred, Runa, Stella and Dotie were all my grandmother's sisters, and there were more where they came from. Absolutely, there was no shortage, and if one was indisposed, another would come out from under a rock somewhere and take her place.

All of my grandmother's siblings looked alike, with the exception of Viola. The other six all had long faces with extreme cheekbones and bone structure, eyes so dark they were nearly black, and, when they were younger, thick dark hair. The things that set them apart, aside from personalities, were just subtle tweaks: eyes set further apart, softer features, bonier features or maybe a longer nose. They were also extremely tall. Even the women. Blanche, my grandmother, had been nearly six foot, the tallest woman in the family, but the others were only a few inches behind her. I'd gotten my small stature from my dad's mother.

Aunt Runa was gorgeous, even in her later years. She had apple cheeks and an all-around more feminine face than the other sisters. But that did not mean she was weak or frail or "girly." She was a determined woman and a true soldier of God, an officer, with her sister Viola, in the Salvation Army. Also— like Aunt Mildred—she had served behind enemy lines during World War I, cooking up the famous Salvation Army doughnuts. She was an original Doughnut Lassie, and when I was a child, she made me memorize the famous recipe that fed thousands of Doughboys across Europe:

7 1/2 Cups Sugar
3/4 Cup Lard
9 Eggs
3 Large Cans Evaporated Milk
3 Large Cans Water

18 Cups Flour
18 Teaspoons Baking Powder
7 1/2 Teaspoons Salt
9 Teaspoons Nutmeg

Cream sugar and lard together, beat eggs into mixture. Mix evaporated milk and water. Add water to creamed mixture. Mix flour, baking powder, salt and nutmeg in large sieve and sift into other mixture, adding enough flour to make a stiff dough. Roll and cut. Five pounds of lard are required to fry the doughnuts. It makes about 250 doughnuts.

I shall be able to recite it from the grave. She was also a suffragette, having marched in Washington and gotten arrested once, which was a whole other story, and she had an entire syllabus of things she'd made me memorize. I can completely recite Sojourner Truth's "Ain't I A Woman?" speech, among many others. She also played the guitar. In my opinion, there was no relative of mine more interesting and well-rounded than Aunt Runa, except maybe Aunt Viola, but Viola had left the state back in 1915 and never came back, except to visit.

Mildred was a bit more masculine than Runa, with a strong jawline, and absolutely flawless skin. Often times when I looked at her I wondered what my grandmother, Blanche, would have been like, had she been given the opportunity to grow old.

Stella, a spitfire in many ways, always had a bit of a mischievous look to her and in her older years wore thick glasses. She loved to take pictures and her house, along with Aunt Runa's, was full of them. She'd had two sons. One had survived everything the South Pacific could dish at him during World War II, the other was killed on D-day. She lived up the road and around the bend, and in her garage sat her very first 8-cylinder, 85-horsepower, 1926 Packard Touring car, with a 143" wheelbase. Stella only drove it on special occasions. One of those special occasions had been the day I came home to Greenhaven from Milton. We'd driven the whole way with the top down.

Aunt Dotie's face, although it resembled her sister's so much, somehow looked kinder. I don't believe there was a harsh bone or a harsh sentiment anywhere in that woman, even after having one of her sons shot down during World War II. His body was never recovered. Somehow, she still looked out on the world with kindness and civility. It was not lost on me how my family had been shaped by events put into motion by men I never met and would never meet, and by events completely out of our control and half way around the world.

It was easy to forget that there was a whole, big, exotic world out there beyond the hills and valleys of West Virginia. We were so isolated here, in more ways than one. But if I became complacent, all I had to do was reflect on the things my family has done, the people we've lost, and I was instantly reminded that the world was knocking on Appalachia's door.

The day was warm, but a nice breeze blew across the back porch. All the little old ladies, with their battle scars firmly tucked away in secret places, sat happily sipping lemonade, tea and Orange Nehi.

Clive took a seat on the edge of the porch railing, but not before snatching a lemon cookie off of a silver tray on a table.

"So, tell us all about Mr. McDowell," Aunt Mildred said. That was Mildred, straight to the point. Aunt Runa had the decency to say, "Well, Mildred, you could be a little more subtle than that. Olivia's going to think that's all you invited her over for."

Aunt Mildred waved a dishtowel at Runa. "Olivia knows she's welcome here any time, although I'd wish she'd wear decent clothing. We've all been waiting to hear this, so why beat around the bush?"

"I agree," Pearl Hargrave said, leaning forward to get her glass of lemonade that she'd set on the porch floor next to her chair. Most of the ladies were all dressed in what I called "high country lady fashion." Cotton sack dresses that hung just below their knees, with no shape to them at all. The dresses had small collars, and were decorated with things like tiny flowers or checks or polka-dots. Aunt Mildred wore an apron over hers. Pearl Hargrave, however, wore a bit fancier dress, still cotton, with contrasting cuffs on her short sleeves, and she finished it off with a tiny hat. "We've been waiting days and days to find out why he's here."

"Liam Tucker says he's a Korean War vet, shell shocked, come to kill us all," Molly Tennyson said.

"Ah, pooh," Aunt Stella said. "Why would he come all the way here and do that, when he coulda killed people anywhere?"

Molly worked her handkerchief between her fingers. "I didn't say I agreed with him, Stella."

"Well, then don't go repeatin' that kind of malarkey."

"Will you two quit bickering and let Olivia talk?" Mildred said. "Go on, honey."

"Uh, well," I began. "He's from Baltimore."

"Baltimore?" Aunt Mildred said, looking taken aback. "Well, what in tarnation is he doing here?"

"He's writing a novel," I answered.

There was an acute sense of astonishment that swept from one end of the porch to the other. I glanced over at Clive, who had finished off his cookie, and smiled at him. He just rolled his eyes, took his cigarettes that he stored in the sleeve of his T-shirt, knowing full well that Aunt Mildred did not allow any smoking or drinking within two-hundred feet of her house. When Aunt Mildred's husband John had gotten drunk and fallen down the privy, she outlawed drinking anywhere on her property. There hadn't been any near-death accidents where smoking was concerned, but Mildred had made it a law in her house, anyway. Clive knew better than to ignore Mildred's Laws.

"Clive Morrison, don't you dare light that nasty thing up on my porch," Aunt Mildred scolded. She took her towel and flicked it at him, catching the cigarette and flinging it into the yard. When Clive got over the shock of Aunt Mildred's quick reflexes, he gave a little snort, jumped into the yard, picked up his cigarette and then quietly tucked it and its case back into his T-shirt sleeve and rolled it up. I looked down at the floor, trying not to reveal that I thought Clive being scolded over cigarettes was funny or that I was once again in awe of my Aunt Mildred. In so doing, I noticed seven pairs of legs, all with broken veins, swollen ankles and worn-out shoes—except for Pearl's shoes. Of course, they were new and shiny—and giggled anyway.

Looking up, I noticed they were waiting for further explanation from me. I cleared my throat. "He's from Baltimore. He's writing a novel," I reiterated.

"He says he wanted to get to the magic land," Clive chimed in.

All the ladies looked at one another, perplexed. "Is he one of them Jehovah witnesses?" Eloise Dille asked.

"I'll bet he's a Mormon," Stella said.

"I'm not sure he has a religion," I said, sending a shockwave through the ladies. Apparently, having no religion was worse than having one with contradicting philosophies from your own.

"Surely you don't think he's..." Aunt Stella began.

I held up a hand in frustration and to keep Aunt Stella from having to say the word "atheist," lest she burst into flames. "I don't know. We didn't discuss religion, or military service, or anything like that."

"Well, what did you discuss?" Aunt Dotie asked.

"Let her speak," Clive said. "Quit interrupting her and she'll tell you."

Molly Tennyson's eyebrows shot up and she looked the other way. "Somebody needs to have a talk with Willie Gene about how his son talks to his elders," she said to the ceiling.

"There isn't much to tell," I said, ignoring her. "He said he wanted a nice secluded place where nobody would disturb him, so that he could write his book. That's all. Apparently, he got the Renshaw house at a good price."

"Yes, but why would he even look for a house *here,* of all places?" Aunt Runa asked.

"Apparently, in Baltimore, they have real-estate agents who will try to find you what you want. I'm assuming, Mr. McDowell told the realtor that he wanted a house that was cheap, in the middle of nowhere, but not too far from Baltimore. The realtor most likely realized that since the Renshaw house had been vacant for years, it would be cheap. I honestly don't know."

"So, nobody knows he's here?" Aunt Dotie asked.

"He says his business associates know he's here, and that he sends letters to his friends. Apparently, he really does not want to be disturbed," I answered.

They were all clearly flabbergasted, for each one had her own distinctive expression to convey this. Lots of open-mouthed stares and rapidly blinking eyes, a hand to the mouth, a wringing of a handkerchief.

"Well, how long will he be here?" Aunt Runa asked finally.

Clive and I both shrugged.

"Is it just for this book or forever?" Pearl asked.

"I didn't ask," I said.

"Well, why didn't you ask?" Aunt Stella inquired.

"I...I didn't think it was important." All the ladies rolled their eyes, made murmurs, shook their heads and in general, resembled a flock of pigeons sitting on a park bench dithering at each other.

"Look, if he's not hurting anything, what does it matter how long he stays?" I said.

"Well, I for one will not sit idly by while a godless war criminal lives in my backyard," Pearl said. Pearl could be a bit excitable.

"Who said anything about a godless war criminal?" I asked. I glanced at Clive. "Clive, help me."

"He was a really nice guy," Clive said. "He's one of those artsy types, that's all."

Now there were audible gasps. "A hedonist!" Aunt Stella exclaimed.

"No, no, no," Clive said. "He's just...he's harmless." Clive looked at me and shrugged.

"Look," I said, trying my best to calm the ladies. "He just wants to write a book. He just wants to be left alone. I don't think he'll cause any trouble."

"What's the book about?" Aunt Mildred asked.

"I don't know, I didn't ask."

"Well why not?" she demanded.

"Because I thought it would be rude. And since I was representing the whole of Greenhaven, I thought it best to mind my manners," I said a little too forcefully, for just as a breeze swept across the porch, so did abrupt silence.

After a few moments, Aunt Runa said, "So, what of his family? Is he married?"

"If he were married," Molly said, "He'd have brought his wife. Men can't do without their wives for more than a few days before they get cranky in the pants."

"Molly!" Aunt Dotie exclaimed.

"For the love of... There are *children* on this porch, Molly Irene!" Aunt Runa pounced. Clive and I weren't children, but neither of us were married, so in Aunt Runa's eyes, topics involving what went on in men's breeches were strictly prohibited.

"He has five siblings; that's all he mentioned," I said.

"Well," Pearl said, clasping her hands. That seemed to signal to all the council that some sort of judgment had been passed and that our interrogation was over. Which I was happy for, because I didn't like the sound of what I heard. I would not put it past a few of the ladies to be rude to Mr. McDowell if he were to take me up on my invitation and show up at the box-social. If that happened, I would die of embarrassment.

The porch swing squeaked with Aunt Dotie's rocking when suddenly Eloise said, "Did you see the size of Lovinia Jones' pumpkin? She says she's taking it to the county fair. I'm pretty sure she'll win. I ain't seen a pumpkin that size since forty-four."

"I know it. And it's not even done growing yet!" Aunt Stella said. "And you know, she gets no help from that no-account son of hers."

"Do you know what he said to me?" Molly asked.

"I'm not sure I want to know," Aunt Runa said.

"Here," Aunt Stella said to Clive. She handed him her camera. "Get a picture of us on the porch, Clive. Go on Molly, I'm listening."

Clive snapped a picture of all of us sitting on the porch with the morning glories snaking up the lattice behind the swing. Molly went into great detail of how Pokey Jones had called her an old biddy. Clive and I smiled at each other from across the length of the porch. We knew we'd been dismissed, but we stuck around long enough to have some of that rhubarb pie that Aunt Mildred had in the oven, and to find out the fate of Pokey Jones.

A Letter to Olivia from Viola Reinholdt

Miss Olivia VanBibber
Route 42
Greenhaven, West Virginia
August 1958

Dear Livvy,

A stranger, to Greenhaven? Did it make the newspaper? It took me several years of saving all of my money to get out of West Virginia; why would he want in? Well, years' worth of penny pinching got me out of Appalachia, but let's not forget a World War and one very romantic German soldier who happened to be my patient! I can't take all of the credit.

A newcomer to our hollow is certainly cause for excitement, though! I'll bet Stella is chomping at the bit to know his whole life story. She was always so nosy.

And, I agree, you are the perfect emissary to receive Mr. McDowell, but bucolic? Never! I nearly spit my tea across the room. Although, I sense you were teasing me, half making fun of yourself, am I right? I have to be right.

Eckhard is doing well. The cold bothers him much more than me. It may be August, but it gets cool here at night. When we lived in Put-in-Bay he was always cold. I loved it. There have been two nights recently that I had to shut the windows because it got so cool.

My book club met last week and we discussed *A Room With a View* by E. M. Forster. Let me know if you've read it because I don't want to spoil it for you, but oh, how I loved it! This weekend The Ladies Auxiliary of Bethesda Gardens of Dayton are working on the most beautiful Lone Star Quilt. We just finished quilting Lucinda Blackhorne's NRA Eagle Quilt. She's had the top finished for almost twenty years, sitting in her cedar chest, and decided that it was an historic piece and should be quilted. It sure brings back memories. I think Mildred may have done an appliqué NRA eagle quilt. You should ask her. Oh, but the fruitcake sale was a disaster. I won't even discuss it.

Eckhard wants my help out in the garden. Apparently one of the trellises for the morning glories has broken. I have no idea what he thinks I can do about it? I am 64 years old, and although I still look fashionable in my mud boots, safari hat and gloves—accompanied with pearls, of course—my knees aren't worth a hoot, they make a grinding noise when I try to get them to do anything, and I can't lift my arms above my head without an emergency run to the toilet! I keep telling Eckhard that he should know better than I how much I've aged, he's the one who has to look at me all the time! (By the way, tell my dear and obstinate friend, Clara, that I know exactly how old she is because we started school together!) Anyway, I'm going to go look fashionable while holding his lemonade for him. Makes him feel better.

And, please, please, you must write and tell me—in less than twenty-four pages, of course—just what your opinion of *Wuthering Heights* was! You threw the English teacher into a tizzy—I must read it! Although, I think I can probably guess, and please don't be too insulting to your teacher. I am of the Victorian age myself, and if you give us half a chance, you'd be amazed at how MODERN we can be! We did get women the vote, after all.

But interesting to note that you feel the need to rebut her rebuttal. What was that you said about people having to convince others of their opinions?

Let me know if there's a new title that you'd like to read. I make a trip to the bookstore now and again. I can get you something. And I sent you that typewriter because I keep hoping you'll do something with it besides write me letters.

Love,
Your great Auntie Viola

Sunday Services

On Sunday, I went to church with Clive, Bessie, my mother and Willie Gene. Humpy had gone to Charleston with some friends and had returned just as the sun was coming over the hill and declared that he wasn't fit for God's house. That was certainly the truth, but not because he'd stayed out late.

It was nearly September and while the days were still warm and sticky, the nights and early mornings were cool and a welcome reprieve. The sun shone brightly, reflecting off of the white paint of the Fairview Baptist Church, making it almost glow against the dark green foliage that surrounded it. There was a mountain in the backyard of the church, and way up on top of it was the cemetery. My grandmother was buried there, along with her mother, and two of my great-great-grandparents. When the church ran out of room, they started burying the dead in a small strip of land across the road from the church that nestled against a creek and was covered by low-hung sycamore branches. Personally, I didn't think they ran out of room on top of the mountain, I think people were just tired of hitching up a team of mules and dragging coffins up there. Not to mention, when they were hauling my Uncle Reggie's coffin up the mountain, they'd hit a rock and that coffin came apart like it had hit a land mine. Pieces of splintered board went in every direction and left Uncle Reggie lying on the ground. It was then that we all learned that once the casket was closed, the undertakers were undressing the dead and keeping their clothes. Aunt Stella swooned and would have hit her head and tumbled down the mountain if it hadn't been for her son, who broke the fall. So, it was probably a good thing that the cemetery was now located across the road.

My mother had insisted I wear a dress to church, and it's the only time I submit to this archaic rule, a remnant of a centuries-old society meant to keep women submissive. As long as a woman wore a dress, she was reminded that she was the "fairer" sex. But my mother did a lot for me, so I gave in on this one thing. It was also the only time I wore my leg braces so that I could stand. Walking was hellaciously difficult in these torture contraptions, but standing was doable. In fact, I sort of liked it every now and then because it put me eye to eye with other people. When you only reach people's navels they tend to think of you as a little kid regardless of how old you are.

The congregation stood and sang, *"There'll be joy, joy, joy up in my father's house, where there's peace, wonderful peace."* I sang along, watching the door with one eye, wondering if Mr. McDowell would indeed grace us with his presence. Aunt Mildred waved at me from two pews behind, clearly approving of my dress, and I waved back as best I could without completely letting go of the crutches.

My mother looked beautiful with her wavy, shoulder-length black hair and bright red lipstick. Her voice was deep and on the occasion that she ever got to use a telephone, people often mistook her for a man. Brother Dixon had begged her numerous times to join the choir because he said he needed a second alto who could reach a baritone note once in a while. Brother Dixon had thought he was giving a compliment, but my mother had been highly insulted and told him that she'd rather slaughter hogs.

Just as we started the second verse, the door to the back of the church opened and little by little the congregation of Fairview Baptist Church all began to falter. Singing voices fell away, some people forgot the words and some shot clear off into another octave. I turned to see what the commotion was about and there stood Jeb McDowell, dressed in a shirt with a tie, and his hair slicked back. The expression on his face bore no resemblance to happiness or peace, but was more akin to sheer terror. As the door shut behind him, he jumped, startled. He glanced around the room, terror gave way to uncertainty and when his eyes found mine, relief overcame him and he made a bee line for my pew. He stepped in next to me and started singing. I glanced at him and he winked at me.

Regardless of the congregation's valiant effort, none of us could manage to find the right notes or the right words to the rest of the song. So Helen Murphy, the piano player, improvised some fancy little ending and managed to finish the song with a smile on her face, as though the lost voices, bad notes and abrupt ending was exactly as the song was meant to be.

We all sat down and I set my crutches between Jeb and me. Jeb leaned around them and said, "I didn't know you could walk?"

"I can't," I said, smiling. "It's an illusion."

Brother Dixon began. "Family, friends, neighbors and..." he glanced at Jeb. "Strangers. Welcome, welcome on this glorious Sunday morning. And why is it a glorious morning you might ask? Well, because the Lord God made it so and we are all alive with the spirit of the Lord!"

Out of the corner of my eye, I could see my sister Bessie lean backward and pretend as though she was fixing the bow in her hair so that she could get a better look at Jeb. I glanced over and she gave me one raised eyebrow as if to say...well, I wasn't exactly sure what she was trying to imply, now that I thought about it. One thing I was certain about, and that was that every person in the congregation, at some point, either hiding behind Bibles or songbooks or just blatantly, had stared our way. I wanted to crawl under the pew in front of me.

Miraculously, Brother Dixon had a sermon all stored up and ready to go for such an occasion. It was not every day that the tiny church of Fairview, sitting in the dell outside the tiny community of Greenhaven, would actually have a stranger visit. Brother Dixon's sermon was all about how we should be kind and be accepting of outsiders. "Be not forgetful to entertain strangers: for thereby some have entertained angels unawares," Brother Dixon began. "Folks, the Bible is full of accounts of strangers, wanderers, people in exile, aliens. Abraham was a stranger. In Genesis chapter twelve and verse one, the Lord says to Abraham, 'Get thee out of thy country, and from thy kindred, and from thy father's house, unto a land that I will shew thee.' So Abraham left home when God called him and lived as a stranger relying on the promise God had given him and trusting in God's people. Joseph was a stranger in Egypt. And really, honestly, what was Jesus but a stranger? He came outta nowheres. Even his birth is an account of a wanderer, a stranger. He was born in a stable because there was no room for him at the inn." Here he paused for dramatic effect.

"Well, folks, I'm here to tell ya, that I reckon—if we could bring those innkeepers to the here and now—they would wish they could go back in time and make room for the savior at their inn. At one point, Jesus says to the homeless, the aliens, he says, 'I was a stranger and you did not welcome me.' Now think about that for just a moment," Brother Dixon said, the sweat beginning to roll down the sides of his face.

At this point my face was beginning to burn bright red. Subtlety was not one of Brother Dixon's virtues, and I could imagine what Jeb McDowell was thinking.

His voice roared, his fist came down and he slapped his Bible. *"They did not welcome the son of God?"* he boomed. "What kinda person would turn away a stranger, let alone a stranger who just happens to be the son of God?" When Brother Dixon spoke the word "happens" he rocked forward on the balls of his feet.

My mother scooted down in the pew and said under her breath, "And he's about to take flight."

I started giggling, which was not a good thing, since all eyes in the congregation kept wandering to our corner of the church every five seconds. On and on Brother Dixon went, further and further he leaned. To and fro and to and fro until at one point, I thought he was going to do a belly flop onto the piano. My mother tried to hide her laughter behind her hanky, dabbing her eyes pretending to search for some errant eyelash or something. Jeb leaned forward and pinched the bridge of his nose with both thumbs and then rubbed his eyes. My shoulders shook with laughter and Jeb, in between silent spasmodic giggling, said, "Will you stop it?" His first Sunday services and my mother and I were about to get him kicked out. I had no idea what Brother Dixon was even saying anymore because my ears felt like they were stuffed with cotton and I was concentrating way too hard on not laughing. All of a sudden Brother Dixon came to a stop, looked straight in our direction and said, "'For we are strangers before thee, and sojourners, as were all our fathers: our days on the earth are as a shadow, and there is none abiding.'" He let his voice echo off of the church walls and was completely silent for the count of ten seconds.

Then, he raised his hands upward and everybody stood. Helen pounded on the piano keys and we all sang, "*Some glad morning, when this life is old, I'll fly away. To that home on God's celestial shore, I'll fly away. Oh, I'll fly away, Old Glory, I'll fly away.*" The congregation began to leave the church, beginning with the back pews, but we all kept singing. "*When I die, hallelujah, by and by, I'll fly away. Just a few more weary days and then, I'll fly away, to that land where joy will never end, I'll fly away. I'll fly away Old Glory, I'll fly away.*" And here Jeb leaned in toward me and sang as deep as he could, "*In the mornin'.*" I smiled and kept singing. "*When I die, hallelujah bye and bye, I'll fly away. Oh, I'll fly away, old glory, I'll fly away.*"

"*In the morning,*" he added again.

"*When I die hallelujah, by and by, I'll fly away.*"

I hobbled along on my braces and crutches, basically dragging my legs, wincing at the pain, and couldn't wait to get outside where my wheelchair was waiting for me. Jeb held the door open as I crossed the threshold and I said as quickly as I could, "I hereby apologize for whatever has happened and whatever's going to happen. It's not my fault."

He threw his head back and belly laughed, just as Brother Dixon made his way over with his hand firmly outstretched. "Well, well, Rosalee," he said to my mother, "Who have we here?"

"Oh, uh, this is Mr. McDowell," my mother said.

"Nice sermon, there," Jeb said, taking the preacher's hand.

"Why, thank you, thank you. It's not very often I get to tell the story of the wandering stranger."

My mother rolled her eyes. After waving good-bye to one of her friends, Bessie made her way over to us as casually as she could. Clive and Willie Gene stood by a tree talking baseball with Arnie Pickens and Gunnar Ryan, who was one of the local deputies and happened to be the older brother of one of my best friends. I'm certain the baseball conversation consisted of whether or not Lew Burdette was going to get to repeat last year's performance in the world championships this year. "And who have we here?" Jeb asked.

I cleared my throat. "This is my sister Bessie," I said. I glanced around, trying to locate my wheelchair, because my back was beginning to ache and my legs were shaking. Aunt Dotie must have seen me looking for it, and suddenly there she was behind me with my chair. I looked up at her with gratitude and she silently walked away.

"Well, how do you do, Bessie?" Jeb asked.

My sister had worn her best dress today and was probably at this moment, thanking her lucky stars she had. There wasn't a hair out of place, her rouge applied evenly and appropriately, and she wore a strand of pearls that Aunt Mildred had given her. Make no bones about it, my sister had a broomstick firmly and positively cemented up her butt. Whatever Jeb would say to her today, she would go home and replay in her head, along with her replies, smiling at herself at particularly witty parts and frowning over things she wasn't sure she should have said. Then she'd get all in a dither about whether or not she had offended Mr. McDowell, convince herself that she'd made a good and proper fool of herself, vow never to be seen in public again, only to forget her vow within a week and start the whole process over again. God, it was painful to be Bessie VanBibber, and I thanked God that it was my legs that had been afflicted, and not my common sense.

"I'm fine, thank you," Bessie said. "So you're the stranger everybody's been talking about?"

Jeb smiled. "Apparently so," he said shoving his hands in his pockets. "Or was Brother Dixon calling me an alien?"

"Don't pay no mind to Brother Dix," my mother said to Jeb. "No matter what, he means well."

"I'm not bothered," Jeb said. Then he turned to me. "You really should introduce me to your aunts."

"My, my what?" I asked.

"I hear that you're related to most of the people in Greenhaven and that you've got a slew of aunts and uncles."

I peered at him cautiously. Had he been checking up on me? "And a slew of cousins," I added. "Although half of them have moved away."

"What's Baltimore like?" Bessie asked.

"Crowded," Jeb answered. "Lotsa people coming to and fro. I used to wash dishes in the Dixie Diner right on Route 40. Met all sorts of people going all sorts of places."

"So you've lived there all your life?" Bessie asked.

"Except for the six years I was in New York going to college. And I hitchhiked to California once."

"Oh," Bessie said, suddenly self-conscious. He was a big city college man.

"Well, you're just in time for the fun to begin," Mom said. She gestured at the tables that were being set up in the parking lot. "We're having a picnic after services, and a box-social. Food. Do you like food, Mr. McDowell?"

"Oh, yes, ma'am."

It appeared as though I was the personal goodwill ambassador for Mr. McDowell, as everybody who approached us would ask me to introduce my new friend. Children scampered all about, running underneath the tables, giggling, sliding to their knees trying to get away from each other. Every now and then I'd hear an exasperated mother call out, "Those are your good clothes!" As if the child cared or had even noticed. To a child, clothes were just something you put on so you wouldn't be naked. Beyond that, it didn't much matter to them until they reached puberty. And even then, given the right temptation of a food fight or a dunk in the creek, most would still forget they were wearing their Sunday best.

People sat down to eat, but I don't think Jeb sat down. Every time he had spare room on his plate, he filled it with something else. He ate three plates of food: potato salad, cole slaw, beet hash, hominy, an egg and olive sandwich, and some fancy casserole dish that Pearl Hargrave had brought. She'd announced, as loud as she could that the recipe had come from her cousin who lived in Chicago. Although I hated to admit it, whatever it was, it was delicious. Jeb ate more fried chicken—complained just a little that it obviously was inferior to "mine"—and then headed for the dessert table.

"I think I might cry," he said, scanning the sweets.

"Why?" I asked.

"Because I don't think I have any room left in my stomach for dessert."

I laughed. "Oh, give it the good old college try."

He breathed deeply and sighed as his gaze swept over the offerings from the sugar gods. I made a mental note to make sure he got a box to take some food home with him. I had a horrible vision that all he consumed up there in that rickety lonely house was whiskey and moldy bread. He filled his plate with angel food cake, lemon pie and then gallantly tried to finish off the apple Indian pudding, but just could not force the last few bites to go down. I honestly thought it was all going to come back up.

Clive had somehow been conned into playing cowboys and Indians with a group of ten-year old boys, and they took quite the delight in killing him over and over. It was most likely because he did such a good job of pretending to die and then rolling down the hill. Then he'd lay utterly still until one of the boys would get up enough nerve to check on their victim, then Clive would jump up, give a war cry and take off running. He was the Apache who would not die, and the kids loved it.

"Your brother seems like a great kid," Jeb said.

I glanced his way. "Yeah, he is."

"Not to be nosy, but you two seem like you're...I dunno, there's this unspoken...understanding between you."

I shrugged. "When I was in the hospital, he worked odd jobs for neighbors. He'd save that money and save it and save it, and then when he had enough he'd take the bus, all by himself, to Milton to see me. He'd spend the whole day with me, and by the time he'd leave, the busses had stopped running and so he'd sneak out into the milking barn and stay all night, get up and take the earliest bus back home the next day."

Jeb nodded. "The milking barn?"

"The hospital sits on, oh, I don't know, two hundred acres, maybe? They grow their own food there, so we always had fresh vegetables and fruit. And they have a big milking barn. Any milk not used for us kids was sold in town. Anyway, Clive would sleep in there all night, without a blanket or anything, just the cows to keep him company," I said. "You don't forget something like that and you don't take it lightly. Especially when your actual blood-siblings never put forth the effort to come and see you, not once. Clive is more my brother than anybody will ever be. Simple as that."

"I'm glad you have him," Jeb said.

"As much as I believe in the bonds of blood, Mr. McDowell, sometimes we are blessed with a spirit-sibling. Sometimes, I think they're sent to us, like angels. To protect us from ourselves and to fill the spaces that members of our family fail to fill."

Just then Aunt Runa and Aunt Dotie made their way toward us. "Here we go," I said.

"Why...Olivia Anne, who do we have here?" Aunt Runa asked.

They knew perfectly well who he was, but I just smiled at their attempt at being coy. "This is Jeb McDowell, who bought the Renshaw place. Jeb, these are two of my great aunts, Runa and Dotie."

"Pleasure to meet you ladies," he said and gave a slight bow.

"Livvy here says you're writing a book," Aunt Dotie said.

"Trying, anyway," he said.

"What's it about?" Aunt Runa asked.

That was not the least bit subtle. Maybe she was picking up some habits from Aunt Mildred.

"Uh, oh, well..." he began, clearly not prepared to answer that question. "It's about a man who doesn't know who he is, really, and he's been all over America trying to find what it means to be from somewhere, but no matter where he goes, he's not from there. He's been through a lot, drinks too much, trying to find where he belongs at the bottom of a bottle. He's been through a lot of women, too, thinking one of them holds the secret to his past—like they're somehow his vessel to that unknown world, but they never do and they never are."

Aunt Dotie and Aunt Runa stood with their mouths open, and Aunt Dotie blushed. It was most likely the reference to having been through a lot of women that did it. While I am certain that amongst themselves the aunties all talked about relations between a man and a woman—I'd overheard a few things that made *me* blush and wish I didn't have such good hearing—but one did not speak of such things in public or with a man, and certainly not with a man in public. Jeb, clearly, was clueless.

Sensing the mood change, Jeb toyed with the edge of his plate. "So, anyway, it's a work in progress. And...um, well, I'm doing some field research for a future book maybe."

"Oh, really?" Aunt Runa asked.

"Yes, I find Appalachia very interesting, the people, the landscape, the *panthers*," he said with a chuckle.

"Don't forget the bears," Aunt Dotie chimed in.

"And bears," he said. "Not to mention the music. I just might have to set a book here someday."

"Here?" Aunt Runa exclaimed.

"Not here as in Greenhaven necessarily, but," he glanced up and around at the sky, the clouds, the trees, the hills, and took a deep breath. "In these mountains. I've become completely besotted."

"Oh, my," Aunt Dotie said. She was most likely trying to figure out if besotted meant that he was going to stay.

It was quiet a moment. Then Jeb said, "So, about those bears. What exactly do I do to get rid of them?"

"Don't leave food out," Aunt Runa said. "Anywhere."

"And throw potatoes at them," Aunt Dotie added.

"P-potatoes? But she just said not to leave any food out."

"Jesse did that once and it worked. Bear ran right off into the woods," Dotie explained.

"Oh, well, I'll have to buy some potatoes," he said, smiling.

"Well, Dotie," Runa said, "I think we best be going our way."

"Nice meeting you," Jeb said.

"You too," they both said and waved.

I looked at him. "Two down, five to go."

"What do you mean?" he asked.

"My grandma died in 1926, way before I was born. She had seven sisters. Not to mention my mother has a sister and a brother and then there's my dad's side of the family."

"Your dad lives here?" he asked.

"No."

He set his plate down on the end of the table. "Where does he live?"

I looked him straight in the eye and said a little too bitterly, "I don't know, and I don't want to know."

He understood he'd hit a nerve and looked away. Just then, Gunnar Ryan walked past the table and waved to me. I waved back. It seemed as though he was going to make his way over to be introduced, but somebody else grabbed his attention. The same thing had happened with Aunt Mildred and Aunt Stella. They never quite managed to get to the table to introduce themselves. "Who was that?" Jeb asked.

"Oh, that's Gunnar Ryan. He's a local deputy with the sheriff's office. He works out of Wellston, but grew up here in Greenhaven, so he still goes to church here. He's one of the smartest people I've ever met. College educated and the whole bit."

"Say, why don't I take you home?" Jeb asked, suddenly.

"What?" I asked, as though he'd grown a second head.

"Yeah, I've got a car. I'll drop you off on my way home."

"Oh, no thank you," I said, imagining him helping me into his car. I'd be mortified.

"Fine, I'll walk you home. I'll walk, you roll, and we'll call it walk-n-roll." He smiled, raising his eyebrows up and down.

I couldn't help but giggle. "That was the worst joke I've ever heard."

"Ahh, but it made you laugh. Come on, you can tell me more about this magic land that you live in."

"This magic land?" I asked, as he grabbed the back of my wheelchair and started pushing me down the gravel road. Back at the church, tongues would be waggling so fast that they'd probably fall off and out of people's mouths. My mother was nowhere to be seen, or I'm sure she would have chased me down the road demanding to know where I was going. "What, you mean, the land with no money? The land that's being destroyed day by day by mining? The land that most of America forgets is here? That land?"

"No, no, no, the land that makes you so alive and vibrant. I want to hear all about that land."

"You do realize that I live three miles that way," I said, pointing.

Jeb just continued pushing.

"Up and down hills," I added.

"I just ate a week's worth of food. I'll be fine."

"You'll die of indigestion," I said.

"I bought a sofa at the used store in Wellston. I'll sleep it off."

We reached the blacktop and he started pushing up hill along the two-lane road. "So, did you start reading the book I gave you?" he asked.

"Oh, yes," I said.

"What do you think of it?"

"Well, it's beautifully written, although clearly Thomas Wolfe did not get the memo from Mark Twain about killing adjectives, but that's okay. It's really brilliant, actually. But, so far, it works more as a lesson in descriptive writing than as a work of fiction."

"Why's that?" he said, huffing and puffing as we reached the top of the hill.

"Well, because so far, I don't really like any of the characters. And if I'm going to read something that's not true, I should like somebody in it. Otherwise, it's too much like doing homework."

He laughed at that and said, "Fair enough."

"I'll keep reading, though. Because some of the passages are quite breathtaking, and maybe I'll like the people more later. But as of right now, it's like reading one long beautiful exercise in descriptive clauses."

"And who are your favorite writers?" he asked.

Without hesitation I said, "Daphne du Maurer and Jane Austen. After that I'd say Ellery Queen, Agatha Christie, and Raymond Chandler. And Hemingway, Poe, Twain. Especially Poe—wait, and Forster. Well, especially Twain. The Brontes, although I despise *Wuthering Heights*. Do I really have to answer that question? It's very difficult."

"What's your sister's story?" he asked, abruptly changing the subject.

"She's waiting for somebody to marry her."

"Does somebody have a name?"

"No, no, anybody will do."

"And your brother? What's his name?"

"Humpy."

"Humpy? Surely that's not his real name."

"Oh, no, uh...Benjamin." We never called him Benjamin and I'd nearly forgotten it.

"And what's he like?"

"He's convinced the world revolves around him," I answered.

"And your mom?"

"Why do you care so much?" I asked.

"You're an interesting person," he said.

"You're the one from civilization. I should be asking you all the questions."

"So, ask me something."

Now that he put me on the spot, I couldn't think of anything. Except the description he'd given of the book he was writing. "Have you really been all over America?"

"Here and there, a few months at a time, but I've only lived in Maryland and New York."

"And now here."

"Yes, and now here."

"Why?"

"I told you why. I'm looking for something."

"What are you looking for?"

"If I knew, I would have found it by now. At least I hope that I would. I don't know, Olivia, I just know that there is something I'm supposed to find, something that holds the answer to all my questions. And it's not in Maryland."

"That seems like a rather unproductive way to go at something."

"How so?" he asked.

"Well, if you don't make a grocery list when you go to the store, you just wander around all of the aisles, not certain of anything, just tossing things in the cart because they happen to appeal to you right then. Only then you get home and find out that you didn't get the main ingredient that you needed for at least three different meals. If you make a list, you know what you're looking for, you save time, energy, money, and you get what you need."

"So, in other words, I shouldn't start looking until I know what it is."

"Or where it is."

"But then, I'd skip right over that jar of peanut butter that I might not have thought to get while making my list, and it turns out to be the greatest jar of peanut butter on the earth and makes me extremely happy."

"Well, there are two sides to everything," I said, wondering if his mind always worked like this. He was exhausting. "I suppose you have to choose which one is best for you. Personally, I like to make a list."

"That's the safe way," he said.

"Practical and productive. I get results."

"No, you only get the results you want to get. But you're completely closed off to any other unexpected results."

"Pragmatic," I countered.

"Why can't you admit that it's the safe way?" he asked.

"Because you make it sound like there's something wrong with that," I said, exasperated.

"There is no right or wrong, Olivia. It just is."

"If there's no right or wrong, then why are you hounding me about it?"

"I'm not hounding. I'm simply stating that if people don't like what they're doing, where they're going or who they are, then they need to take a different approach. Don't complain about a result if you're not willing to change the approach."

"I wasn't complaining. I'm not the one looking for something. You are."

"Are you certain about that?" he asked.

Just as I was getting truly irritated with him, we came around a bend, and a clearing opened to the right. I felt my chair slowing and coming to a stop. "What is that?" Jeb asked.

I glanced over at the clear, clean water bubbling up out of the ground, through a man made pipe. The water spewed over the sides and cascaded into the wading pool. "It's an artesian well."

"For real?" Jeb asked.

"It's the cleanest water that you'll find."

The next thing I knew he had swung my wheelchair off the road and down the hill through the grass. "How does it work, exactly?" he asked, struggling to get my chair through the thick growth.

"Uh, I think it has something to do with the water table being higher than the well, or something. Anyway, this is part of the Pickens property. Arnie's grandfather dug and put the shaft in and now it spits out probably a couple hundred gallons a day. At least that's what I'm told."

We hit a clod of dirt and I grabbed at the sides of my chair. "Where are we going, exactly?" I asked.

"I'm going to go get a drink of that water."

"Oh," I said, and held on tighter. "We have water at the house." But my words were lost on the wind. The ride through the grass went bumpity bump, and grasshoppers, being frightened by our impromptu hike, kicked out in every direction from the ankle-high grass. Jeb pushed me right up to the edge of the water and then stopped with his hands on his hips, catching his breath. His eyes took in all of it. The picturesque little pond, with a surface as reflective as glass, and the surreal blue sky rising up from behind vivid green hills that swaddled every living thing.

"Wow," he said. He removed his shoes quickly and waded through the pool to the center where the never-before-touched-water gurgled from beneath the earth. Closing his eyes, he leaned over, opened his mouth and drank, and drank, and drank. When he was finished he stood up and wiped his mouth on the back of his bare wrist. "That was amazing."

It was not lost on me how exhilarated he was by the most minor of things. Or maybe it was that the well was not a minor thing, but only that I'd grown up with it and was unaware of its value. It made me wonder if all things were like that. And as I sat there watching him take yet another drink, I realized that this must be true. Because I had not understood how much I loved my father until he was gone, or how much I loved to walk and dance, until I couldn't.

"Come on," he said. "Olivia, you have to try some of this."

"Jeb, I've had it before."

"Oh, but have you had some today?"

I smiled and looked away. The next thing I knew, he was sloshing toward me through the knee-deep water with a grin on his face. He swooped me up like one would cradle a baby, and my instinct was to wrap my arms around his neck. He carried me to the fountain and then realized that there was no easy way for me to get to it. He tried bending over so that my face would be close to the pipe, almost fell and overcompensated the other way and teetered over backwards and landed in the water with me on top of him. Immediately I rolled to my stomach and sat up, the water reaching my breasts. It was cold, and my teeth started to chatter, and my skirt *whooshed* out in a perfect circle around me. I imagined that I must have looked like a giant lily-pad; my head was the toad roosted on top.

Jeb came up out of the water with the most shocked look on his face. Then he laughed the most pure and hardy laugh I'd ever heard from a grown man. I mean, the kind of laugh where I could see all of the molars in his head. He slapped the palms of his hands down onto the water and yelled, "Whoooo hoooo. Hot damn!"

I was not as amused.

After a moment he looked at me and said, "What's the matter?"

"I'm wet."

Shrugging he said, "So? At least it's summer." Then he laughed some more.

"How am I supposed to explain to my mother, and every other old biddy who lives within six valleys and five miles, how my dress got soaking wet in your presence? *On a Sunday!*" I said, as if the day of the week mattered.

I had to give him credit. He at least tried to behave as though he had done something wrong. But it only lasted a second, and then he was laughing again, and I was laughing right along with him.

"Well," he said, "We'll just have to improvise."

Five minutes later we were lying in the sun, me with my dress spread out around me so that it would dry faster. Jeb had grown quiet then, as we both just lay there and watched the big white fluffy clouds moving and changing shapes above us. "I really am sorry about getting your dress wet."

"It's okay, it's drying." Although I knew it wasn't okay, because every car that passed on the road was somebody I knew and they all saw me lying spread eagle in the grass with a thirty-year-old stranger lying next to me. My mother was going to kill me. And when she was finished, Aunt Mildred would try and kill me again.

"I could have hurt you."

"Ah, I'm not made of china. You'd be amazed at the things I've done."

"Really? Like what?" he asked.

"Like, at the hospital, me and the kids would go outside after lunch. There was this big, long hill in front of the hospital, and we'd scoot out of our wheelchairs onto the ground and then roll down the hill."

He smiled. "How'd you get back up?"

"We crawled. First person safely back in their wheelchair won."

"You're joking," he said, incredulous.

"No, I'm not. And we used to have archery tournaments. The therapists thought that it was good for us to learn, because it built arm and back muscles, which we really need, since our arms double as our legs. But it also taught us patience and precision. Well, I won every tournament we had. In fact, I can nail a squirrel as it's running up a tree."

His jaw dropped open. "That's amazing." He looked up at the trees with a grin and said, "So, then, I take back my apologies."

"Jeb," I said, suddenly serious.

"What?" he asked.

"What are you *really* doing here?"

In the grass next to me he grew deathly still and quiet.

"There are a thousand and one places you could have gone where nobody could find you. In fact, you would have stood out less if you'd gone to New York City. You come to a place like this and you're going to be noticed. Tell me the truth."

"It's true, I'm writing a book. I also needed to get away, clear my head."

"A woman?"

He paused. "Why do you ask?"

"Nobody clutters up a man's head more than a woman." At least that's what Raymond Chandler implies in all of his books.

He sat up then, and his profile against the ancient mountains was quite breathtaking.

"Have I told you that I have a son?"

"No," I said.

"He's seven. Lives in Louisiana. His mother won't let me see him. His name is Reuben."

"I'm sorry," I said, because I simply did not know what else to say. "Are you married?"

"No, divorced. I always swore if I had a child that I'd be there for him. After what had been done to me..."

"Jeb, I understand all that. What I don't understand is why you picked *here*."

He glanced over at me and smiled. It wasn't a jubilant smile, nor was it a knowing smile. Instead it was sad, wrought with a mixture of emotions that I could not decipher. "Because this is the magic land."

Lunch with Aunt Mildred
September 1958

It was two weeks later, mid-September, when another stranger came to town. This stranger, a man in his mid-forties with a shock of grayish white hair and a lazy left eye, actually took up residence in the next town over. Considering Eva, West Virginia, was a town of about three hundred, a stranger renting a room at the Hill Top motel for an "undetermined" amount of time was news the county over. And it wasn't long before the gossip mill started, assuming that there had to be a connection between Jeb and this newcomer, either that or the world was coming to an end. With each person who came into contact with him the stranger's lazy eye got lazier, until the blasted thing was nearly down to his armpit, and last I heard he was beginning to stoop and grow a hump on his back. Aunt Mildred simply refused to let me visit this new stranger—based on the fact he was staying at a motel and that just wasn't proper— which irritated me to no end, because I wanted to see for myself if the Hunchback of Notre Dame had indeed taken up residence in Eva. He, according to Aunt Mildred, had to be a man of questionable character, or why else would he be at the Hilltop, and therefore we would all pretend as though he didn't exist and he would just go away. Those were my aunt's instructions, anyway.

I was working on a way to get to Eva to see for myself.

Clive had started school, and I wasn't sure which one of us was more distraught. My Aunt Mildred, sensing that I had been feeling claustrophobic and confined, not to mention lonely, offered to take me to lunch with her boyfriend, Edwin. Edwin Mayfair was—what else?—a life-long resident of Greenhaven and had never married. After Aunt Mildred's husband, John, had passed away, Edwin started sitting on Aunt Mildred's porch. Sometimes he even sat on the porch with Aunt Mildred. There was a rumor going around that at one point, back in the day, Edwin had been in love with Mildred, but for whatever reason she had denied him. Then years later she met John and married him. Whatever Mildred hadn't seen in Edwin forty years ago, she seemed to find in him now. Which was a good thing. I liked Edwin, he was a simple man, late sixties, walked with a limp, had sparkly eyes, was always chewing on a piece of Juicy Fruit and wore his pants pulled up to his armpits. He adored Mildred, and my aunt didn't seem so sad anymore. Before Edwin, I would catch her wringing her handkerchief, her eyebrows working up and down, while she clearly carried on a conversation with herself, even if it was just in her head. Since Edwin, I would catch her smiling for no reason, and realized that Edwin had brought her happiness.

Wellston sported a few diners, the public school for the whole county, the sheriff's office, the library—if one can call a building that is six feet by six feet wide a library—and the post-office and newspaper, which shared a building. Most controversial, there was a drive-in theatre. The courthouse happened to be here, also, since Wellston was the county seat.

Aunt Mildred, Edwin and I sat at a table in Mumford's Diner, having a leisurely lunch, talking about the weather and whatnot. Edwin was having breakfast for lunch, as he usually did. The man could eat bacon, eggs, toast and hash browns three times a day. He'd just switch up what flavor jams or preserves he'd put on his toast and called that being adventurous. Aunt Mildred had the club sandwich, while I enjoyed the famous chicken and dumplings. I also decided that in honor of Agatha Christie's birthday, which was today, that I would have a piece of cake for dessert. If I didn't think that Aunt Mildred would consider me completely off my rocker, I would even have put a candle on it. But, I decided there was no point in pushing the limit, seeing as how she already thought that I was odd beyond compare, due in part to the fact that I have a literary calendar that hangs above my bed—one that I painstakingly researched and made myself with birthdates, death dates and publication dates of my favorite authors.

We were halfway through lunch when Edwin dropped a bombshell. "I'm fixin' to get one of those television sets, Mildred."

"What?" Mildred asked. "Well, whatever for?"

I chimed in, "I think that would be wonderful, Edwin!" Admittedly, I had somewhat selfish motivations for agreeing with him. Edwin would, no doubt, invite me over to watch it on occasion.

"Well, I been thinkin' that if I could get that station that shows The Grand Ole Opry, that I might be able to catch a glimpse of Kitty Wells some night," he said. As if we ought to know just how important getting a glimpse of Kitty Wells was.

Aunt Mildred waved a hand. "Oh, pooh, Edwin. Arnie's got a television set and he only gets one station and that's only if his oldest boy is holding on to that antenna thing. That's an awful lot of money to put into something you may not be able to use."

Edwin seemed dejected as he scooped his runny eggs onto his toast. "Well, Edwin," I said, instantly feeling sorry for him. Aunt Mildred's first reaction to everything was often negative. "Can't you get the Grand Ole Opry on your radio?"

He shrugged.

Aunt Mildred had the decency to look embarrassed over shooting Edwin down. "Well, now," I said. "Aunt Mildred's a very smart woman and I'm sure she's just trying to look out for your finances, but she doesn't know everything."

Aunt Mildred cut her eyes around to me, but said nothing. He shrugged again. I knew Edwin would not make a major decision like buying a television set if Mildred didn't give her blessing. They weren't married, I didn't think they were ever going to be married, but Edwin would lay his life on the line for Mildred, and if she really disapproved of something, he wouldn't do it. Kitty Wells or not.

"Olivia, when are you going to bring Mr. McDowell by the house to meet me? I didn't get to speak to him at church last Sunday," she took a drink of lemonade. "With Clive, of course. Bring him with Clive."

"Oh, uh, well I'll have to ask him when he wants to come by. But, honestly, I haven't seen him in a few days. He keeps to himself quite a bit and he doesn't have a telephone, so I only talk to him when he decides to come down the mountain."

She pursed her lips together. "And it'd better stay that way, too."

"Now what's that supposed to mean?" I asked.

Nobody, and I mean nobody, had mentioned the fact that I had lain in the sun with a soaking wet dress for three hours with a man twelve years older than me. At least not to my face. Plenty had been said to my mother, and in fact, I knew she'd received her fair share of boos and hisses from the coven of mothers who all thought they knew how to raise everybody else's children. "How could you let her do that, Rosalee? I know she's a cripple and all, but you have to draw the line somewhere." Those words had come from a neighbor who just thought she was helping out, because clearly, my mother was obviously inept or she would have never allowed the whole incident to happen in the first place. What I couldn't figure out was how my mother was supposed to be able to see into the future to know I was going to fall into the well and need drying out. If she could have done that, she would have been

Mother of the Year and way better than any of her accusers. I had heard my mother on the phone putting people in their places and I'd heard Willie Gene telling her not to worry, that I wasn't senseless, and to let me be. And I'd even heard a whisper of a scandal that Willie Gene had told Pearl Hargrave to shut her trap and mind her own business, while the two were fighting over a side of bacon at Arnie's store. I'm not sure how the progression of subject matter went from bacon to me, exactly, but I would have given anything to have seen it.

At any rate, I was sure that in her own way, Aunt Mildred had just driven home a dig that was meant to embarrass, tame and shame me all at the same time. She was good like that. She had a flair for saying a whole lot in as few words as possible. Like, when she said "apparently" in a specific tone, she was actually telling you how stupid you were and how your ancestors didn't have the brains God gave a slug and that you better keep your opinions to yourself or everybody would know it was true that you were stupider than a slug, and it'd no longer be just a rumor. Then there was the word "dadburnit," which I didn't really think was a word, but when Mildred used it, she was really saying all the curse words and profanity in the book without actually having to say them, so that you'd know how upset she was without her having to betray her cool exterior. And the ultimate word in Mildred's vocabulary was "harumph" accompanied by arms folding under her breasts and ankles clanking together. That actually meant that not only were you and your forefathers beyond stupid but that she wasn't about to waste her breath, nor taint the good memory of *her* ancestors, by bothering to tell you so, and so you should just toddle off into some corner somewhere and shut up.

Believe me, I'd just been insulted and put in my place. But I was going to make her say it anyway.

"Aunt Mildred," I said. "What did you mean by that?"

"You know darn good and well what I meant by that. He's far too old for you. You shouldn't go setting your sights on a man like that, and he should be shot for thinking anything untoward about you."

"Are you serious?" I asked. "There is nothing *untoward* going on between us."

"And it had better stay that way."

"You can't tell me what I can and can't do."

"Oh yes I can, and I just did. You make sure he keeps his distance. After a man's reputation is ruined, people get amnesia. When a woman's reputation is ruined, people never forget."

She bit into her club sandwich like she was taking a bite out of a buffalo hide.

"We don't think of each other like that," I said. "He's very friendly, that's all. He has a very unusual way of looking at the world. Or well, at least unusual in the sense that I've never encountered it. I'm certain that he means to ruin nobody's reputation. And you should give me the benefit of the doubt!"

"Now, listen here, Missy," Aunt Mildred said. But then Edwin laid a hand on her arm and shook his head.

"Olivia's a good girl, Mildred. She's got good judgment. Better head on her shoulder than most. She darn near thinks like a man."

"Why thank you, Edwin," I said. Being told I was anything like a man sort of made my skin crawl, but I realized that Edwin had just given me the highest compliment he could think of, so I accepted it.

Aunt Mildred rolled her eyes, but when she spoke, her voice was somewhat gentler. "Just trying to protect you, Livvy."

"And I thank you for that, too. But trust me, Jeb McDowell means no harm. Besides, don't you believe like everybody else that no man would want me anyway, since my legs don't work?"

Aunt Mildred stopped chewing her food and Edwin swallowed his hard. Almost as if she were in slow motion, Aunt Mildred resumed chewing, and Edwin glanced back and forth between the two of us, unsure if he should say or do something. Then with great difficulty she swallowed, took a drink of lemonade to wash it down, cleared her throat and with tears in her eyes said, "Now, Livvy. Don't you go puttin' stock into what others say about your legs." And that was it. She was finished with that topic.

Just then the door to Mumford's opened and in walked the Hunchback of Notre Dame! It had to be him. He had a lazy eye, and he wore a suit that was so expensive that it was obviously made in New York or Paris or...or China! People stared and anybody who had a seat along the pathway to the counter scooted their chairs a good six inches out of the way so he could pass.

This was my chance!

The stranger sauntered up to the counter, took his hat off and set it next to the napkin dispenser. He cocked a finger at the counter girl, who immediately walked to him and said, "What can I get for you?"

"I'll have the meatloaf," he said. "And pie."

"What kind of pie?" she asked.

"What kind you got?"

I swear, he sounded like Humphrey Bogart, except without the lisp.

"Apple, rhubarb, minced meat and pumpkin."

"I'll take the minced meat," he said.

The stranger chewed on a toothpick as his gaze flitted around the room, until it landed on me. There was nothing unusual in that. People often did that. Like, "Oh, ho-hum, what an ordinary day and an ordinary street and, by Jove, there's a girl in a wheelchair!" That type of thing. I was used to it. I took the opportunity and smiled at him.

Aunt Mildred kicked me under the table.

"Ouch!" I said. My muscles in my legs didn't work, but I could still *feel* everything! "I can't believe you kicked me!"

"I can't believe you smiled at him!" Aunt Mildred said.

"Now, Mildred," Edwin began, unrolling the wrapper on a piece of gum. "Ain't nothin' wrong with being friendly."

Mildred whipped her head around so fast I thought I heard her neck pop. "Edwin, stay outta this."

"No, now, you got to let that girl be sometimes, Mildred. She's not a dog, she ain't got no leash."

"And how many daughters have *you* raised?" she asked.

"None. How many have *you* raised?" he countered, shoving his Juicy Fruit in his mouth.

Aunt Mildred took in a quick breath, because indeed, she'd not had any children of her own, but she had taken care of Blanche's children for the better part of ten years. And I might add that her Victorian morals had not been all that successful, at least where my mother and her sister were concerned. "Edwin George Mayfair!" she exclaimed.

"Aw, Mildred, now don't go gettin' all fired up," he said, instantly regretting what he'd said.

While all that was going on, I had taken the opportunity to roll my chair over to the counter, extend my hand and say, "Olivia VanBibber."

The Hunchback smiled down at me, and maneuvered the toothpick to the side of his mouth without using his hands. He'd had practice at toothpick chewing. His face was craggy, his hair was thick and almost nearly white, but his body seemed spry like a young man. "My name is Clarence Ford," he said, shaking my hand.

"What brings you to Wellston, Mr. Ford?"

He smiled. "What makes you think I don't live here?"

"Because I don't know you," I said. "And one look at that hat tells me you probably spent more on it than most folks around here spend on their whole season's crop. Do you own one of the coal towns? Are you a coal mining official?"

He laughed, clearly amused by something I'd said.

"No, no, I'm just passing through."

"To where?"

He raised his eyebrows.

"If you're 'passing through' then you have to be from somewhere and going somewhere. Otherwise, you'd just be wandering around in circles. You don't seem like the type of person to chase your own tail, Mr. Ford."

He smiled at me. "Protective of your town?"

I nodded. "I suppose."

He sat there for a minute and seemed relieved when his food arrived.

"Well? What's your business here?" I asked. I pushed him a little too hard, I admit, but he was making me angry by the fact that he wouldn't answer me.

"My business here is not your business," he said.

"Do you know Jeb McDowell?" I asked, just on the off-handed chance that the townsfolk's giant leap of conclusions might be true. To my complete and utter surprise, his fork stopped mid-way to his mouth and his eyes cut around toward me. Those eyes said so much, but I had no manual to interpret their language. His lazy eye made me nervous, though, because I wasn't sure which eye I was supposed to look at. I didn't know if he could see clearly out of both of them, and I didn't want to meet his gaze and it be the wrong eye! I'd look like an idiot and all of the tough-girl attitude that I was trying to throw at him would be pointless. Later, I would think about whether or not a girl in a wheelchair could look tough and menacing regardless of how many eyes she was staring at. For right now, I was holding my breath, waiting for his reply.

"I think you need to get back over there with your grandma and mind your own business."

I gave an audible gasp. He *did* know Jeb! *He was here for Jeb!*

How could that be? How could he know him? Why would he follow Jeb here? Why would he care? What would be so important that he couldn't just wait for Jeb to return to Maryland? And more importantly, how could the gossip mill have made the connection and actually been right! Mr. Ford shooed a hand at me, like I was a fly sitting on the counter. Why, the nerve!

"Olivia Anne, what *are* you doing?" Aunt Mildred's shrill voice pierced the diner and bounced off all the windows.

"Just extending a warm welcome to Mr. Ford," I said. Then I rolled back over to the table where Mildred was properly astonished and embarrassed by my boldness. Edwin, however, winked at me, and shoved another piece of gum in his mouth.

Deputy Gunnar Ryan
Colton County Sheriff's Department

Milking the cow was not exactly Gunnar's idea of the perfect way to pass the day, but it needed to be done, and his mother had asked him to do it, and he'd found it difficult to ever tell his mother no. He could see the valley from where he sat on the milking stool, and noticed a change in the air. Autumn would be here soon. Ella, the cow, gave him a nudge with her head. That was her way of telling him he wasn't paying attention, which was true. He was too busy looking out of the barn door at the valley and the mountains as they folded in on the meadow. He wanted to be...out there.

He often went into the woods for no other reason than to be there. The connection was immediate, primitive, bordering on animistic. Leaving Greenhaven and moving to Ohio had taught him one thing. Well, other than people in Ohio didn't pronounce their state's name as *Uhiya,* and that they thought those who did were stupid. It taught him that he would never truly be happy. He was wild at heart and at home among the trees and babbling brooks of Appalachia, but he was equally at home among the wilderness of concrete buildings, bright city lights and the groupings of city dwellers.

He loved the heartbeat of civilization, the pounding of pedestrians on sidewalks, the cacophony of horns and industry. He loved being in both places, never satisfied to be away from the other for very long and always wishing, eventually, that he could wake up in the other.

He had friends in both places, and found that he liked both equally, too. His city friends were from all over the country, with wild ideas and vivid imaginations and outrageous experiences. They talked in terms of what-ifs and why-nots, always challenging him to think outside the box, to think outside of the valley. But his country friends were real, and spoke in terms of what is and what was, without giving too much thought to the what-ifs, and that was somehow comforting. His life-long friends, his country friends, he could sit with for hours on the side of a riverbank and not say a word. Not one word, and not feel lonely or misunderstood. Five minutes of silence with his city friends and they'd explode with the need to communicate, and they made silence seem almost vulgar.

And it was truly heart wrenching, this adoration of both worlds. And he never wanted to compromise. He didn't want to bring the city to this paradise, and he didn't want to bring the country to the city for fear it would water down the effect. He would just have to get used to the fact that he would spend his whole life wishing he were someplace else, even though he loved where he was at any given moment. He smiled at the ridiculousness of the situation. Only he could be miserable by being too happy.

When Ella was finished giving milk, Gunnar set the pan out of the way so it wouldn't get toppled over. He stroked the long side of Ella's ribcage. She had been a part of their family for years.

He couldn't get the conversation with Noah Cabbel out of his head, though. Noah had dozed in and out of consciousness on the way to Charleston. Sometimes he'd recited scripture. Other times the recipe for his moonshine, which Gunnar had promised he wouldn't reveal. And sometimes Noah had just cussed a blue streak. He cussed for being shot in the foot, he cussed because of his no account son-in-law, he cussed at his lot in life and he just cussed for no reason whatsoever other than he liked the sound of it and it made him feel better. But always, Gunnar had tried to bring the conversation around to Andrew Halbrook, Noah's son-in-law. Sometimes it had worked and sometimes it hadn't.

What Gunnar had learned was that, according to Noah, Andrew, with the help of Mosie Gibbon, had been helping himself to the things he was convinced his neighbors didn't need. Mosie was a black man who had never been in trouble with the law before, but who had been homeless longer than Gunnar had been alive. He was invisible to his white counterparts, and he was an outsider, even though Mosie Gibbon had been born and raised here just like everybody else. These invisible laws of who belonged and who didn't, were really starting to tick him off.

As for Andrew Halbrook, well, he simply could not find work, and while Noah had tried to help out where he could, it wasn't enough. Andrew was too proud to move in with his in-laws, but apparently not too proud to be a thief. Gunnar supposed that Andrew could justify one, but not the other. Unfortunately, one was illegal.

He carried the pail of milk back toward his parent's house, where he found his mother sitting on the back porch in the bright afternoon sun, peeling apples. The apples she'd just picked were collected in an old white oak split rib basket that she used for everything. The rounded handle was worn smooth from years of use. She had kept him and his siblings in this basket for the first six weeks of their lives, gathered eggs, carried wool to spin and finished yarn to knit. Apples, eggs, you name it; it all went in the basket. Whenever there was threat of fire, flood or any natural disaster, it was the first thing she grabbed. And then shoved it full of pictures.

"Your uniform is clean," she said.

"Oh, good, thanks," he said. "Look, even though I'm off today, there are a few things I need to check on. So, I'm going to be gone a few hours."

"Be home for supper?" she asked. His mother looked tired, and well over fifty, even though her fiftieth birthday wasn't until this coming January, but then he couldn't really remember a time when she looked any other way. Her blonde hair was mostly gray and her once blue eyes just as gray. It was as if she were a color photograph, slowly fading to black and white. Gunnar honestly didn't know much about how his parents had met, but they had knocked out five kids, one every two years, and they were all blonde-headed and blue-eyed in varying degrees. Gunnar was the oldest with a younger brother and three younger sisters.

"Put the milk on the porch," his mother said. "James is in a right foul mood today."

James was Gunnar's father, but he hadn't called him 'father' or 'dad' in well over a decade. He simply called him James, because to call him 'dad' to his face, made Gunnar want to vomit. At any rate, if his mother said that James was in a foul mood, the translation to that meant that James was on a binge and would try to punch the head off of whomever or whatever entered the house. Sometimes Gunnar wished his dad was a happy drunk, or a blubbery drunk, or hell, even a horny drunk. None of them left bruises. His mother would sit on the porch until his father passed out, because underneath the skin on her face, her bones were a roadmap of James Ryan's drunken destruction.

After placing the pail of milk carefully on the porch, he said, "You need anything?"

"I'm fine," she said, smiling up at him, even though she was anything but fine. But Gunnar could have predicted that was what she would say, because it was what she always said. No matter what. There had been times blood was running down her face.

I'm fine.

Her jaw hanging loose because it had been punched out of socket.

I'm fine.

Fibula snapped in two.

I'm fine, baby. Just fine.

Her fingers broken from fighting back. Earlobe nearly bitten clean off.

I'm fine.

His mother was afraid to admit out loud that she was anything but fine, because then, once the words were spoken, they couldn't be taken back and something had to be done about them. Something would have to be done about those words that now hung in time and space, declared for all to hear. And sometimes, that was more terrifying to her than doing nothing at all. So she was fine. And she would always be fine until James was dead.

With his chore done, Gunnar grabbed several apples out of the basket and shoved them in his pockets and headed toward his car. His sisters, Louise and Mary, had gotten married as soon as they could, to get away from James, and while his brother, Kevin, technically still lived at home, he worked three jobs and was saving every penny for college and nobody ever saw him. Kevin should have enough money to start his education next year, even though most students his age would be graduating already. It didn't matter, as long as he got the education. Gunnar had gotten his the exact same way, working and saving and working and saving, and now it was Kevin's turn. Betty Jo was the youngest and the only other one left at home. She'd be married within the year, he had no doubt, even though she wasn't seeing anybody.

As he pulled the car out of the driveway, he took one last look at his mother in the rearview mirror. She'd sit there until dark if she had to, dinner be damned. They'd all eat peeled apples.

Noah had given Gunnar a few hints as to where Andrew and Mosie were picking up their acquisitions. He wasn't sure what he thought he'd find, maybe he'd catch them in the act? That was a long shot. Still, he couldn't help but follow up on it. If Andrew and Mosie really were stealing from their neighbors, something needed to be done about it. It wasn't as if anybody in this county was rich enough to support the thieving habits of the less fortunate. It also happened to be against the law. Gunnar understood that desperate men do desperate things and sometimes—if nobody was getting hurt—it was all right to look the other way. But, Gunnar could not look the other way when somebody was outright stealing. Helping yourself to apples in your neighbor's orchard that otherwise may fall and rot on the ground was okay, in Gunnar's book. What those two were allegedly doing was nowhere near just picking extra apples.

He also had a sneaking suspicion that Andrew and Mosie just might be the two prowlers that the newcomer, Jeb, had been complaining about.

So Gunnar checked his glove box to make sure he had a bag of candy, and then he drove a few miles until he came to a road that only had a number and not a name. The road was gravel and narrow and it wound back and back, higher and higher, until he came to a squatter's camp. Well, that's what he called it anyway. It was government land, not owned by anybody private, and for about a half a mile along the road, there was one trailer, plywood hut and boxcar after another. Anything that people could use to keep the rain off of their heads. And since it was government land, Gunnar let it slide. The government would run them off once it found out, but that could be years down the road, and for now, these people had a place to sleep, and so Gunnar let them stay. In fact, it was an unspoken agreement among the deputies to leave these people alone. And if the G-men came knocking, he'd swear that all of the squatters had just appeared over night. Shacks and all.

He knew Andrew didn't live here and he knew Mosie didn't, either. Mosie was too wild for anything resembling a community. But some of the residents might know where he was. This, too, was a long shot, because Mosie was usually on the move, but people were creatures of habit and he was certain that Mosie would have places that he liked more than others. He could have gone straight to Andrew's house and talked to him, but he figured he'd be more likely to get information from Mosie. Mosie was harmless; he wasn't so sure about Andrew Halbrook.

As soon as he pulled his car off of the road, barefoot and half-naked children stopped playing ball and tag and came to see the stranger in the "fancy" car. The saddest part of poverty was always the children. These children were so poor that they couldn't even attend school. They had no shoes, barely any clothes. And they were dirty and infested with lice. None of them had electricity so they would have had no light by which to do homework at night. Education was free, but they were too poor to partake in it. And so, the cycle would just repeat unless somebody did something about it.

He opened the glove box and took out the brown paper bag that had gum drops and jawbreakers in it. "Hey y'all," he said, getting out of the car.

The kids were curious, but cautious. It's been said that a lawman walks a certain way and if that were true, these kids knew immediately that he was a deputy. But the brown paper bag caught their attention. "Your parents around anywhere?"

A few adults had come out of the buildings. A couple of dogs, just as skinny as the kids, ran around barking.

"Whatchoo want, Deputy Ryan?" A voice said. Gunnar glanced about and saw a woman, his age, standing in the doorway of a lean-to. In fact, he recognized her, she'd gone to school with him off and on, until she finally had to drop out, either because the family had no money, her parents needed her help, or she got pregnant. Most likely it was all three.

He held the bag out, but the kids just eyed him, warily. Then he stuck his hand in and pulled out a gumdrop. The kid's eyes lit up. "Come on," he said. "Everybody gets one."

The woman rolled her eyes and stepped toward him. "You come all the way out here just to give candy to babies?"

"No, no," he said. "I uh...I can't remember your name."

"Marla."

"That's right, Marla Hopkins," he said.

"I heard you went to Columbus."

He nodded.

"You got to be damned fool crazy to come back here. You ain't stupid, so you has to be crazy."

Gunnar smiled and shuffled a rock with his foot. He'd been called crazy before. Lots of times. "Well, there might be some truth to that."

She smiled. She was tall, thin as a rail, and even through the grime and hopelessness she was still cute with the dimples and curly brown hair.

"I'm actually trying to find Mosie Gibbon. You know him?"

"A course I know him."

The kids had each taken a piece of candy, and a shirtless, shoeless redheaded boy had handed Gunnar back the bag, with half of the contents still in it. The children had nothing, but they took only what he told them they could have and gave the rest back.

"Look, he's not done anything wrong. I just need to talk to him. He's got some information I need and that's it. You know where I might find him?"

"Marla! Who you talkin' to?" a voice boomed from inside the trailer.

Marla's expression dropped. He could have sworn he saw fear at first, but then it was just contempt. "Shut the hell up, Hank, I'm busy!" she yelled over her shoulder.

"Look, I don't want to cause any trouble. Just need to know if you've seen Mosie in the last couple of days."

"Yeah, he was camping up there on the mountain, down the east side, Thursday past. He might still be up there."

"Thanks," Gunnar said. "Any place that he frequents? A place he prefers over another?"

Just then Hank came out of the trailer, twenty years older than Marla, unshaven, wearing what was once a white T-shirt that was now gray with black smudges, and pants two sizes too big.

Gunnar remembered that he had a few dollars in his front pocket. Slowly he pulled it out and handed it to her. She looked down at the money, wanting to take it. He wasn't sure why she hadn't snatched it, unless it was because she didn't want him to think she was desperate. Women were funny like that. "Go on, it's for helping me. But don't let him drink it."

She glanced back at Hank.

"What do you want?" Hank called out.

"Just asking for directions," Gunnar said back to him.

Finally, Marla took the money, it couldn't have been more than four or five dollars, but that would buy a hell of a lot of loaves of bread. She shoved it in the pocket of her dress while facing Gunnar so that Hank couldn't see.

As Gunnar was about to leave, he looked back at the kids who had resumed playing. He motioned for the red-headed boy and handed him the bag. "Now, I'm trusting you to share this, dole it out, fair like, you got me?"

A beaming smile spread from ear to ear. "Yes sir!"

"I mean it, if I hear you weren't being fair, and playing favorites, I'm going to come knock your noggin. You got me?"

"Yes sir!"

"All right," Gunnar said. Then he pulled the apples out of the car and quickly did a head count. Fourteen kids, eight apples. Why hadn't he grabbed more? "You gotta cut these in half, each of you gets a half. Give what's left to any pregnant ladies. Okay?" The kid nodded in compliance.

Gunnar got back in the car and drove on up the mountain until the road wouldn't go any further. He opened the trunk where he kept a backpack at all times. It had matches, a change of shoes and clothes, a blanket, some old army rations that he'd bought at Arnie's, and a thermos full of water. Then he put his pistol in the side pocket of the pack, grabbed his rifle, put his keys in his front pocket and headed up the mountain to try and find Mosie's camp.

He'd been walking about an hour when he found the camp in a small clearing. Mosie had taken a couple of old shirts and sewn them together to make a canopy that he'd tied to four sticks and stuck in the ground. A circle of rocks held the burned contents of a fire, and there were some blankets strewn all about. Gunnar knelt down and placed a hand over the fire. Warm. He took a stick and moved the coals around and found a little bit of red-orange amongst the white ash. Mosie had been here recently.

He could call out his name, but Gunnar knew that Mosie would just stay put if he heard it. If he was guilty of stealing with Andrew, he was going to assume that's what Gunnar wanted him for.

He took another look at some of the things lying about and found an old hatchet that had the name Joe Graham carved on the side of it. Wonder if that was old Joe Graham? He had died when Gunnar was about eight or nine, maybe even ten years old, but he'd been a lifelong resident of Greenhaven, and the great-grandfather of Olivia VanBibber. In fact, Joe Graham had lived his last few years with Olivia's Aunt Mildred. Gunnar couldn't help but wonder how Mosie got the hatchet. Had it been a gift from Joe Graham for a job he'd done for him? He doubted that Mosie could hang onto anything for, what, fifteen years or so? But a hatchet was important for living in the woods, so maybe he had held onto it. Or maybe Mildred had given it to him? Or maybe, he'd stolen it. Some of that booty that he and Andrew were helping themselves to? He made a mental note to stop by and ask Mildred about it.

He looked around for signs of where Mosie would have gone. He most likely would not have gone too far, probably just out to catch a fish or something for dinner. Gunnar found signs of broken leaves and twigs and followed, just like he would if he was hunting a deer. He found several foot prints, partial prints and then he came to the creek. No Mosie sitting on the bank fishing, and no sign that he'd been there fishing, but then Gunnar had to concede that Mosie could have been further up or down stream.

Gunnar crossed the creek without giving it much thought. He'd lost the trail and figured that Mosie had walked in the creek for a while and that's why he couldn't find any evidence of him being on this side of the water. He decided to keep walking, hoping to rediscover the trail. He walked another half hour and reluctantly concluded that he'd have to turn back pretty soon or it would be dark. He had to concede that today would not be the day that he found Mosie Gibbon. Just then, he realized where he was. He had come out of the woods above the old Renshaw place. He was looking down on Jeb McDowell's new home.

"Huh," was all he said. Maybe the prowler that Jeb had reported really was Mosie. Or maybe Mosie was just using this as his quick short cut to the road at Chestnut Hill, and meant no harm. Mr. McDowell would have no way of knowing the difference. Gunnar headed toward the house, and noticed that there was no car parked anywhere. Most likely the newcomer wasn't home. He'd try anyway.

When he got to about a hundred yards of the house he heard growling, and Gunnar pulled up short. He should have known there'd be dogs. Everybody had dogs. The funny thing was, he could hear them, but he still couldn't see them. Eventually one came out from under the porch, a blood hound. He bared his teeth at Gunnar, and Gunnar inched backward. "Nice puppy. I mean no harm. I got lost, is all," he said.

Then the other dog came from around the smoke house. Another blood hound. It was as if revealing their presence had been planned, a coordinated effort. It took unbelievable control, and he realized the hounds must have had excellent training. He frantically strained to see if there were chains on their collars and found none. So, Jeb McDowell turned his dogs loose when he was gone. Well, that said a lot about Mr. McDowell. One, he trusted his dogs implicitly. And two, he trusted his neighbors not at all.

Gunnar kept backing away and when he'd gotten to what he assumed was a safe distance, the dogs quit growling and lay back down. It took every ounce of strength he had, but he turned his back on the animals and walked back into the woods. Even though he was alone, nobody would know if he'd retreated backwards all the way or not, but he would know. And somehow, he didn't want to give the dogs that satisfaction. So, he turned his back on them and hoped he didn't get mauled.

A Letter to Viola from Olivia

Viola Reinhardt
Dayton, Ohio
September 15th, 1958

Dear Aunt Viola,

Well, the Yankees swept a doubleheader against Kansas City and clinched the American League pennant. Not that you are without newspapers and are in the dark on such matters, but Clive insisted that I tell you this, in case you didn't know. You realize, he will be unbearable to speak to until November, and depending on who wins, it could be Thanksgiving before he's himself again.

Jebediah McDowell, the stranger who bought the Renshaw place, is the most amazing person. He finds this place quite intoxicating, and there are times I feel as though I'm in the company of a three-year-old who's just discovering the world. He and I have become fast friends, since he loves to read, and he's the only person within a hundred miles who has read some of the same books as me, and he owns more books than the local library, which isn't saying much, but still. You should see all of his books! He didn't laugh at me at all when I told him about my literary calendar, in fact he pointed out that it was better for me to have an obsession with literary figures than with venomous snakes or gangsters. He loves music, eats as if there will be famine tomorrow, and laughs, uproariously, openly and loudly at the slightest of things. He also has the most unique way of looking at things and is completely convinced that there is nothing anybody can't do, if they truly want it enough. Even women! Even me.

And although he does keep to himself quite a bit, he has become very comfortable with Clive, me and my family. I'm not entirely blind to him, though. I think he's hiding a secret, but then aren't we all?

He came for dinner the other night. My mother made pinto beans with ham and cornbread with fried apples for dessert. You would have thought she'd made caviar. He made so much noise while he ate I thought Willie Gene was going to kick him out of the house. One thing's for sure, he has made me twice as popular as ever, because everybody who sees me stops and asks me about him. And you were right. Aunt Stella has questioned me over and over, asking all these details about him. It's a bit annoying actually. But it's nice to have somebody around who likes to discuss the finer points of what makes a good novel.

Speaking of which; *Wuthering Heights.*

I simply pointed out in my paper that the book did not work as a romance, because all of the characters are so completely unlikeable that I could scarcely understand how anybody could be in love with anybody at all. When Heathcliff isn't brooding, he's full of malevolence and mischief and hate, and when Cathy's not being a tyrannical hell-cat—oh wait, she's *always* being a tyrannical hell-cat. Honestly, by the end of the book, I just wanted them all dead, and nearly got what I wished for. Cathy was ashamed of Heathcliff, and chose not the man she loved, but the man who could give her what she wanted, and so I say, she deserved to be unhappy. The second Cathy's treatment of Hareton is so repugnant, so...loathsome, so...horrid, that I nearly needed to get out a thesaurus just to find new words that mean *awful*. I just think that as a romance this book fails because, well, love should make you kinder and less of a jerk. That's all I'm saying.

The book does have an absolutely brilliant sense of place, so much so that if I closed my eyes I could almost feel the fog of the moors on my face. I was too busy wishing them all dead, though, and really, how am I supposed to be able to concentrate on anything if I'm plotting everybody's murder? Mrs. Hollingberry proclaimed in her rebuttal that there are passages in *Wuthering Heights* that were so gorgeous, so exquisite and sublime, that she could just die—and I say, fine, go to the great moor in the sky with all the other crazies!

In the end, we also have to remember that the story is told second- and third-hand, so we don't even really know if what happened actually happened or if Lockwood just made it all up. Of course, it's all made up, it's a novel. I suppose my real question is why would I want to spend hours and hours and hours with people who make me unhappy and sad and angry, and in the end realize that I've just read a book with no protagonists whatsoever? And I suppose if that's what you want from your leisure time, then have at it.

My point, dear auntie, really isn't about the book, it's about my freedom to have an opinion and express it. When I dare give an opinion that goes against the Dominion of Great Literature, it is assumed that I am wrong. It made me not like Mrs. Hollingberry, just a smidge. Of course it's impossible for me to not like her completely; she's an English teacher.

So, there you are.

There is a dance Friday night. Aunt Runa said she would fix my hair.

Oh, and have I read *A Room With a View?* I have read everything E. M. Forster has ever published. It's also my favorite of all of his novels, so if you have an opinion and want to share it, I would, of course, love to hear it.

Love you bunches,
Olivia

The Dance

"I can't believe it!" Clive yelled the minute he came in from school.

"Can't believe what?" I asked.

"I just heard from Bobby Dailey that the Milwaukee Braves clinched the pennant! I wanted the Reds in the championship, but they were just out of it this year. But you know what this means, doncha?" Clive was clearly excited. His hands were flailing all about. His eyes nearly had fire coming out of them.

"No," I said. "What?"

For a brief moment he looked gravely disappointed in the fact that I didn't know what this meant, but then he realized that my ignorance would give him the opportunity to tell me, and he got all excited again. "It means, two years in a row, Braves take on the Yankees for the championship!"

"Wow," I said, not sure if this was exciting-good or exciting-bad, since he was neither a Yankees fan nor a Milwaukee fan. "So, we're rooting for...?"

"Milwaukee, of course," he said and then thought about it a second. "Dad will root for New York, I'm almost positive. But I'm going with the team that has Lew Burdette!"

Lew Burdette, a fellow West Virginian who was peripherally related to somebody's cousin's aunt, so of course, Clive was going to be on his side. Willie Gene had a tendency to root statistics. He'd go for whoever had the best chance of winning, whereas Clive would go with his gut. He'd root for the team that meant something to him, or had a player who meant something to him. It usually—but not always—meant that Willie Gene won all of their bets. Last year, if I remembered correctly, Lew Burdette was the star of the series, and not without reason. It's not every day a guy pitches two shut-outs in a World Series. He earned his MVP title that year. But, on a deeper, more personal note, it was always nice to see a local boy make it big, and I think that resonated with Clive much more than anything else.

When the occasion arose for me to have a stake in anything like that, I always rooted for the underdog, which said a whole lot about me. Actually, who we rooted for said a lot about all of us. Willie Gene wanted to be right, so he picked the team who statistically had a better chance of winning. Clive wanted a connection to these gods of baseball, so he went the personal route. On some level, I wanted to believe in miracles, so I always picked the underdog.

"Well, here's hoping Lew does it again!" I said to Clive.

"No kidding! I've got to find a schedule. I think the opening game is the first of October, but I need to find out for sure."

He grabbed the keys to my mom's car off of the counter and said, "You wanna come with me? I'm gonna run into town and see if I can find a paper with a schedule." He still had a week at the very least before the series started and I knew if he found out the schedule for the Series today, that he'd be unbearable to live with. I didn't discourage him, though, because there was so very little that Clive would get excited about.

"I don't really need anything in town, but if you'd drop me off at Aunt Runa's that would be great. The square dance is tonight and she said she'd fix my hair."

"Oh, yeah," he said. "I forgot about the dance."

"Are you going?"

"Yeah, I'm going."

"Give me a ride?"

He rolled his eyes. "Well, of course," he said. He didn't seem real thrilled about going to the dance. I didn't push him, I just waited a bit and then he added, "Some of the guys are going to the passion pit, but unless you got a girl, that's no fun."

Ah, the passion pit. The drive-in theatre. "Well, what about actually watching the movie? You don't have to makeout just because you're at the drive-in."

He gave me a look that suggested I didn't know anything and that I'd just crawled out from under some rock somewhere. Not having a girlfriend was really starting to bother him. I never got the impression that he actually liked any one particular girl, but I think he just felt left out. All the guys he hung out with talked about how far they got with what girl, and Clive had nothing to add, nor could he relate.

"Whatever," he said. "Harvey Grose is driving his new Plymouth Fury to the dance tonight. I want to get a good look at it. And besides, at least at the dance you can dance, regardless if you got a girl."

Well, I couldn't dance, but I went just to hear the music, laugh, and talk with the neighbors. Clive seemed to sense that I might take offense at what he said because he looked uncomfortable. "So, come on," he said. "I'll drop you off at Aunt Runie's."

Aunt Runa's house was right at the bend in the road, sitting so close to the blacktop that you could nearly see what was on her dinner table as you drove by. She had plenty of land in the back of the house, which I understood at one time had been important for crops and garden. Most of my aunts and uncles were what I called part-time farmers. They all usually held other jobs, like coal miner, teacher, seamstress, minister, post master, boarding house cook or manager. The farming was what they did on the side because there was no way, especially during the Depression, that their regular jobs could put food on the table. In the twenties and thirties my family didn't go to a grocery store for anything except the things that could not be produced right in their own back yard.

So, I understood Uncle Pete's reasoning for putting the house so close to the road. He wanted every spare inch of the flat land to be used for crops. But, it made me nervous, especially since cars whipped around that turn doing fifty miles an hour, not to mention the coal trucks that went rumbling up and down at all hours of the day. That part of the road had actually become known as Pete's Curve.

Clive dropped me off, and Aunt Runa came out on the porch and ushered me inside. Runa and Pete got married sometime just before World War I, I couldn't remember exactly. They had four kids, who had moved to bigger cities: Charleston and Morgantown respectively. Two of her four children were right around the same age as my mother and her siblings. Aunt Runa had married late in life—well, you know, she was at least thirty—and it had been feared, what with her Salvation Army work and her suffragette activities, that she'd never marry at all. And she'd told me many times that she'd been prepared for that. And then Uncle Pete had come along and changed everything. People had thought for sure once she married that she would settle down and become "normal," but Aunt Runa had shocked them all by leaving her husband and infant son and heading to Europe during World War I to feed the troops. People assumed Pete would scold her or forbid her to go, but he, according to Aunt Dotie, had simply said, "Runie, you go and do what you got to do. Charlie and I will be here waiting for you when you return. Just make sure you return, my jezebel."

I almost swoon when I think of my Uncle Pete delivering those lines to her.

"Up or down?" Aunt Runa said when we were in her kitchen.

"What?"

"Do you want to wear your hair up or down?"

"Oh, maybe up? I'm hoping for something a little more sophisticated, though, so no pony-tails."

Aunt Runa rolled her eyes. "I'd sooner put a pony-tail on a dog."

Aunt Runa's house was always so interesting. There was china in her cabinets that had belonged to her mother, so it was at least seventy-five years old. There was an old Delft spittoon in the living room—sparkling clean, of course—that had belonged to one of our ancestors, and there were photographs everywhere, sitting on doilies that Aunt Stella had made for her, because Aunt Runa didn't really have time for that sort of thing. Although she did make her own lace. There was the "Wall of the Dead" which had photographs of her dead relatives, including my great-grandma Blanche. There was the Soldier's Wall, which had photographs of everything from her Salvation Army colleagues, to her Suffragette sisters wearing their yellow sashes, to her friends and doughboys of World War I, and nephews and neighbors who had fought in World War II. Then there was the Wall of Joy, where photographs of her children and grandchildren were proudly displayed.

Aunt Runa washed my hair in the kitchen sink and then dried it within fifteen minutes, and then she stopped to take a break. Not that she needed one, but she sort of had an easy-going way of doing things. Everything she did was methodical, plodding, as though you could see her making progress with every move she made, but it was done with this I-have-all-the-time-in-the-world attitude. She never seemed to worry about anything, and she never raised her voice. She'd also never laid a hand on her children. Of this, I was certain, because at bingo one night, I'd heard Pearl Hargrave tell Lovinia Jones that the reason all of Stella's children had moved away was because "...she was never stern or strict enough with those children. Why, they grew up thinking they could just do or be whatever they liked. So, of course they're going to get too big for their britches and go gallivanting across the countryside. She never laid a hand on them. Not once. Even when they deserved it." Of course, all of this had been said with an astonished look on her face, and Lovinia had indeed, placed a hand over her lips and raised her eyebrows in response, while neither one of them mentioned the obvious. That Pearl Hargrave's son had also grown too big for his britches, "above his raising" as they so often like to say, and left town. But, according to Pearl, *her* son had left because she had raised him so well that Greenhaven simply had nothing to offer him anymore. He'd waste away and die if he stayed here. The double standard was so evident that I'd nearly choked on it.

Nobody could ever get me to say one bad thing about Aunt Runa. Aside from Pearl, I'd never heard anybody say a bad word about any of Runa's children, either, and they seemed genuinely happy.

"Charlie's coming to visit next weekend," Aunt Stella said as she placed a glass in front of me. She had a refrigerator with the ice-box on the bottom. She bent over and pulled out a long, metal ice tray and pulled up on the lever. The ice broke free in chunks and she put them in my glass. Then she poured me a glass of her home-made strawberry lemonade.

"Oh, that will be nice," I said, taking a drink and savoring every drop.

"I think he's going to make me a greenhouse."

"Really?"

She nodded. "Should be interesting. He's an accountant, for crying out loud. He doesn't know which end of the hammer to use." She laughed at her own joke. But I knew better. Charlie had been raised right here in central West Virginia. He knew his way around tools and such. But his skills were probably rusty. "So, tell me about this Mr. McDowell."

"I've already told you," I said, frankly getting tired of being asked about him.

"Not that stuff," she said. "What's your impression of him?"

"My impression?" I blinked.

"Surely you must have some thoughts about him."·

I took another drink. "He's incredibly intelligent."

"Go on."

"He loves to read."

"No, no, not what he does. How does he make you *feel*?"

I blushed. "Aunt Runa, we're not like that."

"And I didn't mean it like that. Everybody you meet will make you feel something. If they don't, they're dead. And even the dead, if their essence was strong enough, can still make you feel something. How do I make you feel?"

"Wonderful," I said. As her smile pulled some of the loose skin taut across her face, I could see the outline of those magnificent apple cheeks. Under those wrinkles, that age-spotted and sagging skin, was the gorgeous woman who had blazed a trail half way around the world and back.

"What about your mom?" she asked.

"Safe, and sometimes sad. And...satisfied."

"Clive?"

"Happy. Loved."

"So, what does Jeb make you feel like?"

I frowned. "Upside down."

She raised her eyebrows. "Really? How so?"

I set my glass on the table with a trembling hand. "He..."

"Yes?"

"He has such a unique way of looking at things. He makes me feel like all things are possible."

"And what's so bad about that?" she asked.

"Because all things aren't possible, Aunt Runa. Especially for somebody like me," I said. My eyes began to burn, and to my horror, I thought I might actually cry. "And if all things *are* possible for somebody like me, then people have been lying to me my whole life."

Aunt Runa squeezed my hand. "Maybe nobody's lied to you. Maybe in their small little minds they believe what they tell you. Maybe they're not capable of seeing it, that's all."

I gave a wan smile.

"So, do you remember the motto of the *Revolution?*" Of course she meant the suffragette revolution, not the French revolution.

"'The true republic—men, their rights and nothing more; women, their rights and nothing less.'"

She clapped her hands. "You remember!"

"Of course I remember." I was probably the only girl, aside from Runa's own daughter, who grew up thinking the holy trinity was Susan B. Anthony, Elizabeth Cady Stanton, and Mary Wollstonecraft. But the limitations that I felt at that moment, oddly enough, weren't because I was a female, but because I was disabled.

She stood up then and put a mirror in front of me. "Let's get this hair fixed, shall we?"

"Yes."

***

Clive and I showed up at the square dance just as the music was starting. Happily, for me anyway, not all of the music played at these events was square-dances with callers. Some of it was just good old fashioned hoe-down music, and people free-formed dance just as much as they did the rigid do-si-do and promenade, and it was fun to watch.

The dance was held in the gardens behind the courthouse in Wellston. The weather was stunning with cool temps and a gentle breeze, and the smell of wood smoke filled the air. There were big fires lit everywhere and electric lights to make sure the six piece band could see to play, and to make sure the dancers could see where they were going. Red-and-white-checked tablecloths were draped over the tables that had been set up on the perimeter of the dance floor.

In truth, as much as I loved going to the movies, I enjoyed these types of dances more because people of all ages came. The drive-in was just a place where young people went to try and find somebody to go steady with. In one square, at a dance like this, you were liable to find Bernie McCutcheon, who was eighty-two years old this past spring; his wife Nancy, and Arnie and Sue Pickens, who were about fifty and Louise Weaver and Bud Jensen, who had graduated with me last year. I liked the dynamics of it. I liked that the subject matter we would talk about would be diverse. I liked that the whole of my community was represented.

No sooner had I wheeled up to a table than my friend Betty Jo Ryan stampeded over toward me. "Olivia! It's so great to see you." Betty Jo, a diminutive girl, was a genuinely nice person to everybody, and she never seemed to notice my wheelchair. She talked without ever looking at it and never stumbled over it in conversation. She meandered around it physically, too. Like once we were at the school picnic and she had chosen me as her croquet partner. She pushed me and talked the whole time, wove in and out of pot holes and debris and maneuvered my chair so that I could take just the right shot, without ever having to ask me how or where I wanted to go. It was nearly symbiotic. I'd never met anybody who acted as though the chair was an extension of her, not me.

"I got my license, finally!" she said. "And a car. It's an old used car—and I have to share it with my brother Kevin, but I don't care!"

"You did?" I asked.

"Yes," she said, blue eyes sparkling. "Gunnar paid for it, but he won't admit to it. So don't mention that I know it." She wore her blonde hair down, with big giant curls folding in on her face, and perfectly straight bangs. A high-necked plaid dress, accompanied by a white sweater fastened at the neck with a tiny pearl button, and saddle-oxfords completed her ensemble. I, of course, had worn jeans, much to Aunt Mildred's chagrin. Aunt Mildred had happened to come outside to burn her trash, when she saw me leaving Aunt Runa's. She'd nearly broken her neck running across the field to tell me that I'd better not go to the dance, dressed as I was. Aunt Runa had rolled her eyes and shoved me into Clive's car as fast as she could. At least I'd worn a very pretty mint-green blouse to go with the jeans, which seemed completely lost on Aunt Mildred. My hair was pulled back in a French bun, and it made me feel exotic. As if I were Audrey Hepburn.

"I simply have to come and take you driving some time! Maybe all the way to Charleston!" Betty Jo exclaimed.

"I'd love it," I said. "So, who are you here with?"

She shrugged. "Nobody in particular," she said. "Gunnar brought a car load of us."

Her brother, Gunnar Ryan, was a deputy with the Colton County sheriff's department. While Betty Jo was the youngest of five, Gunnar was the oldest, which put him at about twenty-six. We didn't circulate in the same crowd too much, but I knew Gunnar as well as I knew anybody else in Greenhaven. "You wanna sit with us?" she asked.

I glanced around, trying to find Clive. I finally spotted him talking with Harvey Grose at the far edge of the dance floor. Next thing I knew he was walking away with a group of guys, most likely to go look at Harvey's new car. "Sure," I said.

Before I could blink, she'd grabbed my chair and was pushing me across the rim of the dance floor to her table where a group of girls were already seated. Even though some of the girls were uncomfortable with my wheelchair, all were nice and spoke to me. One suddenly announced that she was getting married. This threw the whole gaggle of them into a tizzy punctuated with loud squeals and laughter and lots of clapping and shrieking. Betty Jo and the girls gabbled on and on as I looked about for something to be interested in.

Gunnar took the seat across from me. "Hey, Olivia," he said. "How ya been?"

"Good," I said, relieved to be saved from the girl-talk. "And you? You've been out of town for a while, haven't you?"

He nodded. Gunnar was a striking looking man, with dark yellow hair and piercing blue eyes and a jaw-line that was defined and sharp. He wasn't an overly tall man, but neither was he short. He was muscular, but not beefy. He also wasn't in uniform, which was a rare sight. He seemed to take his uniform and the duty that went with it very seriously. Which, I suppose, was a good thing. You wouldn't want a lackadaisical deputy.

He took a drink of his beer and set it down, nodding his head. "Yes," he said. "I was at Ohio State."

I nodded. "Oh, I knew about that. But recently weren't you off somewhere?"

"Oh, yeah, I was in Charleston, getting more training for a couple of weeks."

It was no secret that Gunnar had languished between the time he'd graduated from Ohio State and the time he joined law enforcement. For about two years he seemed to just float from one job to another, having no direction and not really caring if he found one. At least that was the gossip. Along with that gossip was also the thread that led back to Gunnar's father. An alcoholic who drank the family's money—I could relate to that—Mr. Ryan often spent days on end recuperating from drinking binges, locked up in the bedroom, crying, praying and ultimately lashing out at those he loved the most. He'd managed to keep his job, only because his wife's father was his boss. But the rumor was that Gunnar had given up a job in his field of study in New Mexico because his mother had begged him to return and "take on" his father. There was gossip and there was truth. And there was almost always a kernel of truth to be found in a big bag of gossip. I had no doubt that Gunnar's father had, in some way, been responsible for Gunnar's return to Wellston, and subsequent floundering about.

"Do you like Charleston?" I asked.

"It has its charms," he said and smiled.

"Do you have trouble adjusting to small town life after you've been in a big city for a while?"

He shrugged. "I like both. What about you?"

"The bigger the city, the better somebody like me can get around on my own."

He cocked his head to the side. "I never thought of that. You're stuck out there on that mountain," he said. "You should move to town."

"Right, with all my millions of dollars," I said and laughed.

"I hardly think it'll take millions," he said. "Make it a goal." Just then, Gunnar looked up and the expression dropped from his face. I followed his gaze and found Jeb standing there in a plaid shirt, jeans and brand-new cowboy boots.

"Jeb," I said.

"Am I late for the party?" he asked.

"No," I said. "Um, Jeb this is Deputy Gunnar Ryan. Gunnar, this is Jeb McDowell who bought—"

"The Renshaw place," Gunnar said, extending his hand. "Yes, I'm familiar with who you are."

Jeb shook Gunnar's hand with gusto. Then he put one foot up on a chair and waved a hand in front of his new boots. "Look," he said. "Think I can pass for a local?"

"No," Gunnar said, with a twinkle in his eye.

"No?" Jeb asked.

"Nobody here's got shoes that nice," he said and laughed.

"Damn," Jeb said. "I just can't win for losing." He sat in the chair that his boot had rested upon.

"Want a beer?" Gunnar asked.

"Oh, please," Jeb said and fished in his pocket for money. Gunnar waved a hand at him to indicate that the beer was on him. As he walked away, Jeb looked at me and said, "He's a nice fella."

I nodded. "Most people are, on the surface."

Betty Jo pulled herself from her group of friends, leaned over from the end of the table and said, "Livvy, you must introduce me to your friend!"

"Oh, Jeb, this is Gunnar's baby sister and my good friend, Betty Jo."

"Any friend of Olivia's is a friend of mine," Jeb said.

"You really are as cute as they say," she said.

Jeb looked at me with a big smile. I held my hands up and said, "I never said such a thing."

"No, no, not Livvy, she barely even notices boys. I'm talking about the ladies at the courthouse."

I glanced at Jeb quickly. The courthouse? Why would he be at the courthouse?

"They were all buzzing around like flies on a turd," Betty Jo said. This made Jeb laugh out loud, and blush slightly.

"You're too kind," he said, his right hand over his heart.

The band started playing a song called "Flop Eared Mule" and Betty Jo and the girls vanished in a heartbeat, being pulled by some invisible string onto the dance floor. In a swish of skirts and stomping feet, they grabbed whoever they could find to dance with. Some of the girls danced with each other, because there were no readily available men. For the record, there must be an unwritten law of physics somewhere that states that you cannot clap and stomp without laughing and smiling.

Jeb leaned over and said, "I've never been compared to a turd before."

"Stick around," I said. "Eventually, you'll be compared to a skunk or a possum."

"Really?" he asked.

"It's inevitable."

"Why so?"

"You're a man," I said, laughing.

He looked completely offended. "You think just because I'm a man that automatically makes me a skunk?"

"Until proven otherwise."

His smile faded. "Olivia, don't let your father prejudice you so."

"It's got nothing to do with my father," I said. "It has everything to do with experience. And my experience is, if you give a man enough rope, he will hang himself."

"That could be true of both sexes, don't you agree?"

"Oh, with women, if you give them the rope, they'll call up all their friends and tell them what a horrible person you are for giving them rope to begin with, then they hang *you* with it."

"And which is worse?"

I shrugged. "Guess that's why I'm very cautious with who I dole out rope to."

He slapped the table and laughed heartily. "You are far too pessimistic for such a young age, my dear Olivia Anne. Smart as, how do you guys say it here...smart as a whippersnapper, but pessimistic as hell."

"No, no, no. You have to get the local colloquialisms right. Smart as a whippersnapper, but pessimistic as a turkey the day before Thanksgiving."

Just as Jeb laughed, Gunnar returned to the table with two beers and an orange pop. The pop was for me.

"Having any more issues with prowlers, Mr. McDowell?" Gunnar asked.

Jeb shrugged and gave a quizzical look.

"I saw the report on the Sheriff's desk," he said.

"I'm beginning to think it's just bears."

"Well, good," Gunnar said, taking a drink. "Give us a call, though, if you start to think otherwise. And you know, if you see anybody, please call."

"I will," Jeb said.

I watched the girls dance around the room, laughing and laughing, until I thought for sure their faces would break. I kept time to the music, patting my hand on my knee.

"Did you finish the book, Olivia?" Jeb asked.

"I did," I said. "You can pick it up whenever you like."

"Good, I brought you a new one."

"Fantastic!" I said. "What did you bring me?"

"Don't laugh," he said and pulled the novel from his back pocket.

"*A Little Princess?*" I asked.

"Have you read it already?"

I shook my head no.

"Whew," he said. "I figured you would have."

"Have you read it?" I asked, incredulous.

"I have, actually."

"It figures," I answered, smiling, which made Jeb laugh.

"So, Gunnar," Jeb asked. "What do you do in your spare time? When you're not on duty?"

"Oh," he said and shrugged. "I'm a bit of a history buff. I, uh, I volunteer on archeological digs with the university. Collect fossils. That sort of thing."

"Really," Jeb said. "Sounds very interesting."

Gunnar said, "It's not, really. Well, don't get me wrong, I'm fascinated with the past, but most people, their eyes glaze over when you start talking about anything that happened ten years before they were born."

"Is that what your degree is in?" I asked.

"Anthropology and geology," he said, nodding his head.

"What brought you to law enforcement?" Jeb asked.

"Eh, things," Gunnar said, and took a drink of his beer.

"Well," Jeb said. "There certainly is enough history here in these mountains to keep you busy."

"True enough," Gunnar said. "People don't think about it too much, but there's a lot of history here before people. The geologic history alone is amazing."

"See, Olivia, I'm not the only one who finds this place fascinating," Jeb said, gesturing toward Gunnar.

Just then the band started playing "Foggy Mountain Breakdown."

"Wow," Jeb said. "That banjo player is really boss. How do his fingers do that?"

"That's Harry McClintock. Grew up here, quit school in sixth grade," Gunnar said.

"And my second cousin," I added. Jeb raised an eyebrow. "Mom's dad's side."

"And I'll bet he's never had one music lesson in his life," Jeb said. "Am I right?"

"His daddy taught him. Can't read one lick of sheet music," Gunnar answered. "I've played with him a few times. When he wants, you can't keep up."

"You play?" Jeb asked.

Gunnar nodded. "Fiddle, and a little guitar. And I've been known to pick up my dad's dulcimer on occasion."

"He is fantastic!" Jeb said, watching Harry's fingers move up and down the neck of the banjo.

Suddenly, Jeb slapped his hand down on the table again and said, "Well, you know what? I came here to dance. And I'm gonna dance!"

I watched, expecting him to get out on the dance floor and make some fancy moves like he was one of the Cedar Hill Square dancers or something, but to my shock, and horror, he reached down and unhooked the brake on my wheelchair. "What are you doing?" I asked. "I can't—"

"I'm pickin' my dance partner," he said.

"Jeb, no," I said, cheeks burning. What did he think he was doing? He knew full and well that I couldn't dance. What was he going to do, drag me around the dance floor like a broken doll? Gunnar's expression was one of alarm at first, too, but then something settled in his features. Admiration? Jeb McDowell led me and my wheelchair out onto the dance floor, kicking people out of the way as he went.

At first I wasn't sure what to do. I just sat there in the middle of the dance floor, petrified, stoic, as if there was a spotlight pointed right on me. There was no need for a spotlight, because all eyes were on us anyway. Jeb clapped, then slapped his knees and his boots and made a gesture for me to do the same thing. So, I clapped, slapped my knees and then bent over and slapped my ankles. An exhilarated laugh bubbled from Jeb as he stepped forward, took my hand and then, with the other hand, spun my wheelchair around. Then he stopped the chair with his foot, grabbed both of my hands and pushed me to and fro, and when he did, he sort of stepped off to the side of my chair and bounced his hip on my shoulder! Finally, he took his bent arm, put it through my mine and we do-si-doed. Back the other way. And back the other way again, until I was giddy with laughter and nearly sick from the spinning.

All the people had pushed off to the edges of the dance floor now and were clapping, hooting and hollering at us. As the song was about to come to an end, Jeb clomped away from me, with his arms crossed like he was a

Russian Cossack. Then he turned, ran back toward me, slid on his knees and made a *tada* gesture with his arms toward me.

Raucous laughter and applause roared from the crowd of people, even the band was applauding. Jeb waved a hand at everybody, and then gave a low and humble bow toward me. Through the jumble of noise, he leaned in and said to me, "You can't dance because you say you can't dance."

A Letter to Viola from Olivia

Viola Reinhardt
Dayton, Ohio
September 27, 1958

Dear Aunt Viola,

So much has happened. First of all, I haven't heard from you since the last letter I sent you. Please tell me that you're not feeling poorly! If I don't hear from you in the next week, I'm going to Arnie's to use his phone and call you.

We had quite the scare with Uncle Pete. His rooster attacked the milkman when he came to deliver the milk on Friday, and you would have thought that Freddie Lester, the current milkman, had never seen a rooster in his life. He was jumping all around and kicking and screaming. All because the rooster was pecking at his legs. At one point, Freddie ran all down through the valley between Aunt Runa and Aunt Mildred's houses, milk bottles clanking in the air, screaming for all he was worth, while the rooster chased him and all the hens stared as though they'd never seen a person before. Finally, Uncle Pete was "tired of the nonsense." When Freddie made his way back (he'd done several figure eights by now) Uncle Pete ran out in front of him, snatched the rooster up in one fell swoop, but somehow caught Freddie's left foot and sent him splat onto his belly. All would have been fine, except the milk bottles came down on top of Freddie's head and gave him a nasty gash. Uncle Pete threw his hip out of socket and hasn't walked right since. I'd been visiting Aunt Mildred and watched the whole episode from her back porch. We tried not to laugh too loudly, especially once we saw the blood from Freddie's head. Aunt Runa is concerned because she swears that when "bad things" happen to "old people's hips" that it's "just a matter of time." Whatever that means.

I had a very good time at the dance on Friday, mainly because Jeb was there. He danced all night long and used my chair like it was legs and arms and just led me all around the dance floor. For once I wasn't on the side watching, I was actually a part of it. He has certainly shaken things up here and not just where I'm concerned. It seems all anybody ever does is talk about him. Somehow he ends up in every conversation that I happen to overhear. Even Gunnar likes him, and we all know how "removed" Gunnar can be. Personally, I think being removed is Gunnar's built-in self-defense because people think they can get by with a lot around him because they all changed his diapers or what not. So, I think he tries to keep a distance. But, anyway, if Jeb comes down the mountain, it's nearly reported in the county paper! All the old ladies watch him like a hawk, like they are at once half in love with his beauty, and still not entirely trusting him. Almost like they're angry with themselves because they WANT to trust him, and they have to stop and remind themselves that he is a stranger, after all. Even Brother Dix has come to depend on him to be at church every Sunday to help hand out literature and song books! I think, aside from Clive, he is the brother I should have had. And why does God bother making people who serve no purpose, like my real brother?

I haven't sent my rebuttal to Mrs. Hollingberry. I discussed my feelings with Jeb, and told him what you'd said about not being too insulting to the Victorians. He reminded me of the writers that I loved who were Victorians, although I had to point out to him that, technically, many of them were Edwardian writers and not Victorian at all. He conceded that I had a point on several of them. He also said that people love for their own reasons and that I shouldn't judge the love between Cathy and Heathcliff and just accept it for what it is. The story isn't about why they interact the way they do, it's about what happens because of it. So, I'm trying to think of a gentler way of telling Mrs. Hollingberry that I'm not wrong for having my opinion.

But Jeb says that I am too structured in my admiration of things. That I need to stop expecting things to be a certain way and just let them be what they are. I take too active of a role in it all. I am to let the books happen to me, not me happen to them. I can't say this argument isn't sound, but I will be perfectly happy if *Wuthering Heights* never "happens" to me again. At least I can say that I liked it better than the *Sound and the Fury*. I can't begin to express the amount of torture that I had to endure in the name of Faulkner.

Jeb thinks Walt Whitman is a demi-god. I told him how much I loved Emily Dickinson and he said, in a matter-of-fact tone of voice, "Of that, I have no doubt." What did he mean by that?

Well, that's all for now. I did ask Mildred about the NRA Eagle quilt that she made and she said she'd sent it to the governor in 1942.

Please write, let me know you're well.
Much love, Olivia

Secrets
October 1958

The days grew shorter on Goosefoot Mountain. Cool damp nights replaced warm ones, and the trees were set ablaze with gold, red, and orange leaves. The second of October was one of those days that should have gone down in history as a perfect day. The sky was so brilliant blue that it nearly hurt my eyes to look at it. From the lofty perch on our back porch, all I could see for miles was one orange-red hill undulating into the next, against the backdrop of a cloudless, deep blue sky. I took a full breath, the kind that expands the lungs to the limit, and let it out slowly. Autumn smelled differently than any other season. It must have been a combination of the fresh bed of leaves on the forest floor, stored hay, and firewood being burned.

Today was Graham Greene's birthday. I was jealous of the British author. I wished my birthday was in the glorious days of autumn, instead of the dead of winter. That had to just make you a happier person than most. Today was also the second game of the World Series and Lew Burdette was pitching, and so, after school, Clive would be at Harvey's house listening to the game on the radio. Willie Gene had offered to listen to it with him at our house, but in case New York won, Clive wanted to put some distance between him and his father.

The back of our house was on stilts. And I loved to sit back there because I could see out over the valley and be somewhat on the same level as the birds. My mother and sister were in the middle of one of their famous arguments that went something like this:

Mom: Bessie, you have to get a job and help us around here.

Bessie: I'm not going to live here much longer. As soon as I can get out, I am.

Mom: And how are you going to do that with no money?

Bessie: My husband will have a job.

Mom: Well, you don't have a husband, Bessie. You don't even have a steady.

Bessie: A technicality.

Mom: Well, while you're waiting for your husband, you need to get a job.

Bessie: If I get a job then it will seem as though I don't need a husband and it will put men off.

Mom: Maybe they'll think you're industrious.

Bessie: Or desperate. Besides, if I get a job then I won't have any time to date.

And then my mother would storm off, in tears, swearing under her breath, something about how she didn't understand how people as poor as us could have a child who thinks she's a princess. It was the same argument they always had, just variations on a theme, and so I had no reason to listen to it. Thus, the back porch with the nice breeze, the mountain view and a copy of, ironically enough, *The Little Princess*.

I'd finished my chores for the day, almost before the sun was up. After I'd been reading about two hours, Willie Gene stepped onto the back porch and stretched. It was a Thursday, and Willie should have been at work, but he had a doctor's appointment in Charleston. His left knee had been injured in a mining accident a few years back and it was giving him lots of pain. He walked over to the edge, coffee cup in hand, looking out onto the autumnal majesty, just as I had been. It always made me happy when other people noticed things like how beautiful the moon was, or the colors of the leaves.

"What are your plans for the day?" he asked me.

For the record, Willie Gene Morrison was one of my heroes. He was the same age as my mother, and had been born in the next county over. When World War II came along, he'd joined the service, went off to war and afterward returned to settle in Huntington. He said the quiet of the countryside allowed him too much time to think and he didn't want to think. Thinking led him to remembering things he'd just as soon forget. Like, looking over at the Browning machine gun manned by his best friend, and finding his best friend's head missing. That sort of thing. He needed the fast-paced environment of a city to keep his mind hopping, so it didn't have time to settle on any one thing. He needed to be able to walk outside at three in the morning and find lights, noise and other people. However, by the time he'd met my mother, nearly a decade had passed since the war, and Willie Gene's mind was a bit calmer and less cluttered with ghosts. He'd never found any meaningful work or relationships in Huntington and saw no reason to turn my mother down when she wanted to move back to her home in the country.

The real reason Willie Gene was my hero was because he loved my mother. When my father abandoned us, he actually took two things with him.

The car, and my mother's identity. My mother had been Mrs. Hiram VanBibber, and her whole life had revolved around Hiram and us. Regardless of Aunt Runa's stern and loud preaching of suffragette wisdom, my mother, like so many women, had no identity before Hiram, none during Hiram, and none after. So when my father left, it was like a surgeon had just cut out this huge part of her body and scattered it to the wind. Not only had she been faced with the shock that he did not love her, but that she had given herself so completely to somebody who was capable of leaving her stranded on the side of the road to die. The man she'd shared her most intimate moments with had been capable of just walking away. Most people treated their dogs better than that. It had left her heart as barren as a wasteland, and her mind full of self-doubt. In addition she had to face the fact that Hiram's own desires had far outweighed any love he'd had for his children and that he was a weak and pathetic creature, and she'd *chosen* him. She'd *wanted* him. She'd *pursued* him. She'd also married him while he was drunk, and forgive me for saying so, but if that wasn't a portent of disaster on a monumental scale, then nothing was.

Enter Willie Gene Morrison.

For two years they were just friends. Willie had taken the time to get to know my mother, to woo my mother and to build her up. He didn't want to marry the shell that was Rosalee VanBibber. No, he'd wanted to find the tiny remnants of what had been Rosalee Anne McClintock. The woman who was devilishly funny, had a love for music and was not afraid to play a dirty rotten prank on those who deserved it. And he'd waited, and watered and fed the soul of that woman, coaxing her to bloom. When Willie had met her, she'd been like that Night Blooming Cereus, a cactus that only blooms at night, thus robbing people around her of her beauty. And now my mother bloomed all day and all night. And for that, I would give my life for Willie Gene. People throw that phrase around, but I would.

"I have no real plans for the day," I answered him. "Is there something you need me to do?"

"Pretend that you need something in town and make Bessie take you."

"What?" I asked.

"Get her out of this house before your mother goes crazy. Your momma's off today. She's got two or three days a week where she's not waiting tables with aching feet, and she shouldn't have to listen to the likes of that sister of yours," he said.

Willie had blue eyes, dark hair with a little gray at the temples, and a rather large nose, like the Italians had. I couldn't remember ever having met an actual Italian, but he resembled the ones that I saw in the movies.

"I'm sorry," I said.

He shook his head. "Your mother won't do anything too severe to Bessie, like kicking her out to the curb, which is exactly what I'd do, but she won't because...well, you know. What your father did."

Willie made a fist with his free hand and took a sip of his coffee. I had no doubt in my mind that if Willie Gene ever actually met my father, he'd punch him square in the nose and introduce himself later.

"I know, it shouldn't be up to you to babysit that sister of yours, but—"

"No, no," I said. "That's fine. I don't mind."

I did mind, and he knew I minded, but he also knew that I'd do whatever he asked.

"I'll tell her Aunt Mildred needs something from the store. She'll be less likely to put up a fight that way. Besides, honestly, Bessie loves nothing more than to get out and let herself be seen."

Willie smiled at me and looked out over the mountain that was our backyard. "I'm off to Charleston," he said. "I'll be home in time for dinner."

About thirty minutes later, Bessie and I sat in Aunt Mildred's driveway. My aunts had a habit of giving me their left-over change, because they knew there was no real way for me to earn any money. After saving it for a while, I would accumulate several dollars. So, today, I had five dollars in my pocket, and if Aunt Mildred decided she didn't need anything from the store, I had decided that I would take Bessie out for lunch, so that we wouldn't have to return home right away. Not exactly what I'd wanted to spend my five dollars on, but we all had to make sacrifices for our mothers.

I watched as Bessie knocked on Aunt Mildred's door, and soon she answered it and said that by golly, she *could* use a loaf of bread and how nice it was of her to ask. But we could get a loaf of bread at Arnie's, which was only a few miles down the road. I needed to get her into Wellston. So it looked as though I was going to have to buy her lunch, after all. This went a long way to putting a serious kink in that otherwise perfect day.

Bessie bounced back to the car with a big grin on her face, her pony tail swishing from side to side. When she got in, she held up some dollar bills and said, "Aunt Mildred said to get lunch on her!" I glanced over at the porch and Aunt Mildred, wiping her hands on a dishtowel, waved at me. She was so much smarter than I gave her credit for sometimes.

We drove into Wellston, mostly downhill and around curves, and Bessie paid no real attention to which side of the line she chose to drive on. There was nobody in the oncoming lane, so I assumed she thought it was okay to use it. No sooner had we made it to the first stoplight in town, than we were nearly side-swiped by Harvey and his brand new off-white, gold-trimmed Fury. Bessie swerved into oncoming traffic, and I, feeling my legs buckling and the momentum of my weight moving me forward, lost my balance and nearly ended up in the floorboard of the car. If Bessie had not instinctively thrown her right arm across my chest, I probably would have landed in the floor or bashed my head on the dash.

Bessie slammed on the brakes, leaving the smell of burnt rubber in the air, pulled the car over and jumped out in a flash. The Fury had pulled in behind us. "What's the matter with you, Harvey Grose! You nearly killed us. Where'd you learn how to drive, anyway, 'cause I'd be happy to give you a few new lessons!" I watched through the window as Bessie gave him what-for, with her hands firmly planted on her hips.

"Oh, shut your pie hole, Bessie," Harvey said. "You survived it!"

"Yeah, well my kid sister almost didn't!" she yelled back.

All of a sudden, I saw the passenger side door open and Clive jumped out and came running up to our car. "Good God, Livvy, tell me you're all right!" he said, reaching my open window. His gaze raked over me from head to toe, looking for broken bones and blood.

"And Clive Arnold Morrison, what the devil are you doing? Why aren't you in school?" Bessie asked.

"I'm fine, Clive," I said. "You're in for it now, though. You know Bessie's going to tell your dad."

"We're having a pre-championship game party, that's all."

I caught a whiff of something and sniffed. "You been drinking, Clive?"

"I only had one beer."

"Drinking *and* skipping school?" I asked. "Man, oh man."

"Well, would you rather me drink *at* school?" he asked.

"I'd rather you act like God gave you some sense," I said, reached my hand through the open window and smacked him upside the head. It's not as if my slap hurt. It was more symbolic than anything, but Clive got the point.

Clive looked away and swallowed. Then he glanced back at me. "You all right, though? You didn't get hurt?"

"I'm fine," I said, searching his eyes for whatever devil had suddenly crawled inside him and made him behave so...so un-Clive like.

He started to walk back to his car. "You better be home for supper!" I called out.

"I ain't comin' home for supper. I'm staying at Harvey's."

Harvey and Clive both got in the car, and Harvey pulled out, gunning that V-8 engine until my eardrums rattled, and sped around us. Bessie yelled after them, "Where the hell did you get the money for that kinda car, anyhows, Harvey Grose!"

She got back in the car and slapped the steering wheel. "Well, now that done frosted me but good."

"Calm down, Bessie. I didn't get hurt."

"No, but still. It's the gall of some people, ya know? " As she pulled our car into traffic, she said. "So, where *do* you think Harvey Grose got the money for a new car like that?"

I shrugged. Admittedly I had been wondering the same thing.

"You think maybe he stuck up a liquor or store something?" she asked.

"I think we would have heard about it by now," I said.

"Yeah, probably."

Without asking, Bessie pulled the car into Johnny's Drive-In. She didn't like to mess with taking my chair in and out of the trunk—she said it got dirt on her clothes—and she didn't like to wait for me to get in and out of the car, so anytime we went anywhere together, I usually had to stay in the car. The waitress, Dorothy Craig, a friend of hers from school, came over to take our order. Dorothy stuck her head in the car and said hello to me. Then Bessie said, "I want a cheeseburger, fries, chocolate malt and bring me ice-cream after. Olivia, what are you having?"

"I just want a grilled cheese and a Coke," I said.

She and Dorothy talked back and forth a bit and then Dorothy went to place our order. "I swear," Bessie said to me. "That girl's got more shoes than anybody oughta."

After a few moments, she still had more to say on the subject. "She's got five pair. *Five* pair," she said sticking her hand up and wiggling all five of her fingers. "I mean, what does she do with all of them?"

This was a rhetorical question so I didn't bother to answer.

"I will say one thing, though, she's got this cute pair of brown ones, with the little flap on the top and they tie up. Oh, I'd love to have me a pair of those. And did you see that color lipstick?"

"No."

"When she comes back, you look at it, oh, wait, there, she's walking over to that other car. You see it? Wonder what color that is? You think she'd tell me if I asked? Probably not, knowing her."

My gaze followed where Bessie was pointing and it landed on a blue car parked three empty spaces away from ours. There was something familiar about the back of the head of the man seated in the passenger's side. He was speaking in angry tones and dramatic inflections. Every now and then, the driver would lean forward. The driver was a woman. The more I stared, and the more Bessie droned on about lipstick colors and shoes and what she wanted to do to Harvey, the more I could have sworn that the man in the car was Jeb.

"Bessie, I want to get out of the car," I said.

The woman was infuriated with the man. He was staying a bit calmer, but I could see by the set of his shoulders that he was tense, getting angrier by the minute.

"Why? We're at the drive-in," she said and adjusted the mirror so she could inspect her teeth. I suppose she had to have clean teeth to eat lunch.

"I need to use the rest room," I said.

"Seriously?" she asked and gave me a pained expression. "Do I have to carry you into the toilet? Because I'm not doing it."

"Just shut-up and get me out of this car!" I yelled.

She blinked.

"If I've gotta pee, I gotta pee, and if you don't get me out of here, I'm going to go in the front seat and you can clean it up!"

"Cool it, Livvy," she said. "Good, God, you'd think you'd remember to go before we leave the house."

She got out of the car, yanked and pulled on my chair until it came out with a thud. Then she wheeled it to me. I placed one foot in between the pedals on the ground, grabbed onto the door with the right hand and pulled my body weight onto the chair, lifting at the last second with my left hand so that I didn't scrape my butt on the stupid random piece of metal that had no business being on a wheelchair. Clearly, whoever designed this thing never actually had to get in and out of it. Bessie leaned down like she was going to try and help me, and I put my hand up, shooing her away. "I've got it," I said.

"Don't get your bowels in a kink," she said.

I pushed myself over to the car that had the mystery couple who were arguing. "Where are you going?" Bessie asked. "The bathroom is that way!"

About this time, the man in the car heard Bessie yelling at me and glanced over his right shoulder. It was Jeb, and his expression fell as he saw me rolling across the parking lot toward him. He swung his door open. "Olivia," he said.

"Are you all right?" I asked him.

Clearly, he wasn't all right. His hair was disheveled, which wasn't unusual, but he hadn't shaved in a few days and dark circles smudged the underneath of his eyes. In fact, it looked as though his clothes had been worn for a few days in a row. He glanced around, almost as if he was worried about being seen or recognized. Then his shoulders relaxed, he took a deep breath and smiled.

"I'm fine," he said. He looked over my shoulder in the direction of Bessie. "You out having lunch?"

"Yes," I said and threw a glare at the woman in the car. She took a drag off of a cigarette, glared back at me and then, staring at her reflection in a compact, powdered her nose as if she hadn't a care in the world. "What's going on?"

"Oh, nothing," he said. "Just having some lunch with a friend."

"A friend?" I asked. "I thought you didn't know anybody around here?" I suddenly remembered Clarence Ford and realized that I'd never asked Jeb about him at the dance. I'd been having too much fun. The lazy-eyed stranger had completely escaped my memory. But seeing this woman brought him back.

"I don't," he said.

"Oh, well then, introduce me. I'd love to meet your friends from Baltimore."

"Holly Springfield, this is Olivia VanBibber," he said. "Olivia, this is my friend Holly."

"How do you do?" I asked and smiled. "Is this your ex-wife?"

Jeb sputtered and coughed, but before he got a chance to answer, the woman leaned forward and said, "Not hardly, sugar. I'm not exactly the marrying kind."

Jeb gave a small smile and said, "Why would you think this was my ex-wife?"

I shrugged. "Most of the time men and women don't argue like that unless there are major stakes at hand. And that usually means marriage. Or siblings." I wanted them both to know that I'd seen them arguing. And Miss Holly Springfield had been louder and more vocal than Jeb. I glanced up at my friend, and he didn't seem scared or overly worried, albeit he did seem a bit embarrassed and at a loss for words.

"No, no," he said, finally. "We're just really good friends."

"Well, with friends like that..." I said, and let the implications hang in the air. "Well, ya'll have a nice day. I think my food is being delivered."

"Bye now," Holly said and waved her fingers at me.

"See ya, Livvy. I got something I want you to read," he said.

"Okay," I said. "Any time, Jeb."

Then I stopped for dramatic effect. I could have asked him about Clarence Ford at any point, but decided to wait until I was halfway back to my car. "Oh, by the way, I met your friend, Mr. Ford," I called out. "Seems like you didn't do a very good job of disappearing."

Holly froze and the color drained from Jeb's face. Exactly the effect that I'd been hoping for. Confirmation that Jeb did indeed know Mr. Ford and confirmation that there was something fishy going on between them. But now that I stopped to think about how dramatically they'd reacted, I was a little worried. I waved and left them both staring after me, mouths agape.

I rolled back over to the car as Jeb got back in Holly's. Bessie leaned up against her door, fiddling with the hem on her skirt. "I've got a loose thread," she said. Then she glanced up at me and said, "Are you telling me you didn't have to pee after all?"

"Shut up, Bessie." I rolled over to my side of the car.

"Oh, what, now I have to put your chair back in the trunk again? I just got it out!"

"Cram it, Bessie," I said, getting back in the car.

She huffed and puffed, put my chair back in the trunk and got back in just as Dorothy delivered our food. Shoving my sandwich at me she said, "What's your friend doing with that woman?" she asked.

I tried not to lean forward to look at them, but it was the only way I could see them. I pretended to need something out of the floor board and glanced over to see that their heated discussion had resumed. "I have no idea. Says she's a friend of his, I guess from Baltimore."

Bessie slurped her malt and said, "They don't seem too much like friends."

"I know," I said.

From a distance I heard him say, "Dammit, Holly. Just give me another two weeks!"

"I don't have two weeks!" she replied.

Then Jeb glanced over his shoulder and noticed that Bessie and I were both staring at them. He mumbled something, Holly started the car and they drove away.

"That was odd," Bessie said.

"To say the least," I added and watched to see what direction they were headed.

An Evening with Aunt Runa
October 1958

The World Series, much to Clive's disappointment, had stretched out to seven games. He liked for his team to win as quickly as possible, because he couldn't stand the excitement. As his punishment for skipping school—and as of yet, Willie Gene did not know about the beer—Willie Gene had grounded Clive for two weeks and thus he was forced to listen to the rest of the championship with his father or not listen to it at all. I couldn't stand to be in the same house with them, and Humpy had decided to grace us with his presence, too, so I skipped out to Aunt Runa's. In fact, I'd planned on staying the night. A healthy sense of self-preservation was never a bad thing.

I was in Aunt Runa's side yard, raking leaves, feeling the cool air biting at my cheeks and yet working up a sweat at the same time. Aunt Runa and I worked well as a team, as we often did. I raked up all the leaves within my reach, then—as long as the ground was flat—I'd wheel myself over five feet, and rake all those leaves, while Aunt Runa would come along behind me with a big burlap bag, and gather them to be used later as compost.

Aunt Runa and I had a nice rhythm going, and Aunt Mildred noticed the progress we were making from her kitchen window. She called out something to us, but we couldn't hear her, so after a few moments she appeared on her front porch and began walking toward us. Without warning, Jeb pulled his car into Aunt Runa's gravel drive, and Aunt Mildred—half way to Runa's house—pulled up short. She stood there a minute trying to decide what to do. Return home and not seem like a busy-body and miss out on a chance to speak to Jeb without half the county present, or stay and remove all doubt as to the depths of her nosiness. I could almost see her waffling back and forth but finally, she made her decision and made her way across the rest of the acreage.

Aunt Runa slowly stood up straight, pressed her hands to her lower back, and then threw me a quizzical glance. I shrugged. I had no idea what Jeb was doing here.

Jeb got out of the car, almost bashfully, shoved his hands in his pockets and said, "Pardon my intrusion, ma'am. But I saw Olivia here, out in the yard, and wanted to talk to her a minute."

"Oh, of course," Aunt Runa said. "We're just about finished anyway."

Jeb glanced over his shoulder and watched as Aunt Mildred, beat-up green sweater pulled tight around her shoulders, trotted the final steps up to greet us. "Well, hello," Mildred said to Jeb. "I was just coming over to talk to my sister. Hope I'm not interrupting."

"Oh, no, ma'am," Jeb said, nodding. He put his hand out. "And which one of the Aunties are you?"

"Oh," she said, shaking his hand. "I'm Aunt Mildred."

"She's the oldest," Runa said, mischievously.

"I am not," Mildred countered. "Okay, well, the oldest living, I suppose."

"Nice to meet you, I'm Jeb McDowell," he said with a smile.

"Everybody knows who you are by now," I said, laughing. And in fact, I had to stop and think about it, but it did seem as though he and Mildred had not met before now.

"Well, welcome to our tiny corner of the world," Aunt Mildred said. "I sure hope that everybody has given you a warm welcome."

"Some more than others," he replied.

"I hear you're quite the dancer," she said, with a twinkle in her eye.

"Depends on my partner," he said, smiling at me.

Aunt Mildred and Aunt Runa stared at each other. Each one wanted desperately to know the same thing I did. The "magic land" aside, what was he doing in *our* county? There were plenty of places he could have disappeared to, and probably done a better job at it. There was a tug on my brain and it said; *his being here was no coincidence. He was here for a reason.* And I had the sneaking suspicion that both of my aunts felt the same way.

But neither Mildred nor Runa would ask, although each one tried to silently insist the other do just that. But it didn't work. Both of them were too stubborn.

"Well," Jeb said. "Olivia, I told you I've got something I want you to read. I'll either bring it by for you, or maybe you and Clive could come up and get it? You could bring some of that fabulous fried chicken and I could...well, I can slice tomatoes, if there's any left at the grocer."

I laughed. "Okay, I'll talk to Clive. He's been preoccupied with the championships, you know."

"Oh, I know," he said. "My money's on the Yankees, for what it's worth."

"Lord, don't mention that to Clive," I said and rolled my eyes.

"Well, why don't we call it a date?" he said. "You and Clive. We'll celebrate my birthday."

"Oh? When's your birthday?"

"The twenty-seventh."

"Of October?" I asked.

"Yes," he said.

"What year?" Aunt Mildred asked.

"Hmm? Oh, I'll be thirty-five this year." Older than I thought. He came across much more youthful and unburdened than somebody in his mid-thirties. Although I knew he'd lived his share and experienced a lot more things than I had—college, marriage, divorce and a child—he seemed utterly new at this thing called life. As if, every single thing was a new experience for him. Maybe it was just because he was in a new place. Or maybe it was all an act. He had seemed pretty burdened with Holly in the car the other day.

"Well," Aunt Mildred said. She pulled her sweater closer. "Bit chilly out here. Guess I'll be heading home. It was...terribly nice to meet you."

"You too, ma'am," he said and nodded.

As Aunt Mildred turned to walk back to her house, Jeb motioned for me. I handed Aunt Runa the rake and wheeled over closer to him. "What is it?" I asked.

"What did Ford say to you?" he asked in a hushed tone. I glanced at Aunt Runa who had resumed raking leaves.

"Not much," I said.

"Did he ask about me, directly?"

"No," I said.

"Then how did you—?"

"The townspeople consider it highly unlikely that a man, obviously not from here, would take up residence in a hotel just a mere few weeks after you arrived. So, I just asked him if he knew you."

Jeb smiled down at me. "I didn't know he was here. He must be keeping a low profile."

"Actually, he's not. Walked big as you please right into Mumford's. What does he want? How do you know him?"

Jeb sighed and glanced around. "There are some people who are dead set against me accomplishing my goals. They just can't leave me be. Ford thinks I have something that's his."

"And do you?"

"Not really," he said, shrugging. "If anything, he owes me."

"So, if he thinks you owe him something and he's here. Why doesn't he just come by and collect it? Why all the secrecy?"

Jeb thought long and hard on that question before he answered. "I don't know."

"Well, it makes no sense," I said. "Are you in some kind of trouble?"

"No," he said, but I wasn't sure I believed him.

"Do you want me to talk to Gunnar?"

"No, no, no. I'll go see Ford and get this straightened up."

"Okay," I said.

"So, I'll see you Sunday at church. And then, the Saturday after for my early birthday celebration."

"Okay."

He got in his car and left, and Aunt Runa made her way to stand by me and wave. "He's got a lot of secrets, that one."

I glanced up at her. "It would appear."

"Come on inside," she said. "Let's have some apple cider."

Later that evening, after Uncle Pete had come home and eaten his dinner and smoked his pipe and fallen asleep in the chair, Aunt Runa and I played cards at the kitchen table. As usual, she talked about everything except the game we were playing, as if she weren't paying attention to any of her cards, and yet she managed to beat me at almost every hand. Her Good Morning wood stove was fired up and kept the persistent chill out of the house, replacing cold air with warm, dry, pungent air.

"Aunt Runa, why wouldn't Aunt Mildred marry Edwin the first time he asked? You know, before she met John?"

Aunt Runa shrugged. "Oh there were lots of reasons," she said. "What makes you ask?"

"I don't know," I said. "I was thinking about it the other day when I was having lunch with them."

"Edwin was a bit of a trouble-maker in his day," she said. "One time he decided he was going to play a prank on my daddy. He hid up in the tree, and when my dad came out of the outhouse, Edwin jumped down out of the tree...you know, just to scare him. It backfired, though, Daddy was so startled he kicked Edwin right in the knee and popped it right outta joint. Oh, Lord. Poor Edwin had to wear a knee brace from then on, that's why he walks with a sort of limp."

"Oh, my gosh!" I said, laughing, even though I felt guilty for it. "That's awful."

"Oh, don't feel too sorry for him," she said. "That bum knee kept him out of the service, probably saved his life. But, boy has he calmed down. For a while there...you know how there's this moment that you think a person's life is just gonna be wasted and then all of a sudden, for whatever reason, they just become somebody else."

"No," I said.

"Well, with a lot of young people, it's like one day their minds just decide that they are gonna shed the old skin and get new skin. I think most people are done with this by the time they're thirty. But some, it takes longer. Edwin, one day, woke up and decided he was gonna be different. And by golly, he is." She snapped her fingers. "Just like that."

"So you're telling me that there's hope for Humpy and Bessie?"

"Well, there are miracles and then there are miracles," she said, laughing. My eyes widened at her mischievousness. "Naw, I'm just teasin' you. There's always hope. Anyway, Mildred just couldn't handle what Edwin was when he was younger. Now it's as if, all the things she used to like about him are still there, but the wildness is gone."

"Oh," I said. Maybe this was what was happening to Clive with his sudden drinking and skipping school. Maybe he was going to become somebody else for a while, and come out on the other side a new person. Too bad my father never saw fit to try such a metamorphosis. Somewhere, he's drunk in a gutter, feeling sorry for himself and expecting everybody else to solve all his problems.

"Thing is, sometimes we make decisions for our whole lives during that one short period of craziness," Aunt Runa added, as if she could read my thoughts. She did not defend my father or his actions, but neither was she quick to condemn him. Aunt Mildred and Aunt Stella, on the other hand, held regular gatherings where they burned my father's effigy. An exaggeration, but only just. It wouldn't bother me if they did, one way or another. I didn't care enough to care.

"You know," she said. "I think I've got a photograph of Edwin when he was younger. You could just tell by looking at him how wild his heart was."

That she had a photograph "somewhere" would lead to the best part of the whole night. Aunt Stella and Aunt Runa both were loaded with photographs and family stories. History and lore and legend just seemed to ooze from their pores. I loved it when they got out the big dust-free hat boxes and albums full of pictures. They never sat long enough to gather any sort of dust. Aunt Runa's giant, round hat boxes were full of American history, not just our family history. There was photograph after photograph of suffragette's marches and conventions, and one photograph after another of hollow-eyed homesick soldiers and muddy, squalid trenches of war-torn France. Even the hat boxes themselves, once housing the big flowered and feathered hats of the 1890's, were now antiques.

She disappeared for a minute, the card game all but forgotten, and returned with three boxes. She opened the first one, which was clearly not what she was looking for, and set it in the empty chair next to her. She rifled through another, made some noises, and then finally settled on the third one. When she opened it, it was as if she'd found a treasure chest. Her eyes lit up. Her whole body perked up. She took a handful of pictures and set them on the table. She fingered through them and I immediately caught sight of a picture of my great-grandma, Blanche.

Blanche had been tall and regal and proud, with huge brown eyes and long black hair that reached her waist. In almost every picture I'd ever seen of her, she was wearing a long white dress with a big hat or a big bow. The older the picture, the fuller and longer the dress. By the time women got the right to vote in 1919, she still wore long white dresses, but they were slimmer fitting and slightly north of the ankle. By 1926 when she passed away, she'd begun to wear them a tad bit shorter, but they were still white. However, in the picture that I'd pulled from the stacks of Aunt Runa's photographs, Blanche was wearing a darker, form fitting dress, with high boots that disappeared under the skirts, a tall pointy hat, and what appeared to be jewelry and make-up.

"Oh, I remember that," Aunt Runa said. "Costume party in Charleston the summer before your mother was born." Before women got the vote. Before the Wall Street crash. None of my aunties had ever been what I would call wealthy or even well-off. But before 1929 they'd not exactly been poor, either. After the crash, the family never quite recovered. But then, the entire region had never quite recovered. It was like the rest of America had moved on finally, but not Appalachia.

"Who did she go as?" I asked, mesmerized by the image on the paper.

"Cleopatra, and boy did she set the whole room talking," Aunt Runa said.

"Is it possible to miss somebody you've never met?" I asked.

Aunt Runa glanced at me, still searching through the pictures. "How do you mean?"

"I miss her and I never met her. Maybe it's not *her* that I miss, but the idea of her. It's like there's a vacancy in my heart—in my memories—that she's supposed to fill, and she doesn't," I said, staring at the picture. "Sounds silly, I know."

"No, no," Aunt Runa said. "I understand. Oh, look. Here's a picture of you and my grandson James." The photograph had been color-tinted and in it I wore a red dress. My dark hair had been parted in the middle and braided into pigtails. I couldn't have been more than three or four. James, a year younger than me, had blonde hair and he smiled, squinting into the sun. I had one arm around him and one hand protectively holding his other hand so he wouldn't move for the photograph. I set it aside as she handed me another picture.

It was taking Aunt Runa too long to go through the photographs, and I just started sorting through them myself, not really looking for anything in particular. "Who's this?" I asked. Aunt Runa rattled off some answer about it being her great-uncle's grandson, and how many cousins how many times removed he was. Finally, she found the picture she wanted. It was of a group of people, standing in front of one of the many cliff facings in the area. Off to one of the sides—out of the picture—was probably a small trickling water fall. They dotted the landscape everywhere in this county.

Aunt Runa was busy naming off who everybody was in the photograph, but I'd already found Aunt Mildred. After having had regular viewings of the auntie's old photographs, I could pick out who my aunts and uncles were at all the different stages of their lives. "... and there's Edwin," she said, pointing to the man standing to the left of Aunt Mildred. He was spry and spunky looking, wearing suspenders and a hat sort of cocked off to one side. He also wore a smirk that held more attitude than any words could have ever conveyed.

"When was this?" I asked.

"Before the war."

Anytime any old timers said "the war" they meant the First World War. If they meant any other war, they always specified.

"I'd say about 1915."

"So, Aunt Mildred was what, about thirty?"

"That's about right. Edwin was about twenty-five. Just look at him," she said. "Pocket turned inside out, hat on crooked. What a mess he was. But he sure adored Mildred Anne."

I smiled. "And the rest? I recognize Aunt Colinda," I said, and pointed out the three or four cousins and neighbors that I also recognized.

"Well, that there's Arnie's dad, and on the end, well, that's a feller named Joe Bill, believe it or not. Joe Bill Bishop. His family was from up around Glade Creek. He moved out, went to Charleston, then on to Europe for the war."

"What happened to him?"

"Don't rightly know," she said. "And that there, well that's your Uncle Pete's sister. Boy she was a card!"

And so I got regaled with stories about Uncle Pete's sister, which led to how he and Aunt Runa had met. "Oh, and that's Rhea Webster."

I looked closely. "That's Crazy Rhea?" Aunt Runa nodded. "I would have never made that connection." Crazy Rhea, as the name would suggest, was the local nutcase. An older woman, maybe sixty-five or seventy, who lived way up on a mountain in a house that had belonged to her grandfather. There'd been a massacre there during the early eighteen-hundreds, and she claimed to be able to talk to dead people, animals, and sometimes trees. While I certainly have spent my share of time listening to the trees, I've never answered them, and even though animals appeared as though they understood me, I never understood them. But dead people? Why would you even try to talk to them? She did lots of other crazy things like rifle through your trash and kept the things she thought were important, ran a moonshine still, and embroidered flowers on everything that was made out of fabric. Her entire house was one big embroidered surface. Aunt Dotie told me that when Rhea ran out of things to embroider, that she ripped the old embroidery out and started over. And even at her age, she still quilted, made baskets, canned all of her own food, and butchered her own meat. The only thing she needed help with was putting in the crop in the first place.

Aunt Runa told some story about Crazy Rhea and we laughed and talked a bit more. We went through each photograph, discussing it and the people, as if our life depended on it. As if I'd never heard any of the stories before. Like we were going to get quizzed on it later and win a million dollars. What was so amazing to me was no matter how many nights I'd spent like this, looking at photos and hearing stories, there always seemed to be pictures I'd never seen before and stories I'd never heard. "Who's this?" I asked.

I had come upon a picture of a baby sitting in a stroller with an afghan carefully positioned over the stroller and the baby's legs. "Oh," she said. "Ummm, I think that's one of the Summers' girl's babies."

"He sure is cute," I said.

"Most babies are."

And that's the way the next three hours went. One photograph after another, one story after another. Finally, at about midnight, Aunt Runa convinced Uncle Pete that he needed to sleep in his bed and not the chair, and he toddled up the stairs to their bedroom, scratching his ear and bumping into the wall as he went. I got onto the couch, where Aunt Runa had put down a sheet for me and a big feather pillow, and two old quilts, worn just perfectly so that they were soft and malleable without being tattered or faded. I fell asleep quickly and soundly, dreaming about all the people I'd seen in the photographs: cousins, neighbors, nameless babies, crazy ladies, great aunts and uncles and my grandma, Blanche. Blanche sang to me in my dream. Some old familiar song that I could not name but knew that I'd probably heard as early as in the womb. *"Flow gently sweet Afton among thy green braes, Flow gently I'll sing thee a song in thy praise, My baby's asleep by thy murmuring stream, Flow gently sweet Afton, disturb not her dreams."* I smiled at her and she kept singing. And I kept smiling, utterly happy that Blanche was the one singing it to me. I didn't wake up until dawn, or at least I didn't remember being disturbed in the night, if I did.

A giant coal truck sped down the road, rumbling and shaking the walls, and I woke to breakfast at Aunt Runa's house, wishing that I didn't have to go home.

Detective Gunnar Ryan
Colton County Sheriff's Department

Gunnar shifted his weight to one side because the tree branch that he was sitting on was causing great discomfort to his backside. He had to remain quiet and far enough away from Jeb's house so as not to be noticed. He'd been perched in the tree for about an hour and should have thought to bring a pillow or something to sit on. It's not as if the same thing hadn't happened last night.

It was dark, well after midnight, and Jeb was still burning oil. Gunnar had gone to school with a couple of guys like Jeb. Artistic, driven, intellectual, occasionally self-destructive, and always searching for something. Men like Jeb made you think, because not only did they talk about the "what-ifs" but they held nothing back. It was all on their sleeve. They were always looking for somebody who would listen.

Jeb had taken the dogs indoors with him, just like he'd done last night. They weren't just protection, they weren't just hunting dogs, they were his constant companions.

Last night, sitting in this same tree, Gunnar had witnessed a panther slinking down over the mountain, but then she'd either seen him or caught his scent and stole off into the woods. He'd also seen a family of raccoons scuttling across the clearing. An owl had hooted off in the distance, and at one point, Jeb had come out onto his porch, stretched, scratched his head, yawned and then gone back inside. But Gunnar had not seen hide nor hair of a prowler in the human sense.

And for the record, he liked what he'd seen of Jeb McDowell. He was good to his dogs, and that said a lot. But it was more than that. Throughout town, he'd seen and heard about Jeb doing nice things. Like, he'd given Slim Jackson a ride into town, and nobody gave Slim a ride due to his eye-watering-sinus-burning-stench. Jeb had just rolled down the windows and took it on the chin. He'd fixed the back door on the church for free, and even mowed the grass a couple of times. Brother Dixon was ready to nominate him for sainthood, except he didn't believe in saints. Once Jeb had seen Mildred

McCutcheon, Olivia's aunt, struggling with some firewood, and pulled off the road to help her with it.

But it wasn't those things that made Gunnar like Jeb. Anybody could fake those things if he wanted to impress somebody. And, although Jeb's education was more akin to Gunnar's and he was certainly well-read—always a plus in Gunnar's book—it was the way Jeb treated Olivia that had convinced him that Jeb was a decent guy. And it wasn't only his treatment of her; it was the way he looked at her. You couldn't fake that.

Jeb McDowell, without any doubt, loved Olivia VanBibber with all his heart. And because Gunnar had spent the better part of his life admiring Olivia from a distance, he understood how one could fall under her spell. She was so unassuming and yet intoxicatingly smart. She'd always been smart, even before the polio. And she'd always had those big dark eyes that could damn near put anybody in a trance. But Jeb didn't love Olivia like that. Gunnar could tell that Jeb's love for Olivia was like the love of a father for his child. Or a brother for his sister. Jeb hadn't wanted to own Olivia or claim her or tame her or even brag that she was his. All the tell-tale signs of a man gone googly in the head. No, he wanted to share her. It's as though Jeb thought Olivia was a national treasure and should be adored by all. That was paternal, not romantic. Romantic was much more selfish than that.

When Jeb had taken her out onto the dance floor that night, well, the earth sort of shifted for Gunnar. How many times had he wanted to do the same thing? Hundreds. But he'd been too worried about what people would think, too scared that Olivia would be angry with him. But Jeb, well, Jeb just did it and people be damned. And he'd enjoyed every minute of it. Olivia had beamed so brightly, Gunnar thought she was going to explode.

Jeb *did* things. He was a verb for all intents and purposes, not a noun. Jeb was a thinker, for sure, but he didn't seem to overthink things, it got in the way of his doing. He seemed to go with instinct. While that could certainly have its down side, the plus could not be oversimplified or overlooked. Gunnar realized several things at the moment Jeb and Olivia danced together. One, Jeb had most likely learned the hard way the benefits of spontaneity and the pain of regrets and two, Olivia had been waiting her whole life for somebody to see her. And Jeb hadn't just seen her, he'd shouted it to the world. He'd said, "Here she is, everybody look!" And, in the process, made everybody who'd spent their lives around her appear pathetic.

Gunnar raised his binoculars and took a drink of water from a canteen he'd hung around his neck. All was still on Sassafras Mountain.

He began to doubt whether or not he'd get a glimpse of Mosie Gibbon any time soon, and also began to doubt whether or not he'd ever catch the prowlers that Jeb had reported to the sheriff's department. Mosie hadn't been seen in weeks. Maybe even months. And Andrew Halbrook hadn't been home in weeks either. Supposedly, he was off "working" somewhere. Were they really that concerned about being caught? All Gunnar had planned on doing was giving them a warning and maybe a few nights in jail if their attitudes were cocky, and hoped that would straighten them out. A harsher punishment could come later, if they didn't learn their lesson.

No, the fact that they'd both been AWOL since Gunnar had started looking for them was odd indeed. It meant that there was something they didn't want him to know, something a little bigger than petty theft. At least, that's what his gut was telling him. Of course, alone sitting up in a tree all night could make a man jump to all sorts of conclusions just to have something to do.

No sooner had the thought left Gunnar's mind than he got a glimpse of two figures coming out of the woods across the field from him. It was amazing just how much you could see on the night of a full moon, especially once your eyes had adjusted to the darkness. One of the things he'd missed when he was away at college was the stars. There were still stars in Ohio, but the city lights had dimmed their brilliance. Some hadn't been visible at ·all. Which he thought was a travesty in the truest sense of the word.

He held his breath, watching, waiting. Once the two men looked around to make sure they weren't being followed, Gunnar could see that they were Andrew and Mosie.

His heart quickened, his imagination wandering all over the place, wondering just what these two were up to.

Slowly they made their way toward Jeb's house, crouching down low so as not to be seen if Jeb had been looking. Gunnar would put money on the fact that Jeb wasn't looking. Everybody knew that Jeb was writing a book. He was most likely lost in his thoughts, possibly his drink, and pounding the keys on his typewriter. And Gunnar wasn't one-hundred percent sure, but it sounded as though Jeb had Gatemouth Brown playing on his record player. He'd never hear a prowler over that.

Mosie accidentally knocked over an empty rain barrel, and both of them froze in their tracks. They waited to see if the commotion would bring Jeb outdoors, but it didn't. In truth, it hadn't been that loud. Andrew smacked Mosie upside the head and Mosie shoved Andrew on to the ground. Both were trying to argue with the other without raising their voices, which made for a hilarious pantomime. Andrew jumped back up, arms flailing all about, and Mosie stood, feet spread apart, right arm pulled back, hand in a fist. "Come on," he gestured with the left hand.

Finally, Andrew said something that defused the situation because the two of them quit their charades and headed for the old outhouse. Surely they weren't just out gallivanting and decided to use Jeb's outdoor pot. How ridiculous would that be?

The two went into the outhouse together and Gunnar waited to see what happened. A few moments later, Andrew and Mosie both came out of the outhouse with small bundles in their hands. Andrew slapped Mosie on the chest as if to say, "Good job." And Mosie smacked his knee, smiling. Gunnar climbed down out of the tree, dangling his feet and then jumping the other five feet to the ground. "Stop it right there, boys," he said, gun drawn.

Andrew and Mosie both took off running, which Gunnar had figured they'd do, but it still somehow surprised him. Why didn't he have back up? He didn't have back up because there was nobody in the department who would come and sit out here with him all night on the off chance that he might actually catch Mosie and Andrew in the act of stealing something out of Jeb's outhouse. Gunnar ran after the men, who split in different directions. He had to make a choice and he chose to follow Mosie, because he was older and sicklier and Gunnar knew that if he didn't catch them before they hit the tree-line, he wouldn't catch them. Gunnar pumped his arms, throwing the canteen and binoculars to the ground. He wanted nothing to hinder him as he pushed himself faster and faster. Just as he got to within a foot of Mosie, he called out, "Give it up, Mosie. I know it's you."

Gunnar could almost touch him, almost...he reached a hand out to try and get a handful of anything; hair, shirt, whatever. The tree-line was only a few yards away. He grabbed, managed to get a hold of Mosie's collar, but Mosie kicked like some sort of old mule. Gunnar went down just as Mosie's foot came up and accidentally slammed Gunnar in the jaw.

He rolled about three times, stopping on his belly, scanning the tree-line for any sign of Mosie, but it was too late, he was gone.

"Sonofabitch!"

He flopped over onto his back and saw stars. Not the celestial ones, but the ones floating around in his field of vision. Damn, Mosie had kicked him hard. A pounding, piercing pain shot up his jaw.

After a few moments, Gunnar managed to drag himself up and head back down toward the outhouse, picking up his canteen and binoculars along the way. He tried to imagine what he'd say to Jeb if he came outside and caught him. Gunnar was just doing his job, but this was private property.

He opened the outhouse door and shined a flashlight around. The seat was really more like a wooden ledge with a hole cut in the top of it. He aimed the light down in the hole, a few mice scattered and a very large spider ran and ducked under the ledge. He ran the beam of light up and down the walls, and then stopped when he got to the front door. Above the jamb was a recess and tucked back on the ledge was what looked like two pillow cases. He pulled one down, opened it and audibly gasped.

It was full of money.

Gunnar assumed the other bag was full of the same. He sat down on the ledge of the seat and thought about this for a minute. Why would Jeb McDowell have...thousands of dollars...in his outhouse? Why not put the money in a bank? And was he aware of the fact that Andrew and Mosie had been skimming cash out of the pillow cases? He probably suspected, but still hadn't put the money in a bank, or even put it in his *house,* for Pete's sake.

There was only one reason Gunnar could think of that Jeb McDowell wouldn't want the money in his house and that was because it was stolen. It wasn't his. He didn't want to get caught with it. This way, if anybody found it, he could say he didn't know it was in the outhouse. "Oh, officer, my gosh, you found how much money in my outhouse? That must have been there when I moved in." Gunnar could hear it now. And the only reason he wouldn't put the money in a bank was the same.

Of course, Gunnar couldn't prove any of it, so it wasn't like he could just take the bills, knock on Jeb's door and say, "Hey, I'm taking the cash to the sheriff's office." Because if it was actually Jeb's money, then Gunnar didn't have the right to take it.

Gunnar thought about what to do. It was pretty obvious that Andrew and Mosie had been skimming a little at a time, out of these bags. There had been no hesitation, they knew exactly where the money was and had gone straight to it. There was no doubt in Gunnar's mind that they were the prowlers that Jeb had heard and reported when he first moved in. They'd been smart about it. No big spending, nothing to raise any suspicions.

He inspected the bags, and they were indeed pillow cases. No printing or anything on them to give any clue as to where the money had come from. Abruptly, Gunnar took a single $50 bill out of the bag and stuffed it in his pocket. He would take it to the office tomorrow and see if the serial numbers matched any recent robberies. If they didn't, he'd bring it back and let Jeb know that he needed to put money in a better hiding place. He doubted Mosie and Andrew would be back for any more of the money, anyway, now that they knew a deputy was watching. If the money did match, well, whether he liked Jeb McDowell or not, the man would have a lot of explaining to do.

Confrontation
October 1958

It was just my siblings and me at church Sunday morning. Mom and Willie Gene had decided to sleep in, and so, Clive, Bessie and I had gone to church without adult supervision. Even Humpy, dressed in his cuffed blue-jeans and leather jacket and cigarette stuck behind his ear, had gone too. Jeb, late as usual, came in after the opening hymn and slid into the pew next to me.

People had gotten used to Jeb, just a bit. We didn't field as many stares or strange looks on this morning, except from all the eligible single women who thought Jeb was cute. This allowed most people to concentrate on Brother Dixon. Humpy, of course, thought all the sideways glances and smiles from the ladies were for him. By the time church was over, his chest was so puffed out he looked like a solitary rooster in a house full of hens. It took everything I had not to burst his bubble. And in fact, probably the only reason I didn't was because I would have had to lean across Bessie to do so. That and Brother Dixon's sermon today was about being kind to those who were ignorant and stupid.

As we made our way from the church, the congregation sang, *"Onward, Christian soldiers, marching as to war, with the cross of Jesus going on before. Christ, the royal Master, leads against the foe; forward into battle see his banners go!"* Jeb walked me out and took my crutches from me. I sat in my chair that Clive had parked just outside the door. I'd take the braces off later.

"I've got another book for you to read," Jeb said.

"Really?" I said, excited at the prospect. "What is it?"

"It's a memoir. Do you read much non-fiction?"

"I do, if it's interesting," I said. "Non-fiction books though, they always make me peevish. I have very strong emotional reactions to them."

He laughed for several moments and then said, "One thing I've learned about you, Olivia-you always have an opinion about everything."

"Is that a bad thing?"

"You worry too much," he said, smiling and waving a hand at me.

Just then Humpy came over and a knot formed in the pit of my stomach. I simply never knew what nonsense Humpy would engage in. "Humpy, this is Jeb."

Jeb stuck his hand out and Humpy just stared at it.

"He's a good friend of mine, Humpy," I said, through clenched teeth. If I could have kicked him, I would have.

Finally, Humpy took his hand and shook it. "So, what's a cat like you doing in a hell-hole like this?" Humpy asked.

"Oh, it's not all that bad, is it?" Jeb asked.

"Have you looked around?" Humpy said.

"Yes," he said. "I have. It's a beautiful place. With lots of interesting people. And your music culture, well, it's totally unique. Nowhere else on earth has the style and type of music of Appalachia."

Humpy made some noise that indicated that Jeb was the stupidest thing on the planet. Jeb understood the condescending noise to mean exactly what Humpy had meant it to mean, smiled and said, "So you got big plans? You're gonna leave this place?"

"Hell, yes," Humpy replied. "There ain't nothin' that can hold me here."

Jeb looked down at his feet. "And what are you doing about it?"

"About what?" Humpy asked, as he waved at Lettie O'Neil leaving the church.

"About getting out of here. You got a game plan? Education? Apprenticeship? What?"

Humpy shrugged. "Don't need none of that. I'm just gonna go get a job."

"Where?"

"For now, Charleston."

"Well, good luck to you," Jeb said. "But don't be surprised if Charleston doesn't start to feel just like Greenhaven. It's not the place that offers you nothing. It's the other way around. You won't be happy anywhere you go."

Humpy stared at him for a minute and then started laughing. "Well, why don't you just get bent. What, you think you can come in here with your big city education and big city talk and razz my berries? Well, you can just—"

"Humpy!" Clive said, coming from the other end of the porch. "Just calm down."

Humpy and Jeb had a staring contest right then and there. I have no idea why Jeb decided to be so confrontational with my brother. It's not as if he hadn't been provoked, but still, Jeb usually let things go. Finally, Humpy waved a hand and said, "It figures. My sister always attracts the freaks." After several seconds of direct eye contact with Jeb, Humpy then let his eyes rake slowly over Clive. They got the message loud and clear. Humpy thought they were both freaks and losers and somehow, it had everything to do with me. This was nothing new, although I was mortified that Jeb had been dragged into it.

Jeb clenched his fist, and Clive, without hesitation and without a word, placed a calm but steady hand on Jeb's arm. My brother jumped off the edge of the porch and called out to his friend Randall Hatfield, who'd been waiting in his car on the gravel parking lot. "Let's split," he said as he jumped through the open car window—feet first—without opening the door. When he was situated he looked up at us and smiled and then lit up the cigarette he'd been storing behind his ear. Randall floored the gas, spun the tires and took off down the road, spitting gravel behind him.

"Sorry about that," Jeb said to me. "There's no excuse to be insulting toward one's upbringing."

I shrugged. "Don't worry about it. The only reason he's here at all is because Willie Gene offered to help fix his motorcycle if he went to church."

"Takes all kinds," Jeb said. And then he just stepped off the porch and headed toward his car.

Gunnar Ryan had been standing on the other end of the porch talking to Arnie Pickens. He walked slowly toward me, one thumb hooked loosely on the edge of his pants pocket.

"Everything all right, Olivia?" he asked, staring off down the road where Jeb had just disappeared.

"Everything's fine, Gunnar. Just my brother being a jackass, that's all. Nothing out of the ordinary."

Harvey Grose backed out of the parking lot in his new car and I took the chance to change the subject. "That sure is a nice new car," I said.

Gunnar blinked a few times and said, "Does he even have a job?"

"Last time I checked, no."

"Huh," was all he said.

***

Later that day, Jeb surprised me by showing up at my house. My mother had answered the door and left him standing in the living room to come and get me. When I came out of my room, Jeb was staring at the pictures on the wall. Mom just had one wall displaying a handful of photos on, nothing like the galleries at Aunt Stella's or Aunt Runa's house. "Jeb?" I said. "What's going on?"

"Oh, uh, hey Livvy. I was just wondering—I know this is sort of out of left field, but I was wondering if you could show me how to shoot?" he asked, hands resting casually in his back pockets.

My mother's brows knit together as she glanced over at me.

"You know, with your bow and arrow," he said.

"Oh, well, I suppose."

"The weather is gorgeous, it seems stupid to be inside all day," he said. "And I already know how to shoot a gun. Just thought it would give us something to do and I could learn from the best."

It *was* a beautiful day outside, but the weather report said it was supposed to turn nasty later, so maybe it was a good idea to take advantage of it now. It wasn't unlike him to just arrive unannounced with some surprise request. He'd done it before. But there was something different about him today. Maybe it was the scuffle he'd had with Humpy, or maybe it was something else. But he seemed...a little sad—no, not sad, insecure. He seemed unsure of himself, and I'd never seen that from him before. "Sure."

Mom went and got my canvas bag with the archery equipment and put it on the back of my chair for me. In the meantime, Jeb just kept looking at the pictures. "Who is everybody?"

There were only about eight photographs on the wall. "The top one there, that's our family group, when Hiram was still here. I'm the baby."

"You're so cute," he said, smiling.

"Thanks."

"Your mother is gorgeous."

"Yeah, she was quite the looker. Um, that's Blanche, my mother's mother."

He leaned in and seemed to soak the picture up with his eyes. "She's so striking looking."

"True, nothing gentle about her face, except the eyes."

"And...how did she die?"

"Cancer," my mother said from the kitchen. "Colon cancer."

"That's Humpy on his motorcycle that he crashed. That's me and Bessie on Easter one year."

"Before the polio."

"Yes, the year before." Obviously. I was standing sans braces in the front yard wearing a yellow dress.

"And this?"

"Oh, that's a bunch of my great aunts sitting on somebody's front porch."

He smiled at the photo, and then said, "'*Women sit, or move to and fro—some old, some young; The young are beautiful—but the old are more beautiful than the young.*'" It was Walt Whitman, and he knew that I knew it. He moved to the next picture.

"Those two are Willie Gene's family. And that last one is my mom's dad, Herbert McClintock."

"That's nice," he said. "I love old family photos."

"Me, too, actually. You should see all the pictures my Aunt Runa has," I said. "Shall we head outside now?"

"Sure," he said. He took me down the two stairs on the front porch, and then down the big hill in the back. The bulls-eye practice target that Willie Gene had made me was stored under the porch. Jeb yanked on it, and one of the corners got stuck under one of the loose planks. When he pulled, a nearly empty whiskey bottle came tumbling out. "What's this?"

I stared at it, instantaneously angry. "Probably Humpy's." Hiram used to do the same thing, hide whiskey bottles all over the house, and honestly thought that nobody knew.

"Oh," he said. "Sorry."

I brushed it off as best I could. It was always so disconcerting when I was reminded of the fact that I had a brother or a father.

Jeb set up the target, and I pulled my bow and arrow out of the canvas bag. "The trick is to keep your arm steady, breathe out and hold it, then shoot. And it helps me if I don't stare directly at the target and if I don't take too long."

"Okay," he said.

I pulled back on the bow, feeling the resistance on the string. "Keep your elbow up in the back. Some people have a tendency to forget about the back arm, but that's your shooting arm, so it's important. And if you have to, hook your finger in the corner of your mouth to judge how high your arm should be." I let the arrow fly, felt it whoosh down my arm, saw it fly through the air and hit the center target.

"Damn, girl. You haven't even warmed up!" Jeb said.

"I'm the best in the county," I said, shrugging. It was one of my few bragging points, and maybe I shouldn't brag as much as I did. Aunt Mildred said it wasn't very becoming of me, but I was proud of my shooting skills.

He laughed and clapped his hands together. "You have to show me."

I handed him my bow and let him shoot. A few times the arrow went in the field so far away that I couldn't even see it, and other times it just whistled by the target. All I did was place two fingers on his elbow and lifted, one finger on his wrist and moved, one finger on the back elbow and lifted and moved it out just a little. Just minor tweaks like that. "Your feet are too close together." After a while he began hitting the target, even if it was on the outer rim.

"Now, if you were shooting a big old moose or something, that would be acceptable. If you were trying to hit a squirrel or a possum, you'd go hungry for sure."

He just laughed again. A few hours later, as he was taking me back up to the house, he said, "I really am sorry for the scene with Humpy." When he had me on the porch, he added. "I truly am sorry."

I shrugged. "Don't worry about it. At least you have the decency to apologize. More than anybody will ever get from Humpy."

Jeb and I both took notice as a particularly cool gust of wind blew across the porch. Dark clouds started to roll in over the mountains. The weather was going to turn bad tonight. "Looks like we got in our shooting just in time," he said.

I nodded in agreement.

"You can tell me this is none of my business if you want, but...do you ever see any of your dad's people?"

How could I not see them? I ran into them at Arnie's, and in town. I even saw them at church on occasion, but usually they went to the one farther up on the other side of Wellston. I saw them. And I turned the other way. "You mean...on purpose?"

He smiled. "Yes, friendly like."

"No."

"Why not?"

I shrugged. "They make me angry."

"Have they done something to make you angry or do they just remind you of Hiram?"

I had seen my Grandma V—on purpose—for visits and such up until she died, and I loved her, there was no doubt. But beyond that, I'd washed my hands of all them the year Hiram left. There were many reasons for this, more reasons than I could tell Jeb in a five-minute conversation on the front porch. "Both."

"Absolutely, this is none of my business, but you know, when the cheese goes moldy, you just cut that part off and eat the rest."

I laughed. "Are you suggesting my father is the mold on the cheese? Because if you are, that's absolutely spot-on."

"Yes, I am. I'm also suggesting that maybe the rest of his family isn't moldy. You know, I just see you surrounded by these great people, your aunties and such. But it's all one sided. Nothing, and I mean nothing in this whole universe is one-sided, Livvy."

I just stared up at him, as his dark hair rustled gently in the breeze.

"Thanks for the lesson," he said. "I'll see you later."

I waved to him and watched him walk down the road, waiting until he was completely out of view before I went into the house to finish reading my book. Reading was always better during a storm or when it rained, and it looked like that was how the evening was going to go. I had pretty much forgotten about the incident between Jeb and Humpy, until Gunnar knocked on our front door at three a.m.

***

Somebody pounded on the door—thunder and lightning cracking all about—and I was reminded how much I really hated being in a wheelchair. By the time I could get out of the bed, and make myself decent, Willie Gene and Clive had already answered the door and were engaged in conversation with Gunnar. Standing next to Gunnar was my brother, Humpy, covered in blood and drunk as a skunk.

"What in the...?" I said, rolling into the living room.

Gunnar tipped his hat to me. "Olivia," he said and went on talking to Willie Gene. "Now, Willie, I ain't no saint myself, we all know that. But Humpy can't be out getting drunk and tearing up the streets of Wellston in the middle of the night and starting fights with perfectly good people."

It felt as though the bottom fell out of my stomach. "What did you do?" I asked Humpy.

But Humpy was so drunk that all he could do was raise his head and smile at me. Blood had seeped into the crevices of his teeth and his left eye was nearly swollen shut.

Gunnar looked at me and said, "He picked a fight with your friend Jeb McDowell. Now, I can't really attest to which of them won the fight, since Mr. McDowell pretty much looks just like this." He gestured to Humpy. Then he pulled something out of his pocket and, holding it out to us, said, "But Humpy lost three molars."

"Sumbitch," Humpy said. "Ina kill 'em!"

"Oh, you're not going to do any such thing," Gunnar said.

"Oh, my God," I said. What was Jeb doing in Wellston in the middle of the night? My mind raced through the possibilities. I supposed he was doing what Humpy had been doing. Getting drunk and shooting pool.

Humpy chose that moment to teeter forward and back, and then spit blood onto Mom's clean floor.

"Oh, for the love of Pete," I said. Just then my mother came into the living room, fastening the top of her housecoat as she did. One look at Humpy and the blood drained from her face. Willie Gene held up a hand to her, to try and keep her calm. To try and convey that he had the situation under control. Clive shot me a worried look.

"Now, I know Humpy's not your boy, Willie," Gunnar said, "But, he's kinda your boy. Right? So, you better be doing something with him. Next time, I'm just gonna arrest him and it's gonna go on his permanent record. You got me?"

My mother's trembling hand slowly went to cover her mouth. Then, in a flash, the anger bubbled up until her eyes turned icy cold. Contempt, loathing, anger. That was what had replaced confusion and fear. She ran into the kitchen full speed, letting loose a war cry that I'd heard many times before. When she came back out, she held a cast-iron skillet high over her head. "You good for nothing, no account...why don't you just see how much you can behave like your father!"

"Mom!" I cried.

Bessie stumbled into the living room, still half asleep, hair in rollers and cold-cream caked on her face.

"Rosie!" Willie Gene yelled.

Mom jumped over the couch and lunged for Humpy, who tried to dodge her onslaught, tripped over his own two feet and splatted onto the floor. "Get up, you weasel. Get the *hell* up! Come on, let me beat the other side of your head! Let's make it even!"

"*Mom!*" I screamed.

Willie jumped over Humpy and tried to wrestle the frying pan from my mother's hand.

"Get up from there, go on!" she yelled. Willie pried the pan from her hands, threw it across the room and pinned my mother to the wall. Being disarmed did nothing to quell my mother's rage. She struggled against Willie Gene, a crazed look shot from her eyes, aimed at her no-account son. "Get up so I can beat the ever lovin' devil outta you! You ungrateful mongrel!"

I resisted the urge to run and hide under the bed like I used to when I was a child. For one thing, I couldn't get under the bed. But hot tears scalded my face and my hands gripped the wheels of my chair as I watched the madness unfold.

"Mother! For the love of God, stop it!" I cried out.

"I'm going back to bed," Bessie said and turned around. "Wake me up if anybody dies."

"You're useless!" Mom cried. "Useless! I hate you! *I hate you!*"

Humpy had sat up by this point, butt planted firmly on the floor, legs crossed like an Indian. "Right back atcha, you ol' biddy," he said and tried to wink but couldn't because his eye was now swollen shut all the way. "I hate you, too." He smiled at her, gave her a wave and then vomited right in between his legs.

Clive threw his hands up and said, "Ugh."

I was so embarrassed that I wished the floor would open and swallow me whole.

"Now, Rosie," Gunnar said to my mother. "Rosie, look at me."

My mother collapsed into sobs, all but folding into Willie Gene's arms.

"Rosalee, do I need to take Humpy to jail and let him sleep it off there or can you promise me you're not gonna hurt him if I leave him here?"

Clive shot me a look that said Humpy might be safe around my mother, but not around him. His nostrils flared and he blinked rapidly. Then he started pacing. I couldn't help but feel sorry for Clive. Having step-siblings was adjustment enough, but having one like Humpy was a living nightmare. In any other situation, Clive could have simply walked away from somebody like Humpy, but siblings and siblings by marriage...he was stuck with Humpy until one of them moved out.

Eventually my mother's sobs turned to hiccups and then long deep breaths. "I'm fine," she said. "He can stay here."

"Now, you sure?" Gunnar asked.

"I'm sure!" she yelled and I flinched.

Gunnar asked Willie what he thought, with just a look. Willie nodded that all would be well and Gunnar turned to leave, but not before making direct eye contact with me. I was mortified. Absolutely mortified. And I wasn't sure who I was angrier with. Humpy or my mother! Or Jeb, for that matter. I was going to have a talk with him tomorrow, for certain. Gunnar walked right past my mother and Willie, stepped around the now hunched sack of drunken bones that was my brother, and made a bee line for me. He took his hat off and then said, "Livvy, don't you let this bother you none. You hear me? My father's a way worse drunk than this and I've had my fair share of idiots on the family tree. This has nothing to do with you and don't you go feeling like it does. Okay? Nobody's gonna judge you for this."

I nodded with hot red cheeks, still mortified, unable to actually meet his eyes.

Then he put his hat on, stepped out into the rain, and left us to clean up our mess.

***

First thing the next morning, I made Clive skip school and drive me up to Jeb's house on Sassafras Mountain.

The storm had been pretty wild last night. Fresh clumps of leaves were strewn all about from the wind and the rain, and a few dead branches had blown down here and there. When Clive and I went to make the turn to Jeb's, he slowed the truck down and we could see that the giant weeping willow tree had been cleaved in two by lightning. "Will you look at that?" Clive said.

"Oh, no," I said. "I loved that tree!" When I was a kid and my mother was about to call me in for a bath and bedtime, I would deliberately run to that tree and hide. I'd climb up as high as I could go and just sit quietly. Nobody could see me. That's the beauty of a weeping willow tree. Once you're safely ensconced in its folds, nobody would know you were there. And I'd sit there, trying not to move even though the mosquitoes would buzz around my face and bite my arms. But I'd sit and hope that nobody would find me. And then the wind would blow and I'd feel the tickle of branches. And inevitably my dad or somebody would discover me, because I hadn't realized that they'd all figured out my secret hiding spot a long time ago.

My gaze lingered on the split halves of the tree, the trunk black from where the lightning had apparently caused a small fire. The landscape of my tiny world had just changed.

The truck sputtered and jerked and squeaked as we made our way up to Jeb's house and, as usual, I was never entirely sure that the truck wasn't going to just give up the ghost and call it a day. "What the hell is the matter with Humpy, anyway?" Clive said.

I was really not in much of a mood to dissect my brother's psychosis this morning, and now I could just add the demise of the weeping willow tree to my list of reasons why. But I knew if I didn't say something, Clive would just keep right on talking. "He's weak."

"Weak? He's raised the same as you and Bessie."

"He's the boy, when Dad left—"

Clive glanced over at me.

"It left a hole in him," I said. "He can't fill it up."

"Well, maybe he's trying to fill it up with the wrong stuff. Besides, it didn't leave no hole in you or Bessie. Naw, that's just some lame excuse. If you want my opinion—"

"I don't," I said quickly, and didn't bother to add that Dad's abandonment had left a hole in me and Bessie, too, we just handled it differently. Bessie became obsessed with herself. I lost myself in books and the company of old aunts. Humpy got numb from drink, because he didn't have the character to find a more constructive outlet.

Clive looked at me a little too long and nearly ran the truck in the ditch. It was difficult enough getting up Sassafras Mountain without taking side trips into ditches. The mud from the rain the night before didn't help, either. I grabbed onto the door to brace myself.

"If you want my opinion," he said, again, a little louder, and correcting his swerve. "He's a drunk."

I glanced at him sharply.

"He's a drunk and if you don't stop him now, he's going to be just like your dad."

"As long as he moves away and goes and does whatever it is he's going to do, away from me, I really don't care."

I was in a very foul mood.

"You don't mean that," Clive said.

I rolled my eyes.

"He needs—"

"I don't care, Clive!" I snapped. "And you should be talking. Skipping school and drinking? Just where do you think behavior like that's gonna lead? Huh?"

Clive was quiet a moment and he ground the gears for about five seconds until he slipped it into the right one. He clenched his jaw and glanced out the window at the now half bare, half golden trees, and I was ever so grateful that he hadn't pointed out that he'd skipped school this morning at my behest. Morning sunlight dappled the road and the truck, and a heavy dew covered everything, making it appear as though the world was covered in gold-colored crystals.

"I'm sorry," I said, finally. I was sorry to be so callous and sorry that I upset him, but I wasn't sorry about the context of my sentence. It was exactly the behavior he displayed by skipping school and drinking, that had led my brother Humpy to this moment in his life. It all started so rebelliously innocent. A little fun, a little jab at the parents, no big deal. But all people who found themselves in Humpy's shoes underestimated the power of the drink.

Now, one might think that this was the influence of the suffragette Aunt Runa speaking, the advocate for temperance and all that, but it wasn't. This was me, Olivia, the daughter of a devastating alcoholic speaking, and at times the words I heard coming from my mouth made me cringe. They made me seem so ridiculous, so juvenile, so naive and yet so *old* at the same time. Like I was this little old lady with her chastity belt firmly securing her virginity for all time. Someone who had a paralyzing black-and-white view of the world. But I only had to see my father sell his beloved family dog for a pint of whisky, just once, to be convinced of the evils of drink.

I was not Clive's mother, and that was the part I needed to work on. I was allowed to think whatever I wanted, but it wasn't my place to tell people how to live. But when you saw somebody walking straight in front of an oncoming train, it was so hard to keep your mouth shut.

"No, no," Clive said. "You're right. It's not the occasional beer that's so harmful, it was the circumstances of it. I get what you're saying. Sneakin' around and all that. But Dad just makes me so mad sometimes. Like he knows everything and I'm just stupid."

Before I could respond to that—because I did think Willie thought he knew everything and Clive was not stupid—we pulled into Jeb's gravel drive. Clive turned off the engine, got out, and walked slowly toward the house, a curious expression on his face.

"Clive, get my chair," I called out through the window. "I want out."

He waved a hand at me. "Shh."

"Clive!"

And then I noticed it. The bloodhounds lay at the end of the porch in a heap of brown, and the front door was open. More than likely, Jeb was so drunk when he got home last night that he'd just stumbled in and forgot to close it. If he was half as drunk as my brother had been last night, I was in complete shock that he'd made it up the mountain and into his house at all.

Clive stepped onto the porch, glanced over at the dogs and froze in his tracks. The dogs never even flinched. At that point Clive turned and jumped the porch stairs two at a time and ran back toward me.

"What is it?"

"The dogs," he said. "They're either dead or drugged."

"*What?*" A feeling of cold crept down the length of my body. "Clive, go in and check on Jeb. Go now!"

Clive grabbed the shotgun off of the window rack, nearly smacking me in the head with the barrel of the gun, and ran back toward the house. Within seconds he burst back through the door, face ghostly white, stumbled down the steps and fell to his knees.

"What is it!" I cried. I *hated* being trapped in this truck!

It seemed to take forever for him to get up off the ground and make his way over to my side of the vehicle, but in actuality it had only been seconds. He yanked the door open and said, "Come on, there's no time to mess with the chair, I'm going to carry you in."

"What? Why?"

"Jeb's been stabbed," he said. "He asked for you specifically. I'm going to take you in and then go get help."

I barely realized what was happening. I felt Clive's hand under my knees and the other behind my back and I wrapped my arms around his neck, but it all seemed to happen in a cloud, a haze. Clive spoke to me but I didn't hear it. It was like cotton had been shoved into my ears, or better yet, it was like when I took the therapeutic swims at the hospital, when my ears were underwater and the therapist kept talking. Suddenly it was dark, and I realized that we were inside Jeb's house, but I had no memory of how I'd gotten there.

It took a few seconds for my eyes to adjust to the change of light. Lying on the floor in a pool of blood, with a knife sticking out of his stomach, was Jeb. Clive set me on the floor next to him and I leaned over, not caring that my arm rested in blood, so he could see my face. "Jeb!" I said. "Oh, God." My eyes began to sting and a whoosh of tears sprung forth.

"I'll be back as fast as I can," Clive said. Then he set the shotgun down gingerly on the floor next to me. I glanced up at him and what I saw reflected in his face pounded the breath right out of me. Tears were streaming down Clive's face, and his eyes were full of sorrow. He gave me a knowing nod and then turned and fled from the house.

"Clive's gone for help, okay?" I said.

At first Jeb just stared at the ceiling, like there was something spectacular painted there. As if he was afraid to take his eyes off of it.

"Jeb, Jeb, oh, Jeb, say something," I cried.

Finally, he turned his face toward mine, and it was as if his eyes focused suddenly and he recognized me. "Livvy," he said, and swallowed.

"Yes, I'm here," I whispered. This wasn't happening. This could not be happening. Another wave of tears flooded my eyes and I fought back sobs.

"Livvy, I..." he coughed.

"Shh, shh, don't talk."

"I'm dying," he said.

"Who did this to you?"

"Doesn't matter," he said.

"No, no, it *does* matter. Who did this to you?"

"Don't hate," he said.

I placed my hand on the side of his face and he smiled at the touch. "You're the most extraordinary girl," he said.

"No, no, I'm not. I'm just a girl," I said. The tears flowed down my face now, hot and free. He. Could. Not. Die. "Please, hang on. Clive's gone for help."

"It's all for you, girl. It's all for you."

"What do you mean?" I asked and then wished I hadn't said anything because as he tried to clarify what he meant, a bubble of blood spurted from his nose and mouth. "No, no, shh, shh, just don't speak. Don't speak."

He smiled and tried to raise his hand to touch my cheek. I caught it, grabbed his hand and squeezed. His face was ashen gray, and bruised from the fight he'd been in the night before with my brother. Goose bumps scampered down my spine and arms as the thought occurred to me; *could Humpy have done this?*

"So...so happy I met you," he said. "All of them."

"Just hang on."

I knew it would take Clive at least five minutes to get down the mountain and five minutes to get back up, not to mention however long it took him to get help. Nausea overtook me and I thought I would vomit. I could not sit here like this for twenty minutes while Jeb lay dying. I couldn't do it. Panic gripped my throat and a sob tore from me.

"I...I have no fear," he said.

Oh, my God. My thoughts were so scattered. I just...I couldn't...he...*Think! Think!* What was I supposed to do? What was I supposed to say? I...I...I wasn't even sure I could remember how to speak.

"Just sit...with...me."

"I'm not going anywhere," I said.

He tossed his head back and forth and coughed again. It sounded wet and warm and smothering. All I wanted to do was scream. But I couldn't do that. I had to stay strong.

"Jeb," I said, squeezing his hand. "Jeb."

"Tell my mother...tell her I understand and I...forgive."

"Jeb?"

Somehow he managed to find a surge of energy, he tried to sit up but there was no way he could. He looked me straight in the eye and said, "'a stone, a leaf, an unfound door...O lost, and by the wind grieved, ghost, come back again.'"

"Jeb?"

Then he looked at me one last time and said, "Live, Olivia Anne. Live."

And he was gone. His hand went slack, his body went calm, and the light left his eyes. There was nothing as utterly still as a dead body. And Jeb had gone as still as he would ever be.

"No," I said, tears pouring, streaming down my face. "No. No. No."

I sobbed hysterically, wiping at my tears as if that would make them stop coming. But they just kept coming and coming and coming, and an ache burrowed itself in my chest so deep—so completely—that I was breathless from the pain. Breathing was work. Thinking, impossible. A mind-numbing panic took over and I was glad for it. I welcomed it as I dissolved into a state of paralyzing helplessness.

At some point, noises outside the house brought me back to the living. Scuffling, rocks moving, footsteps on the porch. In my traumatized haze, all I could think of was that whomever had killed Jeb had returned. I'd forgotten all about Clive. I'd forgotten all about the outside world. I had no idea how long I'd been sitting there, holding Jeb's lifeless hand, staring at his chest, the knife, the blood, wondering how he could be here one moment and gone the next. Wondering at the mechanics of it, the unjustness of it, the inevitability of it. I'd gone so far down the rabbit hole of existential thinking that I'd completely forgotten that it was a Monday morning in October and the sun was shining brightly through an azure sky, and all over the country people were going to school and going to work and laughing and talking and loving and existing.

When the door to Jeb's house opened, I picked up the shotgun that Clive had left me and pumped the chamber.

"Whoa!" I heard a voice say. "Olivia, it's me, Gunnar."

I blinked my heavy eyelids, swollen from crying. Shaking, I swiped the back of my hand across my face and eyes, trying to clear my vision. From my place on the floor, Gunnar looked huge, menacing, even though I knew he wasn't.

"Put the gun down, sweetheart," he said. "Put it down. I'm not going to hurt you."

It finally occurred to me that it was Gunnar the deputy, in full uniform, and not Gunnar, Betty Jo's brother and my lifelong neighbor, who stood in the doorway. Gunnar, the deputy, reminded me why I was sitting on a floor with a shotgun. I glanced down at Jeb and realized all over again what had just happened. I'd just watched the life drain from the most amazing human being I'd ever met. The most alive person in all the world was now dead. Jeb was now just a bag of bones, no different than any who had gone before him. I glanced back up at Deputy Ryan, set the gun on the floor and said, "Oh, God."

Then I sobbed.

I vaguely remember Gunnar coming over, putting his hands under my arms and lifting me like a toddler up onto the couch. Then he sat down next to me, pulled me close, and let me cry.

INTERROGATION

Clive and I sat at the Sheriff's station, across from a brand new metal desk, with papers piled all over and a name plate that read: Deputy Gunnar Ryan. I'd been allowed to go home and clean the blood off of me and change my clothes before coming in for questioning. I was grateful for that, but my mother was so terrified by the sight of all of the blood, that I was almost sorry I'd gone home. I was an adult, and Clive was not, and Gunnar allowed me to be Clive's guardian for the questioning, since my mother was too terrorized to be here—after all, her son was the prime suspect, her daughter and step-son discovered the body—and Willie Gene was deep in a mine shaft somewhere.

Sitting next to Deputy Ryan was the Sheriff, Arlo Cunningham, and another Deputy, Lyman Boland. Sheriff Arlo Cunningham was about forty-five, had lived here his whole life, and always came across as an understanding but firm man. Deputy Boland, on the other hand, was a jerk from Dayton, Ohio, who made it as plain as he could that he thought all of us here in the valley were a bunch of uneducated, in-bred, morons. Of course, that didn't stop him from partaking of the fruits of the young, well-developed uneducated, in-bred, teenage girl morons. A classic example of how people equate my gimpy legs with mental retardation, or deafness, was how Deputy Boland had sat at Mumford's Diner with my brother, and me, and explained to Humpy in great detail all the things he'd done to one of the residents of Wellston, and she'd only been fourteen. "Yeah, Humpy. They might be dumb here, but they are soft and round in all the right places. And a certain amount of dumbness goes a long way in helping me get what I want." Then he laughed, to my horror my *brother* had laughed, too, and it was as if I had not been sitting there at all. So, I'd just kept eating, forcing food down into my queasy stomach, wondering if either one of them realized that Deputy Boland had even committed a crime.

And now, Boland sat on the edge of Gunnar's desk, up high, above the Sheriff and Gunnar, trying to be as intimidating as he could be. I'd made my mind up that I'd behave as though he wasn't there, unless he spoke to me directly.

"So, why'd you go up to Mr. McDowell's house?" Arlo asked. He had short cropped, dark hair, with an occasional white one rebelliously sprinkled throughout. A nicely moderately round belly indicated that his wife was a good cook, but that he'd maintained some sort of self-control throughout the years. His eyes were kind and it was clear that he felt sorry for me by the way he kept tilting his head to one side and speaking in a sing-songy tone.

"He got into a fight with my brother last night," I answered.

"So, you were going up there to check on him?" Arlo asked.

"Well, I suppose," I said. "No, actually, I was going up there to give him what for. I can't abide that type of behavior and I was angry with him."

There was silence.

Clive chimed in. "If Olivia doesn't think it's okay for Humpy to behave like a jerk, she isn't going to make no allowances for Jeb."

"Why weren't you in school?" Arlo asked Clive.

"I asked him to go in late, so he could drive me up there," I said. "I don't get around on my own very easily."

A cold smile spread across Deputy Boland's face as he said, "You and this McDowell fellow...were you two an item?"

"What?" I asked, incredulous. "How do you mean that?"

"Meaning, were you having your brother take you up there for a rendezvous—you know, for some hanky-panky," he said.

I was impressed that he even knew how to use the word *rendezvous*. But I'll bet he couldn't spell it. Before I had the chance to tell him what I thought about his ridiculous line of questioning, Clive jumped to his feet. "You shut the hell up, Boland! Olivia and Jeb were just real good friends, that's all. You take that back! Take it the hell back!"

"Clive," I said. "Sit down."

Clive clenched his fists and begrudgingly sat down.

"So, if there's nothing going on between you two," Boland said, "Why'd you two spend so much time together?"

"He was a writer, I am a reader. I guess he just thought..."

"If you moved to Russia or somethin' and you found one person in your village who spoke English, you'd hang around them all the time, too. Simple as that. Olivia spoke Jeb's language," Clive answered.

"Are you calling me a Commie?" Boland asked.

"Nice try at maneuvering the subject away from the fact that Clive just gave you an answer that made sense," I said. I realized with some self-contempt that I was failing miserably at ignoring Boland. "None of this matters, anyway."

"Oh, it always matters," Boland said.

"All right," Gunnar said, speaking for the first time. "That's enough of that line of questioning. Livvy, when did you see Humpy last?"

"Last night when you brought him home. In fact, when I went back to bed, he was still lying in the living room floor."

"So, you didn't see him this morning?" Arlo asked.

I glanced at Clive and we both shook our heads. "I assumed he was in bed sleeping," I said.

Clive shrugged. "Uh, no he wasn't in his bed, in fact, it didn't look like it had been slept in all night. Well, except the pillow case was missing off the pillow, but that was it. I assumed he'd slept the night in the living room, got up and went to hang with his friends, like he always does," Clive said. "Although, now that I think on it, that would be kinda early for him to be up after an all-night binge."

The silence in the room was as accusatory as it was deafening. I hoped with all my heart that my brother had been with his friends and they could vouch for him. I thought this, not with so much loyalty to Humpy, but because I couldn't bear the thought that my brother had actually killed a wonderful human being. If Jeb had not become friends with me, he would not have met Humpy. Even though the end result was still that Jeb was dead, I could deal with it better if it was a total stranger who'd killed him and *not my brother!*

"Was Jeb alive and well the last time you saw him, Gunnar?" I asked.

"Yes, he was. Jasper and John took him to his house, while I was taking Humpy home," he said. Jasper and John Fitzwater, brothers and deputies. "They said the dogs were fine and they walked Jeb into his home and all was well."

Which meant at some point after that, between three in the morning and about eight in the morning when Clive and I arrived, he'd been attacked. A five-hour window. Could Humpy have sobered up enough to get up off the living room floor, trek up the mountain and attack Jeb an hour or so before Clive and I got up there? Or had there been somebody else, waiting in the bushes, waiting to attack the dogs and kill him?

"What about the dogs?" I asked.

"What *about* the dogs?" Boland asked. I ignored him and looked straight at Gunnar and waited for a reply.

"They were drugged," Gunnar said. "They'll be fine."

"Who's got them now?"

"Arnie Pickens has them in the two empty pens behind his store. You know, where he used to have his German shepherds until they got old and died. He said he'd keep them until I could find a permanent home for them. Shouldn't be too hard. Any number of people around here could use a couple of good bloodhounds."

"I'll take them," I said.

"What?" Gunnar asked.

I glanced over at Sheriff Arlo. "I'd like to have them."

"You better clear that with Willie Gene first, Olivia. If he says it's all right, then I suppose it's all right," Arlo said.

"What about a funeral and such?" Clive asked.

"I suppose his family will take care of that," Arlo said.

His family! I wasn't sure where any of them even lived. Whoever they were, wherever they were, they were about to get very unwelcome phone calls.

"What is it, Livvy?" Gunnar asked.

"Well, he said he didn't tell anybody he was coming here, other than a few business associates, so I don't know how to get a hold of his family."

"We'll figure all that out," Arlo said. "In fact, Maggie said that Jeb had just been in at the courthouse filing a new will a few weeks ago. I'm sure he mentioned them."

"He did?" I asked. "Isn't that sort of an odd thing for a perfectly healthy thirty-five year old man to do?"

"You don't know that he was perfectly healthy," Arlo said. "He coulda been real bad sick and just not told you."

I had to concede that he had a point, even though I'd never seen Jeb act sick.

"Besides," Arlo said. "He'd just acquired new property. He probably just wanted to bring things up to date. I wouldn't read too much into that."

"Back to the body," Gunnar said. I flinched as the image flashed in front of my eyes. "Did you notice anything unusual while you were there? Did he say anything to you?"

"I was so...upset, Gunnar, that I didn't notice anything." It was odd, actually, how it had been as though the edges of the entire room had just blurred away, and the only thing that had been in focus was Jeb and the blood and me. "Um, but he did say a few things."

"Like what?" Gunnar sat forward.

"Well, I asked him who had done this to him and he told me it didn't matter. I...I think I asked him twice, and neither time would he answer me. He had ample time, in fact, he, uh...he quoted a book."

"A book?" Gunnar asked. "Which one? Maybe it's a clue."

"I'm not sure. And I'm even less sure if it matters."

Arlo sighed. "That's a bit confounding. You'd think you'd want to see to it the right people got what was coming to them."

"Unless he didn't want Olivia to know who'd done it," Boland said. "Like, he knew if he told her it was Humpy that she'd get upset about that."

"Or maybe he just had other things to say," Clive chimed in.

"Really?" Boland said. "What else could be more important than who killed you? Maybe he did tell her and she's just covering for that person. You ever think of that?"

Clive did not want to make an enemy of Deputy Lyman Boland and so I placed a hand on his wrist and shushed him. Clive looked down at my pale hand, stark against his tanned skin. He was at the breaking point. He was always a bit claustrophobic and so he took a deep breath. And I had to remember that he was Jeb's friend, too, and he'd seen just as much horror this morning as I had.

Deputy Boland glanced down at my hand. "What's going on?" he said. "Are you screwing your sister, Clive?"

Clive flew out of his chair, but Gunnar jumped to his feet, slapped Boland across the face, turned him around, grabbed his arm and shoved him against the closest wall face-first. Arlo had managed to grab onto Clive's shirt to keep him away from Boland, but Clive fought hard, the whole time screaming, "You sonofabitch!"

"I must have struck a nerve!" Boland said from his position against the wall. "All these mountain folk mate with their siblings."

Gunnar slapped Boland upside the head again, and said, "Cool it, Lyman."

"Shut that shit up," Arlo said, "Don't think I won't suspend you."

Boland relaxed, but Clive was still wiggling. "Now, son," Arlo said. "Don't take no account of the words coming out of an idiot's mouth."

"He needs to apologize to Olivia," Clive said. "I don't care how much he insults me, but to suggest that Olivia...why, if I get my hands on him, I'll turn him into a heifer!"

I just shook my head, wondering how many more posturing scenes I was going to have to endure.

Gunnar yanked Boland by the shirt and threw him out the office door into the waiting room. "Find something to do, Lyman."

Clive relaxed, shrugged Arlo's hands off of him and then all but fell into the chair next to me. I couldn't make out everything he was saying, since he was talking under his breath, but Lyman Boland was getting called every choice word Clive could think of.

Gunnar looked straight at me with those blue eyes, the no-nonsense-I-ain't-foolin'-around-eyes, and said, "What was so important?"

"What do you mean?" I asked.

"What was so important that Jeb would rather tell you than who his own damn murderer was?"

I shook my head to try and stop the tears from coming, but they did anyway. I took a deep breath and tried to compose myself. That was just it. He hadn't really said anything all that important. When I spoke, I spoke through tears and with a trembling chin. "He, he said he wasn't afraid. And then he said, 'Live, Olivia. Live.'"

I decided that I would refrain from telling them the part about me being an extraordinary girl. It would only lend credence to Boland's accusations. And besides, I wanted to save that part, just for me. The fact that some people assumed that Jeb and I had a sexual relationship was both typical and curious. Most of the time, women didn't have "friendships" with men. We had fathers, brothers, cousins, teachers, in-laws, bosses, and...husbands. There was always a title and a reason for our relationships with male counterparts, otherwise we had to be sleeping together. Friends were almost always exclusively female. So, it was difficult for people to wrap their minds around the fact that Jeb and I could just be friends. However, the fact that people thought that I—the deformed cripple—was having that type of relationship with an attractive older man, sort of made me smile. Because at the end of the day, it meant that in their eyes, I was still a woman. A she-devil capable of wicked things.

"Do you know anybody, aside from Humpy, who'd want to hurt him?" Arlo asked.

"Uh...as far as I know everybody around here liked him," I said. I looked to Clive for back-up.

"Yeah," Clive said, composing himself. "I ain't heard nothin' about anybody having any sort a grievances toward him. He's a right nice person."

"I know that he was divorced and had a son," I added.

"Really?" Gunnar asked.

I nodded. "They live in New Orleans, I think, and he hadn't seen them in years. And he had a friend named Holly Springfield who was visiting a while back, and, uh, the gentleman at the Hilltop Motel, um...Clarence Ford. Otherwise, just us."

Arlo stood up then and adjusted his belt to hold in his belly instead of hovering below it. "Okay, well, we'll be in touch, Olivia, Clive. I'm sure as this investigation goes on there will be more questions we're gonna need to ask you."

"All right," I said. "Will somebody let me know if his family is taking him back to Maryland for burial and funeral, or if they're going to do it here?"

"Sure," Gunnar said. Then he nodded at Clive. Clive took that to mean we'd been dismissed and that he could wheel me out of the station and take me home. Which is exactly what he did.

MELANCHOLIA

I cried for three days.

On the fourth day, I went to Jebediah Joseph McDowell's funeral. His family had swooped in from Maryland and completely arranged everything at the eleventh hour. I found it odd that they weren't taking him back to Maryland to bury him, so he could be with his family. When I had inquired about this, a peculiar look had crossed my mother's face and she'd said, "I heard from Charlie Lucas that his will stipulated he was to be buried in the cemetery by the creek, across from the church, where his services are to be held, too." Charlie Lucas was one of two lawyers in the whole county, and apparently, had been the one Jeb had chosen to rewrite his will.

I'd decided to wear my braces to the funeral, since Jeb always encouraged this, and Clive helped me up out of my chair so that I could walk inside and file past the casket, like everybody else. Charlie Lucas stood at the end of the church with the McDowell family. He was a very large man, well over six foot with hips as wide as his shoulders. He couldn't have been more than thirty because I could clearly remember being a child and attending a bonfire in his honor because he'd caught the winning touchdown that had put Wellston in the run for state championships. He hadn't been quite so big then.

There were several things that set Jeb's family apart from everybody else. One, they were the only strangers present, and two, they were all dressed in very expensive suits and dresses. They were huddled together, looking out upon the townsfolk of Greenhaven with amusing curiosity and just a touch of anger.

When I had entered the church, there had been a hush that fell upon everybody. Many of the locals were present, including my great aunts and anybody who had come into contact with Jeb. Law enforcement was there, too, but that could have been curiosity as much as respect. They could learn a lot by who did and didn't show up at a funeral, and how a person behaved. Even Crazy Rhea had made an appearance. Suspicious or not, people really liked Jeb. Once I had broken the ice with him, it had only been a matter of weeks before he'd completely disarmed the entire community.

Clive and I had found the body, and everybody knew that Jeb and I had been good friends, not to mention it was already a foregone conclusion among most that my missing-in-action brother had been the one to murder Jeb. It was no wonder that silence dampened the room like a wet blanket when we entered. Everybody was waiting to see if there was going to be a casket-side spectacle of tears and hysterical crying. I'd cried so much already that I felt certain that I had no more tears left to cry, not to mention I was slightly dehydrated. As I approached the end of the pews, Jeb's family parted and stepped aside, casting not so subtle glances my way, staring at my legs and whispering amongst themselves. Clive helped me lean over the casket and I touched Jeb's cold and lifeless hand. It's always a shock to feel dead flesh, no matter how many times you've felt it. Beside me, Clive sobbed gently.

In my hand was a letter I'd written to Jeb. I placed it in the pocket of his suit jacket. Then I fingered a lock of his hair, and to my utter dismay, shed more tears. It was not lost on me that he was being buried on his birthday. Clive stuck by my side all the way back to our pews. My mother, Willie Gene, and Bessie filed by after us.

What followed was a blur and will probably remain so the rest of my life. Somewhere on the peripheral edges of my consciousness I realized that Jeb's family kept turning around and staring at me. But mostly, I just stared at the floor, sang when I was supposed to, and wondered if there would ever be a day that I didn't feel as though there was a storm cloud hovering above my head. Jeb had waltzed into Greenhaven and turned on a light for me. Right now, the pain was so severe that I almost wished he hadn't. I might still be in the dark, but at least I'd be numb.

When the funeral was over, my aunties descended on me like a bunch of mother hens. They tried to soothe me with "there, there" and "it'll be all right" and "there must've been a reason" and "he's in God's hands now" and, although I knew they meant well, I didn't want it to be all right. Somehow, I felt if everything were all right, or would be, then Jeb would be forgotten. But, to my surprise, their ancient voices and powdered faces and warm hugs did actually make me feel a little better, which I promptly felt guilty over.

Aunt Runa kept touching her hanky to her nose because she had apparently been crying. Aunt Mildred seemed distracted, staring at Jeb's family at the end of the church. She didn't want trouble. She didn't like outsiders or strangers and always thought they meant our little community harm. Maybe she thought they were going to blame us all for Jeb's death. Whatever it was she was thinking, I knew it bothered her because she studied all of them, with a great intensity, grinding her jaws as she did so. Aunt Dotie had put a hand around my shoulder and wouldn't budge. Aunt Stella, with a coy little smile said, "I brought Delilah. We're going for a ride when this is over."

In a distant, wispy voice, Aunt Mildred said, "What a lovely idea, Stella."

I smiled at Aunt Stella because riding in her Packard Touring car was always a treat, and for her to bring Delilah out was her way of trying to make me feel better.

Most everybody had, at some point, gone up to the McDowell family and briefly with a quick nod of their heads said a curt, "We're sure sorry for your loss," and moved on. They were words that meant absolutely nothing. *We're sorry for your loss?* Of course people were sorry. Most normal people didn't rejoice in another person's pain. But the community couldn't very well *not* acknowledge his family. That would be rude. And when mountain folk were rude to a person it was usually because they believed that person deserved it. No, they had to make the effort, the show, because it was the right thing to do.

Edwin appeared out of nowhere and in a public display of affection that I wasn't used to, cupped Aunt Mildred's hand in his and guided her toward the McDowells to pay their respects, too. I suppose that meant that I couldn't get out of it. But his family kept throwing glances my way, even when they were being comforted by the town's residents. It made me not want to speak to them.

Aunt Stella, sensing my hesitation, moved in and said, "I'll walk up with you."

"Okay," I said.

Every step felt huge and seemed to take forever and not just because of the braces. When I reached the woman I assumed to be Jeb's mother, I stopped and extended my right hand. She looked at it for the longest time and then took it, fresh tears glistened her eyes.

"I...I'm Olivia VanBibber."

"I know who you are."

"I...I...I can't seem to find the words," I managed. Aunt Stella had made her way around all of the other relatives of Jeb's and finally came to stand by my side and acknowledged his mother with a nod. In a way, though, she was declaring that she was my protection and that Mrs. McDowell had better not say one mean thing to me or else. "Are you Jeb's mother?"

She nodded. She was a small woman, with dainty hands and delicate features and salt and pepper hair, coiled perfectly in a knot at her neck. A tiny black hat with a black veil sat perfectly cocked on her head.

"He spoke kindly of you," I said. Which was not exactly the truth. He'd really never spoken of any of his family at all other than to say they existed. But I couldn't bear to say the *I'm sorry for your loss* nonsense. So I focused on something good.

"Really?" she asked, surprised.

"Yes," I said, searching through my mental catalog. In fact he had said one thing, in general, about his past and I felt I should use it here. "He said that he'd had a very happy upbringing."

She softened a little. "You were with him when he died?"

I nodded.

"I can see that you loved him," she said. "I'm glad he had love in his last moments."

I had no idea what to say to that, so I said nothing. Aunt Stella placed a protective hand on my back, as if to say, "You've done your duty; let's go."

"I don't know what I was expecting," Mrs. McDowell said to me.

"What do you mean?" I asked. I glanced over at the people I assumed to be Jeb's siblings. They all abruptly looked away.

"Jeb was such a lost soul," she said.

I didn't dare tell her that I completely disagreed with her.

"Always searching for something he couldn't name. Something he couldn't quite find. But it was always the thing that he thought would heal an imaginary wound. The moment he came into my life I knew he was never going to be happy. He'd never be at peace."

She wasn't describing Jeb at all. Had she maybe come to the wrong funeral?

"As a boy, he spent his days drawing things he'd never seen, daydreaming about people he didn't know, writing stories from made-up people's points of view. There were times I thought that he'd never actually been himself one day out of his whole life. His fictitious characters could say and do the most amazing things, he could submerse himself so completely in something that didn't exist at all, but the real Jeb could not express love enough to keep his own son."

By this point I was shaking my head back and forth. She was wrong. She was completely wrong. But then I heard Jeb's words; *Nothing, and I mean nothing in this whole universe, is one-sided, Livvy.*

"He'd been gone a while," she said. "Wandering around being no place and doing nothing. I could feel his gratitude toward me when he finally returned, but he didn't speak it. Then he disappeared again, and came here."

"Gratitude...?"

She smiled and waved a hand. "Family affairs, you know."

"I...he..." I floundered. I didn't know what to say. I wanted to tell her that he had changed, that he was wonderful; that he expressed himself better than any person I'd ever met. I wanted her to know that somehow, some way, at some point, I think he'd found what he'd been looking for and he was truly happy. But at the same time, if I told her this, she might take it the wrong way and be full of resentment, and I didn't want to cause her more pain than she was already in. Finally, I said what I thought could be taken in the best possible way. "I think he was on the path to being truly happy."

"It would appear," she said. "Thank you for being his friend."

"It was my pleasure," I said, struggling to hold back tears. "Oh, and he also...his last words. He asked me to tell you that he understood and that he forgave."

The color drained from her face. "Forgave what?"

"I...I don't know. He didn't say. He—" I took a big cleansing breath. "He was struggling by that point. He didn't get a chance to explain. Just thought you should know." Then as Aunt Stella and I turned to leave, I remembered something Mrs. McDowell had said. "Wait, I'm sorry, what did you mean by 'I don't know what I was expecting?'"

"Well, when I'd heard that Jeb had left half of his estate for some crippled girl to run a library in West Virginia, I suppose I was expecting some bedridden, filthy, sickly child," she said. "But you're nothing like that. You're vibrant and intelligent and surprisingly beautiful."

It was my turn for the color to drain from my face. The palms of my hands grew sticky. "I...I'm sorry," I said. "What do you mean by half of his estate? What are you talking about?"

"He left half of his estate to his son, and the other half is to go to build a library here in Wellston and you are to run it. Well, surely you knew this."

"N-no, I didn't." Aunt Stella placed both of her hands on me to steady me.

Mrs. McDowell sized me up for a moment and then finally spoke. "Well, it's not a lot. Jeb had no fortune, that's for sure. But if he left it to this town, to you, it's because you managed to give him something nobody else could."

"And what's that?" Aunt Stella said, suddenly, protectively.

"Hope," Mrs. McDowell said.

Deputy Gunnar Ryan
Colton County Sheriff's Department

Sometimes things just didn't make sense, and there was no making sense of them. Gunnar didn't like that. He liked to have options. Lots of them. And when the only option was that you weren't going to know something, he found that unacceptable.

As he drove down the winding road, he thought of the petroglyph of the Piasa bird on the rocks overlooking the Mississippi. Father Marquette had discovered the petroglyph and described the creature as being as large as a calf, with deer horns, red eyes, a man's face, a lion's beard, wings, a long tail that wrapped all around its body and that it was green, red and black. The Illini Indians had named the bird the Piasa, and had many legends about it and believed it had been a real creature. Of course, the largest depiction of the Piasa had been on a giant piece of limestone and so it had been blown up by quarrying operations. It seemed as though the settlers had been hellbent on destroying everything in this country. But, the point was whether or not the Piasa had been a real creature. It drove Gunnar crazy that he would never know. Oh, he doubted that it was ever real, but then, it had to have represented something important to the Illini Indians to have been so prominently displayed. So, what did it mean? What did it represent?

And there were all sorts of things like that throughout history that he could not know the answer to, and so when it came to things that he *could* control, things he could find the answers to, he made it his business to get to the bottom of them. It was his way of balancing things out. So he might never understand who built Stonehenge, or what the Piasa had represented, but he could find the answers to smaller, more local questions. It made him feel better to accomplish smaller things.

Gunnar put on his blinker and turned onto a gravel road just outside of Wellston on the east side.

The murder of Jeb McDowell wasn't exactly what he'd call "small," but neither was it on the scale of the Piasa bird or Stonehenge. In fact, aside from when Lou Reynolds had shot and killed his wife because she was cheating on him, this had been the only murder in the county in five years. Murders in this part of the world tended to be pretty straightforward. Somebody caught somebody cheating, somebody wanted what you had, or somebody got drunk and did something stupid, which was more like manslaughter than murder, but still, a life was taken, so Gunnar counted it.

What he'd learned from this was sleep in your own bed, be happy with what you've got and don't get drunk, and all would be well. But nobody ever listened to him.

What bothered him about the murder of Jeb McDowell was that Gunnar didn't think any part of it was going to be straightforward. Well, yes, on the surface one could imagine that Jeb came home drunk after an all-out brawl with Humpy VanBibber and interrupted Mosie and Andrew while they were sneaking into his outhouse once again to take more money, and they killed him. Or that Humpy had gone up the mountain to finish what he'd started. Or that Clarence Ford killed him for some yet unknown reason. On the surface, those would seem the most likely scenarios. But, there were so many other aspects to this. For instance, the fact that Jeb had had a fight with Humpy and now Humpy was missing. The fact that Gunnar had a tough time believing Andrew and Mosie capable of murder, but he acknowledged that people had done horrible things in the name of money all down through history and so he couldn't really disregard Andrew and Mosie just because he didn't think it was in their characters to kill.

Six hours after the murder, Mr. Clarence Ford had checked out of the Hilltop Motel and disappeared. That was strange, indeed, and quite worrisome. Gunnar felt in his gut that Clarence's flight was indicative of suspicious behavior.

But, Gunnar couldn't even be certain that Mr. Ford had even had a conversation with Jeb McDowell while in the state of West Virginia. He only had what Olivia had told him and the fact that Jeb had confessed to her that he knew the man and that Ford was in the area for him. It seemed more like Clarence Ford had just watched Jeb, rather than interacted with him, but Gunnar couldn't know that for sure.

One of the first things Gunnar did after Jeb's murder, after he'd sat with Olivia on the couch and let her cry for a good ten minutes straight. After he'd made sure she was okay and that she wasn't going to pass out or be sick. He went straight to the outhouse, got the two pillow-cases of money and threw them in the trunk of his squad car. It had been so strange to him to discover how absolutely all-out pissed off he'd felt. He was angry that anybody would kill Jeb, angry that anybody would hurt Olivia in the process. And the notion that somebody in this county thought he had the right to take a life and was arrogant enough to think he wouldn't get caught, irked him right down to the marrow. After his anger had subsided, he'd thought about Harvey Grose and his brand-new car that he'd somehow managed to purchase without even having a job. And he thought about how he should go and see what sort of lies Harvey could come up with to explain the purchase of the car.

Gunnar pulled into the driveway of the Grose home and turned off the engine. He checked his gun, made sure it was loaded, and double checked to make sure he had his cuffs and they were in working order. These were tools of his job that he rarely had to use and he needed to make sure they were ready.

He was met by a couple of scroungy but happy dogs, and he made his way up to the front porch with them nipping playfully at his heels. It was a small house, but neat and tidy; Mrs. Grose was a very industrious woman. Harvey's mother answered the door and said, "Well, hello, Gunnar, what can I do for you?"

She was about fifty, pink cheeked and had a plump, round body. She'd borne thirteen children in her life—Mr. Grose was apparently very industrious as well—and yes, raised them all in that tiny little house. They must have slept one on top of the other. "Hello, Mrs. Grose," he said and tipped his hat. "I noticed that Harvey's new car is parked in the driveway. He's home, I'm assuming?"

"Why, yes, he is. What do you need him for?"

"I just want to ask him a few questions."

"About?"

"About Jeb McDowell," he said.

Her expression dropped. "Well, he didn't know that fella. I'm certain of it."

"I just need to ask him a few questions."

Just then, Harvey Grose stepped up behind his mother and said, "What's this about?"

"Good afternoon, Harvey," Gunnar said, "I'd like for you to come on out on the porch and answer a few questions for me."

Harvey, a scrawny kid who was right around twenty, with lots of acne and more grease on his hair than in a car engine, suddenly looked nervous. "It's not a choice," Gunnar added.

Harvey stepped out, shut the door and walked all the way to the edge of the house and onto the lawn so that nobody would overhear the conversation. "What do you want?" he asked.

"Where'd you get the new car?" Gunnar asked.

"From Abel's car lot in Charleston," he said.

Gunnar rolled his eyes. "Where did you get the *money* for your car?"

Harvey's dark gray eyes flicked, his gaze went from one surface to the next, careful not to land on Gunnar. "I uh...I saved up for it."

"You saved up for it," Gunnar said with his hands on his hips. He leaned in and boxed Harvey on the ears. It wasn't meant to hurt, necessarily, just meant to let Harvey know he wasn't talking to an idiot. "You saved up for it? You'd have to work 'round the clock for the last five years to save up for a car like that. What kind of fool do you think I am?"

Harvey grew ever more interested in the grass between his feet.

"Now I'm gonna ask you again," Gunnar started.

"It ain't none of your business," Harvey said, making eye contact with Gunnar for the first time.

"Oh, yes but it is," Gunnar said. "You see, I got a murdered man who had a lot of money. A lot of cash hidden on his property and some of it went missing. Suddenly, Harvey Grose has a new car that he couldn't possibly afford to buy. So you see, I think it is definitely my business."

Harvey started to sweat. "M-m-my uncle died and gave me the money."

"Really," Gunnar said in a condescending tone. "Then I'd be expecting that you've got some paperwork, estate papers, papers from lawyers to prove that?"

Harvey wiped the sweat from his brow.

"You stole money from Mr. McDowell, didn't you? Were you in on it with Andrew and Mosie?" Gunnar asked, inching closer to him.

With the mention of their names, Harvey seemed to cave in. As if he knew the jig was up. He leaned back against the house and rubbed his face. Then tears came to his eyes. "Am I going to jail?" he asked.

Gunnar thought about that for a minute. He could arrest him and press charges, but he had other things in mind. "You tell me everything you know about that money and Mr. McDowell, and you give the car up, and I won't arrest you."

"Give the car up?"

"You bought it with stolen money. It's got to be returned, because it's not yours."

Harvey seemed to weigh that for a minute, but then Gunnar assumed that he realized he couldn't really drive that fancy new car if he was sitting in prison. "M-Mosie had been squatting at the Renshaw place for a couple of months. He, uh, when Jeb moved in, he went back up on the mountain, but, well, he missed being able to shit under a roof, you know? He didn't like being all out in the open. So, he used to go down and use Jeb's outhouse. No harm done. One day he noticed these bags above the door. He looked in and found the money."

"Go on," Gunnar said.

"Well, you know Mosie, he's sort of soft hearted, so he wouldn't take all the money because then he felt like Jeb wouldn't have any. So, he just thought he'd take what he needed."

That actually made sense, knowing the things that Gunnar knew about Mosie. He was not a bad guy, not a criminal, but definitely opportunistic, and had pretty much been like that as long as Gunnar had known him. If a homeless person wasn't opportunistic, he wouldn't survive. "Go on."

"Andrew found out. Saw Mosie with a fifty dollar bill! Andrew threatened to turn him in, if he didn't tell him where he got it. Mosie could have lied and told him he stole it out of somebody's jar in the kitchen and there wasn't any more to be had, but no, Mosie told him the truth. So, Andrew went down there with him and got the bright idea that they should just take a little at a time, every week, so that Jeb wouldn't get suspicious."

"Okay, and I'm waiting for the part where you come along," Gunnar urged.

"Well, Jeb must have caught on, because he started moving it. He moved it to the smoke house, and under the porch. One time, he dug a hole and buried it and the only way we knew he'd done it is because the land had been disturbed and the money was missing. We dug, sure enough it was there."

"Okay, but how did you get involved?"

"I was back up on the hill, hunting squirrels, I came out on the clearing there above Jeb's and saw Andrew and Mosie. I went to tell them to get off the land because I figured they were up to no good, and noticed money sticking out of Andrew's pocket."

"And you, in turn, threatened them that you'd tell if they didn't cut you in, and thus, now you were up to no good."

He nodded, staring at the ground.

"All I wanted was a new car. I took money that day, and went back two other times, that's all."

That's all. As if stealing three times was somehow not as bad as stealing ten times.

The fact that the money had been moved around definitely meant that Jeb was aware of it, and Gunnar thought for sure that Jeb had come upon it illegally. The more he thought about it, the more he felt like it had to be stolen. Otherwise, Jeb would have brought the money inside, safe with the dogs, or deposited it in a bank. But he didn't want to get caught with it. So, why didn't he just spend it? Nobody around Wellston would have thought anything of it. They would have assumed he was just a rich author come to spend some time in the back country. There was more to it. One thing was for sure, if Jeb hadn't been murdered when he was, that money would have become the worst kept secret in all of Colton County and it would have eventually disappeared altogether.

"Anybody else know about the money?" Gunnar asked.

Harvey was quiet, tears staining his cheeks now.

"Harvey, anybody else? What about Humpy?"

He shrugged. "I don't know. I might have mentioned it to him, but...honestly, I don't remember."

Gunnar sighed heavily and gave Harvey a look as if he was the stupidest goldfish in the tank. "You realize this makes you a suspect in his murder."

"What?" Harvey said, looking up. His eyes were wide with fear and Gunnar couldn't help but notice the pulse pounding in his throat.

"Look, I don't think you killed him," he said. "Did you? You didn't kill him, did you? Because if you did, you'd be better off to tell me now, than for me to find out later. It'll look good if you cooperate with the investigation. Your sentence could be lighter."

"My *sentence?* Jesus, Gunnar. I didn't kill him. I was with Ginny Perkins that whole night. In the barn. You can ask her."

"I will," he said. "Well, I'll work on clearing your name. In the meantime, don't get any scratches on that car. You got me?"

"Yeah."

"And you better be coming up with some lie to tell your mother as to why you're going to have to give up that car, to cover the first lie you told her on how you got it."

He nodded, swiping at tears.

"All right," Gunnar said and walked back to his car. He watched Harvey slink into the house and he thought about the conversation as he turned over the engine. He made a mental list of things to do. One, find Humpy

VanBibber. Two, find Clarence Ford, and three, make sure that the money from Jeb for the Wellston Library was legitimate money. If Jeb left stolen money for that library...after getting Olivia's hopes up, Gunnar was pretty sure he'd dig him up out of the ground and re-kill him. But what if the money in the outhouse wasn't Jeb's? What if he was holding it for somebody? What if that person came back for it, only to discover it wasn't all there?

Letter to Viola from Olivia

Viola Reinhardt
Dayton, Ohio
October 1958

Dear Aunt Viola,

Jeb is dead. Murdered! I can barely see to write, the tears are so thick.

I feel that I'll spend the next year with only Emily Dickinson and Jane Eyre. I don't want to talk or see another living human. My chest hurts with sadness. I leave you with Lord Byron, for he says it better than me: And thou art dead, as young and fair, As aught of mortal birth; And form so soft, and charms so rare, Too soon return'd to Earth!

OAV

Limbo

For weeks, I was in a state of maudlin shock. I sat on my back porch, with Jeb's dogs, Wolfe and Ernest, watching the last of the fire-colored leaves float to the forest floor, and said nothing to anybody. Half the time I didn't even realize that the temperatures were barely reaching forty, or that all the leaves had finally been defeated and had vacated their temporary homes until spring. Today was different. Today I noticed. It was nearly winter now, and the mountains resembled the heads of old men, with matchsticks for hair. And my heart was nearly as barren.

Today, the difference was that I'd finally decided, at the urging of Clive, to read the letter from Jeb. It had been in the legal papers that he'd left with Charlie, along with a manuscript, and I had not been able to bring myself to read it. But since Jeb had entrusted me with this library project, I figured the answer to why lay in the letter. I had been given the job of running the whole library, according to his lawyer, even though I didn't know the first thing about how to do the job. The Dewey decimal system was easy enough, I supposed. He'd given a copy of his last book to Charlie and had sent another copy on to his agent. The sale of that book or any royalties earned were also supposed to go directly into the library fund so that I could continue to purchase books, pay the salaries of employees and so forth. Right now, I had to make a decision on whether or not to build a new building or just purchase an empty one to house the library. How could I possibly make these decisions? If he were alive, I'd slap him.

He had also, oddly enough, left me his dogs, which I had already asked for, and he also had left me all of his books, which was absolutely no surprise. In fact, if I could have been able to see into the future and know that he would die, his books would have been the only thing I would have predicted he would have left me. Jeb's son received eight thousand dollars, the Renshaw place (which was to be sold) and all the royalties off of any previously published works.

I opened the envelope with shaking hands, and Ernest and Wolfe instantly moved to sit by me, one on each side of the chair. It was almost as if they could sense that the letter had been from their former owner. In a penmanship that was surprisingly legible and nearly feminine, I read his words:

Dearest Olivia,

You most likely are wondering why I have chosen you to lead my library project. You have touched my life beyond words. I arrived here looking for something and although I knew it was here, it was you who unveiled it: the spirit of the mountain people. You, with your eager and cautious eyes, your desire to learn new things and yet your inclination to keep those things tucked away, were a reflection of myself at a younger age. It was my intention to build the library myself and open it to the great people of this region, but if you're reading this letter then I am unable to do so, either because I am in jail or dead, and I believe you are the perfect person for the job.

I believe as we walk through life, we have three duties. One is the easiest of all and yet somehow seems to evade us in modern society, and that is to witness the basic miracle of life. We should witness our time and our world, for it will not stay the same. At first, it might be just small subtle changes but eventually, some mountains will erode while others grow taller, and the rivers will stop running, and the moon will stop orbiting around the earth, and the only reason anybody will ever know that any of these things ever existed, is because we witnessed and took them with us into the great beyond. The second thing is to love and forgive, for those are the apex of the human experience. And three is to make a positive influence and contribution whenever possible, even if it means maybe sacrificing a little of ourselves. Because only then is the contribution truly heartfelt.

I hope I've achieved these in my time on this earth, and I hope that you do, too. Forgive me for preaching but it's only that I know what you can achieve if you will get out of your own way. And you must bring down those imaginary walls that you, and your loved ones, have built around you. Those walls dictate you will never be a wife or mother. They say, you will never be anything more than the eccentric relative who spends her days reading. The walls seem at first to keep you safe inside, but they will eventually lead to the phenomenon where the body keeps living long after the soul. Those walls are only there because you built them. Your family have handed you the bricks and mortar, and you dutifully built them one by one. And only you can take them down. Wasn't it your Elizabeth Cady Stanton who said, "The isolation of every human soul, and the necessity of self-dependence, must give each individual the right to choose his own surroundings?" Would you choose those walls for yourself, Olivia, if your family hadn't suggested to you that they exist? We are so alone as it is, why deliberately make yourself more so?

And although you play the game of contentment, and you wear your mask of nonchalant indifference, you are full of anger and resentment, and in some ways, Olivia, that is the hardest mortar of all.

You might remember that I had something for you to read. My lawyer will give you a copy if something should happen to me before its publication. It is my memoir. Once you read my book, your ability to forgive, at least me, anyway, will be tested. There are things that you'll learn that may upset you. And no doubt, some of it may make you angry, because it may appear as though I lied or kept things from you. It's simply that I had no other way to tell you.

All of this may sound as though I knew my death was coming. Well, it's always coming, Livvy. The one constant of life is the inevitability of its end. Death is your little friend that walks three steps behind you. On some days it creeps up and holds your hand, only to let it go and return to its place behind you once again, but it is always there. Let's say, let's hope, this letter was written as a premature divulgence. The scribblings of a man who fears the door to the afterlife may be closer than he would like. I just wanted to say these things and make things right.

If you would, on the occasion of my death, please go through my personal things and choose a few items that you think my son might want. My mother will have some things to give him, as well. And I leave to you the decision of what to put on my tombstone.

And, please, keep anything you like.

It was always my intention to make you my head librarian, to give you a job so you could be independent and so that you could share your knowledge and love of the written word with others. I have no doubt that you will be the best librarian the world has ever known.

Yours, humbly,
Jeb.

I placed the letter on my lap and cried.

***

"Are you going to read that book he gave you?" my mother asked from the doorway.

I was seated at the window in my bedroom, looking out, begrudgingly realizing that it was probably too cold for me to sit on the porch. Ernest and Wolfe were asleep on my bed, snuggling together on the pillows. It was no secret that they slept better and more often than I did. And I'm not sure why. It's not as if they did anything to make them tired. I reached out a hand and stroked Ernest's leg which was hanging off the side of the bed.

My mother sat on the bed, shoving Wolfe down two feet, so that she would be directly in my line of view. "Livvy?"

"What?"

She nodded to the pile of white paper on the nightstand. "Are you going to read it or not? It's been sitting there for days."

"Eventually."

"What are you waiting for?"

I shrugged. But inside I was screaming; *I'm petrified to read it!* I didn't want my view of Jeb to change.

"He wanted you to read it for a reason."

"I know."

"So, how long are you going to wallow around in self-pity?"

"Self -pity?"

"You're drowning in it. And I've never seen you do this before. Frankly, I hate it. It's not you. It's not my little girl."

I rolled my eyes. She went on. "Look, somehow you managed to get all the good things from my kin, like being spunky and brave and intelligent, but the good Lord managed to make sure you got a good dose of self-discipline to go with it, so that you don't go around acting like an idiot when the world falls apart around you. You are the most even-keeled person I know."

"Mom, you don't understand. I can't really do crazy things. I can't pick up a frying pan and chase Humpy around a room. I can't run after my drunken husband in the middle of the night, chasing the car down the road in my bra and panties. God didn't give me a good dose of self-discipline or anything like it. He gave me a virus! And that stopped any stupid behavior right in its tracks. There is nothing superior about me or my behavior. This just happens to be all I can do."

Tears spilled from my mother's eyes, and for a moment I thought she just might smack me. "I...I have never, not once in seven...eight years, have I heard you talk like that, and I don't like it. I hate it."

"Well, I hate being me!" I shouted at her.

"You don't mean that," she said, swiping at the tears. "Baby, I'm so sorry. If I could go back in time and keep you from going swimming that day, I would. If I could trade places with you, I would."

"No, you wouldn't." My cheeks were burning hot, and my heart pounded in my chest.

Now my mother was sobbing. "Oh, baby, I would. No mother wants to see her children suffer."

"And what about fathers?"

"This isn't about your father. This is about me and you. And I would die for you, Olivia. That was the deal I made when I became a mother."

I took a deep breath. My mother could be dramatic. In case the frying pan incident wasn't proof enough.

"Now, I know you loved him. Good Lord, we all loved him in one way or another, I took an instant liking to him. But you tell me, did you trust Jeb's judgment?"

I nodded.

"Then trust him on this. He gave the town of Wellston that money for that library so that we could all learn and prosper and so you could make something of yourself. Or at least so you could live independently. So you could earn your own way. And he gave you that book to read for a reason. He desperately wants you to know something, Livvy. He is trying to tell you something, share something with you that maybe he didn't know how to come right out and say, and that book is the only way he knew how. So, now, this sitting around and moping and staring at these ugly dogs, is nothing more than self-pity, and I'm not gonna sit around and watch it. Not from you."

I smiled. "And what are you going to do about it?"

"Don't you get smart with me," she said, a grin tugging at her mouth. "Willie Gene and I discussed it and we think you should move to town. To be near the library once it's opened."

"I'm not going anywhere," I said, although inside my mind was racing. Did my mother really just suggest I move out?

"Why not?" she asked.

"Well, I can't just leave you. My income from the library could help out here."

She shook her head vehemently. "I think you and Clive should move to Wellston. Get off this mountain, baby, and go to a town where you can come and go as you want. You need a taste of freedom. You need to be on your own. And, I know, Clive being with you, you won't exactly be on your own, but I think for the first year anyway, it'd make me feel better to know that somebody was with you, in case you fell."

That was my mother. Even though she was encouraging me to move out, which I was still having trouble comprehending, she still had to remind me that I could fall out of my chair and be stuck in a bathroom for five days with no food and water. She didn't go into that kind of detail, this time. But in the past, that's exactly what she would do. She usually even threw in a couple of broken bones and some blood. Maybe a concussion.

"I'll think about it," I said. But in truth, that was exactly what I knew I would do.

She smiled then, happy. She stretched across the bed, picked up the big stack of paper that was Jeb's book, and handed it to me. "Now read."

JEB

There is a dream I've had since before I can remember. So vivid and textured that as a child, I honestly believed I was dreaming somebody else's memories. Ridiculous as that may sound there was no other way that I could make sense of it. Why was this particular dream so real and vibrant, infused with warm color and brilliant sounds, and with painfully sharp images, while every other dream I had was boring and drab by comparison? I could only come to one conclusion, and that was that it wasn't a dream at all, but a memory.

It had to be from a life before...but before what? I was only a child.

I was born on the twenty-seventh day of October, 1923, in Baltimore, Maryland, to William and Hannah McDowell. I was the youngest of six very healthy, happy and highly functional children. It would become apparent later that I was the black sheep of the family, the only child that did not conform entirely, although my sister Ellen definitely had her rough patches, as did my brother Sam. But they outgrew their "trying times," as my father called them. I did not. My siblings seemed to find what they were looking for, while the thing I was trying to locate was always just out of reach.

My first encounter with this memory, as best as I can determine was May of 1927, when I was three and a half. I remember the exact date because it was the night after my brother Max's birthday party. We'd had cake for him in the backyard, with pony rides and the neighborhood kids all in attendance. My brother had received a stuffed bear for his birthday and he clutched it in his sleep, as if it were going to run away in the middle of the night.

Earlier at his party, some kids had been digging in the dirt, making mud pies and caves...and mounds. I can clearly remember sitting in the grass, staring mesmerized at a mound of dirt. It triggered something, that heap of soil, for that night I had the dream, and it went like this:

I am riding in a Model T, along a curvy, winding road. Sunlight dapples the windows as it peeks through the variegated leaves in different shades of green. Light to dark, big to small, the leaves wink at me as they rustle gently on the wind. There is a woman, seated next to me, with dark hair pulled back at the nape of her neck, and she has lovely, flawless, skin. She sings to me, an ancient hill-folk song that had been carried across the ocean on the voices of hopeful but homesick immigrants.

In the seat between us is an oak egg basket, covered with a blanket.

The dream shifts, and we arrive somewhere without me really knowing how I got there. All I know is that I'm no longer in the car. The woman is holding my hand, walking me across an expanse of land, with the basket in the other hand. In the distance I see a large mound of dirt that seems to reach the sky. Rows of dirt are etched around the base of it, and it is covered with grass, a worn path, curving around to the top of it.

Waiting at the base of the mound is a man. When the woman sees him she begins to run. My little legs have so much trouble keeping up that I nearly stumble. She runs into the arms of the man and he grabs her around the waist, spinning her around and around until they're both laughing. Then he stops, looks down at me with emerald green eyes, and kneels to my height. He calls me by a name I don't recognize. It's not my name, and I can't hear what he says. I only know that it starts with an "A" or maybe it's an "O," possibly even an "E," but I know it's a vowel. He hugs me close and then we're eating our picnic lunch under a tree on a blanket, with the big earthen mound behind us. I'm playing with a toy soldier while munching on a carrot. I am suddenly and keenly aware that the sunlight is intoxicating.

Without warning, the dream changes again, like shifting sands through fingers. Suddenly, I'm scared; the woman yanks me up from the blanket, clutching at my body as if I'd fly away. Two men walk toward us, and when they reach the edge of the picnic blanket, they pull out guns and shoot the green-eyed man dead. He falls to the ground, the woman screams and runs to him, sobbing. She presses her forehead against his and sobs some more. I'm so scared by this that I wiggle from her arms and start to run. And I run as fast as I can, across the park to the earthen mound. Up the mound I go, not stopping to look back over my shoulder. I hear the woman scream behind me. She calls my name, the one I don't recognize, but it's lost on the wind. And then, I'm at the top of the heap, scared to be so high up, but happy to be away from the dying man. The woman runs after me and when she reaches me she says, "It's okay. Shhh." But her face is covered in tears and streaked with blood and everything is anything but okay.

The next thing I know we are pulling up to a big, two-story building. With lots of windows and doors and rooms. A porch that runs the expanse of the building is covered with climbing ivy and morning glories struggling with each other for the right to grow. A big white star in a dark blue circle is carved from *wood and affixed to the siding, just under the roof ridge. The upper floor has a porch too, with white lattice railing. Rising up behind the building are worn and ancient mountains, covered in green, hissing with long forgotten legends, witnesses to eons of time. In the yard is a massive oak tree, and a large flat boulder sits off to the left before we enter the gate. There are people milling about, some speak to us, some don't, but I notice that many of them are thin and wearing thread-bare clothing, while some are dressed in nice suits and hats.*

We go upstairs and the woman with the dark hair, throws herself across the bed and cries. She keeps looking at me and every time she does, she cries even harder. I am not sure what's happening or what to do, but I remember crying with her because she is so upset. Her pain is palpable.

She smells like rosewater.

I am back in the car again and the woman is still crying. We drive and drive and drive and I make some comment about being tired. "I sleepy." She cries harder. We pull up in front of another building and we sit there until it is almost dark. Five times she opens the door, comes around to get me out, but gets back in. And then she cries. She looks at me, strokes my hair, mouths something, but I don't understand it. And then she begins to write on paper that she'd brought with her. It grows dark, but still she writes until there is no light left and she cannot see and is forced to stop. And then finally she retrieves me from the car and carries me toward the corner building with five arched windows on the side, knocks on the door, and speaks to the woman who answers. She speaks quickly and rushed, and then she hands the nice-looking lady the papers she'd written, a basket of things, and me. The nice woman in the black dress smiles down at me, but it's a sad smile. Then, the woman with the dark hair turns to leave, covering her face with her hands. And I watch her drive away.

That is pretty much how the dream goes, although sometimes there are different things that happen before the trip to the earthen mound and sometimes things are out of order. Sometimes I'm sitting on the floor in a big kitchen while the woman with the dark hair is cooking food in big pots. She's cooking things like chicken and dumplings, ham and beans and cornbread, pork chops, hominy and crowder peas cooked with pickled corn. An older gentleman, whom she calls Doc, plays the fiddle and sings a tune. I love this music, and when he begins to play I always go and stand between his legs, getting as close to that magical sound as I can get, feeling the tap of his foot vibrate on the floor. He smiles at me and loves it when I dance.

Sometimes there are people making apple butter in big giant black pots next to a stream. And sometimes, I'm in the back of the buggy with the man called Doc, while we ride through the mountains being pulled by a team of horses. But the dream always ends the same, and the green-eyed man is always murdered at the mound.

Oddly enough, the fact of the violence and the way the dream ends, don't bother me. At least, not at first and not any more. Somewhere in my teenage years it did, and I'd try to wake up before it got to that point. By the time I was eight, I realized one thing.

The woman in the dream was my mother, the man who was murdered was my father, and the people that I called mom and dad were not the people in the dream. Somewhere along the line, I'd gotten lost and ended up where I wasn't supposed to be. And this is the story of how I found me.

A Letter to Olivia from Viola

Olivia VanBibber
Greenhaven, West Virginia
November 1958

Dearest, Olivia,

The news of Jeb McDowell's murder sent me into a depression and I didn't even know him! I could tell from your letters and conversations with my sisters that he meant the world to you and quite a bit to other people as well. And murder? Death is one thing, but to be murdered is quite another. Who would do such a thing? Poor girl, don't for a minute think that Humpy had anything to do with this. I know Humpy's a lost soul, but really, to think he was responsible is simply ridiculous! Why? What would he have to gain from it? He's been on the losing ends of fights before and never thought to kill those people, so why start now? No, you just stop worrying right this instant. (You might be able to tell that I talked to Stella yesterday. Through all the noise and static and somebody's bleeping pig, I could make out that she seems to think you're convinced that Humpy was involved. Really, Arnie should have a quiet booth at his store for folks to talk in!)

I had not written to you in a while because Eckhard was not feeling well and you know how old men get; only their wives can take care of them. I will say it sort of reminded me of our days in France, only more private and not as loud. No mortar shells exploding all about. He's feeling better now, so don't fret. And now I have more free time. He was laid up for several weeks and I swear that he was trying to see if he could kill me by sending me up and down the stairs forty or fifty times a day! I finally told him to make a list of requests, give it to me three times a day, and let me get as much done in one trip as possible, or he could hire a nurse!

I simply do not know what to say to you, dear child. There are no words of comfort that I can offer. Although, may I suggest you read Austen while recovering, instead of a Bronte. She's a bit on the sunnier side. My reading group and I are going to read *Bernice Bobs Her Hair*, this month. It's short and it's Fitzgerald, so, it should go swimmingly.

    With all of my love and prayers,
    Your devoted Auntie Viola

Gunnar Ryan
Deputy Colton County Sheriff's Department

Thanksgiving. Gunnar's brother Kevin had spent all day yesterday in the woods hunting turkey or pheasant or anything resembling a large bird for their mother to pluck and put on the dinner table. He'd succeeded. Around dusk his brother had dragged the twenty-five pound turkey into the house and, with a broad smile, plopped it onto his mother's table. She'd been so proud of him that she hadn't even yelled at him for flinging blood everywhere.

Today, he and Kevin were down at the creek. A heavy fog was rolling up the water, which concealed the tops of the mountains almost as if they didn't exist at all. Combining the morning dew with the fog made it soaking wet outside, so much so it may as well have been raining. There was no reason for Kevin and Gunnar to be out at the creek this early in the morning other than they just wanted away from the house. James was home today, and in a right civilized mood, and the fewer men in the house, the more likely James was to just keep to himself and let their mother get dinner in the oven.

Time passed, close to half an hour, and neither one of them had said anything. Gunnar and Kevin were like that. Silence sometimes had been their best friend. When James was on a tear, you kept as quiet as you could. Most of the Ryan kids had learned that. Everybody except Betty Jo, who just couldn't help herself. But instead of Betty Jo inciting the wrath of her father, she seemed to be the only one who could calm him down. Sometimes just the right word spoken from her would change his whole mood. But she was the only one who could do that. The other four had always paid the price for drawing attention to themselves in the middle of one of his rages.

Finally Gunnar said, "You going to be ready for school next fall? You think you'll have enough money saved?"

"I think so," Kevin answered. His younger brother was a talented kid. He could play any instrument he picked up and for a few years had thought about pursuing a career in music. He had been all about heading to Nashville. Gunnar thought he could probably make a decent living at music, but he'd talked him out of it anyway. He wanted Kevin to have a secure future, away from any sort of "high life" that could lead him down the same road as their father. Kevin had fought him for a few months, and then their father had engaged in one of his greatest benders of all time and that had made all the difference. So now Kevin was going to study chemistry. And he wouldn't be coming back to Colton County to live, that was for sure. There were no jobs in this county for anybody with a chemistry degree.

Gunnar hadn't seen Kevin in what seemed like weeks since his brother was always working and until recently he'd slept in the barn on most nights. Once it got too cold to be comfortable in the hay loft even with a blanket, Kevin started sleeping in the house again, but Gunnar still hadn't seen him. He'd heard him come in after midnight and he was gone before six the next morning. At twenty years old, Kevin was more devoted, more focused on his goals, than Gunnar had ever been. He was an inch taller than Gunnar, leaner, stronger, smarter and with a greater sense of adventure. His movements were sure and precise and yet done without any thought whatsoever. He might have only been six years younger than Gunnar but, standing on that riverbank Thanksgiving morning, Gunnar felt decades older.

"But," Kevin said, and Gunnar's heart skipped a beat. "I'm thinking about studying in Chicago instead of Ohio."

Gunnar stopped. It would be more difficult to visit with him if he went to Chicago. "Why Chicago?" he asked as nonchalantly as possible.

"It's farther away," Kevin said as he picked up a rock and skipped it across the creek.

Gunnar nodded. Just what he'd expected. "That all?"

Kevin shrugged.

"More expensive?"

"Possibly."

"That means you'll have to work more hours."

"So?"

"You don't want your grades to suffer."

"It would be worth it. I don't want any reason to be talked into coming back here."

Gunnar sucked in a breath. That stung. That was exactly what had happened to him. He'd been talked into coming back. No, not talked into, begged and begged was more like it, but what was he supposed to have done? Kevin might have been able to get out on his own without Gunnar's help, but it would have been harder. Kevin would've had to spend more time doing chores around here and placating James, which would have taken time away from his studies and work. His sisters would have suffered. There wouldn't have been as much money in the house. Nobody to get between their father and them, except Kevin, who at the time was still very young. And his mother...well, his mother would have suffered the most and it was her pleading voice on the telephone that had finally been Gunnar's undoing. He simply could not tell her no. Kevin's world would have been very different if Gunnar had gone on to the desert to study the Indians, rather than come back here. "Don't forget, you have a mother."

"I know," Kevin said. "But I got my life, too."

And I don't? Gunnar thought.

"I...I don't mean...Look, the only reason I have a life, a chance at a life, is because of you. For more than one reason."

Gunnar swallowed but said nothing. That statement was truer than true.

"Don't think I'm not grateful for that. And I love Momma, I love my sisters. But if you're truly going to make a sacrifice for me, then I have to make a clean break and make sure it wasn't for nothing."

Gunnar shuffled rocks with his right toe. Then he nodded. "I understand."

Kevin turned on him, eyes intense and pleading. "I want out of here so bad I can taste it. And I can't come back. You bring the girls to come visit me, but I'm never coming back."

Gunnar nodded again, fighting the lump in his throat. The biggest difference between Kevin and Gunnar was not size, speed, determination...nothing like that. Kevin had no romantic notions whatsoever of his past, his people, his culture. None of it meant a damn thing to him. He did not love the land, at least not like Gunnar did. He was not sentimental in any way. When he picked up a fiddle and played some old tune, he never once thought about who he learned it from, where the song had come from, the journey it had made across an ocean with a migrating people. Never, not once. But Gunnar did think of those things. Gunnar was sentimental, Kevin was not.

Gunnar knew at that moment that was what Kevin what trying to tell him. He was saying, *I have a deep sense of responsibility to kin. If you use that against me, it will work. Please don't use that against me. Cut the strings.*

Gunnar sighed and said, "I understand, Kev."

"Do you really?" he asked. Relief poured over him, softening his expression.

"I honestly do."

They walked along in silence for another half hour or so when Gunnar put a hand on his brother's shoulder. "Chicago is good," he said. "Colder than the arctic, but it's a good choice."

Kevin smiled and took a deep breath.

They continued their walk, crossed the creek at the boulders and traipsed back the other way.

Around noon they found themselves reaching the clearing, the house they grew up in off in the distance. They came to the small, arched bridge that they had built with their father when they were kids and crossed it, Gunnar leading, Kevin following. Betty Jo rang the dinner bell as they came over the hill. They'd timed it just right.

Before Gunnar had a chance to fantasize about eating the turkey in the oven, Kevin had flicked him on the ear and ran past him. "Turkey!" he yelled. Gunnar gave chase and Kevin sped up. "I'm gonna eat all the turkey!"

"Like hell," Gunnar said.

Legs and arms pumping, Gunnar and Kevin raced to the porch like they'd done so many times as children. Gunnar had always won then, being six years older. But not today. Today was Kevin's turn, even if it was by seconds. But it was enough to send Kevin into all sorts of hoots and hollers and celebrating.

To stop his momentum, Gunnar grabbed the porch railing and spun around, knocking into Kevin as he did. Kevin knocked him back and smiled. A moment Gunnar would cherish in the years to come.

They made it inside the house just as their mother removed her apron. She smiled and held her hands out as if to say, "Look at that glorious bird." Both boys hugged and kissed her and they washed up to eat. Gunnar's other two sisters wouldn't be joining them; they were celebrating with their husband's families. When Betty Jo eventually got married and Kevin went off to Chicago, would his mother have to suffer through holidays alone? Just her and James?

Of course not, Gunnar thought. He would be here. While the moment was bitter, just a little, because he wanted to go study the Pueblos, it was also oddly comforting to know that no matter what, he had a place he belonged. He grabbed his mother, hugged her again, and said, "The turkey looks great."

When James entered the room everybody's gaze flicked about to each other so as not to land on him for too long. He was in his *I'm so terribly sorry, I'll never drink again* part of the cycle. His hands shook like he had palsy, and when he spoke, his words were clipped as though somebody was tugging on his throat from the inside out.

"Looks good, Sally," he said.

"Thank you, James," she said.

James Ryan was a very big man. Well over six feet, with long legs and a short neck so that his shoulders seemed higher than they should be. He lumbered wherever he went as opposed to walking, and the thought of his mother on the receiving end of his brutality choked like acid in Gunnar's throat. But he swallowed that thought. Today was Thanksgiving and he was not going to ruin it for his mother in any way, even if it was just with a bad attitude. No bad thoughts. Not today.

"You boys out all day," James said. Gunnar wasn't sure if that was a question or an accusation.

"Went for a hike," Gunnar said.

He pulled the chair out and saw his mother's old basket in the seat. "Making Kevin a sweater to take away to college," she said, moving it to the counter.

"Pass me those taters," Kevin said. He rubbed his hands together in anticipation.

Gunnar handed the bowl to Betty Jo, who passed it to Kevin with a beaming smile on her face. The family would enjoy this while they could. It wasn't every year that James was in the "down" side of his cycle on a holiday. When he was humble and sorry and spent. They got lucky this year.

And as Gunnar took the knife to carve the turkey, he couldn't help but think that this would probably be the last Thanksgiving that he would ever spend with his brother. And the look on his mother's face said that she understood that, too, but she smiled anyway. Because she was fine. Everything was fine.

Errands for Aunt Stella

Today was Louisa May Alcott's birthday. The twenty-ninth day of November. She'd be one-hundred and twenty-six years old today if she were living. I'd often wondered if she and I were related, since she was born in Germantown, Pennsylvania, and my VanBibbers had been one of the six founding families of that community. It was a small world. I liked to think it was possible. In honor of the occasion, I had thought briefly about pulling my beat-up copies of *Little Women* or *Under the Lilacs* out of the box in the closet, but realized just as quickly that I had to finish reading Jeb's book, Little Boy Found, before I could start anything else. Not that I haven't been known to read more than one book at a time, but I needed to give Jeb's my full attention. I literally never knew when something he said in the book was going to turn out to be an important clue in discovering his true identity, or maybe help find his killer.

I figured that last part would be a long shot. Gunnar was going to find Jeb's killer with good old fashioned detective work, and I didn't see how anything I did or said was going to make or break his case. That was my hope anyway. And it was my fervent hope that the killer would not turn out to be Humpy. But if it was, then so be it. My brother should rot in jail for all eternity, if he was guilty. And it would keep him from eventually ruining the lives of the wife and children he didn't yet have. I knew that sounded horribly pessimistic of me. But really, how could anything he touched turn out otherwise?

At the moment, Bessie was not speaking to me, hallelujah. She was beyond jealous at the thought that I would be earning my own money and might be moving out, while she was still stuck here. Not to mention, she'd already run through her mind all the lipstick colors I could buy once I started earning a paycheck and told me so. "The only reason he did any of this is because you're a cripple. Wish I was a cripple," she'd said. At that point, Clive had lunged for Bessie and told her in no uncertain terms that if she wanted to be a cripple so badly that he would certainly help her along. Willie Gene had pulled him off of her and told Bessie in the iciest voice I'd ever heard, "Take a walk, while you still can." And she'd stormed out of the house, but not before calling out over her shoulder, "You're just a spoiled rotten brat, Olivia Anne. Ain't nothin' special about you!"

That had been two weeks ago and she had not uttered one word to me since, which of course, suited me just fine. I could think better when Bessie's mouth was shut anyway. She'd refused to leave the house for Thanksgiving—not wanting to be seen with me—and so she ate cold leftovers that we'd brought back from Aunt Mildred's house. Willie Gene, Clive and I had not wanted to bring anything back for her, but my mother had insisted. There was just something really pitiful about people who tried to boycott something based on what they thought was a true principle, when in reality they were wrong and nobody cared. Her righteous indignation at my "lucky windfall" was nothing more than a temper tantrum of somebody who wanted everything for nothing because she thought she was somehow owed it. Never mind that a man had to be brutally killed—possibly by her own brother—for me to inherit it, and never mind that—according to her—I had to spend a lifetime in a wheelchair to have earned it. No matter how hard I tried, I couldn't think like her. And I was afraid if I tried too hard it might actually work and then I'd be shallow and petty, so I quickly realized that maybe I wasn't meant to understand her and stopped trying.

At any rate, it was a Saturday and Aunt Stella had asked Clive and me to run some errands for her, so we got in the truck and drove down to her house. Since Uncle Reggie had died and her son, Matthew, had moved to Texas, Aunt Stella was dependent on nieces and nephews and neighbors to do the things she wasn't up for. She was only sixty-six, but she'd had an accident a few years back, fell down a mountain, and hurt her knee, and every now and then it caused her a great deal of pain. My fear was that she would move to Texas to be with her son and I'd never see her again. An extremely selfish fear, but it was there nonetheless. She had no grandchildren, which was why she'd stayed here in the valley as long as she had. She loved being around all the younger kids, since she had no grandchildren of her own to spoil.

The front door of Aunt Stella's house was level with the porch, and the porch just had one little three-inch step that I could manage myself. I knocked on her door and she let us in. The living room was a mess, which was not like her at all. It only took me a few moments to realize that she had brought all of her Christmas decorations out from the smokehouse—which she now used for storage—and piled them all in the living room. She was getting ready to put up her Christmas tree, as soon as she cut one down. For that, she'd take my cousin

Arthur out into the woods, choose a tree, have him chop it down and carry it back for her. My Grandma VanBibber had always given us grandkids a couple of axes—in retrospect, not the most brilliant thing to do—and told us to pick out the ugliest tree there was. But, Aunt Stella, no, she had to pick it out herself and it had to be pretty.

"Oh, Livvy, let me get those boxes out of your way," she said.

"Oh, that's all right," I said. "I'll just shove them out of the way with my chair." Which I did. Clive and I made it to her kitchen, where she was making a "mess of squirrels." In other words, she was making squirrel stew. Which meant those scrambled eggs she had for breakfast this morning most likely had squirrel brains cooked in with them. Mountain folk wasted nothing.

In the middle of her kitchen was a water-well, with a pump, right there, indoors. I'd always thought that was the height of convenience. It was an original fixture of the house, built about 1870, by the Morrow family.

"Mmmm, that smells good, Aunt Stella," Clive said. "Where'd you get the squirrels?"

"Shot them myself," she said.

"You went in the woods by yourself?" I asked. "You know that knee could have gone out on you."

"No," she said. "I put some peanuts out there on the picnic table. When they come up to get them I shoot them from the back porch. Simple as that."

Clive raised his eyebrows; a new-found respect for Aunt Stella had just been born. I just smiled because I knew she'd always been a resourceful woman. She was also a mixed bag. She had that big extravagant Packard in the garage, she had fancy clothes and attended fancy parties when she had lived in Charleston. At Christmas her house would be all lit up and every inch decorated. In the spring and summer, she would put out glass gazing balls in her wondrous garden. She made her own lace, knitted, tatted, quilted, embroidered and knew all the refined skills of a lady of her time. On the flip side, before the trouble with her knee, she'd hunted, caught fish with her bare hands, could deliver babies as well as a doctor, and smoked a corn-cob pipe. You just never knew which Aunt Stella you were going to get when you shook the bag.

"So, how's that scarf coming?" she asked. She was referring to the one that I'd been trying to knit for Clive.

"Twirly."

She laughed. "Your tension's too tight. Bring your bag of yarn back over and I'll help you out."

"I will. I think I dropped a couple of stitches, too. Every now and then there's like this little hole."

She just laughed again. I made a mental note to try and get back to her house in the next week to have her help me with it. But it wasn't knitting that I wanted to learn, although I did believe that it was an important skill and thought it industrious of women to knit during otherwise wasted moments. Like when riding in a car, or waiting in a doctor's office. A person could get a lot of things accomplished that way, and I wanted to be more like that. But it was Aunt Stella's crazy quilts that I really longed to learn to make. She'd made two big ones and a few pillows, and probably more that she'd given away. It was the crazy quilts that I'd look at for hours, running my hands over the buttons and beads and laces and trims, and the stitches. The stitches were amazing. And all the colors and the textures were hypnotic. There were so many surprises on a crazy quilt, hidden around every corner of fabric. It was a road map of luxurious beauty. Somehow, the knitting seemed less intimidating and more practical, and I did love the yarns and colors, so when it came down to it, it was the knitting that I'd asked her to teach me.

"This stew's not quite ready, ya'll want to stick around and eat some of it before you go runnin' off for me, or do you want to eat some when you get back?"

"Both," Clive said.

Aunt Stella laughed. "How about when ya'll get back?"

"Okay," I said. "Where do we need to go for you?"

"I need you to take those two boxes to the post office and mail them to Matthew for me. It's his Christmas presents. I made him some divinity and fudge, and stuck it in there with the sweater I knitted for him. Of course, it's not very cold in Texas, except at night, so I made sure the yarn wasn't too bulky. I also knitted him some socks. Those he can use no matter how cold it is."

"Okay, no problem," Clive said.

Aunt Stella handed him some money. "I need you to stop by Arnie's store and get my pictures for me. Got a roll developed. That should be enough money to cover the pictures and the postage, and get yourselves a pop."

"Is that it?" he asked.

"No, no, it's not. Now, this favor I know you may not want to do, Clive, because I know Crazy Rhea gives you the shivers..."

"She doesn't give me the shivers, she gives me the hell roarin' trots!"

"Now, Clive," she said in that even, patient tone.

"It's true, Aunt Stella. Every time he sees her, he's in the outhouse for an hour," I said, chiming in for his defense.

"Now both of you, stop. She's not dangerous, she's just not right in the head, that's all. I want you to take this box of food to her. I made her some mulled cider, oatmeal cookies, fudge and a raisin cake. I don't think she cooks anything fancy anymore, and everybody ought to have something special in December."

"You want us to drive up to her place?" Clive asked. "I don't think I even know where it is."

"Here, I'll draw you a map," she said, and began scribbling on the back of an envelope.

Clive made eye contact with me from behind Aunt Stella's back. He wasn't happy.

"Now, you deliver this stuff for me, and not only can you have some of this stew, but I'll send home a whole tin of divinity for you. All right?"

Clive's stomach always got him into trouble. I could see him caving in. "Well, all right," he said. "But if she touches me or if she even looks like she's gonna put a hex on me, I'll be outta there faster than you can say hiss cat."

"Hiss cat," Aunt Stella and I both said at the same time. Then she tugged on his ear and gave him a slap on the rump.

We pulled out of her driveway a few moments later, but not before having downed a few pieces of chocolate fudge and a glass of water. In Wellston we headed to the post office first, then stopped by Arnie's and got her pictures and our pop. I got orange Nehi and Clive got a Coke. Then we backtracked and went right by Aunt Stella's house, and all the other aunties' houses, and ours, up the big mountain, down the other side, and headed toward Charleston.

Crazy Rhea lived way back in the woods on a mountain in an area that didn't really have a name. She lived on Fourteen Stone Creek, named so for the number of big rocks that altered the creek's direction. Most people just called the creek Fourteen. I'd never actually been to her house, and had only been on the road to her place maybe once in my whole life. It would take about thirty minutes to get there.

"So, you been reading Jeb's book?" Clive asked.

"Yes," I answered, looking out the window onto a solemn day. The trees were all bare now, the grass had turned brown, and today there was a blanket of gray that went from horizon to horizon.

"What's it about?" he asked.

I shrugged.

"Well, it ain't personal if he's getting it published. I mean, the whole world's gonna know what it says, so why don't you tell me?"

"I don't know, Clive. I guess because I don't like the way it makes me think."

He was quiet a moment and shifted gears on the truck. "Come on, tell me."

"Well, it's a memoir, and it opens with him talking about how he's had this one dream his whole life, starting when he was like three and a half. Sometimes the dream changes, or it starts out different than other times, but it always ends the same."

"And what is the dream?"

I sighed heavily. "He's dreaming about something that happened to him when he was two and a half or three. I don't really know the exact age."

"And what was it?"

"His father was brutally murdered in front of him and his mother."

"Oh my gosh. I knew he said his father was dead, but I thought he said he had a heart attack. Or do you think he made up that whole murder thing for dramatic purposes?" Clive asked.

"Oh, no, it's not made up. Then at some point his mother takes him and gives him to another woman. From what I can tell, she dropped him off at an orphanage."

"Are you saying that Jeb was adopted?"

I nodded.

"I think he witnessed his father's murder as a child. Very intense emotional things can trigger dreams, even in small children. The thing of it is, for whatever reason, Jeb latched on to it, and wouldn't let it go. He sort of kept the dream perpetuating every night by obsessing over it. Most of us would have let it go and it would have just buried itself in our subconscious, but he didn't. He grabbed at it, groped for it, held on for dear life, because somehow he knew those dreams were all he had of who he once had been. Once he realized that he was dreaming about his real family, he started having all sorts of problems."

"Like what?"

"Well, according to the book, he confronted his mother over it and she denied it. When he was eight, he told her he wasn't going to call her mother anymore until she told him the truth."

"What happened?"

"After five years of him drawing these images from his dreams, asking for things they didn't have, like some object that he'd owned before and didn't realize it, and singing songs none of them knew, she finally realized that she had to tell him the truth because she was afraid he would think was insane."

"Are the other kids adopted, too?"

"Just Ellen and Sam. The other three are biological. But Ellen and Sam were adopted as babies. They had no experiences with their former families. Jeb did, and it was a highly emotionally charged one, so it stuck with him. Anyway, so I'm to the part where he just graduated from high school, which was punctuated with all sorts of bad behavior, wild parties, and trying to kill himself without killing himself. He just couldn't let go of his past. He couldn't accept his present."

"So, why does this bother you so much?"

"What do you mean?"

"You said you don't like the way the book makes you think. Why?"

"Because I honestly believe that the reason Jeb came to Greenhaven is because he's from here. I think he was either born here or his parents were born here. Or at least somewhere in central West Virginia. I think he came to find his family."

"Wow," he said.

"Who do you think it is?"

"I have no idea."

"Do you think he learned who it was?" he asked.

"I'll find out when I finish the book, I guess."

"That is too much for me to take in," he said. "I wonder if he just had an idea of the vicinity of where he was from and thought if he came here it would trigger other memories? Maybe he didn't have a clue who his parents were."

"Could be," I said.

"But...there's more to it. What else is bothering you?"

I shrugged and picked at my thumb nail. "I just can't help but wonder why, Clive? Why would a woman give away a two or three-year-old boy?"

"Times have changed, Olivia. Women used to give children away simply because they were sick and couldn't take care of them, or because they lost their farm and couldn't feed them. There could have been all sorts of reasons. Sad but true. In fact, my grandpa lived in an orphanage for two years and then, later, lived with his oldest sister when she finally got married and had a place for him. My great-grandpa had died and my great-grandma had tuberculosis. Wasn't nothin' else his momma could do with him."

I knew he spoke the truth, but it still bugged me. Maybe what really bugged me was the raw emotion that his mother so obviously showed in the dream that he captured so realistically with such few words. I could feel her pain, her terror at having to hand him over to the woman at the orphanage. And I didn't like that feeling. I didn't like what it evoked in me. Maybe it was because I wasn't unlike Jeb in being abandoned at a hospital for three years, wondering if I was ever going to go home. Maybe it allowed me to feel too much of what my mother must have felt at leaving me there. And as Jeb had pointed out more than once, I preferred the safe way of doing things. The safe way of thinking meant that I shut down all those thoughts that made me unhappy.

"I think this is the road," Clive said, and saved me from going down that path in my mind.

Even without leaves, the canopy of trees was so thick that as soon as we turned onto the road, it was considerably darker in the cabin of the truck. We went up a small hill, around a bend, back down and then up a bigger hill. We passed a few old abandoned homesteads, and a few that weren't abandoned but should have been. Buildings with towels hanging in the windows where there should have been glass. Buildings with leaky roofs and broken planks. Buildings that leaned so far one way or the other that one good gust of wind would topple them over. And all of them with families living in them, cold and damp to the core, eking out some sort of existence. My family was certainly not wealthy. We drove ten-year-old cars and lived in a tiny house and rarely got anything new. But I was always reminded of how wealthy we actually were when I drove by houses like these. Finally, we came to the end of the road. There was a private property sign that had little smiley faces painted in faded blue pigment against dark wood. There was a sign that said; *Dont enter witout permishun.* And yet another sign that warned us of dogs, snakes, bees, wasps, pigs, and spirts.

"Beware of dogs, snakes, bees, wasps, pigs, and spirts?" Clive asked. "What's a spirt?"

"I believe she means spirits. Ghosts, you know."

"Aw, Livvy, there ain't no divinity in the world worth going on her property. She's plumb crazier than a bed bug."

"Hey, you're the one who told Aunt Stella you'd do it."

"Next time that woman wants me to run errands for her, I'm showing up on a full stomach."

"You do that, Clive," I said, laughing. "But in the meantime..."

Begrudgingly, he drove the truck down and over a dry creek bed and then up the other side. We made our way through more trees, and then eventually we came into a clearing. In front of us stood Rhea's house which looked like nothing more than an old tobacco barn. The building was square, two stories with no siding, just wood planks that had turned gray from weather. A chimney protruded from the top of the building, a swirl of smoke curling into the sky beyond. The front had a protective awning that protruded out from the house and over the front door, but there was no porch, no concrete slab, nothing. The front door literally opened onto dirt. The outhouse could be seen in the distance, her actual barn was off to the left, that same weathered gray color to the planks, with just a scant remnant of red paint clinging to corners and seams. Her cellar was separate from the house and dug into the ground. When we pulled up, Rhea Thurgood was sitting on a stump, peeling potatoes, wearing a thick flannel jacket, a scarf on her head that was tied under her chin, and an old dirty quilt wrapped around her legs. Chickens squawked all about and one kept pecking at the quilt by her ankles and she kept shooing it away.

She stood, set the big bowl of potatoes on the stump and walked over toward us, with the quilt slung over one arm. I rolled the window down as I could tell she was about to speak. "What in the hell done bring you all up here to my place?" she asked.

"Stella Davies wanted us to bring you some Christmas baking," I answered.

Rhea peeked in the back of the truck and saw my wheelchair. "You Blanchie's granddaughter," she said, with a surprised look. I was taken aback by this because most people didn't acknowledge me as Blanche's granddaughter, considering she'd been dead since 1926. I was usually known as Rosie McClintock's daughter or Hiram's daughter, or somebody's niece or cousin. All of my grandparents, even the ones who'd lived long enough for me to get to know, were all gone now, my Grandma VanBibber having passed just a few years back.

"Why, yes I am."

"I loved that ol' Blanchie dearly," she said, her milky eyes tearing up. The woman did not have one tooth in her head. Her face was crisscrossed with wrinkles and her hair was so white it was nearly translucent. But she was the picture of health. Not too fat, not too thin, she had a nice pink glow to her skin and even her joints appeared only mildly inflamed from arthritis. When she walked, she was stooped shouldered, but she moved with quickness and ease. "Good lawd, she was a prankster."

Clive and I had no idea how to react to her mini-trip down memory lane, so we just waited for her to finish.

"Well, don't just sit there. Boy, you get that contraption outta the back that truck and git this girl in the house! S'cold out here. Ain't you got sense God gave a poke?"

Clive all but jumped out of the car, considering he'd just had his intelligence compared to that of a paper bag, and within moments we were in her house.

The inside of her house was, to my utter astonishment, quite lovely. The walls were a butter yellow, with some sort of green vine painted around the windows and doors. The floors were clean, like she'd just been inside spit shining them before we pulled up. There was no dust anywhere, not even on her collection of dolls. An old spinning wheel sat in the corner of her living room, and she had an old stone hearth that wrapped around the front of the fire place. I'm not sure who was more shocked, me or Clive.

And true to the rumors I'd heard, everything was embroidered. Stitchery adorned the pillows on the sofa, curtains, samplers and in the kitchen, the cover for the coffee pot, the tea pot and the cushions on the chairs. Every fabric surface was embroidered. And the stitching was all happy stitching. Smiley faces, suns, flowers. Lots and lots of flowers. Hanging on the south wall was a sampler that read: *Home is where the hart is.*

I just smiled.

Clive ran back outside to get the box of goodies for Rhea, while she fussed and got me a blanket and put on the kettle. Being inside of her very clean, very cozy and inviting home sort of put a different slant on Rhea. Next time I saw her with a dead possum in her purse, I might think twice before thinking she was completely crazy. Maybe she was just partially crazy. Anybody who lived with this much order and neatness had to have some control over her senses.

The quilt she gave me to put on my lap—because everybody always assumed my legs were cold—was not old and beat up and faded like the one she'd been using outside. This one was newer, crisp cotton, made with warm colors of red, gold and brown with perfect points. I wasn't sure the exact name of the pattern, since I hadn't paid that much attention to sewing when I was a kid, and my mother no longer had time for it. I had been too busy climbing trees and running through creeks away from imaginary packs of wolves or Indians, to sit still on a porch with a needle and thread. But, it's possible that it was something called flying geese.

Clive came back in with the box and stood there like a dummy until she told him to put it in the kitchen on the table, which he did. Then he sat down on the sofa and looked over at me with an uncomfortable expression. Rhea came back in with hot tea in real china teacups and said, "I already sweetened it for ya, 'cause I knows how much is too much and what's not."

"Thank you," I said and took a sip. I could tell Clive was worried he was about to be poisoned.

"That's awful nice of your aunt to make me them goodies. Tell her I'm much obliged."

"I will," I said.

Silently, Clive was trying to communicate to me, "Stella didn't say anything about having to stick around and have a conversation with Crazy Rhea!" I knew that's what he was thinking, just as sure as if I could read minds.

"What did she send?" Rhea asked.

"Uh, fudge, cider, cookies and...a raisin cake," I said.

"A raisin cake!" Rhea said, jumping to her feet. "What in God's name is she tryin' to do to me! You can't give nobody a raisin cake for Christmas. Doesn't she know about the curse?"

"W-what curse?" I asked.

But Rhea didn't hear me because she had already run into the kitchen. I could hear her rummaging through the box and then, fast as lightning, she ran through the living room with the cake and threw it out the front door onto the lawn. Then she shut the door, clapped her hands together twice and said, "Get thee evil spirits away, be taken on the wings of birds to other places."

Clive just glared at me.

"I'm sorry, Rhea, I uh..."

"Well Stella Graham Davies sure knows better. What in tarnation got into her? You think she's tryin' to make me sick?"

"What is wrong with a raisin cake?" Clive said, his patience wearing thin.

"Now, don't you go gettin' snippy with me. If ya'll don't know, then I'll tell you. You know down in Stokes County, North Carolina, on Christmas day of 1929, Charlie Lawson done been taken over by evil spirits, took up a shotgun and killed his wife and six kids. Youngest one was just a coupla months old, head bludgeoned in by the butt of that gun. Somethin' terribly evil jumped that man's bones to make him do such a thing. How's a man in any good standings with the Lawd go and do something so evil? A tiny baby, layin' in its cradle. Imagine! And then there his girls were playing outside, shot them dead.

.

Little boys hiding under beds and behind stoves, bashed in their brains. Oh, Lawd, such a terrible occasion."

Rhea was pretty worked up now and I was about to ask her a question to try and get her to calm down, but Clive beat me to it. "So, what has any of that got to do with a raisin cake?"

"Marie, that oldest Lawson girl, she done made a raisin cake for Christmas. It was still sittin' on their table when the deputies came in to get them bodies. The horror of that day was baked into that cake."

"But, the cake Aunt Stella made you is not the same cake that Marie made," Clive said.

"Doesn't matter!" Rhea said. "Anybody got any kind of good sense knows better than to tempt the devil with a raisin cake at Christmas! You'd think ain't none of you been to church a day in your life."

"Oh," I said. I had heard about the Lawson murders, so many years ago, as most of us in the area had, simply because there had been several folk ballads written about the event. A recent one had just come out a few years ago. But, I had never paid that much attention and didn't know all the details.

"Well, don't go a worrying none, now. I done took care of it. The chickens'll eat it."

"The chickens to the rescue, who'd have thunk?" Clive said and rolled his eyes. I threw imaginary daggers at him, but they hit home, because he straightened up and put a smile on his face.

"Well, now that unpleasantness is over," Rhea said. "Olivia, I just wanted to tell you that I was sorry 'bout that feller friend of yours, but there wasn't any way that was gonna be turnin' out okay. You can't just go traipsin' through other's backyards and not expect to stumble over their dogs, now ain't that right? Funny thing is, I don't feel him hangin' around like I do some folks. He had no unfinished business. He went right on to where's he's supposed to go."

"Won't the raisin cake hurt the chickens?" Clive asked, clearly not ready to move on with the conversation.

"No, 'cause they ain't got human souls," Rhea said. "They's got different kinds of souls. The kind that ain't affected by Satan."

"Oh, that's good to know," he said.

"Rhea," I said. "What do you mean there was no way *that* was going to turn out okay? What is *that* exactly?"

"His comin' here lookin' for kinfolk."

The hair nearly stood straight up on my arms. "What do you mean he came here looking for kinfolk?"

"Well, I knew it, first I seen him. I said, Rhea, he's a lost soul, lookin' for kin. I never helped him none with that, and he never asked. I figured, if he's supposed to find 'em, then he's supposed to do that all on his own. But yes, as sure as the sky is blue, he was looking for somebody. That, and he was runnin' from something awful."

"Awful?" I asked.

"Awful," she declared.

Clive rubbed his eyes with his hands and said, "Just awful." Then he mouthed, "Can we go now?"

"What sort of awful?" I asked.

"The kind of awful that makes a man's colors turn murky."

"Murky?" I asked.

"Colors?" Clive asked. "We have colors?"

"Course we's got colors. Damn, boy. Didn't yer folks teach you nothin'?"

Clive didn't get to answer. Rhea went on.

"Now that feller, that Jeb, he wasn't like Blanchie. Naw, Blanchie she still hangs around, talks to me, says I supposed to keep an eye on you, Olivia, but I told her you had plenty a eyes on you, what with Runa and Mildred, Stella and Dotie. You girl, you can't take a breath without those aunties knowin' about it. I'm not sayin' that ain't a good thing, I'm just sayin' that, Blanche, her worries are ungrounded."

"You talk to Blanche?" I asked.

"Well, she mostly talks to me."

"Back to the colors..." Clive said.

"Dammit, you, anyhows, you just tryin' to make me forget what I'm sayin'. Now, Clive, I know you's a good kid. Stupid, but good, so don't be tryin' my patience. Only reason I let you in here is cause I know you got a heart a gold. Now, I done took a backset to that cold I had last week and I ain't in no mood to be fooling with you. Are we clear?"

Clive looked sheepish. "Yes, ma'am."

"Now don't be actin' like ya'll don't see those colors. Everybody's got 'em and those colors is what helps me knowed they good or bad. That Jeb feller, he had good colors. He was green. But there was big holes in his color and it was dark. Now that don't mean he was turnin' evil or something silly like. It just means that something was after him or he was runnin' from something. Hang on a minute, I've got to answer the pig."

Clive and I exchanged curious glances. Rhea went out the front door and Clive ran over to the window to watch where she was going. I wheeled over to the window myself, and leaned over to get a view. "What do you think she's doing?" Clive asked.

"Answering the pig," I said.

He glanced at me. "Can we leave now?"

"Yes," I said.

I folded the quilt and set it on the arm of the couch and we made our way out the front door. Clive started pushing my chair really fast. "What are you doing?" I asked.

"Getting out of here," he said.

"We can't leave without saying good-bye," I said. "Where are your manners?"

"Manners?" he asked. "She's talking to a pig!"

I placed my hands on the tires of my chair to stop myself. "No, Clive, she was a gracious host, I'm not leaving without saying good-bye."

Rhea came walking back up the hill, away from the pig pen and stopped when she got in front of us. "Ya'll done go on and tell Stella Davies I said thank you much, and we'll just overlook her little indiscretion of tryin' to get me possessed by the devil. I'm pretty sure she didn't mean to do it. Clive, the john is down over the hill that way seeing as how you're needing to use it. Olivia, I really hope you didn't set that quilt on the arm of the couch. It makes the cushions all flat. See ya'll later." She headed for the house and then turned back around. "Olivia, I like your color these days."

Clive just looked at me and said, "We. Are. Leaving."

Awkward Moments

Clive relished every bite of his squirrel stew, maybe more so because he felt he'd earned it.

Aunt Stella and I were doing dishes, she was washing and I was drying. "Rhea was quite upset that you baked her a raisin cake for Christmas." I said.

"She fed it to the chickens," Clive added.

Stella just laughed. "Didn't even occur to me that she would get upset over that. Good, golly, it's been almost thirty years since those murders happened."

"Well, they don't call her crazy for nothing," Clive said.

Aunt Stella took two steps and flicked Clive on the back of the ear. He squealed. "Now, she might talk about some unusual things like people's colors and so forth, but she's harmless. In fact, after Reggie died, Rhea helped me find his song book, you know, the one that Uncle Clem had written? Clem autographed it to Reggie. Reggie loved those songs. That book had been one of his prized possessions. Uncle Clem was a very talented song writer. Anyway, I couldn't find that thing anywhere. No matter where I looked. Well, one day after church, Rhea came up to me and said, 'The song book is in the extra cookie jar in the top cabinet.' Sure enough, that's where it was."

"So, you're saying that you believe she can talk to dead people?" I asked.

"Why was the song book in the cookie jar?" Clive asked.

Ignoring Clive, Stella answered, "Only the dead folks who haven't moved on."

"You're joking," Clive said. "You believe that?"

"Look," Aunt Stella said. "I know she says we all have colors, which I don't believe, and I know she says that the trees talk to her..."

"And apparently pigs," Clive added.

"But any time she's ever given anybody a message like that, 'the book is in the cookie jar'...It's always been right. And there's no way she could know these things."

"She says that Blanche hasn't moved on and that she asks her to keep tabs on me."

"Then she probably does," Aunt Stella said, with tears glistening in her eyes. Blanche had only been four years younger than her and they had been very close.

"Malarkey," Clive said.

"Now, Clive!" she began.

"Aunt Stella," I said. "He doesn't have to believe it if he doesn't want to." Stella looked a bit shamed and handed me a plate to dry.

"What's her story?" I asked.

"What do you mean?"

"I mean, how did Rhea get this way?"

"Well," she said, but didn't get to finish her sentence. There was a knock at the door. "Who could that be?"

Favoring her bum knee, she walked into the next room, wiping wet hands on her apron. Clive had spun around from his chair and said, "I don't care how good her stew is, if she flicks me on the ear one more time, I'm gonna—"

"Olivia, Sheriff Ryan is here to see you," Stella said.

I glanced up, a bit taken aback. "Oh, Gunnar," I said. Immediately, I was worried that they'd found Humpy.

Gunnar was in his official uniform, hat in hand. "Olivia," he said. "I was wondering if you'd take a ride with me up to Jeb's house. All the evidence has been bagged. It's not a crime scene anymore. I'd just like to take you up there and see if you notice anything out of place. Since you've visited him before when it wasn't a crime scene."

"Oh, uh..."

"Clive can come, of course," he added, quickly.

He took my hesitation to mean something other than I'd meant. I wasn't worried about appearances, I was simply surprised to see him, and worried that he was bringing news about my brother. I also didn't want to go back to Jeb's house. Ever. Crime scene or not. But, I realized I was going to have to go to his house, eventually, because I needed to go through his things. May as well get it over with.

"Actually," Aunt Stella said, "I've got a few more jobs for Clive to do."

"What?" Clive asked.

"I need help hanging those Christmas lights around the fireplace and such."

"Oh," I said. "Well, that's fine. I don't need Clive to go with me."

I handed Aunt Stella the towel and wheeled through her house and out the front door. I glanced over at the vehicle that Gunnar was driving and sighed in relief. It was the squad car, low to the ground. So I didn't need help getting in and out of it. I wheeled down the sidewalk, stopped when I got to the car and opened the passenger side door.

"Hang on," Gunnar said. "I'll get that for you."

"No, I've got it," I said, a bit testily.

"Livvy, I'd open the door for any woman, not just one in a wheel chair. Don't be so defensive."

My cheeks burned and I found that I couldn't look him in the eyes. "Sorry, I...I can do it, that's all."

He lifted his hands as if in surrender. "You just tell me what you need me to do."

"Just stand behind the chair in case it slides." I locked the wheels and then lifted myself into the passenger seat, one hand firmly on my chair and the other on the squad car upholstery. Once my butt was safely in the seat, I then lifted my legs with my hands and rested my feet on the floor board. "It folds up. Just put it in the trunk."

Gunnar did what I instructed and within a minute was seated in the car beside me. "Now, I know you're not thrilled about going up there, Olivia. But, it really should be done. And I know there are some things you need to go through. So, I brought some boxes. We can fill them and I can drop them off at your house after we're finished."

"Sure," I said, suddenly very uncomfortable.

Gunnar made the turn up Sassafras Mountain and I immediately noticed that the ride was a tad bit smoother in a squad car than in our old dilapidated truck. "You and Clive out running errands for Stella?" he asked.

"Yeah," I said. I realized then that, in addition to wearing jeans, I was wearing an old flannel shirt—tied at the waist—Clive's old denim jacket and my hair was pulled up haphazardly in a ponytail. I tried to nonchalantly, pull on the ponytail to get it to tighten up. But that only caused little ridges to form on the top of my head.

"Have you heard from your brother?" he asked.

No less than six times had Gunnar showed up at my house in the past few weeks asking if we'd seen Humpy. And all six times we'd all replied no. "I haven't seen him since the night you dumped him in our living room floor with half his teeth kicked out of his head. I have not heard from him. No letters, no calls." We didn't have a telephone, but Arnie had one at the store that people would use and he'd take messages and give it to you the next time he saw you.

Humpy had not called there, either. For anybody. All of his friends had been interviewed and they had all said they hadn't seen him.

"If we don't catch a break on him soon, I'm thinking we may have to list him as missing and endangered."

"He's fine," I said.

"How can you be sure? Maybe in his drunken stupor, he wandered in front of a train."

"Have you found a mangled body on the train tracks?"

"No."

"Then he didn't wander in front of a train. Any other great theories?"

"Livvy, why you being so short with me?"

Because I didn't want to go to Jeb's and I didn't want to talk about Humpy. I was mortified that I was even related to Humpy. But all I said was, "Sorry."

"Is it like Humpy to miss Thanksgiving?"

"It is if he's drunk enough and horny enough."

"Olivia," he began but I cut him off.

"What? Humpy does what Humpy wants. If he shows up to church or to Sunday dinner it's because he either wants a favor or he needs money. He never just comes to visit us because he loves us or misses us or wants to spend time with us. He uses us. Right now he must be getting what he wants from somebody else and we're not needed. That'll change. Just give it time."

"But, it makes him look guilty."

"You know, he may not even know Jeb's dead. He could have left here that night and gone to Charleston or wherever and hasn't heard the news."

"Jeb was not an unknown writer. I did some checking. He wasn't all that commercially successful but in the literary crowds and the universities, he was pretty well known. I think it would have made the papers."

I laughed. "Humpy doesn't read. I don't even know if he knows how."

We were both quiet for a few seconds. "How are the dogs?" he asked, wisely changing the subject.

"Good," I answered. "When we go outside they always look west toward Jeb's. It's like they know."

We had made it to the top of the mountain and Gunnar pulled in front of Jeb's house. "They're putting it on the market next month," Gunnar said, motioning toward the house that had so quickly gone from being known as the old Renshaw place, to Jeb's. And just as quickly it would become known as somebody else's house. But for me, it would always be Jeb's.

To give Gunnar credit, he tried to get my chair out and bring it around as casually as possible. Like most people who've never taken me anywhere, he hovered, though, afraid that I wouldn't remember how to get myself out of the car. I had to instruct him on how to get the chair up the porch steps, but he performed the act smoothly and flawlessly. He had plenty of muscles to make it seem easy.

I glanced at the edge of the porch. "The dogs were lying there," I said.

"Whoever his killer was, they couldn't get near the house or the porch, because of the dogs, so we think that sometime when Jeb had them indoors, or he'd taken them with him, the perpetrator slipped the drugs in their water bowls. Then there is evidence that they were given a shot of something to really knock them out cold, after being drugged. So, we're looking for somebody who has access to narcotics."

Gunnar slipped the key inside the lock. "That could be anybody. All the farmers can get access to things like that, from the vets," I said.

"I know," he said. "It doesn't really help us all that much. Plus, they could have just as easily stolen the drugs. But it does say one thing."

"What's that?"

"It was premeditated. Which makes me think it wasn't Humpy."

"Humpy's not smart enough, is that it?"

"No. There's no way in his drunken state he could have pulled off anything like what was done here. Especially when you consider the dogs. The only way he could have been involved is if he was the distraction. You know, he was paid to get drunk and start a fight with Jeb, so that when Jeb went home, he'd be slow to react. The only way Humpy could be involved is if the murder was committed by a group of people and Humpy was just one of the people. And that seems unlikely."

It took a moment for my eyes to adjust once we were indoors. Gunnar left me alone in the house for a few moments while he went back out to get some boxes. I tried not to look at the floor where Jeb had died. My hands started to shake and the walls seemed to move in closer. Just as I thought I was going to fall to pieces, Gunnar came back in. He glanced around and said, "Huh. I should have remembered that most of his stuff is still in boxes. He never unpacked it. Well, that makes it easier."

I glanced toward the kitchen and noticed that there were one and a half bottles of whiskey left on the counter. Meaning, in the three months that he'd lived here, Jeb had drunk one full bottle of whiskey and a half. My father could have finished that in two days. "Take the whiskey," I said to Gunnar.

"Why?"

"I've got no need of it in my house," I said. "Give it to Sheriff Cunningham if you can't think of anybody else."

Gunnar nodded and walked toward the kitchen. "Do you see anything out of place?"

I rolled my eyes. "A housekeeper he wasn't."

"I mean, do you see anything missing that he normally had? Or anything added that you don't remember being here?"

"Well, I've never been upstairs, so I can't help you there."

"There's nothing up there."

"What do you mean?" I asked.

"I mean, he slept on the couch and lived out of boxes. He never bothered to move anything up there."

"He was too busy writing," I said. An image came to mind of Jeb sitting at the table feverishly typing away. "I think he was planning on 'settling' in after he finished the book."

"Well," Gunnar said. "Let me take a few of these boxes that are already packed out to the car. If you want, I'll bring Clive up here tomorrow and we'll start bringing some of the books down."

I nodded.

Gunnar took a box out to the car and I wheeled myself around the room, trying to make sure I didn't wheel over any of the blood stains on the floor. I ran my fingers across the keys on his typewriter, knowing that he was the last one to have touched them. Somehow it made me feel as though I'd made a connection with him, across time, space, and the afterlife. Somewhere on the other side, Jeb got my message. At least I hoped he did. "I am here," was all that gesture meant. And that's all I wanted him to know.

I found a calendar opened to October, the last month he ever knew. On it were strange notes in short hand. "Prwlr." When I sounded the word it out, it came out, "Prowler." I flipped the page back to September, same thing. And August. Jeb had documented every night that he'd had a prowler. I remembered suddenly hearing him speak to Gunnar about it at the dance. How, on that first visit, he'd met Clive and me in the driveway with his gun over his arm.

When Gunnar came back in I showed it to him. "Have you interviewed Clarence Ford?"

"He checked out of the motel the day Jeb was murdered. Since Jeb was from Baltimore, I've got calls into the Baltimore police, thinking maybe that's where Clarence was from."

I stared at him.

"There are a lot of Clarence Fords in America, Olivia. We're trying to run him down."

"You know something you're not telling me."

"If it's the same Clarence Ford, he has a criminal record."

"Why would the prowler keep coming back? It had to be somebody who was watching him for a reason."

"Like what?" he asked.

I thought a moment and remembered Holly Springfield. "Maybe Jeb got mixed up in something illegal back in Baltimore."

Gunnar's eyes looked up from the calendar and met mine. He looked away. After a moment he said, "I'm gonna keep the calendar. Maybe these notes are nothing more than deadlines, personal things."

"That's a good idea."

"Oh, and here," he said, handing me a book off of the counter. *Leaves of Grass* by Walt Whitman. "It was under the bottle of whiskey."

As he turned, a piece of paper slipped from the pages of the much-loved and used book and floated to the ground. I pointed toward it, but Gunnar had already seen it, and was bending over to pick it up. He glanced at it and said, "I think this has something to do with you."

He handed me the piece of paper, and my hands began to tremble as I took it. I hated surprises, and it seemed that where Jeb was concerned, there was always a surprise of some sort. At first the piece of paper made no sense. It was just a list of names. Colinda, Mildred, Hazel, Runa, Dotie, Stella, Viola, and Blanche.

Then I realized that not only was it the list of my great-grandma's family, but the names were even in order according to their birth. I glanced sharply at Gunnar.

"Mildred, Stella, Dotie, Runa... does he mean your aunts?"

I nodded. "He means all of them."

"I don't understand. Why would he have a list of their names?"

I shook my head. "I'm not sure."

Gunnar took a box out to the car, along with the calendar, and left me to ponder the meaning of this list and stare at Walt Whitman's beautifully craggy face. Why have the list? Why bother making it? I tried to remember if there had ever been a point when I had listed all of the Graham children for him. *Think, think.* Yes, there had been one time. Jeb had taken Clive and me to the soda shop, and I had mentioned an aunt on my father's side of the family. Jeb had said he was confused and didn't understand where she fit in. The memory became clearer in my head. I'd said, "My father has four sisters and four brothers, who all live within a thirty mile radius. My mother has two sisters and a brother." Jeb had shook his head and said, "So, your Aunt Stella, she's your mother's mother's sister. Now, wait. Name them for me." And I had rattled them off, in order, because it was easier for me to remember them that way. Not to mention, that's the way they were listed in my Grandma's bible.

That one time I had named them for him. In that busy soda shop with dishes clanking and the people milling all about, he had zeroed in on that. He'd remembered it, gone home and written it down. That was the same day I'd told him about the Graham family. Well, as much as I knew anyway. How the immigrant ancestor of my Grandma Blanche and her siblings had come to this country an indentured servant from Ireland, but before that, the family had come from Scotland. He'd asked me where in Scotland and I'd told him I didn't know exactly, only that it was northwestern, somewhere in the highlands. And that we'd had a plaid. He'd hung on my every word. And then I'd told him as much as I knew about their mother's family, the Millers. It had been German originally, with some Irish and Cornish, and even the rumor of a Cherokee. But in this neck of the woods, there was always a rumor of a Cherokee or a Shawnee in every family, and as a result, I usually took it with a grain of salt.

Gunnar came back into the house then, startling me. I jumped as the screen door banged against the frame.

"Are you alright?" he asked. "You look like you've seen a ghost."

"I'm fine," I said.

"I've got a domestic I need to take care of, can I leave you here and come back or do you want to ride along?"

"I'll ride along," I said.

Things Hidden In Plain Sight

Gunnar and I drove in the squad car toward Charleston. I shuffled through a few things that had been in one of the boxes from Jeb's house because not only was I curious, but I needed something to keep me busy. It had been my experience that nothing brings out just how much you don't know a person as much as being in the car alone with them. Gunnar and I knew each other, but we didn't know each other, and this could have been a very awkward car ride. I had managed to lay my hands on what I assumed to be Jeb's pre-kindergarten artwork that he'd written about in his book. I can see why the drawings disturbed his mother. One was of two men with guns—not just handguns, but what looked to be machine guns—shooting a man standing under a tree. Blood spurted from the man's body, and his mouth—a perfectly round 'o'—was open in horror. They were just stick people, but they were stick people with lots of detail. There was a drawing of an earthen mound, and even a drawing of a lynching. He hadn't mentioned *that* in his book. There was a drawing of what I assumed was his biological mother. She sat in front of a mirror, twisting her long dark hair up onto her head. And there was a depiction of the building that he had so vividly described. I lay my head back and watched out the window as one leafless tree blurred into the next. I suddenly felt sorry for Jeb. As a child he must have thought he was truly insane. And just as suddenly and just as overwhelmingly, I felt sorry for his mother, thinking she'd taken him away from the orphanage and the horror of his past, only to have Jeb unable to let it go.

We passed the road to Crazy Rhea's in silence until I couldn't take it any longer. "So what's going on?"

"Hm?" Gunnar asked.

"Where are we going?"

"Oh, I got a call that there are two farmers arguing over a cow and one is brandishing a shotgun. Not unusual. I just show up, tell them to calm down and leave. Most people put their guns down on their own, but if I show up then they know there's a witness to what's going on. By the time I get there it'll probably be over with anyway."

"Why do you say that?"

"Most people out here don't have phones. Maybe one out of six houses. By the time somebody gets to a phone to call the sheriff's office and I actually get there, the situation has usually fizzled on its own," he said. Then after a moment he added. "You guys got a phone?"

"No," I said. "Aunt Mildred does, though. So, we're not too far from one. And there's always Arnie."

"God love Arnie."

I smiled.

"Do you know how to shoot, Livvy?"

I glanced at him out of the corner of my eye. "Am I in danger?"

"No," he said, chuckling. "It's just, you know, with your brother and all, and now Jeb being murdered. I was just curious if you needed to..."

"I'm actually a pretty good shot with a gun, but the only way I can really shoot is if I'm secured pretty good. There's too much kick and if I'm not careful, it'll knock me right over. But, you can't beat me with a bow and arrow."

"Really?" he asked, smiling over at me.

"Yeah, I learned at the hospital. And it doesn't matter if it's a moving target or a still target. I can nail it at fifty yards."

He laughed and said, "Do you own a bow?"

"Yeah, Willie's got his, but he gave me one for Christmas a couple of years ago. I usually keep it in the truck behind the seat or under my bed."

Now he just outright laughed.

"What's so funny?"

"Oh, girls usually get things like record players, transistor radios, and pretty dresses for Christmas. Or Elvis records. You...you get a bow and arrow."

"And books, don't forget those," I added. Books were my favorite gift.

"I just find that..."

"What?"

"I don't know, charming, I guess."

"Charming?" I said. "Well, I never said I *liked* getting a bow for Christmas. Maybe I wanted a new dress."

He glanced at me. "Fat chance."

I smiled. "Well, for the record, I don't really like shooting things that move. That usually means it's living, and that bothers me. But, I have before and I will again, if I have to."

"You've been hunting?"

I nodded.

He gave me an incredulous look.

"What? You think because I can't walk I can't go hunting?"

"I uh...well, I uh...well, yes, that's exactly what I think. How'd you...?"

"If you want to know so badly, you'll just have to take me some time," I said, and then realized that he might misconstrue that as me *wishing* that he'd take me, which was not at all what I meant. I floundered about trying to think of a way out of what I'd just said when suddenly, on my right, an old abandoned building appeared like a ghost ship out of the fog. "Stop the car."

"What?" he asked.

"Stop the car!"

Gunnar slammed on the brakes and pulled the vehicle into the gravel driveway. "What is it?" he asked.

But I could barely hear his words. They were all muffled and lost, as if they were traveling down a tunnel. The window was foggy and I wiped it with my sleeve, but that didn't help the moisture pebbles that had formed on the outside of the window. I fumbled for the handle and slowly rolled down the window. It was as if I'd unveiled a secret hiding place.

"Olivia," Gunnar said. "What's going on?"

"That's it," I said pointing to the building. Goosebumps danced along my arms and legs.

"What?"

I rummaged through the papers on my lap until I found the drawing of the building. The building that Jeb had described in his book as having lots of doors and windows and lots of people dressed in many different ways. The one with the big tree and the boulder to the left. The one with the big white star in a circle, hanging under the roof ridge. "It's a boarding house."

"Yeah, Olivia. It's been there for ages. I think it was built in like the 1880's or something like that. Haven't you ever seen it before?"

Of course I'd seen it before. Every time I'd ever been to Charleston and back, I'd seen it. In my defense, I hadn't been to Charleston that many times in my life and the last time I'd been this far down this road had probably been two years ago. But I had seen it, several times, and there were even photographs of it in my aunties' ancient hat boxes. It had never registered to me as being any place important. It was just another ramshackle Appalachian building disintegrating from years of neglect, crumbling right before our very eyes. It was a monument of days gone by and a monument to the Kanawha valley's lack of money and the people's disdain for anything old and no longer useful. It harkened back to the time of the "company store" when entire towns were owned by coal companies and families were paid with coal script instead of cash, which could only be spent in company owned stores and boarding houses.

But this boarding house was special.

"It was owned by the Lewis-Baker Coal company," I heard Gunnar say. "Since it sets right here in a bend of the Kanawha River, they just called it the Bend house."

"The Bend house," I repeated.

The Grahams had all worked at the Bend house at some point. Some earlier, some later in years, and some, for decades.

"Olivia, what's the problem?"

"I uh...well, you wouldn't understand," I said, since Gunnar had not read any of Jeb's book. "But, this is the same building as this." I pointed from the piece of paper to the building that stood watch over the mountains and the river.

"What is that?" he asked, pointing to the paper.

"It's a long story, but this is a drawing that Jeb did when he was four or five."

"How do you know it's the same building?" he asked.

I pointed to the tree, which was still there, only much bigger and more all-knowing. I pointed to the boulder and its unique flat shape. And then I pointed to the star under the roof ridge. It was still on the building, faded and crooked, but there all the same.

"How can that be? I thought Jeb was from Baltimore."

"I've got a lot to tell you," I said.

Jeb

When I was twenty-five, my mother finally gave me the handful of things that had been left with me at the St. Vincent's Infant Asylum. A crocheted blanket, the clothes that I had been wearing, even the shoes, a wooden toy truck, and a letter from my birth mother.

My mother tried to explain that she hadn't meant to keep these things from me but that she thought to give them to me would have made my issues worse. When it became clear that nothing was going to make me worse and that any smidgen of my past would give me hope, she'd given me the box. Well, that, and I'd volunteered for the Korean War and was shipping out in three days, and she was afraid I would die without ever having seen those items. I could tell that it pained her to give them to me. And she'd even said to me, "Jeb, we love you. This is your life here. Can't you try just once to put this behind you and be here, with us, while you can?"

What my mother didn't know—what she could never understand—was that I could never be here until I knew the before.

The question wasn't whether or not I was loved or if I was safe. My parents' love for me was never in doubt. They loved me as any parent would love their child. I never doubted their devotion or their sacrifices. And while I was theirs in most respects, I came from somewhere else. There was a before that had nothing to do with them. I made a journey to St. Vincent's without the McDowell's. Without that journey and without that "before" they could not have had me to love.

The question was simply, who am I? Asking that question did not in any way reflect on my upbringing. In some desperate rationalization on my parent's part, they thought they had failed me somehow, that if they had loved me just a little bit more, I would not care about where I came from. The truth is, aside from the obvious input of our surroundings, our loved ones, our friends, our enemies, we are an accumulation of the secrets we don't know.

It was a question of nature versus nurture on some level. And there was a good and solid standing for both sides of that argument.

I was unique. I was a blend of both worlds. But my mother was only content as long as I was hers alone.

But I needed to know my kinfolk. While I had siblings with whom I had shared all of life's major moments, whom I loved as much as I would any who had been related by blood, and while I had cousins, aunts, uncles and even grandparents, my family connections stopped there. My adopted mother's ancestral journey had no bearing on me. And that is what I really longed for. I wanted to walk among my kinfolk, look out upon their landscape and hear their music. Because that was uniquely and magically all mine. And I couldn't know that history without first knowing the answer to who am I?

In some ways it was cruel that my mother had waited until three days before I was to leave for Korea to give me these things. Because then I had to do my entire tour with this newfound knowledge and no way to investigate it. But I think, on some deeper level, my mother also knew that by giving me these things, my desire to hunt these clues down and to find the answers, would keep me alive in Korea. I would survive, by sheer willpower, so that I could come home and answer that single question of identity.

And it worked.

For all through Korea, I had kept this letter from my birthmother, folded and in my pocket. I would take it out and read it every now and again. And it is so stained and torn and ragged now that one can barely read it. But I don't need to read it anymore. I have it memorized. It said;

"I have just a few moments to tell you a lifetime's worth of things. I have only a few moments to impress upon you my undying love for you. It's a task I will surely fail. I want you to know so many things. I want you to know that I loved your father with all my heart and soul and that he was a good man. Your father had been a soldier in the Great War and he returned injured and broken, but still able to love. He was honest and forthright, and although his life may have been scrutinized by others, he always did what was right, eventually. And it was that righteous sense of duty that was his undoing. I want you to know that I am just an average girl from the hills, a poor girl who worked in boarding houses and coal companies, and I have many siblings who would have loved you if life had dealt you different cards. I have memorized the color of your eyes, the texture of your hair, the wrinkles and dimples on your hands. I cannot imagine a day without you and yet I know if I live to be an old woman, there will be many, for I cannot raise you. I will think of you every day of my life. My heart breaks as I write this, and I cry so hard that no sound comes out. You must

know that I love you so much that I would rather another woman raise you as her own, than to raise you myself and risk your well-being."

And those are the words I carried off to war.

A Letter to Viola from Olivia

Viola Reinhardt
Dayton, Ohio
November 30, 1958

Dear Aunt Viola,

My brother would have to have a soul to be lost. I'm off to celebrate Mark Twain's birthday.

Love, Olivia

Deputy Gunnar Ryan
Colton County Sheriff's Department

Gunnar pulled his squad car into the Baltimore Police Department's headquarters. Right after Jeb's murder he'd made a call to the Baltimore police, giving them the names of Clarence Ford and Holly Springfield, and made a request that they be picked up, if they could be found, to be questioned in a murder case. Last night he'd received a phone call saying that Holly had been brought in for questioning, she was awaiting his arrival. He'd driven up to Clarksburg immediately, hopped on Route 50 and took it all the way to Maryland, skirting right by the Monongahela National Forest. Any other day he would have stopped and detoured, but not today. He'd driven for hours, he couldn't even remember now what time he'd left, and was tired and cranky. The crankiness was due to the fact that he was hungry. He'd been so intent on getting there that he'd completely forgotten to eat anything.

He'd brought along the Jeb McDowell case file, complete with crime scene photos, because he was most likely going to stay overnight in a hotel before heading home, and he wanted to keep everything fresh in his mind.

He carried the file under his arm as he made his way into the police department, asked for Detective O'Leary and took a seat on a very uncomfortable chair. He opened the file and read through Jeb's specifics. Age, height, weight. His writing credentials were listed, along with some of his other odd jobs that he'd had. What school he'd gone to, the names of his family, known friends and last, the cause of death were also permanently recorded. The coroner's report took up three or four pages, and then the photos. Gunnar scanned the report, taking note of key words like intoxicated, busted lip, broken nose, cut above eye, multiple bruising on body, two broken knuckles, defensive cuts on the palms of his hands and forearms, and four stab wounds to the chest and torso. None of his major arteries had been severed or nicked, but he'd still bled to death. He'd just done it slowly. The coroner was quick to note that most of the damage on Jeb's body had been inflicted by fists, not a knife, and concluded that the man had been in an altercation either right before he was stabbed, or it was part of the stabbing.

Gunnar rubbed his eyes. He was aware of that point, all right. And that altercation had been at the hands of Benjamin "Humpy" VanBibber, Olivia's brother. It didn't take much of a leap to think that maybe Humpy had gone up there and finished Jeb off. Except that he'd been so drunk he couldn't even stand up, and Jeb's murder had been premeditated. Even counting both of those things, his boss, Sheriff Cunningham, and fellow deputy, Lyman Boland, liked Humpy for the murder because there were three hours between Gunnar dropping Humpy off at Olivia's and the murder. They thought he had time to sober up. Gunnar thought they suspected him because it was easy. Open and shut. He wasn't saying that Humpy wasn't capable of murder; he just didn't do this one. Gunnar could feel it in his bones. Although a court of law could have cared less what Gunnar Ryan's bones felt, so he had a lot to prove.

He glanced at the crime scene photos, trying not to focus on Jeb's open eyes. The knife was still sticking up out of his chest, buried up to the hilt in flesh and blood. There was blood located throughout the living room, but that was it, it hadn't been found in any other part of the house. Jeb had been intoxicated enough that he hadn't been able to fight that well. In fact, it had seemed to Gunnar that the first stab had most likely caught him off guard completely. Then he tried to fight off the second and third strike, and was unable to defend himself on the fourth. Down to the ground he went. The whole attack probably lasted less than three minutes.

He glanced at the blood on the lefthand side of the body. It was smeared and smudged. Olivia had been sitting on that side, holding his hand, crying. God, it made him want to kill something himself when he thought about it. Nothing in his twenty-six years had prepared him for walking in and finding Olivia covered in blood, shaking, crying...and then she'd raised that gun and pointed it right at him, completely prepared to shoot. The look in her eyes had said, "Okay, you sonofabitch, come and get it." Although he hadn't been the killer, the one she'd been hoping would come through that door. But he had no doubt, based on the look in her eyes, that she would have pulled that trigger and worried about the consequences later. She had been half out of her mind with fear and adrenaline. If she hadn't been able to place his voice, Gunnar thought for sure she would have shot him.

He'd seen her face every time he'd closed his eyes since the murder. It wasn't Jeb's face that haunted him, it was hers. And in some ways, that was worse.

Gunnar examined one of the close-ups of the blood on the right-hand side of the body. Jeb's left. The side Olivia wasn't on. It was odd. A small pool of blood with a pattern in the center. Like something had been set in the blood, but it wasn't a handprint or a footprint, he couldn't get that lucky. Right in the center of the pattern was a ridge. So, blood on the outside, a pattern section inside that, and a ridge inside of that. What could make that type of mark?

"Deputy Ryan," a voice said. Gunnar looked up to see a man about thirty-five, with a short, military style haircut, motion for him to come into his office. "I'm Detective O'Leary."

Gunnar put the pictures and such back in the folder and made his way toward the detective with his hand outstretched. "Nice to meet you."

"So, fill me in," O'Leary said as they went into the office. In addition to beige furniture and beige walls, there was a framed photograph of a very attractive woman by the phone, and a large 11x14 framed photo of the capitol building in Washington, D.C., hanging on the wall.

"I've got a white male, thirty-five, originally from Baltimore, who was found stabbed down in Colton County, West Virginia. He bought a place there. He's a writer, came to our neck of the woods to write, or so I'm told. I think there might be more to it than that."

"Why's that?" O'Leary asked, subtly swirling his chair back and forth with his feet.

Gunnar pulled out the fifty-dollar bill he'd found in Jeb's outhouse. He'd received a call from Charleston that the serial numbers did indeed match those of a robbery in Maryland. Luck had been on his side that Charleston had gotten back to him just before he got the call to come here. "This is from a robbery here, Moulton Bank of Baltimore. This money was found on the property of the dead man."

Detective O'Leary leaned forward and picked up the bill.

"What can you tell me about that robbery?" Gunnar asked.

"I can tell you that a man named Clarence Ford is suspect number one. He has committed a string of robberies in this state, was convicted and just released last year sometime. When Moulton got robbed, I thought nothing of it, until I read the specifics. Everything—the guns he used, what he wore, even the things the suspect said—everything was Ford's style. But the perp got away, no money has surfaced and I can't connect him—with evidence—to the robbery. Are you telling me you think your dead man did this? What's his name?"

"Jebediah McDowell. Do you know of him?"

"He's a bit of local celebrity, down on his luck. His last two books tanked. Everybody thought he just retired."

"You think he was 'down on his luck' enough to stick up a bank?" Gunnar asked.

"I guess it's possible, but I'd have a tough time believing that. And if it was him, he mimicked Clarence Ford's style to a tee."

Gunnar thought about that for a second. Had Ford pulled off the robbery and then stashed the money at Jeb's? Were they friends? Did Ford have something on Jeb, something to blackmail him into keeping the money for him?

"So, why did you want to speak to Holly Springfield?"

"She visited Jeb while he was in West Virginia. And Jeb introduced her as a friend of his."

O'Leary stopped rocking his chair.

"And, Clarence Ford was in our county, as well. Not in the same town, but he was there. Left about six hours after the murder."

"Interesting," O'Leary said. "Holly Springfield is a known associate of Clarence Ford's. She served a short prison term for helping him on a robbery eight years ago."

It felt like the bottom dropped out of Gunnar's stomach. "I just want to question Holly Springfield."

O'Leary nodded his head. "Of course. Any information you can get from her for me to prosecute the robbery, the better."

Gunnar shrugged. "Sure. As long as I get my murderer first."

O'Leary started to protest.

"Murder is a bigger crime than armed robbery. I want him put away forever, if he's guilty. Then you won't have to worry about him robbing anymore banks. Right?"

O'Leary turned his palms up and said, "If he's guilty of murder, he's yours. If not, he's mine for the robbery. Providing of course, you or I can make a connection."

Gunnar agreed with a nod of his head and O'Leary stood and led him to the room where Holly Springfield was waiting. When Gunnar walked in, Holly immediately smirked. She was thinking "hillbilly sheriff" and relaxed. He could read it on her face.

She had long fingers and a bony face, with coarse dark hair that curled in a big wave under her chin. Fingernails were painted a bright color that had begun to chip around the edges. It's been said that you can tell how much a woman has lived by her eyes, and in Holly's case, Gunnar thought that just might be the truth. Small, brown eyes were knowing and curious and cynical all at the same time. They were the most striking feature on her face because they spoke loudly and callously about what she thought of the world. She crossed her arms and said, "Can we please hurry this up, I'm hungry."

"Me too," he said. "So, we both don't want to mess around here, then."

"So the police said that you wanted to ask me some questions about a murder?"

"Yeah, I understand that you know a man named Jeb McDowell?"

"Yes," she said. There had been only a slight flick of her gaze when Gunnar mentioned Jeb by name. She'd probably been expecting this.

"Well, you know he was murdered."

She nodded.

"You didn't attend the funeral?"

"I didn't find out about it until after. His mother didn't like Jeb's friends. She always tried to keep him for herself."

Or maybe she had reason not to like his friends, Gunnar thought. "Miss Springfield, do you know a man named Clarence Ford?"

She smiled. "You know I do."

"How do you know Jeb McDowell?"

"We went to college together."

"And what is your degree in?" Gunnar asked.

Holly narrowed her eyes at him. "English."

"So, you decide to aid and abet criminals instead of... what, teaching?"

She smirked again. "Do you know how much teachers make?"

"Yes, yes, I do," Gunnar said. She rolled her eyes. "They make about as much as I do."

"Is there something you want to know specifically?" she asked. "Your line of questioning is juvenile."

"How did Jeb McDowell get mixed up with Clarence Ford?" he asked, ignoring her jab.

She clenched her jaw and raised her chin a notch.

Gunnar spread the crime scene photos out, one at a time. "Take a look at him, Holly. Jeb was a good man, a talented man. He's gone now. He's left behind a son, parents, siblings, friends. How did he know Clarence Ford?"

"I want my lawyer," she said. Which meant that if she answered the question of how Clarence and Jeb knew each other, it would incriminate her in some way.

"Fine, you can have your lawyer. But you're going to answer this question anyway. Eventually."

Gunnar slowly picked up the pictures to return to the file. "Because I'm going to offer you clemency. You tell me how they knew each other and I'll promise not to prosecute you for whatever involvement you had with the Moulton robbery."

She said nothing.

"Your lawyer will agree to that, I'm sure."

Gunnar's heart was pounding in his chest. O'Leary had not given him that authority and since Gunnar was law enforcement from another state, he couldn't give her this promise anyway. But he was hoping she would think that the two law enforcement officers had already worked that out between them.

He'd picked up all of the photographs, except one. It was a close up of Jeb's beaten and swollen face. Open, lifeless eyes staring off into oblivion. Every time he saw that picture he remembered Jeb's smiling, glowing face the night of the dance when he had do-si-doed with a girl in wheelchair. He tapped the corner of the photo with his finger and said, "Get a good look at that, okay? That was your friend. He died a horribly brutal death."

The first sign of remorse slipped into Holly's face. Her chin trembled and she looked away. "I can't believe Clarence would do that. I just can't."

"Why not?" Gunnar asked. She was talking. This was a good thing.

"Clarence is a lot of things...but a murderer?"

Gunnar gave a half-hearted chuckle. "Nobody ever thinks their loved ones are capable of the things they are capable of. I'll let you make that phone call to your lawyer now."

Gunnar made it all the way to the door and for one brief and excruciating moment he really thought she was going to keep quiet. He'd have to wait hours for her lawyer to get here and then negotiate with O'Leary about not pressing charges against her if she incriminated herself in the questioning...or worse yet, not answer at all because her lawyer told her not to. His hand reached for the doorknob and she said, "They didn't know each other."

Gunnar turned around. "What's that?"

"They didn't know each other at all. That was the beauty of it."

"Of what?"

"Clarence needed a get-away driver. He wanted somebody he didn't know, somebody he'd never worked with, never met. Nobody who could be traced back to him. He asked me if I could get him a driver. Somebody..."

"What?"

"Trustworthy."

"And that was Jeb," he said.

She nodded. "I didn't tell Jeb what was going on. I simply asked him if he could do a favor for a friend of mine. Pick him up at a specific address on a specific date and take him to the bus stop. I told him I'd buy him dinner and we'd go to the symphony. My treat. I just needed him to do this favor." Her voice trailed off.

"You mean to tell me Jeb picked Clarence up from a bank robbery and didn't know that's what was happening?

She nodded. "He picked Clarence up on the street corner. When Jeb realized what had happened," she said with a smile, "in typical Jebediah fashion, he punched Clarence in the face, opened the door and kicked him out and drove off with the money."

"He stole the money from a thief," Gunnar said. An odd surge of pride filled him. He could just see Jeb kicking the thief out of his car.

She shook her head. "Then he panicked. He wanted to turn the money in right then and there, but..."

"But what?"

"Jeb had a record. Some bullshit charges his ex-wife had lodged against him in Louisiana. And there was me. He knew I'd go back to jail. How would it sound to the police? 'Oh, officer, a friend of mine asked me to pick up a bank robber, but I swear I knew nothing about it, and neither did she.' I mean, he'd have to tell them who I was, if he didn't, they'd suspect him. If he did tell them, then I was headed back to jail. So, he had bought a house in West Virginia and he thought he'd just take the money with him until he could figure out what to do about it. I told him just to give it to Clarence, but he said if he gave it back to Clarence he'd be an accessory."

"So, what, you drove down to Greenhaven to persuade him?"

"I begged him to give the money to me and said I'd give it to Clarence."

"Do you know if Clarence ever actually spoke with Jeb while he was in Greenhaven?"

She shrugged. "I think Clarence was just watching Jeb. I think Clarence was completely thrown by Jeb's actions. I think he was waiting for the right moment, then he'd move in and take the money."

"So, Jeb was planning his trip to West Virginia before this happened," Gunnar said.

She nodded. "Yes, that's exactly right. He said he'd be gone for a couple months, maybe even a couple of years, and that maybe he'd never come back," she said. "Picking up Clarence was just a last minute favor for a friend before he went off to start his new life. When I visited him, he said he couldn't think about the money until he was finished with the book. He just needed a few more weeks."

Gunnar stared at her for a moment. He wanted to say something profound, but he could think of nothing. As the seconds drew out before him he wished he could think of anything to say, profound or not. But still, nothing would come. She'd taken advantage of a man whom she knew was kind enough, thoughtful enough, to do her a favor. And, in return, he'd gotten nothing but a bunch of trouble.

"Where is Clarence Ford at this time?" he asked.

"I don't know."

Gunnar gave her an incredulous look.

"I swear, I do not know."

He turned to leave and she stopped him again. This time she had tears in her eyes and she struggled to speak. "That idiot told me that there were so many poor people in Colton County, that he'd thought about keeping the money and giving it all to them, except it wasn't his money to give. It belonged to equally hard-working people up here in Maryland. But wouldn't that be just like him, a regular Robin Hood?"

Gunnar opened the door and left her sitting there to think about her actions. Jeb the dreamer, the Robin Hood. He'd been taken advantage of in a way that Gunnar not only found despicable but pitiful. If Ford killed Jeb, Holly was just as responsible as if she had stabbed him herself. And if Mosie and Andrew had killed Jeb, in a roundabout way, she was still responsible. In fact, if Jeb was killed over that money at all, she was responsible. She knew it, too. Maybe she'd have trouble sleeping at night. Maybe she'd think twice before asking a nice guy to do a dirty favor for her again. Well, that was the way it would go if this were a movie. But it wasn't, and Gunnar just wanted some dinner to concentrate on so he wouldn't have to think about Holly and what a pathetic excuse of a person she was.

Who needed enemies with friends like her?

A Trip to the Big City

Two days later, Betty Jo Ryan showed up at my house.

"Hey, girl," she said with that wide genuine smile as I answered the door. "I'm headed to Charleston today. When I said I was thinking about asking you along, my brother said that was an excellent idea because you had something you wanted to research at the big library down there. So, you want to go?"

I couldn't help but smile. I loved the library in Charleston, even though I couldn't check anything out. I didn't live in the city limits, and I would have had no way to return the items anyway. I had told Gunnar about Jeb's book and expressed an interest in doing some research at the archives. Surely there had to be a record of a man being gunned down in broad daylight. While Gunnar found this information really fascinating, he didn't see how it connected to Jeb's murder. He encouraged me to learn what I could, but he was going to drive up to Maryland and speak with Holly Springfield, and he was going to track down some "loose leads" on Clarence Ford.

"I'd love to go," I said. It was only about nine in the morning and I had just gotten dressed.

"Great, let's go. I'm gonna stop by Arnie's to get us some snacks."

Before I even realized what was happening, I was in Betty Jo's car—her brand spanking new twelve-year-old used car—and we were in the parking lot of Arnie's store. Arnie's was a general store in the truest sense of the word. He had two gas pumps, and a small garage that he could perform minor repairs in. He stocked groceries—dried and refrigerated—fabric, buttons, personal items like soap and toothpaste. He sold magazines, comics, and tools. In the back he carried seeds, like for tomato plants, and soil and pots. And one couldn't forget the post-office drop off and pick up, and his telephone messaging service. And somehow he even managed to have a little counter top and a soda fountain so you could get sandwiches and ice-cream. All of it fit into a building that wasn't much bigger than Aunt Mildred's house. But Arnie's was the heartbeat of Greenhaven other than the church.

I was so used to people just leaving me in the car when we came to places like this that I was completely taken aback when Betty Jo opened the car door and had my wheelchair right there. "Come on, girl. We ain't got all day."

She had me in the store in a matter of minutes. "Hey, Olivia!" Arnie called out from behind the counter. He wore his usual Dickie's and a striped shirt with a battered and stained apron over it. He was a jack-of-all-trades after all. One minute he was butchering a cow, and the next he was fixing your car or making you a root-beer float. He did have a few employees, namely his two sons and a neighbor.

"Hi, Arnie," I said. "How's it going today?"

"Good. Tell Willie Gene I got that new hunting rifle in for him. I was gonna go up there tonight and tell him, but since you're here, you'll save me the trip."

"All right," I said.

Just then my Aunt Mildred and Edwin came around the end of the aisle. Obviously there to do their shopping, Edwin had a side of bacon secured under his arm. "I thought I heard Arnie say Olivia," Edwin said.

"Where are you going?" Aunt Mildred asked.

"Oh, I'm going to Charleston today with Betty Jo Ryan."

"Really?" she asked, smiling. "Does your mother know?"

"Mildred, Betty Jo is Gunnar's sister, I think Olivia will be safe with her," Edwin said.

"What are ya'll going all the way down there for?" she asked, ignoring Edwin.

"Oh, Betty's got to go there for something and wanted to know if I'd like to go along. She's going to drop me off at the library so I can do some research."

"On what?" Aunt Mildred asked. On one arm, she had her purse strap secured in the crook of her elbow, and on the other arm was a wooden box that she always brought with her on her shopping excursions. Sticking out of the container was a box of cornflakes, which made me chuckle. Edwin didn't like it when she ate cornflakes, because Edwin loved cooked breakfasts and thought everybody should have an eight- course meal to start off the day. She also had a gallon of milk and some flour and sugar. She was about to start her Christmas baking and I couldn't be more excited about that prospect. I reminded myself to drop hints to her for a pineapple upside-down cake.

"Oh, uh...I'm going to research a murder."

"A murder!" she scoffed. "What type of subject matter is that for a lady to be reading about?"

"Well, it's important."

"How so?" Edwin asked.

"It just is," I said. "It took place back in the twenties."

"Olivia!" Betty Jo called out. "What kind of pop do you want?"

"Orange," I answered her.

"Got it. Let's go, it's a two-hour drive," Betty Jo said from the front counter.

"Well, I've got to go," I said to Aunt Mildred, who was staring off toward the front door. "Aunt Mildred?"

"What?" she said.

"I've got to go. See you later."

"You be careful," she said. "No talking to strangers. You drive careful, Betty Jo Ryan!"

I rolled my eyes, but smiled anyway. On some level, it was sweet that she worried about us. Betty Jo and I pulled out of the parking lot a few minutes later. Once she was settled on the road, I handed her the open bottle of pop. We passed the Bend boarding house, but I said nothing about it. Betty Jo talked for the first half hour, non-stop, mostly about three different boys that she had a crush on. Her dilemma seemed to be which one she should pursue. The one who liked her, the sweet one, or the really good-looking but dangerous one. And why was it that the one who liked her was never cute, dangerous or good-looking, but plain and boring? A question, I'm sure that has been echoed down through the ages of young love.

I liked Betty Jo. We'd been friends since I was a kid, before the polio. She was lively, energetic and so impossibly positive that a person couldn't help but feel good in her presence. I wondered about that. How do I make people feel? I hoped I wasn't one of those people who made others groan just by entering a room.

"I suppose plain and boring is better than mean and hateful. Or creepy," she said. "Like that awful Lyman Boland! That man is a disgusting pig. You wouldn't believe some of the things he says to girls. Or just the things he says in general. My brother almost punched his lights out the other day..."

"The other day? What happened?" I asked.

"Oh, uh, nothing."

I glanced at her and her face flushed. Had Boland said something inappropriate to her? Clearly, nothing was something. "What? You can tell me."

"Well, no, it's just..." she stammered.

"What?" I asked.

"I don't want to upset you. Forget that I said anything."

"You won't upset me. Honestly, you can tell me anything."

"Are you sure?" she asked.

"Of course, what could you possibly say that would upset me?"

"Lyman told my brother that you didn't like boys. That you *couldn't* like boys," she said.

"What do you mean I *can't* like boys?" I asked.

She was quiet a moment, then she ventured. "You know..."

"Know what?"

"Please don't take this wrong way, Olivia, but...you know. Can you *do* things with boys?"

"I can do all sorts of things with boys," I said. I played baseball with Clive and his friends. I'd bat and then I'd wheel to the base. And I could catch balls, I just couldn't field them well if they grounded first. I could fish and hunt and...Then I realized, painfully, what she was talking about. My face turned blood red and I could feel the heat radiating off of it.

"You know," she said. "It. Can you do it?"

I cleared my throat. "If you mean sexual relations, I don't see why not. I mean, I haven't as of yet, but I assure you everything works fine."

"Everything?" she asked, cheeks turning an even deeper shade of red.

"Everything is normal. Everything works."

"Well, good," she said. "That's a relief."

"Why is that such a relief and why do you care?" I asked.

"I told Gunnar that you were just like everybody else."

"I *am* like everybody else."

"You know what I mean. Lyman told Gunnar that everybody knew you'd never get married and...I'm making things worse aren't I?" she asked.

I was mortified. The gossip of Greenhaven had been whether or not my reproductive organs worked? I wanted to open the car door and jump out! I cleared my throat again and fought back a tear. "I'll have you know, and you can shout it from the mountaintops, if you like, that I don't have any dates, because boys don't ask me. And the reason they don't ask me has just been made perfectly clear. And I don't flirt because I don't know how. It seems counterproductive. My not dating has nothing to do with whether or not *things* work." I was livid. I went from being mortified to angry in the amount of time it took me to finish that thought out loud. "*And* I don't see how any of it is Lyman or Gunnar's business!"

"Oh, don't be angry with Gunnar. Lyman's the one who brought it up. I heard that they were in the lunch room when somebody asked Gunnar about the murder investigation," she said.

"How did I end up being the subject of conversation?" I asked.

"I don't really know. I wasn't there. Anyway, when Lyman started talking about you the janitor had to pull my brother off of that no-account Lyman. That's what I hear anyway. That's the talk. Of course, when I asked Gunnar about it..."

"What?"

Betty Jo smiled and changed the subject. "So, the big question floatin' around Greenhaven and Wellston is whether or not you're going to move to town?" she asked.

"Are you sure?" I said, still miffed. "Are you sure that's the *big* question?"

I had this horrible image of Betty Jo running home tonight and calling a pow-wow with all her girlfriends and setting the record straight on whether or not all of my plumbing worked properly. I wanted to die. Just right here and right now. Dig a hole and shove me in it.

"Don't be angry with me," she said. "Please? I sure as pie didn't mean to upset you. You know I'd never want you to be upset. And I'm not gonna tell anybody, unless of course they start spreading lies and then I'll tell them truth."

"Please don't. Just don't say anything," I said.

"Are you mad at me?" she asked.

"No," I said.

"Good. So are you gonna move to town?"

"I've been thinking about it," I said, hoping that my coloring would return to normal soon. "Maybe Clive will move with me."

She smiled. "That would be fantastic. You can get out more and do more things without having to ask that nasty sister of yours for anything."

"True. True that I could do more on my own and true that my sister is nasty."

"You think you'll ever leave Colton County?" she asked.

"Probably not."

"Why's that?"

"Family."

"Some people want to get away from their family," she said, a little too seriously. I'd never heard any talk about Betty Jo or Gunnar fighting or any of their siblings not getting along. I was pretty sure she'd meant her father, in particular, when she made that statement.

"You know, Betty Jo, it's the oddest thing. But I love my family. Okay, not Humpy or Bessie, although I wouldn't ever want anything bad to happen to them. I could just care less if they ever speak to me again. But, the rest of the family—I love my aunts and uncles and cousins. I love where I'm from."

"You do?" she asked, giving me a quizzical look. Her blonde pony-tail slapped the side of her head when she turned in my direction.

"I do," I said. "I can't imagine any other scenery for the setting of my story. Well, not permanently, anyway. I could see a change of pace now and then, but this is where I belong. I just have to somehow make my way in it."

Betty Jo smiled.

"What?" I asked.

"My brother said that you weren't an empty-headed kewpie doll, which of course, I already knew."

"Oh, he did?" I asked. "And why was he talking about me this time?"

"Oh, uh...I dunno. He came home Saturday and said that he'd taken you up to the crime scene to have you take a look around. He just commented that you were really smart, which everybody knows, and that you weren't no empty-headed kewpie doll. That's all."

I always managed to alienate people. It was either the chair or my brains. The chair usually alienated women, and the brains usually alienated the men. At least that had been my experience anyway, although after the conversation we'd just had about boys, I needed to reassess my thoughts on that. Well, I would not apologize for my smarts. And it wasn't as if I was Einstein or something. I was just more widely read than most people I knew. It was sort of funny how I probably had less life experience—aside from spending three years in a polio ward and almost dying—than most of the girls I knew, and yet they seemed not to notice things right in front of them. Maybe I wasn't smarter, maybe I was just more observant. Or I read more books. Or I had more time to think about things. Maybe I just vocalized my thoughts more, where other girls kept their mouths shut so the boys would like them. Well, whatever it was, if Gunnar thought I was odd because I was smart, let him. It wasn't as if talking to him was the highlight of my day or anything.

We switched subjects and she started telling me about a movie that she'd seen at the drive-in. We talked about movies and James Dean until we made it to Charleston.

Apparently there was a medical condition that Betty Jo's father had, that nobody was aware of, and she had not shared the exact details with me, either. But it brought her or somebody from her family to Charleston once a month to pick up supplies for him that either could not be mailed to their home in Wellston, or the family didn't want mailed because they didn't want people to know about them. Postmen did not take a vow of silence or anything of the sort. Aunt Runa knew that Molly Tennyson's son had been wounded in Korea before Molly did. Uncle Pete had delivered the telegram.

So, Betty Jo dropped me off at the library and went on her merry way. She said she'd only be gone about an hour at the most. Once in the library, I found the microfilm readers and loaded the reel that had the newspapers from spring of 1926. Jeb had been about two and a half when the incident at the mound had occurred. And he remembered everything being green and sunny, so I was betting that the murder of his father occurred between March and September of 1926.

I found what I was looking for in the paper dated 30th of June, 1926.

MAN GUNNED DOWN IN PARK IN FRONT OF WITNESSES

Rufus Peebles, 38, was found shot to death at the foot of the Criel Mound in South Charleston on Sunday afternoon. Peebles, an ex-convict recently released from prison on what many believe to be bogus charges, was meeting a friend for a picnic lunch. Two men, rumored hired guns for the Lewis-Baker Coal Company, walked up to Peebles and opened fire.

Peebles was killed instantly in front of an unnamed woman, an infant, and a young boy, suffering no less than thirteen direct shots to his torso and head. Peebles had been instrumental in organizing a labor union for coal miners at Lewis-Baker. He was involved in a dispute that left twenty men dead, six who had worked for Lewis-Baker and fourteen who were "scabs." Although his involvement in the incident had never been proven, he was convicted of killing two men, detectives for the Freedman Detective Agency out of Morgantown; Lawrence Bradley and Edward Nunley. He had served three years of his twenty-five year sentence when he was unexpectedly released from prison.

I had been sitting on the edge of my seat, holding my breath while I read the article. Now I leaned back and let it out. This had to be the incident that Jeb had dreamed about over and over. It wasn't as if this crime would have been common knowledge in Baltimore. He would've had to be looking for this information to have found it. Unless he'd just happened upon it. *Had* he happened upon it? Did Jeb, at some point, find this very same article and read it, knowing that this was his father? I was sure the book would tell me, but I just hadn't gotten that far. The combination of emotion he must have felt would have been mind boggling. Even I, without ever having experienced the dream, was sitting here, a mixed bag of emotions. I was exhilarated at finding the article. Yes, I had *found* them. And then sad; the man was dead and a woman and child had witness his murder. And an infant? Who was the infant? Jeb's younger sibling? Jeb must have been both exhilarated and sad, and what else? Justified? After all, this article was proof that he wasn't insane all those years. It had all been real.

I wrote Rufus Peebles' name down on a sheet of paper that I'd brought with me. I also wrote down Lewis-Baker Coal Company. I'm not sure why I wrote them down, it wasn't as if I would need this piece of paper to remind me of these names. I would never forget them.

I scanned through the newspaper a little more. An article published a few days later about the funeral for Rufus Peebles stopped me cold. This time the article went in to a little more detail about the original charges against Peebles and how he had gone away to prison the third week of March 1923. Jeb's mother would have just probably learned that she was pregnant. The coal companies used to hire people, sometimes private detectives, and plant them as spies, to see who among their workers were pro-union. The detectives would also go in and evict miners and their families from their company-owned houses and just in general tried to make the lives of the workers as miserable as they could, so they would go back to work and quit complaining. Apparently two of these detectives—and I use that term loosely because that doesn't seem like anything a private detective would ever agree to do—turned up dead in a car in 1922, shot through the head at point-blank range, just after having given the coal company the name of the union organizer, Rufus Peebles. Charges were brought against Peebles and with no physical evidence against him whatsoever, he was found guilty and given twenty-five years to life. An investigator later learned that the jury had been rigged and all of them had some sort of interest in Lewis-Baker Coal Company. Then evidence came to light as to who the real shooter was, and Rufus Peebles was released from prison.

The thing that stopped me cold was a photograph taken the day of the funeral. There was a casket and flowers, with lots of miners and men staring at the ground and looking properly sad. In fact, I'd never seen so many people at a funeral. I assumed that they were all the coal miners that Peebles had tried to help over the years. But it was the woman standing off to the right, holding a little boy—it was her image that raised the hair on the back of my neck. It was

Jeb, being held by his mother, looking over his shoulder at the photographer. Big eyes, sad and scared. He probably didn't understand that the man in the casket had been his father; after all, the man had been in prison all of the boy's life. I'm certain he probably didn't understand much of what was happening at that moment at all. But he must have understood the mood, and understood his mother's tears. And the look he gave the camera was unmistakable. His mother had one hand clutching him to her side—poised on her hip like all women down through the ages have held their children—while the other hand tried to hide her face as she cried. I couldn't make out her features, since most of them were hidden behind her hand. But she did have very dark hair, just as Jeb had said in his dream. And once I compared her to the men in the photograph, I noticed that she was tall and thin. This had most likely been the last photograph of Jeb and his mother ever taken. Because at some point after this, she took him to the orphanage.

It was true. It had all been true. Jeb's dream had indeed been a memory of his former life. A very sad, tragic memory. Some of it had been so raw and so horrifying that it had imbedded itself somewhere in his tiny, barely formed subconscious. It had taken a seemingly innocuous event of little boys playing in the dirt, building mounds and caves, at his brother's birthday party to trigger his memories.

What I really wanted to know was the name of Jeb's mother. I wasn't aware of a Peebles family still in Wellston, so Jeb didn't come to our county looking for his father. He came there looking for his mother. Call it a gut instinct, but something told me that Jeb's quest for his father's identity had ended right here in a library very similar to this; he'd found that part of the story. It was the more elusive angle of his mother's identity that had driven him to purchase the Renshaw house on Sassafras Mountain. Women's names didn't ordinarily appear on land records or estate papers, census records or even tombstones. It was their husband's names, always. Their first names were available, usually, but never their surnames. It was as if women weren't anything until the day they married. Their clan was deemed unimportant.

A sudden adrenalin rush at discovering this information nearly took my breath away. I wanted to know more and more.

"Olivia!"

I glanced up to see Betty Jo walking toward me.

"Hi!" I said.

"You look...flushed. Are you hot?"

"Oh, I found out so much!"

"Well, good," she said. "You want to get something to eat before we head back home?"

She had already walked behind me and had grabbed the back grips of my chair and started to push. I didn't want to leave. I didn't want to go home. I felt like Miss Marple, only not quite so old or British.

"Yes. Do you think we could take a drive through South Charleston?"

"I don't see why not. Why?"

"I'd like to go by and see the Criel Mound," I said.

"Okay," she said, happily. "We went there with school one year on a field trip. I think it was seventh grade."

I would have been at the hospital at the time.

"Any special reason why you want see it?" she asked.

"I just want to."

**

Betty Jo and I gazed up at the Criel Indian burial mound. Thousands of years ago, this part of West Virginia was populated by what was known as the Adena culture. The mound had been conical in shape at one time, but the top had been removed and flattened to make a nice little stand for the horse racing judges. Was it any wonder that the Native Americans were so angry? It wasn't enough that we waltzed in and took over the land, but we took a sacred burial ground, chopped the top off, ran horses around the base of it and used the top for the place where the judges could see all the action. It would be like somebody moving into the Vatican and installing roulette wheels and blackjack tables.

Inside Criel mound had been the remains of several native peoples, buried in the ceremonious ways of their culture. They'd gone to the afterlife, never thinking their resting place would be so defiled. How could they? They could not in their wildest dreams ever imagine what lay beyond the oceans, and how it would come here one day. As silly as it was, it made me wonder what lay beyond our solar system and if this same thing would play out at some distant time in the future, only then it would be people from other galaxies. That had to be what it was like for the Native Americans.

This mound was not the only one left of the Adena culture. There was one in Moundsville, and the top of it had been spared. And for about eight miles along the upper terraces of the Kanawha River flood plain, there had been about fifty smaller mounds. This valley had been a major gathering place for those people. I knew this because I'd listened to Gunnar give a talk during history class two years ago, and I'd immediately gone to the encyclopedias at school and looked it up.

I glanced around and took a bite of my cheeseburger that Betty Jo and I had bought from a diner. We'd gotten the food to go, so we could get here and see this before having to return home. "My brother's really into all this stuff," she said.

"All what stuff?" I asked.

"Indian stuff."

She would be talking about Gunnar, not Kevin. "I know. He gave a lecture once."

She nodded. "Oh yeah, I forgot all about that. He wanted to go to South America, but...you know things don't always go like we plan."

"No, they certainly don't." I had never planned to get polio.

"I tried to tell him that there was plenty of things he could study here," she said.

"But he can't really study them, like he should, as long as he's wearing that badge," I said.

"I know," she said. "Momma's hoping it's just for a little while. We've got to get Kevin through school. Then Gunnar can get back to his Indians."

I smiled.

"So why did you want to see this?" she asked.

I shrugged. "I've never been here before," I said. Which was true. But I also wanted to see for myself the place of Jeb's tragedy. Today was a day like any other day. There was a lazy feel to it, with the sun shining and a ripple of flat clouds here and there. How many times had people stood here and thought about the native population, wondered about who built this mound, gazed up at flittering birds against blue skies and white clouds? How many times had people sat here and discussed a new dress they would buy or a movie they wanted to see? How many times had people eaten lunch under the trees, never realizing that on one specific day—June 30th 1926—something happened that changed the course of one little boy's life forever?

And devastated one woman.

"Olivia?" Betty Jo asked.

"What?"

"You were off somewhere in your mind, weren't you?"

I nodded.

"You miss him?"

I glanced at her.

"Jeb?"

"Terribly," I said. But it was more than just missing him. I was wrought with sadness at the thought of what he'd been through, only to have it all taken away again just as he had come to terms and made his peace.

She reached over and squeezed my hand. "It'll get better."

Knitting Night at Aunt Stella's

It was knitting night at Aunt Stella's house, which I had forgotten about. No sooner had I'd made it in the door from Charleston with Betty Jo than my mother handed me my bag of yarn and needles and booted me out the front door. I was about to make the turn from our driveway onto the side of the road to head down the mountain to Aunt Stella's house, when my mother came out onto the porch. "Hang on, I'll take you down!"

She grabbed a jacket and came out with a baking dish. "I made a cobbler," she said. "You should take it with you."

As if there wouldn't be all sorts of cobblers, bachelor pies, sweets and candies already there. Aunt Stella's house was past Aunt Mildred's and Aunt Runa's and around that sharp turn in the road, Pete's Curve. Then the road straightened out just a bit. Aunt Stella 's house was in flat bottom land. In fact, her home had nearly flooded from the creek on more than one occasion.

Mother pushed my chair and I held the warm pie on my lap. The sun was about ready to set and I suddenly realized that I was tired. It had been a very long day. "So, did you find what you were looking for at the library?" Mom asked.

"Yes. Which just led to more questions."

"Isn't that the way of it?"

"How am I getting home tonight?" I asked. The trip down to the aunties' houses was not difficult unless there was snow. The trip back up could be challenging, especially if I was already tired. At one time, I would have never tired. At the hospital we were constantly pushing ourselves physically. As I said, pulling myself back into my wheelchair from the ground after rolling down a hill had been easy as pie at one time. As soon as I left the hospital and moved home, things got softer. People did more for me. And there just wasn't as much need for me to haul myself up into my chair. As a result, I tired more easily. I made a mental note to come up with a way to remedy that. "Will you come and get me?"

"Either me or Clive," she said. "He's out with some friends, but he can stop by on his way home."

"As long as it's not too late. Last time he didn't show up until midnight and Aunt Stella was ready to shave his head. If he's later than eleven, tell him not to bother and I'll sleep on her couch."

Mom laughed. "It won't be that late, he's got school tomorrow. Have you finished Jeb's book?"

"Almost," I said. "His accounts of the war were harrowing. In fact, I wanted to skip them, but wouldn't. It was so difficult reading those scenes, knowing that it's all real. Knowing that he experienced those things. He didn't know until he got to Korea that his girlfriend was pregnant with his son. It's very odd..."

"What is?" she asked. A car went by and honked, we both waved without really knowing who the driver was.

"It's like he kept trying to find his mother in other women. You know?"

"No," she said.

"I think he thought if he could figure out the mystery of women, any woman, that she would somehow lead him to understanding his mother. He says about one girlfriend, and I quote, *'In Maria was the whole of all her mothers. And maybe just one of them had known mine.'*"

My mother was quiet.

"Anyway," I said. "I should probably finish it in the next few days."

"It's taking you a while to read it."

"Well, it's a long book, but I'm also paying close attention to everything he says. That takes longer than when you're just reading for fun."

We were quiet a moment, the sun now totally behind the mountains. "Mom, what year did your dad die?"

"He died the year I was born, nineteen-nineteen. Why?"

"No reason. It's just sad how some people have kids and then don't get to be with them."

Aunt Stella's house appeared on the right and Mom dropped me off on the front porch. "See you tonight," she said. "Have fun."

Upon entering Aunt Stella's house, I was taken aback by the festiveness of her living room. She'd managed to get a tree and get it decorated, and all of her lights and greenery were up, snaking around every surface that would hold them, due in part—a large part—to Clive. The living room was resplendent with holiday glow and the aroma of coffee and baked goods were sweet, buttery, warm,...intoxicating.

All the seats were taken with the knitting ladies and several called out my name. In attendance were: Eloise Dille, Pearl Hargrave, Molly Tennyson,

Aunt Dotie, Aunt Mildred, Aunt Stella, Aunt Runa, Gunnar's mom, Sally Ryan, and a few "young" folk, namely, Sarah Gerhard, Maddie Wilcox and Mary Anne Newkirk. The last three were in their late twenties to early thirties. There were about five or six other women who usually came to Aunt Stella's knitting nights and they would most likely arrive later in the evening. But, I was—by a good eight years—the youngest member.

But that was okay. I loved the old ladies. I loved the lines in their faces, the sounds of their voices, the way they smelled of vanilla, lavender toilet water and Mum deodorant. (Except, Pearl of course, whose son had bought her Chanel No. 5 in Charleston.) I loved the stories they told, the food they cooked—special flavors that only they seemed to know the secret ingredients for—and I loved the sense of safety that I felt around them. As if no matter what, a blizzard, a war, a plague or a flood of Biblical proportions, they would take care of the situation and all would be fine. Because they already had.

And I realized suddenly that even though I was in no hurry to get old, I wanted to be one of these old ladies someday. But you don't get to be all wise and knowing, nor do you get to be as comfortable as old leather, without having lived through all the trials and tribulations that they'd survived. That was a sobering thought.

I handed off the cobbler to Molly who passed it to Mary Anne, who passed it to Aunt Stella, who took it to the kitchen. Then I found a comfortable corner of the living room and parked my chair next to Sally Ryan. On the radio Bill Monroe was singing "Blue Moon of Kentucky."

Apparently, I had come in on the tail end of a story that Eloise was telling and it ended with, "I liked to never got that cow poop out of her hair." Everybody laughed, but nobody laughed harder than Eloise herself. It made me wish I'd been there for the beginning of the story. I pulled out my knitting and began my knit stitches. In comparison to the other ladies, I seemed to have been born with nothing but thumbs. My sticks clanked together and I was constantly dropping stitches and having to stop and go back and find them. I was determined to finish this scarf before Christmas.

Mrs. Ryan leaned over and said, "I see you're back from your trip with Betty Jo. Everything go well?" she asked.

For the record, I liked Gunnar's mom. She was pale and washed out, but there was a warmth to her as if she had a fire in her heart. Her hands worked the needles like a professional, every now and then she'd pull the rusty brown yarn from the basket next to her feet. She had a strong, square jawline and an intense way of looking at you when you talked, like she was actually listening to what you were saying and not just the words you were speaking. She had a familiar look about her, especially in the set of the jaw and through the eyebrows. Not unusual when you were talking about mountain people whose families had been in the same valley for hundreds of years. People start to look alike. Her father had been the Superintendent of the school district at one time. One of the great unknown questions of the valley was why Sally, an educated woman who was the daughter of two teachers, had ever ended up with James Ryan.

And, everybody else knew that her attendance at these social gatherings relied entirely on whether or not she had bruises.

"It was lovely, Sally. And it was nice of Betty Jo to think of me and ask me to go along."

"She's a doll, isn't she?"

"Yes she is."

"Gunnar's sure been talkin' about you a lot lately, too. I guess well, what with all that...business, you know. Sure am sorry about that."

"Yeah," I said. "Gunnar's a nice person, too. Well, all your kids are nice people."

"The only thing I've ever done right," she said, smiling. And the smile was genuine.

I looked down at the mess that I called a scarf. Pearl was knitting an Aran sweater, a cabled cardigan of beautiful gray wool. Maddie was making a sweater for her little boy that reminded me of the folkwear in Eastern Europe. Aunt Dotie was working on a vest for her new great-grandson to wear for Christmas. "What a lovely sweater," I said to Pearl. Pearl could be a sour puss on a monumental scale, but I noticed that if somebody complemented her as soon as they came in, she was a bright ball of sunshine and most of that cantankerous behavior could be side-stepped.

"Why, thank you," she said. "In Ireland and Scotland, the fishing wives would knit a specific pattern into their husband's sweaters so that they could be identified in case of a fishing accident."

"Oh, that's a bunch a hooey," Aunt Runa said from across the room.

Pearl set her needles down on her lap, and leveled a no-nonsense glare over the rim of her glasses at my Aunt Runa. "I beg your pardon?" Pearl asked.

"I said, that's a bunch a hooey. That's an old wives' tale. Legend. Myth. You know the Irish," Aunt Runa said with a chuckle.

"And just how would you know?" Pearl countered.

Uh-oh.

"Now, Pearlie don't go gettin' in a snit," Aunt Dotie said.

"I'll have you know," Pearl said. "That I have a mind like a steel trap. Are you sayin' that I don't, Runa Montgomery?"

Aunt Runa laughed and said, "Nobody's saying you don't remember it right, I'm saying that your information was wrong to begin with. I traipsed all over the coast of Scotland and Ireland, and what you said about those patterns being used to identify dead husbands is folklore."

Pearl picked up her knitting needles and resumed knitting, but not without making a very agitated sound in the back of her throat. She didn't inquire as to how Aunt Runa actually knew that information, though. Had that been the first thing she'd asked when she got off the boat? It seemed unlikely. Still, Pearl would sit and stew on it and I guarantee you that at some point in the near future, she'd corner Aunt Runa and ask her that exact question. Maybe that's why Runa said it. To see how long it would take Pearl to challenge her.

Social catastrophe number one had been avoided for now. But I knew, and everybody there knew, that Pearl wouldn't forget it.

Molly held up the sweater that she was knitting and one side was much larger than the other side. "Holy cow, Molly!" Aunt Dotie said from across the room. "What did you do to that sweater?"

Molly started laughing and laughing and finally she said. "It's all lopper jawed, ain't it?"

Pearl Hargrave rolled her eyes and kept knitting, hands moving at inhuman speed. She was still pouting at Aunt Runa's audacity, but everybody else laughed.

Personally, I was happy to see that I was not the only knitter on Goosefoot Mountain who was less than capable of pulling a string together with sticks and having it resemble something wearable. Knitting seemed to deny the laws of physics. I looked at everybody's projects and it seemed to me that they were all completed by a good dose of magic.

On the radio the new Kingston Trio came on to sing "Tom Dooley." It made me think of murder, which made me think of Rufus Peebles. This was the perfect time to ask about him.

The oldest person here was Eloise Dille, who had been born in eighteen-seventy eight. She'd turned eighty this year. I leaned over and said, "Eloise, I was wondering if I could ask you a question?"

"Sure, honey," she said.

"You've lived here all your life, haven't you?"

Somebody over by the kitchen said something funny and several of the ladies all laughed.

"No, no, I was actually born in Kentucky. And then we moved to Logan County when I was about ten. My Uncle Noah, though, he was a member of the Logan Wildcats."

"What's that?" asked Maddie, who was sitting in between Eloise and me. Maddie was about twenty-six, married to the local farrier, and had three children already. I never saw her when she didn't look completely exhausted.

"Oh, those Logan Wildcats, they's a bunch of hoodlums," Eloise said.

"They were a Confederate guerilla unit," I said. "Sort of like the Dalton gang. Only the wildcats were founded by Devil Anse Hatfield."

"Never heard of the Daltons, either," Maddie said.

"Well, my Uncle Noah, he was a right mean old guy," Eloise said. "He wanted to keep on killin' even after the country was done bled to death."

Not that Eloise would remember that exactly, since she wasn't born until about twelve or thirteen years after the Civil War had ended. But she would come closer to having memories of the aftermath of war than anybody else here. She was six years older than Aunt Mildred, even.

"So, when did you move here to Greenhaven?" I asked.

"Oh, 'bout nineteen and fifteen," she said. "Came up here with Teddy, God rest his soul. Came up here for logging work."

"Logging?" I asked. "Did he work with my grandpa McClintock?"

"Oh, yeah, he knew Herbert real well," she said. "Do you know that I was at Devil Anse Hatfield's baptism?"

"Really?" Maddie asked.

"Yessa, we were right there on the banks of Island Creek, there was a bunch of us in the river with him, too. I wouldn't go in the water, though, 'cause I was afraid that the water would start boiling as soon as he stepped his foot in it and I didn't want to get boiled to death. He was, after all, a good friend of the devil's. But I was right there on the bank. That was nineteen and eleven," she said. "He came up out of that water an entirely different man than when he went in. God won that day, and the devil lost. As it should be. If you get baptized in the waters and you don't come up feelin' different, it didn't work and you better redo it."

Maddie, Sally and I laughed.

"Well, I was curious," I said. "Are you familiar with a Peebles family?"

"Peebles?" she asked. "Not from around here. But there was a bunch of Peebles down in Logan County."

My pulse quickened. "Really?" I asked. "Did you know a Rufus Peebles?"

All the voices in the room seemed to hush at the exact moment that those two words came out of my mouth, as if there was a giant vacuum that had just sucked all the air and life right out through the window. I glanced around and every knitting needle whose owner was over forty grew completely still. Like they were all in a movie and somebody just shut off the projector.

"I think we need some pie!" Aunt Stella said. And with those words life returned to the room.

I glanced over at Eloise. "What just happened?" I asked.

Maddie glanced between Eloise and me. "I have no idea, but that was strange," she said.

"Now, Olivia, what would you want to know about that business for?" Eloise asked in a hushed tone, glancing over my shoulder at Sally. I cut my eyes around and noticed that Gunnar's mom had sped up her knitting to what seemed like super human powers.

"So, you knew him?" I asked.

"Not personally," she said. "That whole mess was in the papers."

"What whole mess?" I asked, just to see if she was thinking what I was thinking.

"I don't want to talk about that kind of violence on knitting night," she said. "Now, you go on and think of something else to talk about or I'm gonna find a new place to sit."

And that was that, she totally clammed up. Her jaw was set firm, and she was clearly agitated because she had to rip out five or six stitches. "Now, look what you done made me do. Purling when I shoulda been knitting."

Just then there was a knock on the door. Maddie leaned back and glanced out the window. "It's Crazy Rhea," she said.

"Now, Stella Davies, why'd you go inviting that woman?" Pearl Hargrave said.

"Now, now, Pearlie, I'm just being neighborly. If she wants to join in on knitting night, I'm sure we can find it in our hearts and my living room to let her in."

But the mood in the room had changed, rather quickly. I, for one, was shocked she came. Stella had been inviting Rhea as long as knitting night had been going on, and she'd never, not once, actually showed up. Stella opened the door and Crazy Rhea stood on the threshold in men's boots and a man's flannel coat. When she took the coat off, she was wearing a red and white checked dress that she had embroidered big blue flowers all over, and green stockings. She was also wearing an old slave turban wrapped around her head, embroidered with those same blue flowers. In her hands she carried her giant bag, and I could just barely see her knitting needles sticking out of the top of it.

Everybody said polite hellos and then Rhea reached in her bag and everybody held their breath. You simply never knew what Rhea was going to have in her purse. She pulled out a big bottle of whiskey—a homemade brew—and held it up with a toothless smile. I busted out laughing and Rhea winked at me.

"Well, all right," Aunt Stella said. "It's a cold night. A little won't hurt."

"Well, I never!" Pearl said from her throne on the couch.

"And maybe that's your problem," Eloise said under her breath. Then to Rhea, "I'm in!"

And so the eggnog had an extra special *oomph* to it that night. I tried some, just to be polite, but I felt dizzy within minutes and thought I should probably not finish it, so I gave it to Rhea, who downed it in one gulp. Aunt Runa and Aunt Mildred definitely turned their noses up to it, Aunt Stella had a little too much, and Aunt Dotie had just the right amount.

"Stella, I couldn't help noticin' that you got some ornaments out in the trash," Rhea said.

"Help yourself to them," Stella said.

"But they're broken," Pearl said.

"One man's junk is another man's treasure," Eloise added in a sing-songy voice.

"Where does she put all the stuff she gets out of the trash?" Maddie asked me.

"I'm not sure," I said. "But definitely not in her house."

"No?" she asked.

I shook my head. "No, her house is immaculate. Top to bottom. She's got a lot of knick-knacks, but there's nothing junky about the inside of her house."

Maddie just shook her head.

As the evening wound down and people started leaving, I got out of my chair and on to Aunt Stella's couch. I curled up there, with my feet under me, and continued knitting. Maddie sat next to me, working diligently on the sweater for her son. "It's taking me so long to finish this sweater, I'm afraid he's gonna outgrow it before I can give it to him!" she said, laughing.

Pearl, Eloise, Molly and Aunt Dotie had left already, and I was just waiting around for Clive to stop in to help me home. Sally had grabbed her basket, hugged Stella and hitched a ride with Aunt Dotie, since Dotie was sort of going her way.

"See you later, dear," Sally said to me.

"Look at all those photo albums," Maddie said, pointing to a shelf in Aunt Stella's living room.

"I know. She and Aunt Runa are big on pictures. Hand me that red one, no, no, the big one."

Maddie handed me the photo album that I requested. It must have weighed five pounds. Inside was an envelope of pictures that she hadn't put away into the new album. I opened the envelope and they were recent pictures. I flipped through them. There was a picture of Aunt Dotie, with her swollen ankles and hair pulled back in a bun, sitting on her porch with two of her nieces. One was on each side of her, hugging her neck, crumpling her gingham dress. Another photo was of Uncle Pete whittling wood and smoking a pipe, leaning up against a fence post. Sometimes Stella just took "everybody smile" pictures, and then other times, she really tried to compose the photograph and catch ordinary moments in people's lives. Among the "everybody smile" pictures was one that she'd taken at the picnic lunch back in August. It was of me, Jeb, my mom and Bessie standing on the front porch. And then another one of me and Jeb on the opposite side of the table from her, with our heads together, Jeb holding up a heaping plate of food and smiling. And it was a genuine smile, and he wore it naturally. If the pictures had been in color instead of black and white, I would have been able to see that vibrant green of his eyes.

I nearly choked; the sob was out of my mouth before I even knew what happened.

"Are you all right?" Maddie asked.

I swiped at my tears, glancing around the room, making sure that nobody else witnessed that.

"I'm fine," I said. "It just startled me. Wasn't expecting it."

I placed the pictures back in the envelope and made a mental note to ask Aunt Stella for the negatives so that I could have copies of those two pictures. I flipped through the big red album, because I knew it was full of old photographs.

There was the picture of Aunt Stella sitting in the graveyard with a bunch of her cousins. I always loved that picture. All the women were wearing their Sunday best, with big hats and pearls, sitting scattered amongst the tombstones.

Another photo was one of many school yard pictures, where the teacher had lined all the kids up in front of the schoolhouse, or maybe in a field. I knew this one well, and could recite who all the kids were. My grandma Blanche was third row, fourth from the left. The tallest kid in the picture.

But this time, there was a photograph that caught my eye that I'd always passed right by before. I'd gotten used to being told, "Oh, that's a cousin." Or "Oh, that's a neighbor." And if I didn't really know the people, I would just move on. Unless it was a really outstanding photograph for whatever reason. For example, any pictures that my aunts had of World War I, I had completely memorized. Hours and hours of staring at every face, every torn uniform, ripped jacket, worn boots, haunted eyes, the ancient motorcycles and cars, the horses that most of the war had been fought with. I didn't know any of the soldiers, but I still could not stop studying them.

But this picture, the one that caught my attention, was not a photograph from the old war. This was of a boy, sitting on a blanket in the grass, holding a wooden horse, looking up at the camera with an expression of amused curiosity. I tried to remember what Aunt Stella had told me about this photo. Was this one of the "oh, that's a cousin" photos? I pulled the picture from its black triangle edging that had held it in place for who knew how long. I peeked at the back. It simply said, "My boy. 1925." I wasn't sure whose boy he was, but I knew one thing: it was Jeb McDowell. The same baby whose image had stared back at me from the newspapers.

A Letter from Aunt Viola to Olivia

Olivia VanBibber
Greenhaven, West Virginia
December 1958

Dearest Olivia,

I do hope this letter finds you in a bit of a better mood and spirits. I feel to write to you of mundane things would be to trivialize what Mr. McDowell meant to you, but then I also believe that as soon as you can return to normal routines the better.

How did you celebrate Mr. Twain's birthday? Both of the boys were here for Thanksgiving, it was lovely to see them and their families. I spoke to Mildred Anne yesterday and she told me all about your Thanksgiving celebration. It seems as though she and Edwin may end up tying the knot after all. After years of "courting" they may make it official, I am told, by spring. Of course this is a very poorly kept secret, which half of the county already knows, so you absolutely cannot tell anybody. But if there is a wedding, I guess I'll be coming for a visit.

Of course, she also told me at length about Mr. McDowell's plans for a Wellston Public Library and how you are to head it. Livvy, my dear, I can't think of anything more perfect for you. Or for Wellston. How gracious of him. Now the county will have an actual library, not an outhouse with a few books crammed in it, and you will have a job for as long as you want it! Make no mistake that he has given you an incredible opportunity, but that you will be the one doing the work. This isn't a hand-out to you. He's just opened the door. Take full advantage of it.

When you feel like resuming our regular correspondence of book reviews, let me know. I do hope that Gunnar puts this whole mess to rest soon. I've only met him once or twice when I was back home visiting, but he seems a very capable man, and certainly a better one than his father. Of course, I suppose I shouldn't really say such things. Men who are "sick" with drink don't really behave like they would if they were well. The trick is to not get "sick" in the first place.

Chin up, dear girl.

Lots of love,
Aunt Viola

Precariousness

On his way to school the next day, Clive dropped me off at the Sheriff's office in Wellston. My mother had to be at the diner she worked at before six in the morning and would be getting off from work at one in the afternoon and agreed to come take me home. So, at eight in the morning I wheeled into the sheriff's office and asked to speak to Gunnar. He was busy.

So, I sat in the tiny waiting room, watching the people walk by on the streets outside. It was cold, the first honest to goodness cold day of the year, and flurries floated to the ground with no real determination. A Greyhound bus stopped across the street to pick up passengers, kicking up slushy gray stuff as it came to a stop. Wellston didn't have public transportation, but the Greyhound did make a stop twice a day on its way to and from Charleston, and in the opposite direction to Morgantown and Wheeling.

"Well, well, look what the cat drug in," Deputy Boland said. I glanced up to see him leaning against the wall with a cup of coffee in his hand. I couldn't find suitable adjectives for how this man made me feel. His thick lips always seemed to have a pasty coating of something in the corners, and his eyebrows were like bushy wooly worms that moved in waves across his forehead. Disconcerting as those things may be, they hardly made him a bad person. No, it was his eyes that told me what type of person he was. They were at once cold and hungry, and I knew that he would never be warm or satiated.

"It's 'dragged,' you moron." I looked out the window.

I couldn't see what sort of effect my words had on him because I was too busy watching the shoppers passing by on their way to purchase Christmas presents.

"So, how's your boyfriend, Clive?" he asked.

My face flushed, but I still stared right out the window, although I was so incensed that I didn't actually see anything anymore. All I saw was a blur of red.

"It's okay, Olivia," he said. "It's not like he's actually related. I see what you see in him."

I began singing in my head, *T is the season to be jolly. Fa la la la la, la la la la.*

"Of course now, I'm not real sure what he sees in you, exactly. Other than you can't run away."

"No, more like that's your fantasy Deputy Boland," I said and unlocked the brakes on my chair. I wasn't going to sit here and listen to him. I was going to run right over him.

"Sorry about that," Gunnar said, suddenly from the doorway. "I was on the phone."

Gunnar exchanged glances with me, and then he looked to Boland. "Don't you have something to do?" he asked him.

Boland just smiled.

"I can find something for you to do," Gunnar said.

Boland turned then, to go back to his desk, and Gunnar sat down on the bench that was next to me. "What did he say to you?"

I just shrugged, too angry to speak.

"He said *something*. Your whole face is red."

"I'm fine," I said and took a deep breath. "But don't you have to sort of be, I don't know, a good guy to be in law enforcement?"

Gunnar laughed, but not too loudly. "Sadly, no."

"Well, that's just ridiculous. It should be a requirement."

"I'll mention it at the next staff meeting. What brings you in? Is everything okay?"

"I wanted to talk to you about Jeb. And what I learned."

Gunnar glanced around. "Okay," he said. "Let's go down the street and get some coffee."

"I don't drink coffee."

"Then you can have tea," he said, smiling.

Gunnar grabbed his coat and then we headed outside. He walked along beside me, never offering to push my chair, which was weird. Everybody pushed my chair. So, I gladly pushed myself, using small hand towels so that I didn't get the winter slush all over my hands. "My sister said she had a good time with you yesterday," he said.

"Delightful," I said. "I'm very keen on your sister. She treats everybody the same."

"She said you wanted to see the Criel mound." He walked with his hands in his pockets, nodding occasionally to people that he passed. "I love the mounds. Have you ever seen any of the Indian petroglyphs?"

"Only in pictures."

"My Grandpa found one years before I was born and showed it to me when I was just a kid. I've never told anybody about it and as far as I can tell, none of academia even knows about it."

I glanced up at him. His cheeks had turned ruddy from the cold. He nodded to a passerby, then looked back down at me. His blue eyes sparkled with excitement. "It's a man and he has the weeping eye motif. Do you know what that is? What it looks like?"

"Yes, I do," I said.

"I wish you could see it."

Just then we came to T.J's Diner and he opened the door for me. I pushed myself in and took the first table that was free. "You do realize that this is where my mother works," I said.

"Oh, that's right. Well, we can go someplace else."

"No, this is fine," I said, smiling.

Within minutes my mother made her way over to our table, and without looking asked, "How y'all doing? You like some coffee?" Then she handed us the menus and stopped. "Olivia."

"Hi, Mom."

"I'll have coffee, Mrs. Morrison," Gunnar declared. "And some pie. Whatever sort you've got."

"And I'll have a cup of hot tea," I said.

She gave us both a quizzical look and said, "Be right back."

"Rosie! Order up!" I heard the cook say from behind the counter.

After spending a few moments settling in and taking in the surroundings, I met Gunnar's gaze. He'd been watching me; studying me, like I do with other people. It was not as unpleasant as I would have thought, but it made me feel peculiar.

"Well, what I've got to tell you...it might upset you."

"What?" I asked.

"You were right. Jeb did get mixed up in something illegal."

"What?" I said. A heaviness settled in my chest.

"Well, from what I can tell, Clarence Ford is the number one suspect in a high-profile bank robbery in Baltimore. He's been in prison before for this very thing. The police that I talked with said they've not been able to get proof that Ford was involved, so they haven't arrested him."

"What's that got to do with Jeb?"

"He was tricked into driving the getaway car. He had no idea what was happening. He panicked and brought the money with him here, to Greenhaven."

I worked my lower lip between my teeth.

"What are you thinking?" he asked.

Mom came back with our coffee and tea. Gunnar thanked her, but Mom looked uneasy. As if she wanted to say something to him, but not with me sitting there. After a moment she left.

"How do you know this?" I asked.

"I interviewed Holly Springfield," he said. "And I spoke with the Baltimore police."

"So, Ford was here looking for the money?"

Gunnar nodded. "Or for revenge. Either way."

"So you think Clarence killed him?"

Gunnar took a deep breath. "I think it's a good possibility."

A thought suddenly occurred to me. "You don't think..."

"What?"

"That the money Jeb left for the library—"

"No," Gunnar cut me off. "I've already checked. The money he left was his money, legitimately. He honestly had done nothing with the money from the robbery, except stuff it in the outhouse."

Relief swept over me. I would not be able to live with the fact that Jeb had given money, no matter how good the cause, if it wasn't his to give. I should have known better. Jeb McDowell may not have always made honorable decisions in all aspects of his life, but somewhere along the line, he became honorable. So, I took a deep breath and filled Gunnar in on what I'd learned at the library in Charleston about his father's murder and my suspicions that his mother, or her family, was still living here.

"Have you ever figured out what the quote was from the book? The words he said when he was dying?"

"No," I said. "I don't know how I would ever figure it out, unless I just happened upon it. To be honest, it's most likely a Thomas Wolfe quote."

"Why do you say that?"

"Wolfe was one of his favorite authors," I said. "And the language...it sounds like him. I don't know that it meant anything, other than he wanted the last words that left his mouth to be those of his idol. Just as easily could have been Whitman."

"Except his very last words were about you," he said.

I glanced down and fought back tears.

"So, do you think Jeb knew somebody here? Like, he'd come here for help, if he got mixed up in something bad?" Gunnar asked.

"No," I said. "I think he strictly came here looking for his mother."

Gunnar ran his thumb around the rim of the coffee cup. "Any idea who that might be?"

I smiled. "No, but my Aunt Stella knew whoever it was. I found a picture of Jeb, as a baby, in one of her photo albums."

"How do you know it was him?"

"I've seen other pictures of him as a baby. It's him."

"Could his mother have been your Aunt Stella?"

I shrugged. "Right now, Gunnar, I think it could have been anybody. You know Wellston and Greenhaven are a close-knit group. All I know is that at some point, nearly all of my aunts and uncles lived in Charleston, except Dotie. And most of them worked at the Bend at some point, too. It can't be Viola because she'd already moved to Cleveland before 1923—the year Jeb was born. So, those three are out."

"So you think it's one of your great aunts?"

"I'm going to have to seriously sit down and make out a time-line of all of my aunts' lives up until 1927. Gunnar, it could even have been my grandma, Blanche."

"Really?" he asked.

"Her first husband died in nineteen-nineteen, second husband was dead by nineteen-twenty-two. My mom's youngest sister was born in nineteen-twenty-two and Jeb was conceived sometime around February of nineteen-twenty-three. Blanche died in December of 1926. If she knew she was sick, and Rufus had just been murdered..."

"You really think Jeb could have been your uncle?"

I took a deep breath and nodded. "He could have been. And it would certainly explain why he latched on to me so quickly."

Gunnar looked down at his coffee and laughed.

"What?"

"Maybe Jeb 'latched on to you' because you were the first to befriend him. You were the nicest person and most approachable person in the county, and you're a big reader. That's sort of a plus with writers. I think he just liked you."

I took a sip of my tea. "Chances are, we were related. I feel it in my gut."

"I'm not doubting that. I'm doubting that the *only* reason he took to you was because you were kin. After all, if he was a relative of yours, then he was related to a hell of a lot of other people, too."

I shrugged.

"What about your dad's family?"

"What about them?"

"Could he be related on that side?"

"I doubt it."

"Why?"

"If he is related on that side, he's got more character in his pinky than all of them put together."

Gunnar smiled up at me without fully lifting his head. He suddenly appeared boyish, charming, and I found it disconcerting. I needed him to be Gunnar, The Professional. I wanted to feel secure in the fact that he was going to get his man.

"Besides, none of Hiram's family ever lived in Charleston, nor did they work at the Bend. And even though my dad's family knows my mom's family, none of them have ever given my Aunt Stella a picture of their baby before. No, it's my grandmother's family, I'm sure of it," I said.

"And how does that make you feel?"

"I don't know," I said. "I don't know how I feel. I want to know the answer of who he is. Yet, now that it's my family I can't help but wonder if I should just let it lie. As long as it was somebody else's family that I was going to trample all over and turn upside down, I didn't give it much thought. It's different somehow, when it's my own."

"Olivia, you are the most honest person I know," he said, smiling.

"I don't know how else to be."

"I know," he said. "That's what makes it so great."

I was uncomfortable suddenly. "Well, what evidence do you have from the crime scene?"

"No fingerprints, not a lot, really. Some smudgy footprints."

"And the murder weapon? It was still lodged in his chest."

"Just your average hunting knife that you could buy anywhere. Shoot, Arnie's probably got four of them on the shelf right now."

"So, what about the prowler?" I asked.

"I've pretty much figured that out, but I'm not at liberty to say right now. It's an active investigation, Olivia."

That sort of irked me. I was sharing all of my information with him, after all. But I thought about it a second and realized that this was his job, and if telling me somehow compromised his case, I'd never forgive myself. So, I let it go. But, now I really wanted to know what he knew even more than before!

"So, how does somebody go into a person's house, struggle with him, kill him and leave nothing behind but smudged shoeprints?" I asked.

"Infuriating, isn't it?" he asked. "Maybe you could come by the station sometime and look at the evidence that was collected from his house. See if anything stands out. You know, something that was obviously not his."

I nodded. "Of course."

"That might be easier than trying to see if something was missing."

"Just say when," I said.

"So, are you going to tell me how you go hunting?"

I smiled at him. "You want me to tell you my secrets?"

"I'm dying to know how you get up in the hills."

I grew still then. I wasn't so sure I wanted to tell Gunnar this. It was personal. And it only highlighted my handicap all the more, and since I was forever trying to behave as though I didn't really have a handicap, telling him seemed counterproductive. But he sat there, waiting patiently, smiling a gentle smile, slowly moving his thumb back and forth across the rim of his mug. What would he do with the information? Nothing. It wasn't as if he was going to make fun of me, or run and tell everybody, or put an article in the paper. What could it hurt? Nothing, except he would know and that somehow seemed like a violation.

Would I have told Jeb if he asked? Yes, in a heartbeat. But Gunnar wasn't Jeb. Gunnar was the brother of one of my best friends. One of my only real friends. He was a neighbor. He was a deputy in the sheriff's department. He wasn't the man who had bared his soul to me and changed my life like Jeb had. It came down to one thing. Gunnar was a man. And I didn't trust men. Willie Gene, Clive, Uncle Pete, Jeb, the list was pretty small. But Gunnar had never given me any reason not to trust him. He just hadn't passed any tests because he hadn't been given any. Never had any reason to.

But hadn't he just told me about the petroglyph? He'd trusted me with that.

"Willie Gene straps me onto his back, like a papoose," I said quickly and quietly. There it was out. Now he could laugh or make fun of me or belittle me or whatever he wanted. I took the chance, I said it out loud.

His expression dropped. "What? How do you mean?"

"He straps me onto his back. I face away from him and carry the weapons. Then he just walks into the woods. It's not like we go far or that he's carrying me for miles. There are a few tree stands that we use, but most of the time we just set up on the forest floor. I wait for whatever prey to come along and voila. I'm hunting. To be honest, I just like to be in the woods. And once, there was this huge buck that came into a clearing one morning. I'll never forget it. There was frost everywhere, and just a dusting of snow. He was so beautiful and so majestic with all of his points. I begged Willie Gene not to kill him."

"And did he?" Gunnar asked.

"No, he let him go. To tell you the truth, I think he was just as awed as I was at that moment."

Gunnar smiled and shook his head. "Don't take this the wrong way, but that can't be easy. I mean, you *are* a wisp of a girl, but still. What are you, five foot?"

"Five-foot two."

"And...a hundred pounds?"

"Give or take five."

"Climbing these hills with you on his back... That's impressive for an old man."

"He says it's no different than carrying the dead deer," I countered.

"True. So how does he get the deer out if you get one?"

"Sometimes we have Clive with us, and he gets carcass duty. Other times, he just carries me out and goes back in for it."

He leaned back and crossed his arms, smiling at me. "Huh," was all he said. But there was something going on behind those blue eyes. And he hadn't laughed or made fun of me.

Analyzing

Aunt Viola had been correct. I needed to read something light and happy so I chose to reread *A Room With a View*, rather than *Jane Eyre* and wished at once that I could move to Windy Corner and be neighbors with Lucy Honeychurch. It got my mind off of so much negativity. I knew I should finish reading Jeb's book, but just couldn't bring myself to do it. The last chapter I'd read he had met the woman to be his wife and had his son. Reading these extremely intimate and personal scenes, for me, felt like I'd been given my own personal keyhole into his life. It was heart-wrenching.

I just flat-out didn't want to finish Jeb's book. Because his book was the last conversation that he and I would ever have. It was one long confession to me, told over days and days, but it was his words, with his sentences, his phrasing, his keystrokes, and his brutal honesty. And when I was finished with it, then Jeb would really be gone. I just kept putting it off. Besides, I really didn't think it was going to tell me who his killer was and I couldn't for a moment believe he'd actually give the name of his mother. He would have had too much respect for that. So, why finish it? I procrastinated and kept reading other things.

Lucy Honeychurch and George Emerson were good enough company for me right now. I hoped Jeb would forgive me.

Presently, I was at Aunt Mildred's sitting on her back porch, reading, in my opinion, Forster's best book. The weather simply could not make up its mind if it wanted to remain autumn or plow into winter. Today was an autumn day, about fifty degrees and unseasonably warm for December. So it was tolerable to sit here and read, as long as the sun was shining on me. Of course, I could read at my house, but there was always the chance of running into the calamity known as Bessie VanBibber, and I avoided calamity at all costs, even if it meant sitting outside in the winter. I swear she was like a plague.

I glanced up and saw Aunt Mildred walking down by the creek. She was gathering kindling, which was not unusual. She always said that the branches that fell by the creek were better for kindling because they'd been lying there longer. I have no idea if that's true. I think like so many of us, she just liked to get out and about. And she moved well for someone who was seventy-something. Edwin must have knocked on the door and hadn't gotten an answer, because just as I was about to put my nose back in the book, he stepped around the corner of the house.

"Hey, Olivia."

"Oh, hi, Edwin. Sorry, I didn't hear you knock."

"That's all right," he said. "I figured youse were out back."

He stepped on around, and grabbed the rail to help him up the porch steps. I was reminded of what Aunt Stella had told me, how he'd hurt his knee jumping out of a tree trying to scare my great grandpa. It sounded like something he'd do. In an odd way, he and my Aunt Mildred were a good match. I wondered about the letter Aunt Viola sent, and weighed whether or not I should mention the fact that I knew about the wedding, but then thought maybe they wanted to make a "surprise" announcement and didn't mention it. Christmas was coming up and people did a lot of announcing things over the holidays, since everybody was together. It saved having to tell the story over and over. "Where's Mildred?" he asked.

I nodded. "She's down getting kindling."

"What?" he asked and whirled around. "What in tarnation is wrong with that woman?"

"She's not an invalid," I said, smiling.

"It's winter."

"It's warm."

"She'll catch her death."

"It's warm," I repeated.

"It's winter! Don't matter if it's warm or not."

"Technically, it's still autumn."

He hobbled down the steps pretty quickly, if one could hobble quickly, and got about halfway between Aunt Mildred's house and the creek and yelled, "Mildred Anne! Whatcho you doing, you crazy woman?" Then he limped the rest of the way to the creek.

I laughed, but took that break to go into the kitchen and get something to drink. I sat at the kitchen table mulling over all the things Gunnar had said to me the other day, and things I'd said to him. I needed to make a time-line of my great aunts' lives because I was seventy-five percent sure that one of them had been Jeb's mother. Not that it mattered. Did I believe one of them killed him? No. Why would they?

So then why did it matter to me who his mother was?

Because it had been important to Jeb. He'd come all the way down here to find her. And the truth was I wanted to know, simply because I couldn't stand not knowing. It wasn't as though I had to tell anybody what I found out, and probably wouldn't. I thought about it seriously for a moment. Was it really one of my relatives? Aunt Stella had worked at that boarding house, she could have befriended any number of people who could have been Jeb's mother and sent her the photograph. It could have been a neighbor, a cousin, a church member, or a hundred different boarders or employees. The problem was, I couldn't just ask her, even though that would certainly be the most straightforward and logical way of discovering the truth. But if Stella or one of our relatives really was Jeb's mother, that would put her in a very awkward position, and she could end up lying about it anyway.

It hurt my head to think about it. But still, I found myself grabbing a pencil and a notebook from Aunt Mildred's counter and making my list. When I was finished I had eliminated three of my grandma's siblings. Runa was married during the years 1922-1923 and living right next door in the house she'd lived in since before going to Europe. Not to mention, she'd just given birth to her daughter about three months before Jeb was born. So, it wasn't Runa.

Dotie, also happily married, was about thirty-one years old and in between having child number five and six. I didn't think it was too believable that she could have had an affair with Rufus Peebles under the eyes of everybody. Not to mention, if she did, why not just pass Jeb off as her husband's? I'd have to check but I didn't think she was employed at the boarding house during those years, either. She would have been far too busy with her own family. She had worked there more around 1912-1916.

The last one that I crossed off was Aunt Viola. She had gone to France in 1918 when she was only eighteen years old. She met Eckhard during World War I while nursing him back to health. They stayed in France until about 1921, then went to Germany, where Eckhard put his affairs in order and said good-bye to his family. They returned to the states in late 1922, stayed in West Virginia for a few short weeks, then moved to Ohio. I knew this because Aunt Viola and I had just discussed this very thing about six months ago. So, it wasn't Viola.

I had serious doubts about Aunt Colinda, although I hadn't scratched her off the list entirely. In 1923 when Jeb was born, she was 38 years old. She'd been married to Uncle Clem since 1907. I supposed there was always the chance that she could have had an affair with Rufus Peebles. He would have been about the same age as she was. But how could she have hidden a pregnancy from her husband? And again, if she found out she was pregnant, why not just pass Jeb off as her husband's and keep him? Aunt Colinda and Uncle Clem had died childless. I can't help but think that if she was Jeb's mother, that she would have kept him. She'd have had no reason to give him up. Unless Clem knew he wasn't his father, knew she'd had an affair, and forced her to give him up. But they were living in Charleston at the time. So, a good distance from Greenhaven, and a good distance from the Bend. She was a possible candidate, but very unlikely.

So, that left Hazel, Mildred, Stella and my great-grandma, Blanche. Blanche was a widow at the time, so a very real possibility. Hazel was in between husbands, and would have been about thirty-three at the time. Also a very good candidate. Aunt Mildred would have been on the older side, thirty-seven, but she was single at the time. She didn't marry Uncle John until she was forty-something. She'd never had any children. Still, her age made me hesitate, not to mention, she might not even have been here: she'd gone to France during World War I, and I'm not entirely certain when she had returned. She may not have even been in the country by 1922. I'd have to check on that, too.

And lastly, Aunt Stella. She would have been twenty-seven, but she was married at the time. However, she was the one who had Jeb's picture in her album, which lent a lot of credence to that theory. All four women had worked at the Bend off and on from about 1910 all the way up to about 1938.

So, I realized with a big sigh, that I'd have to find out who worked at the Bend from 1922 to 1926. I'd bet money that Rufus met Jeb's mother at the boarding house. Jeb was conceived in 1922. But Jeb can clearly remember the boarding house as late as the night she surrendered him, which would have been 1926. It was a three-year window.

How was I going to figure this out? I couldn't ask any of the remaining women on the list, and my great-grandma was dead anyway. So, I needed to ask one of the women I had eliminated, or somehow find some sort of records for the boarding house, if they existed. If I could find a birth certificate for Jeb, that would certainly answer the question, but I had no idea what his birth name was. Would he even have been born with the last name Peebles, or would he have been born with the last name Graham? Or the last names of my married aunts? Still, that was a possibility. And I'd have to know what county he was born in. But still, I could check all the courthouses in the surrounding counties, and just check every birth record for 1923, providing of course, nobody lied about anybody's names on the records. And I'd have to actually get somebody to take me to the courthouses

Just then, Aunt Mildred and Edwin came in from outside, her gray hair wispy and standing out around her head, all tousled from the wind. "I'm just saying that you should at least put a scarf on yer head, Mildred," Edwin said.

"What are you doing, Olivia?" Mildred asked. "Would you like some tea or cocoa?"

"Oh, just something I'm working on," I said. "No, I think I'm going to get going."

"How are you getting home? Clive's not out of school for another hour or two."

"Oh, I'm going to call mom at the diner and have her pick me up on her way home. She should be getting ready to leave."

"You want me to just take you on down there?" Edwin asked. "I gotta run into Wellston for new tires anyway. I just come by to see if Mildred needed anything or if she wanted to go along. Or I can just drop you off at your house."

"Uh...why don't you just take me to Wellston. That sounds like a good plan."

Deputy Gunnar Ryan
Colton County Sheriff's Department

Damn. Gunnar hated knowing bad things about people. Especially when it was going to hurt a completely innocent person.

He had found Humpy VanBibber, and he was on his way to talk to the idiot now.

Several weeks ago he had put out his feelers in Charleston, not certain he'd get a hit, but he finally did. He knew Humpy pretty well. He'd gone to high school with him, although Humpy had been a freshman the year Gunnar was a senior. But he knew Humpy well enough to know what kind of man he was, what he did when he got a little cash under his belt, the types of places he'd hang around if he was trying to lay low. The Sunday Humpy had had the fight with Jeb he'd mentioned that he was going to Charleston, and Gunnar took him at his word, because Humpy would have been too stupid to have thought of anything else. Not to mention, if he was not Jeb's killer—and Gunnar was pretty sure he wasn't—he probably hadn't even known about Jeb for the first few days.

Charleston was the biggest city Humpy could disappear in quickly. If Gunnar had been Humpy, he would have gone to Charleston for a short while and then moved on to Kentucky or Ohio, possibly even Pennsylvania. Only a fool would stay in West Virginia. A fool and somebody who depended wholeheartedly on his friends for survival. And Humpy was both.

Shortly after Jeb's death, Gunnar had gone down to Charleston and dropped off copies of Humpy's mugshot at a few of the hotels and dives and had followed up on the "wanted" ad with the local authorities there, too. Humpy's picture was all over Charleston, although not out in public, because Gunnar didn't want to scare him off. Humpy was a drunk and a womanizer, all Gunnar had to do was wait. Humpy had to get arrested sooner or later. But enough time had passed that Gunnar had almost given up and decided maybe Humpy was actually being smart. Maybe he'd grown a brain between those two giant cauliflower ears of his and cleaned up his act. But then, Gunnar had gotten a phone call this morning from the owner of an establishment of questionable reputation, and Gunnar's hope for a painless end to this story went flying out the window.

No, Humpy had not grown a brain. In fact, he'd gotten stupider.

The back of the photos that Gunnar had handed out had Humpy's vital statistics listed on the back. Including aliases: Benjamin Dorsey VanBibber, Ben VanBibber, Benjamin Dorsey, Humpy VanBibber, Humpy Van and Gunnar's personal favorite, Humpy Bibber.

These were all the names that Olivia's brother had been arrested under, or names he was using at the time of his arrests. All of the arrests had been for petty things, Gunnar realized, such as misdemeanors and drunk and disorderly, but still, Humpy had a record. In a town the size of Wellston, Humpy was just about as close to a bona fide criminal as they usually got.

And what happens to small-time fish when they get into a big pond? They usually go a little crazy. And often, they start bragging about things that they've never done. So, Roddy Jennings had given Gunnar a call and told him that there was a guy staying in one of his rooms by the name of Benjamin Dorsey and that he'd only surfaced long enough to buy more booze and pick out a different prostitute for the night's entertainment. The last prostitute had gotten a little worried when, Mr. Dorsey told her that he'd robbed a bank and was wanted for murder. She also reported that he'd had a bag full of cash.

Humpy, the dumb ass, was on a month-long bender with stolen cash from the Maryland bank robbery. Either that or, stupider still, he had committed a robbery between Wellston and Charleston, and had just moved up the ladder from petty criminal to actual criminal.

How would Gunnar break this to Olivia? To her mother, Rosalee? Gunnar didn't even want to think about it, so he went back to watching the river.

The Kanawha River looked especially beautiful this morning, as he drove along the winding road. The early morning sun sparkled off of the water, and Gunnar took note of his anticipation that every bend in the river brought. What lay ahead? It was winter, so it wasn't as though there was a lot of color, but winter held its own beauty and served its own purpose. He loved spring all the more because there was a winter. He could never live in a place that had no change of seasons. He'd grow bored before the year was out. It was the ever-changing face of Appalachia that he loved, and yet, it was the seemingly unchanging view of the mountains and the rivers that kept him grounded. He had made the drive to Charleston before. But not often enough to have it memorized, so the drive was still interesting.

He realized with a heavy heart that he would be enjoying the drive much more if he had more pleasant business to attend to. He really hated drunks. And he had wondered more than once if maybe he was the wrong person to come down here and retrieve Olivia's brother. Was he too close to this one because of Olivia? Was he biased because of his father? Would Olivia be mad at him for finding Humpy like this? Would Humpy fight him? Would he be drunk? Because if he was drunk, Gunnar thought he might just pummel him right then and there. And that wouldn't be good.

Gunnar was not prone to violence. You live with a violent alcoholic long enough and you become one of two things; just like him, or just his opposite. Gunnar was pretty much the opposite—at least he hoped—but every now and then something just flipped his switch and made him so angry that he honestly felt like he wanted to hurt somebody. And that scared him. He'd kept it in check pretty much his whole life, except for that one incident when he'd been away at school in Ohio and he and a friend had gotten jumped on the way out of a nightclub. But their lives had been on the line. He wouldn't apologize for that incident, no matter how many times it visited him in his dreams. No matter the guilt he felt for how badly he'd hurt the two men. It had been self-defense.

But that incident in Ohio had taught him one valuable lesson. Hurting one individual never hurts just the one individual. Every person on this planet had a deep and far-reaching root system and it led to lots of other people, attached and tethered by their own root systems. And nowhere was that more obvious than in small towns. Whatever transpired between Humpy and him, in the next few hours, it could affect more than just the two of them. And that was what he dreaded the most.

He made a few stops first. Since he was here, he thought he may as well purchase a few Christmas presents. It took him all of forty-five minutes to do so, because he knew exactly what he was looking for. Besides, Humpy was on a bender. He wouldn't be awake until noon, and so he wasn't going anywhere. Then Gunnar pulled over and filled up the gas tank.

Maybe you could pull out the fishing rods and go fishing, too, while you're at it, you idiot. Good Lord, how ridiculous could he be? Stopping for Christmas presents? He was stalling and he knew it and yet, he couldn't help himself. All it did was delay the inevitable. The moment when he would cease to be Olivia's friend and the moment he would become the big bad law enforcement officer who found her brother in a flop house, wasted beyond measure. But this was his job, this was his case, and he sure as hell wasn't going to allow anybody else to come down here and get Humpy.

Gunnar finally pulled into the diner parking lot at about eleven-fifteen in the morning. The building looked like it was concrete, painted white, dingy and sooty in the corners and the edges. The words ROD'S GRUB were painted on the big window in white letters, shadowed in blue. Inside, people were eating breakfast. Although the clientele were of the lower income and social category, judging by the cars in the parking lot and the clothes the customers wore, the place was pretty respectable and fairly clean. On the upper stories, the windows were smudged and dirty, and Gunnar had the distinct impression that Rod hadn't put as much effort into cleaning the "hotel" part of his building as he had the restaurant. He wasn't actually sure this place could even be considered a hotel, motel or even a flop house. It looked more like dorm rooms. He got out and checked his weapon, and headed around the back. He found an entrance that had no actual door any longer. The hinges were still there, and he thought he saw what might have been the door, leaning up behind the trashcan about fifty feet away. Once inside, he found stairs leading up to the rooms beyond. Taking a deep breath, he double-checked his gun, holstered it, and headed upstairs. He was looking for room number four.

It was quiet. All the residents had either gotten their use out of the rooms in the middle of the night and left, or they were all in a drug and alcohol-induced stupor. He was banking on the latter.

The pungent smell of urine was so thick and heavy that Gunnar gagged. He shook his head, cracked his neck trying to get his focus back, and quietly crept down the hallway to room number four. Slowly, he pulled out his gun, stepped next to the door and stood off to the side to listen. He honestly didn't believe that Humpy would shoot him through the door, but honestly believing that somebody wasn't going to hurt them had been the last thoughts of too many people just before being shot to smithereens.

He'd thought about how to do this. He wasn't going to knock, but he also doubted the room was unlocked. He walked down to the end of the hall and tried the door on one of the other rooms to gauge how flimsy the locks were. The door was thin, but not thin enough that he thought he could bust it down without injuring himself and giving Humpy a chance to get away. The best he could hope for was that Humpy would jump out the window and break a leg, saving Gunnar the trouble of chasing him, but that probably wouldn't happen.

He slunk back down the hall and made his way to the diner. He'd try the easiest route: getting a key from the owner.

A skinny, elderly waitress came up to the counter. It was the same waitress who'd been working the day that Gunnar had distributed Humpy's pictures. "Hep you, sir?"

"Looking for Roddy," Gunnar said.

She nodded at a booth, and Gunnar went over, glancing around to see if Humpy just happened to be eating breakfast, but no such luck. He sat down in the booth across from Roddy, the owner of this fine establishment, and said, "Gunnar Ryan, Colton County Sheriff. We spoke on the phone."

Roddy was a young punk, which totally threw Gunnar off. He'd been expecting some old balding guy with a beer belly, but instead, he'd gotten an ex-con. He could tell by looking. Roddy was about thirtyish, but had all the tell-tale signs of somebody who'd been living for half a century: massive amounts of crow's feet, deep pocked-marked skin, a missing bottom tooth, greased-back hair that curled at his neck. In general, his coloring looked like he hadn't seen the sun in ten years, pasty and shiny all at the same time. Roddy looked up from his crossword puzzle and gave Gunnar the once over. Sizing him up, judging him, just as Gunnar had done to him seconds before.

Roddy then glanced around the diner. "I don't wanna be no tattle tale," he said. "But I'm on the up and up, now. You got me? I want no trouble and I got no patience for a wanted man in my place of business. Yeah?"

"Yeah," Gunnar said. "I understand."

"I done my time and I'm honest now."

"Sure, all right," Gunnar said

"But I also can't afford to become known as a tattle tale. Yeah?"

"My lips are sealed. Just give me the key to the room."

Roddy sucked the air through the gap in his bottom teeth and shook his head, as if he just couldn't believe what he was about to do. He got up and made his way to the counter, pulled out an old metal box that squawked when he opened it, and handed Gunnar the key. "Bring it back, it's the master. They all got the same lock."

"Sure," Gunnar said and smiled.

"Appreciate you had the decency not to come in the uniform, but you're so squeaky-looking it won't matter."

Gunnar wasn't sure if that was a compliment, an insult or just an observation, so he said nothing, but just nodded a thank you, again, for the key.

He headed back up the stairs, stood in front of the door to room number four and thought, *This is it. No turning back.* He slipped the key in, turned the lock, opened the door and found Humpy and some naked woman lying on a filthy cot on the floor. He quietly shut the door behind him and took stock of the room. There were enough empty booze bottles to pickle about thirteen livers. Damn him.

But no weapons that he could see. That didn't mean there weren't any, they just weren't visible. And other than the cot, there was only one table and one chair, so there weren't exactly a lot of places to hide any weapons either. Gunnar picked up a shoe and threw it at Humpy's head. The two love birds rolled over and made some general grunty-sleepy sounds. Humpy was also, Gunnar noted, naked as a jay bird. This was going to be interesting. It was entirely impossible to arrest a naked man without somehow or another touching the family jewels. Great, just what he wanted. Maybe Humpy wouldn't fight.

And the Queen of England wasn't British.

Gunnar picked up the other shoe and threw it at Humpy's head, just a wee bit harder this time. Humpy tried to sit up but the woman, a natural blonde, Gunnar noticed, was sort of intertwined in Humpy's arms. In fact, it sort of seemed like there were about five limbs too many tangled all over that cot. They were both tall and thin, guess that made the difference. Finally, Humpy managed to get the woman off of him and sat up, though at first he took no notice of Gunnar standing there. Finally, he saw Gunnar's feet. His eyes focused, he ran his fingers through his hair and raised his head with great effort.

"Hey, Humpy," Gunnar said.

"Aw, shit," he said. He tried to run. Gunnar would give him credit for that, but Humpy couldn't manage to get up off the mattress. Everywhere he moved the leggy blonde had him pinned, then at one point it seemed as though Humpy was tangled in his own two feet. It was like watching ugly naked wrestling. Gunnar reached out and grabbed him by the arm, and hauled him up.

"You're coming with me," Gunnar said.

Humpy looked back down at the blonde. "But what about..."

"What about what?" Gunnar asked

"Melinda," Humpy said, scratching his head and seemingly unaware that he was naked.

"Her name is Melba," Gunnar said, even though he had no clue what her name was.

"Oh, damn, I knew it was an 'M' name," Humpy said.

"I think she'll be fine without you. By tomorrow, you'll just be a distant memory."

"You think? I mean, because wow, did we ever..."

"Get dressed," Gunnar said.

"Okay, okay," he said, looking around. "Just let me find my clothes."

He found his jeans and put those on without bothering to put on any underwear, and Gunnar thought Humpy probably didn't have any anyway. Then he found his shoes. He faltered a moment trying to find his shirt, picked up something and put it on over his head, only to realize that it was Melinda/Melba's pink sweater.

Gunnar found something plaid lying on the floor, picked it up and threw it at him. "Oh, thanks," Humpy said.

After he was dressed he stretched and he yawned and he scratched his belly and he stretched some more. Then he looked at Gunnar and yawned yet again. "What the hell do you want?" he asked, as though he just realized Gunnar was standing there.

"You are a suspect in a murder case," Gunnar said.

And then he ran. *Thank God he put his clothes on first,* Gunnar thought, and then took off after him. Humpy bolted down the hallway with his head tucked down, like a football player going for broke, headed toward the end zone. His running posture must have thrown off his balance, because he knocked into one side of the wall, backed up, ran and knocked into the other side of the wall. Gunnar was right on him, snatched him by the shirt and threw him up against the end of the hallway, just in front of the stairs.

Humpy turned, threw one punch that missed, but landed the second one in Gunnar's gut. The wind went out of Gunnar, Humpy scrambled, but Gunnar held on, and then finally, he clipped Humpy right on the edge of the chin, bouncing his head into the wall behind him. Gunnar slapped him across the face, "Stop! Just stop!"

But Humpy put his head down and tried to ram Gunnar; then he took a slight opening and ran for the steps, tumbling down the last half of them. Gunnar all but jumped over four steps at a time to get to him and landed with his boot right next to Humpy's head. He gave him a swift kick in the side, and felt no guilt for it whatsoever. Then he yanked Humpy to his feet by the hair of his head.

"You piece of shit, stop running!" Gunnar yelled. Then he threw the skinny, good-for-nothing twit onto the pavement. "I really don't want to keep fighting you, now stop."

"Get bent, you asshole!" Humpy said from the ground.

Gunnar kicked him again, Humpy rolled farther into the back parking lot, coughing and spitting something onto the ground beneath him.

"For God's sake, stand up and face what you've done like a man!"

Humpy slumped to the ground, rolled over, and lay back staring up at the sky for what seemed like an eternity. Gunnar hoped Humpy was indeed finished fighting and running, because he didn't like this part of the job. Even though there were times that the job called for violence and even though there were times Gunnar felt as though it was deserved and justified, afterward, it always made him feel like a Neanderthal. Before Gunnar could register what was happening, tears poured out the sides of Humpy's eyes, and splattered onto the gravel. Great heaving sobs poured from Humpy and Gunnar, stunned, just stared at him. "I didn't do it," he said, swiping at his tears.

"What's that?" Gunnar said towering over him with his hands on his hips.

"I didn't kill that poor bastard, okay?" he said. He raised up, hands clawing at the pavement. He screamed so loud it caused the blood vessels in his neck to stick out. *"I didn't kill him!"*

Gunnar, hands still on his hips, glanced around the parking lot and the streets beyond. "Well, then, I reckon this is the point where you're desperate to tell me your side of the story, huh?" he said.

Humpy rubbed his eyes, wiping the tears away. "Whatever."

"What's that?" Gunnar asked.

"Whatever you want," he said. "I'll tell you whatever. Just...turn off the sun. It's just hanging up there in that sky, just being bright for no damn good reason at all."

Humpy was ready to talk. And Gunnar was hungry. Well, they may as well do both. Gunnar hauled Humpy to his feet and headed toward the car. He wasn't about to eat in the same diner where he'd just apprehended his suspect. He handcuffed Humpy to the steering wheel long enough to run in and return the master key to Rod. Then he returned, uncuffed Humpy from the steering wheel, and made a left toward one of the burger joints that were in the general direction of back home.

They stopped about ten miles out of town at a place that had no name. At least if it had a name, it wasn't painted anywhere on the window or the door, and there was no sign. That was alright. Gunnar had learned that most often, those were the type of places that had the best food. In fact, once they were inside, the food smelled so good he ordered the daily special and pie. He always had to have pie.

About halfway into his beef stew, Gunnar said, "So, explain yourself. What happened after I dropped you home that night?"

Humpy clearly had thought Gunnar had forgotten about questioning him, because his shoulders sort of slumped at the sound of the words. Gunnar studied Humpy. He didn't really look like his sister Olivia. Humpy was sort of chuckle-headed, with eye-teeth that protruded beyond the rest. He had dark hair, like Olivia and Bessie, but his eyes were the color of three-day old dishwater, which neither of the VanBibber girls had. He was scrawny, but fairly tall, taller than Gunnar. His ears were way too big for the rest of his head, which was saying something, because his forehead was huge. What did he have in that skull, rocks? He should have been a genius with a brain that big.

About the only resemblance that Gunnar could find between Humpy and Olivia, aside from the hair, was the shape and expression of the mouth. Both had an upper lip that was just slightly fuller than the bottom, and both had a pronounced upward curve to their lips. Gunnar shook his head, lost in his own thoughts. Where had this guy gone wrong? He'd been given a perfect example of what not to be. A great example of how lying, cheating, and drinking could ruin a family. And yet, he'd chosen those vices anyway.

Maybe he'd chosen them because he felt like he wasn't good enough to be anything else.

Gunnar had felt that way at times. He'd fought that self-destruction, like one would battle an addiction: with desperation and determination, fighting each battle as it came simply because to not fight it was the same thing as giving up. The difference between Humpy and him, not to put too fine a point on it, was that Gunnar would rather prove his father wrong than prove him right. *That* he would fight for.

Humpy took a drink of coffee and with elbows on the table, made a steeple with his fingers. "I slept for about two hours, then I woke up."

"As drunk as you were? What woke you up out of a sound sleep in your own home?"

"I dunno. The storm maybe? There was all kinds of thunderin' and such. But I woke up. Then I got to laying there thinking about how pissed off I was at the jerk and how I remembered somethin' that Harvey Grose had told me."

Harvey Grose? He'd figured as much. "What's that?"

Humpy shrugged. "About how that idiot, McDowell, had a bunch a money in his outhouse. Harvey told me it was damn near a million dollars!"

It was more like one-hundred-and-twenty-six thousand dollars, but Gunnar wasn't about to correct him.

"So, I thought, well, he don't need no whole million dollars, especially if he's keeping it in the crapper, so I might as well go up and get it. Teach him a lesson. Who the hell keeps a million bucks in the crapper?"

"What do you mean—a lesson?"

"He knocked three of my teeth out. I figured he could pay to fix them."

"Really," Gunnar said. "Three teeth are worth a million dollars?"

He shrugged. "Whatever. So, I got up there..."

"You walk?"

"Yeah, took me forever."

"Was it light or dark when you got up there?"

"Just before it got light," he said. "Anyway, so I get there and he's got those two dogs, you know. Harvey had told me that he usually had them inside with him, so if they was outside, he wasn't home. Even though he wasn't home, you didn't want them dogs outside, because he kept them unchained. So, I figured, the dogs would be inside with him because he was so drunk he wasn't about to go nowhere. But, when I got up there, the dogs were on the porch."

"Awake?"

Humpy narrowed his eyes. "Yes," he said.

Which meant, nobody had been by to drug them yet. "What did you do?" Gunnar asked.

"I ran like hell and hid in the outhouse."

"How long were you in the outhouse?"

He shrugged.

"Well, how long did the dogs bark?"

"Just a few minutes. So, I sat down in the corner to wait for them to stop. Only I fell asleep."

"And?"

"And I woke up when I heard Clive coming up the hill in Willie Gene's truck."

"How did you know it was his truck?"

Humpy gave him an expression that told Gunnar to trust him. "I know the sound of that dumb truck, I drove it for years."

"Okay..."

"Okay what?" Humpy asked.

"What then?"

"I shoved a bunch a money in my pockets and my pillow case I'd brought along. Clive left a few minutes later, and that's when I took off through the woods. I ran until I came out down at Dutch Bottom where all those homeless people are—at that camp. Then I hitchhiked to Charleston."

Gunnar studied him. Was he telling the truth?

"What's a guy like that got a million dollars in the crapper for?" Humpy asked again. "Who does that?"

"And you expect me to believe you didn't hear a sound? The man was brutally murdered, and you were asleep in the outhouse through the whole ordeal and didn't hear anything?"

Humpy's expression was one of panic.

"I swear I didn't hear nothin'. Not even the dogs."

"Did you notice anything unusual on your way up the mountain?"

His eyes got huge. "It was doin' some serious rainin'," he said. "Damn, that willow tree was struck by lightning, right in two. Just two humps going each way to the ground. Suzie Belle always loved that tree."

"Suzie Belle?"

"Olivia," he said.

Gunnar thought a moment. If he could figure out what time that tree was hit by lightning, it could narrow down the time frame that Humpy was talking about. Humpy kept right on talking. "You know, when she was little she'd hide in that tree 'cause nobody could see her. She thought she was safe from the world in there. And I'd go lookin' for her sometimes, or Dad would. One time, I'll never forget this as long as I live, we were going to my Grandpa's funeral, but she didn't want to go. So, she ran and hid in the tree. Mom sent me after her. I found her and she was sitting up in the top branches like, I dunno, like it was her throne and she was queen of the tree. She couldn't been more than five. I think the reason I remember this so much is because the sun had lit up the whole tree, it was, like, glowing and there she was...a little dark spot. Dark hair and those black eyes, in her pretty dark blue dress. And she looked at me and she said, 'How did you find me? You're not supposed to be able to see me.' And I laughed and I said, 'I found you 'cause I know your nature.' And then she made me climb up there and get her because she refused to come down. So, I suppose that's what you do, huh, Gunnar? You know people's nature?"

Gunnar was stunned by the moment. The fact that Humpy shared this, had the insight to understand it, the fact that, whatever he had become, at one time he had loved his little sister. And yes, he was right. Most of this job was knowing the nature of the people involved. But no matter what, Gunnar knew that even some of the best people could be reduced to committing awful acts if the situation was threatening enough.

He cleared his throat and continued. "Did you see anybody else on the road, on your way up?"

Humpy thought about it a moment. "Nobody in cars."

Gunnar leaned forward. "But you saw somebody walking?"

Humpy shrugged. "I have no idea if they was headed to that idiot's house or not. I just know that I saw somebody cross over the road and down the other side."

"Headed which way? Toward town or away?"

"Away," Humpy said. "But it was dark and I was a drunk as a skunk, there's no way I could tell you who it was. So, don't even ask."

Somebody was out walking along the road on a Monday morning before dawn in the pouring rain. It was possible that it was somebody who was headed to work and had a long walk ahead of him. Gunnar wondered if he could hunt that person down, because he might have seen Jeb's killer and he would have been much more alert than Humpy. Or they could have *been* Jeb's killer.

"Was he moving fast? Slow? Singing? Humming? Did he seem worried that you saw him? Did he duck behind a bush? Come on, give me something."

"Uh, well he scared the beejesus outta me. Wasn't expecting nobody on the road...other than that, nothing. He stopped when he saw me. I probably scared him just as much. Then he just mosied along. Slow like...I swear that's all I know."

"And you're sure it was a man, not a woman."

"He was dressed like a man. Pants. Hat."

"What did he smell like?"

"Smell like? I didn't get that close to him, and as if I gotta say it again, I was drunk!"

Gunnar studied him. It was difficult to tell if Humpy was lying. Addicts were expert liars, and they even got irate that you dare question whether or not they were lying, knowing they were lying the whole time, but just angry because you caught them in the act. It was enough to make a person want to hit something. The bottom line: there was no way to know for sure. But Gunnar's gut told him that Humpy was most likely telling the truth. Or at least a version of it. But no matter the version, Gunnar was pretty sure the part about not killing Jeb was on the up and up.

"She's doing fine, by the way," Gunnar said.

"Who?" Humpy asked, eating another French fry. "What are you talking about?"

"Your sister. Olivia. One of her best friends has been murdered. She found the body. In fact, while you were hiding out in the john and running through the woods with your stolen loot, she was inside Jeb's house, cradling him as he took his last breath, covered in his blood, you selfish little prick. Just thought I'd let you know."

"How was I supposed to know she found the body?" Humpy asked, irritated. Irritated was good. That meant that Gunnar's words bothered him. If they bothered him, it meant that he felt a little guilty. And if he felt a little guilty, that meant that somewhere in the giant rock-filled skull of his, he had a conscience. "And how good a friends could they be? She only knew him a few months."

"They were very good friends, actually," Gunnar said, fighting back the urge to punch him right in the face. There were a few spots on his ugly mug that weren't covered in bruises, nobody would know the difference. *Down, Neanderthal, down.*

Humpy shoved the last of his fries in his mouth, and said with potato squirting out through the sides of his lips, "So, what happens now? Can I go?" He swallowed.

Gunnar chuckled. The nerve of him. *Don't punch him. It's not worth it. Don't punch him.* "Uh, no, son. I'm arresting you for stealing from Jeb. Charges might not stick, but I don't care. I'm going to let you dry out in lock-up for a few weeks."

Humpy sat back and rolled his eyes to the ceiling.

Gunnar really wished that there was a prison sentence for being a shit, but there wasn't. Chalk it up as one of the great injustices of the world.

Decisions

I was sitting at T.J's waiting for my mother to get off from work, when through the big picture window I saw a familiar figure meandering through the streets, stopping to investigate all of the trash cans. It was Rhea. I glanced around the noisy diner, looking for Mom to try and get her attention. She was busy handing off lunch to some customers. No fewer than four plates were resting on her left arm, and she swiftly and easily delivered each plate to the correct customer. There were three orders still in the window. She was going to be a few minutes

I made my way to the double doors and was happy that one door opened in and one out, so that I could just push the OUT door with my pedal and not have to maneuver an inward-swinging door. "Rhea!" I called out.

She looked up and down her side of the street, without glancing over at me. I went to the corner and crossed the street on the crosswalk. I'd learned in Huntington what happened to girls in wheelchairs who didn't use the crosswalk. Nobody could see me coming, and I'd nearly caused an accident and several heart attacks. I'd only made that mistake once. I reached the other side just as she was making her way to the next trash can. "Rhea!"

She glanced up again, clearly agitated that somebody was calling her name, but as soon as she saw me she smiled. "Blanchie's grandbaby!" she said and waved.

Why did she always call me Blanchie's girl or Blanchie's grandbaby? Did she know my name? I couldn't remember if she'd ever used it, but it was annoying. "How are you?" I asked when I'd managed to get to her. I was out of breath. That last part had been uphill.

"I'm good. How are you? You feelin' okay? Your colors are kinda muddy, today."

"I feel fine," I said.

"You shouldn't be worried about that Jeb feller. He's done moved on."

"I wasn't…I'm not worried about him," I said. "I was wondering if I could ask you a question."

Rhea stopped, looked completely incensed and said, "Look at that. Somebody done threw away a perfectly good pen!" She marked on her hand with the end and it, indeed, did still work. "Now who'd go and do somethin' that plumb wasteful and stupid?"

I shrugged.

"Whatchoo wanna know?"

"Did you ever work at the Bend house?"

Her eyes narrowed. "Yes."

That was it. A one word answer.

"What years were you there?"

"Off and on as a kid. Worked so my momma could buy fabric. Later...uh, oh, nineteen and eighteen to after the war. Twenty...four, I think. Why you want to know?"

"Did you work with any of my family?"

She nodded her head. "Yeah, I surely did. Blanchie was there during part of that time, but then she got so sick and moved to Charleston. Mildred and Stella were both there."

"What years?"

"Well, Mildred worked there, Lawdy, way before me. Then she left for a while, came back and then worked there some more until about nineteen and seventeen, then she went to Europe."

"When did she come back?"

"Nineteen. After that, she was there until the place closed. Stella was there off and on. Pretty steady, like, between nineteen twenty to twenty-six."

"Do you...?"

"Do I what?"

"Nothing." I did not know how to ask her what I needed to know. "Anything unusual go on during those years?"

"You mean aside from all those mine wars and killings and such?"

"Yes, aside from those," I said.

"Let me tell you, Olivia. The Bend house was smack in the middle of a lot of goings on. This and that and all sorts of stuff."

"Like what?"

"Stuff."

"Stuff isn't really an answer, Rhea. You're using a word with a broad definition and I need specifics."

"Well if I don't speak perty enough for you, why don't you just go ask your aunties?"

She had me there.

"Oh, by the way, I need you to give somethin' to Gunnar." She reached into her big bag and pulled out something off-white. As she handed it to me, a flush crept up her cheeks. "Found those in Jeb's trash when he first moved in. Big city fella like him, I thought he might be wantin' to get rid of some stuff that I might need. Rich people have interesting trash. Went down there when he first moved in and he had those two perfectly good bags in the trash bin. Guess he was gonna burn them with all the other stuff. They's perfectly good. No holes, no nothing.'"

I unfolded the fabric and found that I held two cloth bags. Bank bags. With Moulton Bank of Baltimore stamped across the side.

"Now I figure, what with what happened to that poor fella, this might be meanin' somethin' important. I just couldn't—in good conscience—keep them. Well, that and Blanchie told me that they'd look plumb awful with blue flowers on them. I disagreed with her, but she insisted. So, if I can't be embroiderin' them what's the point in keepin' 'em? Right?"

She honestly believed that my dead grandmother had discussions with her on what to embroider. I'd ponder that later. These two bags would be the connection Gunnar needed to the bank robbery and Jeb's involvement, voluntary or not. "Rhea, thank you for coming forward. These are actually very important."

"Really?" she said. She puffed up like a cobra, proud of herself.

"Yes, thank you."

"Youse good people, Olivia."

She did know my name. That was comforting.

"Now, as for that Jeb feller."

"What about him?"

"Just be careful what you go digging up. A head of a snake can still bite you after it's dead."

With that she spit on the ink pen, polished it up with the tail of her shirt and handed it to me. "That's a right nice pen. You get more use outta that than I will."

And then she walked away.

It occurred to me then that I happened to be right in front of the courthouse steps. I could go in and see what births they had listed for October of 1923. I could. I could clear this up right now, providing Jeb was born in this county and not one of the surrounding ones. I didn't need to ask anybody, question any family members. I didn't need anybody's permission to do this and I didn't need anybody's help. I could answer this with my own actions. But Rhea's words echoed in my head, bouncing off my skull, warning me. Not that she was insinuating that Jeb was a snake, just that actions had long reverberating consequences. How would that information change me once I learned it? I couldn't unlearn it, that was for sure.

I glanced up and down the sidewalk, lost in my thoughts, wondering how I could possibly make this decision right here, out in the open. People milled about in their own little bubbles of their own little worlds. Doing their shopping, mailing letters, keeping appointments, visiting friends. I felt like I should yell, "Stop! I'm about to make an important decision!" Everybody went on about their business and the moment became more and more surreal. This was it. This had been my first opportunity to get to town on a day the courthouse was open. I could answer this question right now, providing Jeb had been born here.

I stopped the next person I saw, a man in his mid-fifties, walking briskly by. "Would you do me a big favor?" I asked.

His expression softened as he looked down at me. "Why sure, little lady."

"Would you go in the courthouse and ask the guard to come out here for me? Let him know I want to come in but can't get up the steps."

"Sure." He jogged up the concrete stairs and came back within seconds with the security guard. I thanked the man, and asked the guard to take me up the steps, which he did without hesitation. He refused to let me wheel myself to the vital statistics room and insisted on pushing me there. So, I let him. It made him feel better. People were like that. They felt guilty because I couldn't use my legs and they could, so for them to do something for me made them feel better. Less guilty. *Look, I helped a crippled girl today.* The only problem was that it helped perpetuate the myth that I needed the help. But sometimes I did.

As the security guard left me at the desk, I realized that there was no going back now. My heart thudded and my palms were suddenly slick. When an elderly woman with black eyeglasses waddled up to the counter, my voice left me.

"What can I do for you, today?" she asked.

"I..."

She raised her eyebrows as if that would somehow help me speak.

"I...n-need to..."

"Yes, honey?"

Then the words rushed out of me. "See the birth records for the year 1923."

There, I'd said them.

She walked away, leaning heavily to one side. My mind buzzed like an alarm clock. I tried not to think about it. I tried to just think about all the work it took to build this building or how shiny the floor was or why I didn't mind my own business. When she returned, she pushed the thick rimmed glasses up on her nose and said, "It's a big book, you want me to just put it in your lap?"

"Uh...sure."

She came around the counter, placed the book in my hand and said, "Let me know when you're finished."

So, I sat there in the middle of the room with this amazingly large book, twelve by twenty inches at least, and my hands shook at the realization. Information was power. And anybody could have it. And what I was about to learn could tear my family apart. And yet, I opened the book anyway, turned to 1923 and followed the entries with my finger. Down the page, down, down, October. October 1923. October 27, 1923.

Jeb's birth name was Owen Charles Peebles.

A Letter to Viola from Olivia

Viola Reinhardt
Dayton, Ohio
December 1958

Dear Aunt Viola,

I don't know how to begin this letter. Nor, I should think, will I know how to end it. And come to think of it, the middle is not getting any clearer for me, either. Oh, Aunt Viola, what will I do?

What is your advice to somebody who suddenly finds herself in possession of knowledge that she would have been better off not knowing? And yet, I think, well why shouldn't I have this knowledge? It's my family. People I loved were involved. But then I think, I'm a busy-body, a gossip hound...a terrible person.

Clive is here with me now, sitting next to me, soothing me because I have cried for the last three hours.

Well, so far I've done a terrible job of beginning this letter, so we'll consider everything I just wrote as an annoying prologue.

Aunt Viola, I know who Jeb's mother is. I found his birth record. I know, I know, I know, it's not as if the information just fell out of the sky and landed in my lap, I went looking for it, so it's my own fault. I actively pursued this information and now that I have it, I don't know what to do and wish I didn't have it.

I'm writing to you because I know you know who his mother is. They all have to know. I don't know how they can't. His mother had him for three years and during that time there were several sisters working at the Bend house together. The entire family has to know, so I don't think it is that great of a secret and yet, since nobody's ever talked of it, it must be a secret on some level. At what point does a secret become common knowledge enough to go ahead and share it without dire consequences?

I haven't told Clive. I haven't told anybody, but Clive knows that I know something because my eyes are swollen from crying and I look like Bessie looks when she eats nuts. All puffy and splotchy, only a tad less hysterical.

Anyway, I'm writing to you because you will most likely be hearing from your sisters in the immediate future and I wanted to let you know that I am the one who discovered the information. Me. I'm to blame. I don't want anybody trying to take the blame for me or make it out like it wasn't a bad thing to do just because I'm in wheelchair. People tend to do that, you know. Quite unfairly, I might add.

I suppose I'm writing also to tell you that I have to divulge this information to Gunnar. I have to. It could work into the investigation in some way. Probably not, but you never know. I promise never to desire that which I shouldn't know ever again.

And yes, I'm looking forward to being a librarian (referring to your earlier letter). It has been my dream job since I can remember. That is, if anybody will ever speak to me again.

I'm off to finish reading Jeb's book.

Love, Your Terrible Niece,
Olivia

Gunnar Ryan
Colton County Deputy

Gunnar sat at the kitchen table going over the crime scene photos one more time. He'd only looked at them a thousand times, and he guessed he'd look at them a thousand more if that was what it took. His mother was in the living room knitting the sweater for Kevin. She had taken the news that he was going to Chicago for school instead of Ohio well, at least at first. But then as the days wore on she got more and more quiet, knitted faster and faster.

After a few minutes she came into the kitchen with her basket and set it on the table. "You still lookin' at those pictures?" she asked.

Gunnar nodded. "The answer is here, I just can't see it."

"My advice?" she said.

"Sure, what?"

"Section off a little piece of the picture at a time and see just what's in that part. Separate from the...body."

He did as she suggested as she got herself a glass of milk. He even went so far as to place blank pieces of paper over the rest of the photo so that he couldn't see the whole picture. After about five minutes he'd found in the photographs an empty soda bottle under the chair, wadded pieces of papers lying on the floor around the desk. A pack of gum by the couch.

Then he noticed the blood next to the body. The odd markings just to Jeb's left...He was certain they weren't from Olivia. She said she'd only touched the things to Jeb's right.

His mother got a piece of cornbread and jammed it down into her glass of milk, got a spoon and started eating it. "I saw Olivia the other day. At Stella's knitting night."

"Yeah?" Gunnar asked.

"She's a smart girl," his mother said.

"She's pretty excited about the library. Although I think she's just as nervous," he said.

"I would never want anything bad to happen her. She's been through enough. Polio and her dad..."

Gunnar stopped and studied his mother's face. There was something she was trying to get to without being too obvious. "What is it?"

She studied the contents of her glass and shrugged. "I think you like her."

Gunnar took a breath and sat back. "I do like her. As you said, she's extremely smart. And very direct and honest. None of those games you get from other girls her age. You can have an actual conversation with her and not have to wonder what her ulterior motives are."

His mother swallowed her bite of cornbread and smiled at him.

"What?" he asked growing testy.

"She's also quite beautiful. Those big dark eyes..."

"Is there something you want to say?"

"I get it," his mother said. "She's a very pretty, unique girl. But don't lead her on."

"What are you *talking* about?"

"Don't make her think she means more to you than she does. Do her a favor..."

"And what?"

"You're a very handsome man. A man of authority and you've got a good job. Just do me a favor and whatever your relationship is or whatever it turns into, you be as honest with her as she is with you. She's young, she could misconstrue...She comes from good stock, Gunnar. Those are good, *really good,* people."

Gunnar started to say something but he didn't get to finish. At that moment, James dragged himself up the steps on the porch and all but kicked the front door in. He stood there, completely inebriated, swaying back and forth like a tree in a hurricane. He wore an expression of impatience, intolerance, malevolence.

"Sally!" he roared.

"Yes?" his mother said. Her kitchen chair nearly toppled over backwards from the speed with which she'd jumped up.

"Where's my keys?"

"Now, James, you know..."

"Keys, Goddam you, woman!"

"You're not allowed keys when you're like this," Gunnar said in a steely voice.

"And who the hell are you to tell me what I canna do?" James said.

"Well, for one thing, I'm an officer of the law and I'm telling you that you're not driving when you're like this. I'll arrest you, if I have to."

Gunnar's heart hammered. They'd known it would only be a matter of time before the cycle started back up. His mother silently pleaded with him.

Shut up and don't say anything else. Don't make him angrier! But it didn't matter when James was like this. James was just as likely to get angry if you gave him exactly what he wanted. He was deranged, a psychopath when drunk. A total Dr. Jekyll and Mr. Hyde, because there was never a meeker man in the world when he was sober.

James all but fell into the kitchen, landed on the table with all of his weight and knocked the whole thing over. Milk and cornbread went into the floor. Crime scene photos, the basket with the yarn for Kevin's sweater, both followed. His mother screamed, "My basket!" Just as the words left her mouth, James stepped on it and snapped the handle in two.

Gunnar gasped and he tore his gaze from his father's oblivious face, to his mother's broken one. The tears spilled from her eyes as her mouth made a perfectly silent "Oh!" Nothing came from her. No noise whatsoever. She couldn't breathe, she could make no sound. And then before Gunnar could stop her she lunged for the basket and caught James' knee in the chin as he was clumsily trying to get his foot out of it. Gunnar heard her teeth snap together from the impact, but the whole time her hands groped for the basket.

Finally, an inhuman noise tore from her lips. It sounded at once primeval and animal as she tried to put the pieces of the broken basket back together. James kicked her then, "Get the hell up, you stupid bitch," he said.

And with those words, something broke in Gunnar. A perfect cleavage of a new self from his old self. The sane self from the enraged. Like he was outside of his body looking down at the situation. The table on its side, the photos of a bloodied dead man strewn across the floor, his mother heaving great sobs of ancient pain, his father's ridiculous drunken swagger, the beloved broken basket, and Gunnar standing in the middle of it.

Gunnar lunged for his father, a shriek tearing from him, echoing off of the kitchen walls. Clutching the remnants of the basket his mother scrambled away and under a kitchen chair. James was completely taken off guard and Gunnar drove his father into the wall with his shoulder, like a football lineman would tackle his opponent. James shoved Gunnar back, smiled at him and said, "Oh, you want to do this? So *you want to do this!* Are you man enough, finally?"

Gunnar punched him and his father's head snapped back. When his eyes met Gunnar's, they had briefly cleared from the alcohol haze and Gunnar could tell James knew exactly what he was doing. Blood ran down James' face and onto his lips. "You think you're big enough to do this, boy? Huh?"

And the Gunnar who was watching told himself not to take the bait. But the Gunnar who was physical kicked his father in the groin, grabbed his dad by the hair of the head and bashed it into his rising knee. James was startled at first, but soon gained his composure and landed a few punches of his own.

By this time, Betty Jo had come racing into the kitchen, having been upstairs asleep. "Oh my God!" she cried.

But Gunnar paid her no mind and punched his father, hard, to the solar plexus. James immediately vomited, spewing alcohol and stomach acid all over the place, but Gunnar didn't stop. He would take it no more. No more would his siblings hide in the barn even on cold nights. No more would this tyrant terrify everybody for the sole purpose of enjoying it. All because he was pathetic and weak and scared, and he couldn't stop himself. And so Gunnar punched him again. And again. And James answered every punch with a punch of his own. They bashed around the kitchen breaking dishes as they went, knocking things off of walls. Betty Jo tried to get to her mother, but Sally would not come out from under the chair.

"Take my hand, Momma!" she cried. But Sally did nothing but cradle that basket and cower under the chair. So Betty Jo shielded her mother by spreading her body across the front of the chair, arms out to the sides, watching her brother and her father destroy the kitchen.

All this Gunnar knew, because the version of him observing it all could see. There was blood everywhere now, too. His blood, his father's blood, not that it mattered whose it was since it all ran together. Gunnar picked up one of the wooden kitchen chairs and as he reared it over his head, it was if his two halves came back together, melding unwillingly, but having no choice. The physical Gunnar had no excuse, he knew what he was doing, now, and he hit his father with the chair anyway.

The chair splintered and Gunnar grabbed one of the legs and hit James in the face with it. James sputtered and coughed and laughed. *He laughed.* "What's so Goddam funny?" Gunnar yelled. He was half crazy, demented, blind with rage and years of living this life. And he hit James again. He hit him and he hit him and he hit him until his father's face was no longer recognizable. From somewhere off to his left he realized that Betty Jo pulled and yanked on his arm.

"Stop, Gunnar, you're going to kill him!" Betty Jo screamed.

Gunnar was down on one knee, leaning over his father, chair leg poised high over his head, ready to keep hitting him. Wanting to keep hitting him. He flung the chair leg across the room and stood, staring down at his father.

"I'm done," he said. "I'm done, we're done. Do you hear me, you sonofabitch? We will not cower to you anymore. Do I make myself clear?"

But James only laughed.

Gunnar grabbed his father by the hair of his head and got within inches of his vomitous bloody mess of a face. "Do I make myself clear? I'm the head of this family now, not you. You lay a hand on my mother again, and Betty Jo or not, I'll kill you. You got it? I. Will. Kill. You."

His father looked at him, then. Really looked at him. Gunnar suspected that everything before this moment had been somewhat of a game to James. A healthy father-son sparring match. But when James looked at the murderous hatred in his son's eyes, he realized that Gunnar meant what he said. And tomorrow those bruises and broken bones wouldn't be a joke any longer.

Gunnar stood then, casting his gaze around the kitchen. He looked at his father's body, realizing that had it not been for Betty Jo, he quite possibly could have killed James. Was this what happened to Jeb McDowell? Had somebody just gone to talk to him and became so enraged that he just couldn't stop? There had been no Betty Jo or anybody there to pull and yank on Jeb's killer's arm. Gunnar shivered. He had wanted to kill his father just then. He wanted to kill him for years of neglect, years of abuse, years of making Gunnar feel unworthy to breathe and for years of terrorizing his mother.

But it would have still been murder.

The reality sunk in. He could feel the color drain from his face. He looked around for the crime scene photos but they were all over, covered in blood and vomit and broken glass and cornbread and milk. Then he looked again at the way his father's body lay there. And he saw the marks in the blood where his knee had been.

The odd markings to the right of Jeb's body was where somebody had knelt. Only the killer's knee had left a unique marking.

Gunnar began to shake. He had to get out of the house before his father saw him. If he sensed any weakness, any regret whatsoever, James would pounce on it and all the territory that Gunnar had just gained would be lost as if the battle had never been fought. He turned, saw his mother still crouching under the chair and found Betty Jo leaning up against the over- turned table top. He traipsed through the living room to his bedroom and got his gun and a clean shirt. When he came back into the kitchen, Betty Jo looked up at him, with pleading eyes. He handed her his gun. "If he gives you any trouble, shoot him."

"Where are you going?" she asked. Her voice sounded quiet to him. Maybe he just couldn't hear her for all the rage rushing through his ears.

"I...I have to leave now. I'll be back to clean this mess up."

He stalked out of the house, jumped the stairs on the back porch and headed for his car. By the time he was on the road he was sobbing, slapping his steering wheel every time he saw his mother's stricken face and the broken basket. He wished he would have hit James just a few more times.

Before he realized what he was doing, he had pulled into the gravel drive of Olivia's house. What was he doing? He couldn't very well knock on the front door, bloody, covered in his father's vomit. Could he? Why not? Who would understand better than Olivia and her mother, Rosalee Morrison?

He took his shirt off and wiped himself up as best he could and then pulled the new one on over his head. The adrenalin pulsed through his body at such high amounts that he didn't even feel the nip of the cool night weather. Nor did he notice the swollen knuckles or the black eye he would surely have tomorrow. None of it hurt. He felt nothing.

He opened the car door and then thought better of it, but realized that Clive was sitting on the front porch and had already seen him. "Gunnar?" Clive said.

"Uh...yeah," he answered, trying to sound normal.

"What's up? You find Humpy?"

Gunnar wiped at his eyes with his hands. "Yeah," he said. "He's resting in the Wellston jail."

"You want me to get my parents?"

"Actually, I was wondering if I could just have a few moments with Olivia?"

"Sure," Clive said in the dark. He hesitated before turning to go. "Everything all right?"

"No," he said. "Got into a fight with my dad."

After a moment, Clive finally spoke. "I'll be right back."

When Olivia came out onto the porch, she was by herself. He couldn't see her real well, but he could see that her long dark hair was down and curling around her shoulders. "Gunnar?" she said.

"Olivia," he said. "Can I...can I just talk to you for a minute?"

"Of course," she said. He made his way to the porch then—he hadn't dared move before she gave her permission. He could see her face a little better in the moonlight now that he was closer, but he didn't want her to see his. He sat down on the step in front of her and looked out upon the yard and the mountain across the road. It was suddenly very quiet.

She said absolutely nothing. She just sat there and let him speak when he was ready to speak. Finally, after what must have been a full two minutes, he finally cleared his throat. "I beat my father within an inch of his life tonight," he said.

"Are you hurt?"

"I'll live."

"And your mother, Betty Jo?"

"Terrified, but okay."

It struck him that she hadn't asked about James. Her concern had been for him and his mother and sister. "I could have killed him," he said. "I would have killed him had it not been for Betty Jo."

Olivia said nothing at first. "Gunnar?"

"I know you must think I'm a terrible person."

"No, I don't. These kinds of situations...they're not what life is supposed to be. It's difficult to exist in these kinds of climates and retain all of yourself. My mother took a coat hanger to my father once. Beat him until he bled."

"Really?" he asked. "Why?"

"That was the time he sold our dog for a pint of whiskey. You don't want to know what he got for the horse."

Gunnar shook his head. "I found Humpy. He's in the Wellston jail right now."

"Oh, God," Olivia said. "What did he have to say for himself?"

Gunnar thought about how Humpy had relayed the story of Olivia in the willow tree. It was such a tender moment, something shared by siblings and it had apparently affected Humpy deeply or he would not have remembered it all these years later. He didn't think telling Olivia about it, at least right now, would make her feel any better. "He didn't kill Jeb."

"No?"

"No," he said. "But I wanted you to know that I did find him."

"I never doubted you for a second," she said.

"I have things, about the case, that I think you should know."

"I have some things to tell you, too."

"Can we just wait until tomorrow? I...I don't want to think about any of that right now. I almost killed my father."

"But you didn't."

"Only because Betty Jo was there."

"You would have stopped," Olivia said. "I have no doubt."

"How do you know?" he said. He swallowed the sob that was building in his chest.

"Because you're not your father. And you have nothing to fear."

With that, he leaned over and rested his head against the cold metal of the wheel of her chair. It was a forward move, he knew, but somehow since it was in the dark he thought maybe it wouldn't count. She couldn't see his pain and he couldn't see her sympathy and somehow that made it erasable. Tomorrow they could pretend this moment never happened.

But then Olivia reached down with one small hand and ran her fingers through his hair and shushed him like one would a suffering child. And he broke, and he cried, and he knew that neither of them could pretend that this never happened.

History Becomes Real

It was December tenth, Emily Dickinson's birthday. My heart was heavy with knowledge and I couldn't help but think of her poem, Melancholy.

A midnight bell, a parting groan—
These are the sounds we feed upon:
Then stretch our bones in a still gloomy valley,
Nothing's so dainty sweet as lovely melancholy.

My mother and I sat parked in the car in front of Aunt Mildred's house on a gray, cold day. The fog had settled in the valley overnight, leaving a suffocating blanket on my otherwise picturesque part of the world. We were waiting for Gunnar. We were waiting because I had told Gunnar what I knew and I'd confided in my mother, as well. Jeb McDowell was Aunt Mildred's son.

One might not think that this was a police matter, but in light of the fact that Jeb had been murdered—and the fact that I was completely convinced that he had found out his mother's identity—Gunnar believed that this time, it was a police matter. He wanted to hear her story, but he didn't want to confront her alone. That would be improper. She needed family there, and who would be better than my mom, Rosalee, who had been her surrogate daughter?

It was so quiet in the front seat of our car that I swear I could hear the dew running down the glass. Mom did not dare speak, and I barely breathed. She'd not taken the news well. The color had all but drained from her face and her whole body had sagged as if the weight of the world had been gently, but firmly set upon her shoulders. She simply nodded that she would go with me and Gunnar, and that was it. She hadn't spoken since.

I sat there fidgeting with the trim on my skirt wondering how long Gunnar was going to be and why Aunt Mildred had not come out onto the porch to see what we wanted? Maybe she knew.

When my mother finally spoke, it sounded like a mountain slide. "I cannot believe that he was...That Jeb was...Owen. I played with him.

Pretended he was my own baby." And then she sobbed. "I would have loved to have told him that."

"And he would have loved to have heard it," I said and swallowed down my own despair. There were so many things I would have loved to have said to him, had I known who he was. Had I known he would die.

"You don't really think that Mildred knows who killed him? Or killed him herself, do you? She adored that child. I mean, utterly and completely adored him. Why would she kill him now? I won't believe it."

"I don't think she killed him."

Mom wiped her eyes. "Why?"

"It was too physical. She couldn't have done it."

"Then why must Gunnar confront her? She'll be mortified."

"Because there might be something she knows that could change everything. Point him in the right direction."

"It seems cruel," she said. And then Gunnar pulled in behind us.

It felt like the bottom dropped out of my stomach.

Mildred answered the door after one knock, wearing her Sunday best and her only pearl earrings, with her hair perfectly fixed. "Gunnar," she said. "Guess you'd better come in."

Gunnar removed his hat and my mother and I followed him in. My mother went to her and took her hands. "Mildred, Gunnar needs to speak to you about something."

"I know why he's here," she said. Her dark eyes cut around to mine. "You discovered it, didn't you?"

I looked away.

"It's all right, no point in worrying about it now. It had to come out eventually."

"Mildred, I'm sorry for this intrusion, but it's come to light that you were Jeb McDowell's mother." Gunnar said.

She nodded. Something in my mother broke then. As if she had been holding out hope that I had been mistaken. That Jeb really wasn't the little boy that she'd played with as a child. When Aunt Mildred nodded, the sobs broke from my mother and it took everything I had not to join her. Aunt Mildred simply patted her hand. "Well, I guess we'd all better sit down," Mildred said.

Gunnar looked over at me. The scars from last night clearly showed on his body. His hands were bruised and scabbed over. His eyes were bloodshot from crying and lack of sleep. A jagged cut traced from the corner of his mouth to the edge of his chin. I took a deep breath and he nodded at me. As if to say everything would be all right. Then he took a seat, and my mother, clasping her hands protectively around Mildred's, sat down with her beloved aunt.

"I hope you've got a while," she said. "Because I have a long story to tell."

Mildred's Story

Things were so different then. The boarding house was my whole world. I'd worked there for a while when I was younger, then I went to France in 1917 and patched boys younger than me back together so they could go home to their mommas. Their mothers wouldn't care if they were missing an arm or a leg, or even an eye. They'd just be happy to have their precious boys back on their home soil, able to love and heal.

There was nothing quite as detestable as seeing the damage done to a young healthy body by a bullet or a mine. Or a bayonet plunged, twisted and sliced through the side. There was no fixing that. No patching him up, no apologizing or patting him on the head with a chipper, "It'll be all right, lad. Don't you worry."

No, in those moments they could read it all over your face, no matter how hard you tried to disguise it. And all you could think of when you looked at that mangled, war- ravaged body was somewhere there was a mother who had worked day and night on this masterpiece for nothing.

For absolutely nothing.

For somebody else to use as fodder.

An acceptable casualty in somebody else's fight.

Acceptable.

There had been nothing casual about any of those boys. They had been handsome and brilliant, lively and musical, rowdy and funny. They had been our future.

And in my own way, I fell in love with every single one of them. The ones who died, the ones who came back in pieces, missing limbs and full of holes. I loved them all and I swore that if I ever had a son of my own...well, I would never let him be somebody else's acceptable casualty. If it meant I had to hide him, tuck him away, that's what I'd do.

On the return home from the war, I met an American soldier sunning on the deck of the ship. A bullet in the thigh was what he'd suffered, and although he might not have thought it was nothing, I knew that he'd been lucky.

He asked me to sit and talk to him. He said, "I've seen you walking the deck every day for three days now. You nearly tripped over me yesterday and never even noticed."

I begged his forgiveness and then he smiled up at me, revealing green eyes that were the color of the Irish hills. And I saw in them all of the terror he'd just escaped, all the love he'd been born into, and all the hope he held for the tomorrows. I loved him almost instantly.

Every day of the two-week journey, we met on deck, spending almost sun up to sun down with each other, talking, laughing, sometimes even singing. He'd even tried to dance a jig for me, but his injured leg made it nearly impossible. His favorite thing was to read to me. He told me that literature was the one true art form in this world. "In a book I can be any character I choose to be, and participate in any adventure I want to, solve any problem, mourn any loss that the author chooses to share with me. There is no closer communion than a reader to his author. And what is art but somebody inviting you to partake in their vision?" He read Huckleberry Finn *to me, making note that he wanted to ride a raft down the Mississippi some day, and he read* The Tell-Tale Heart *out loud as well and held my hand when I'd become anxious and scared.*

I felt like a young, giddy girl when he was around. I was already in my thirties. I'd never had an experience like this one. Never had I ever thought about another human being as I drifted off to sleep, and thought of him first thing the next morning. I had always assumed my life was meant for other things and not for love, and I'd accepted that. Until I'd been shown the possibilities.

I was like a blind person who could suddenly see. And I never wanted to close my eyes.

To my surprise I learned that he was from West Virginia—farther south than where I lived, but still it was a relief to know that, if he should want to visit with me once we were home, it wouldn't be impossible. We exchanged addresses when the ship docked in New York, and he was all I thought about on the train to Charleston. Every time I closed my eyes I saw him pressing his address into my palm, brushing his lips across the back of my hand, promising to write and visit. He had an errant lock of dark hair that continually fell into his face, and I had to make a conscious effort not to reach up and brush it away. I wanted to throw myself at him, beg him to come home with me. But I was raised with more decorum than that and I simply smiled, told him how much it would mean to me if he would visit, and swiped away the tears as my train pulled out of the station.

All the way home I saw him in my mind's eye, head tilted up toward my window, searching for me. When his gaze had found mine, his smile transformed his face—he'd seen me one last time—and he'd waved, heartily at first and then...he'd just stood there, like a lost child in disbelief that I really was leaving.

He was not scheduled to return home for another week, something to do with the army, otherwise we would have most likely had another day on the train together, too. Before my train pulled into the station in Charleston, I had penned my first letter to him.

I returned to work at the Bend house almost immediately. I suffered from the trauma of the trenches almost as much as the soldiers. I had nightmares, entire nights when I couldn't sleep at all. Doc would play his fiddle for me and I'd fall asleep sitting up in the chair. My sister Hazel brought me flowers every chance she got and Blanche would take me on long walks with her girls. Eventually, I settled into a more peaceful state and lived for the letters that Rufus and I sent back and forth.

And then one day, Stella came running up the steps and almost knocked over the lamp in the hallway. "Mildred! Mildred!" she said. "There's a man here to see you."

"A man?" I asked.

"It's him," she said. "The one you met on the boat."

My knees buckled and Stella had to grab me so that I wouldn't fall. When I realized that Rufus was outside, standing on the porch of the Bend house waiting for me to come out, I nearly ran as fast as Stella had, burst through the screen and stopped abruptly. Stella smashed into my back and knocked me a few feet closer to the edge of the porch. And closer to my green-eyed soldier.

"Mildred," he said and removed his hat.

"Rufus," I said.

"I...I was wondering if you had any rooms to let?" he asked.

And that was how he'd come to Bend house.

Our romance blossomed and he became a union organizer for the coal miners. Rufus earned everything he'd ever gotten in life. He had taught himself to read, he'd saved up and bought a little farm, and then when he'd gone to France he had given the farm to his sister in case he didn't return. When he did come back, he'd lived with her and worked the mines, until he decided to move a little farther north to see if the girl of his dreams would have him. At least, that's what he said. And of course I would have him.

He was instantly liked by all of my family. Rufus was a few years younger than me, but the war had aged him in ways that didn't show. And at night when he would wake, screaming for somebody named Charlie, I would leap from my bed and race down the hall to his rooms. It wasn't very becoming for an *unmarried woman to run to the aid of a man she was not married to while still in her nightdress, but I couldn't help it. His cries reminded me of the cries I'd heard in France and something in me just fell into place and Nurse Mildred took over. Rufus's nightmares cured me of mine.*

One night while I sat on the side of his bed, holding his hand, he told me the story of Charlie. Charles Broward, a soldier in his unit who had become his best friend. Charles had been from Connecticut, and was at least five years younger than Rufus. They'd played checkers and cards and sang silly songs just to keep themselves from going crazy in the muddy, cold, and mildewed trenches. One night Rufus had noticed that Charlie had a book in his left breast pocket. Loving to read, Rufus had asked him what it was. Charlie pulled it out, handed it to Rufus and told him to read it. It was a hardback version of Longfellow's The Song of Hiawatha.

And he wooed her with caresses,
Wooed her with his smile of sunshine,
With his flattering words he wooed her,
With his sighing and his singing,
Gentlest whispers in the branches,
Softest music, sweetest odours,
Till he drew her to his bosom,
Folded in his robes of crimson,
Till into a star he changed her,
Trembling still upon his bosom;
And for ever in the heavens
They are seen together walking,
Wabun and the Wabun-Annung,
Wabun and the Star of Morning.

And so Rufus took the book to read it and when the Germans attacked the next day, Charlie had been shot right through the heart, right through the breast pocket where he'd kept the book all those months. Rufus became convinced that if he'd had his book with him, Charlie would have lived. Nobody will ever know, will they? But, still, it haunted him, every night. Charlie lived and died in Rufus' dreams every single night. Slowly Rufus became obsessed with fate and chance and choices.

I still have that book in my cedar chest next to the bed.

Dark clouds hovered on the horizon of our healing. The mine wars were in full swing and things with the officials and the company owners and the miners had declined to the point of violence. Random shootings and attacks, protests and strikes became the language of men, as it often does. Rufus, who had done his fair share of shooting and killing, and being shot and suffering, had sworn the union would go peacefully or he'd die trying. Eventually there was some killing that went on and somehow my beautiful Rufus ended up in the middle of all of it even without wanting to be. One night he came tearing through the Bend house after dinner, covered in blood, a wild look in his eyes, yammering on about a shooting and how everybody was going to think he had done it. I said, "Rufus, did you kill somebody?"

And he said, "No, no, you must believe me. It was Stokes. It was Stokes, but Mildred, my love, they'll never believe it." And then the authorities burst in and arrested him. They pulled him from the Bend house, his legs and arms finding purchase on whatever they could. "Mildred!" he called out to me.

"Rufus!" I fought the men, but they tossed me aside down to the floor where I'd hit my head on a table. When Rufus realized that they would hurt me, he stopped fighting, stood stock still and told the men that he would go peacefully.

I crumpled in a heap of tears, sobbing so hard I could barely take a breath.

At his trial I sat stoic and nauseous, with my sister Stella holding one hand and Blanche holding the other. I had only just realized that...that I was with child and had told Rufus only the night before. And when the gavel came down and the judge announced that Rufus would be serving twenty-five years in prison, my heart all but stopped beating. I don't remember it, but Blanche and Stella both said that I screamed like a banshee and brought the entire court room to stunned silence. Blanche had said it was a blood-curdling scream, a universal scream by all women through history who have lost love unjustly to the hate of men. But I don't remember that scream at all.

I remember that in the silence I heard his voice. Strong and sure. "It'll be all right, Mildred," Rufus said. And then they took him away and nothing was ever all right again.

My days ran together and I existed in a state of numb denial. And my belly grew. Stella and Blanche knew, of course, they guessed. There was to be no wedding for me. My son would be the bastard child of a convicted killer. I tossed about wild ideas of what I should do, where I should go. Panic and denial were at war in my mind.

When Owen was born, I was torn between loving him so much that I was exhilarated and missing his father so much that I could die. It was an odd sort of existence, wishing to be dead and wanting to live, happiness and sadness cohabitating side by side. But I did it. And every day I grew stronger and every day I loved Owen more and more. And in a letter to Rufus I had told him that

I had named the baby after Charlie Broward. When Rufus wrote back he said that he'd cried for hours when he'd read my letter. He said, "Truly, there is no better woman in the world, than you, Mildred Anne."

I had finally had my own masterpiece: Owen Charles.

I didn't know you could love something so much. Nobody ever told me that part.

So, I went about making a life for Owen and me. People talked. Some people accused me of being a godless hussy, but Owen didn't seem to mind. He loved me no matter what. And the entire boarding house helped to raise him and all my sisters took turns spoiling him. He would play with his cousins; Rosie was his absolute favorite. She was four when he was born and she pretended that he was her baby. Owen had affectionate nicknames for all of them. Stella was TeeToe and Colinda was Linda and Blanche was his beloved Banchie. We were, in our odd little way, our own family.

And then one spring afternoon when the cherry blossoms hung heavy and thick on the trees, a girl showed up on the back porch of the Bend house. A blond girl—dirty, shoeless, ready to burst with child, and hungry. She could not have been more than sixteen. Vacant blue eyes stared at me as she said, "Are you Mildred Graham?"

"Yes," I said cautiously.

"Rufus didn't kill those men. But I know who did."

Immediately, I ushered her into the kitchen and fed her some cornbread and crowder peas. I didn't understand how a girl could be so skinny and have enough strength to stand up. Then she told me that she'd been living in Rhea's shed. Since she'd discovered she was pregnant she was afraid to return home. So Rhea told her she could stay with her and her family, but the girl refused, saying that she didn't want to cause any trouble for Rhea, but that she would sleep in her shed on nights she had nowhere else to go.

The girl had worked in the private home of Stuart Stokes, the manager of the coal mine. The night the two detectives were murdered, Stokes had left with his guns, returned later, splattered in blood. The girl couldn't prove anything, but she knew Stokes had killed them and made it look like it had been Rufus. Then, two years later she overheard Stokes talking about how Rufus had seen him kill those two detectives. The way the girl explained it, Stokes had arranged a meeting with the detectives and Rufus and made sure people heard they were meeting. Then he showed up, shot them dead in front of Rufus, who then turned and ran to the Bend house.

At this point in the telling of her story, the girl began to shake and wail and glance about the kitchen as though she was being watched, because Stokes was the father of her baby and she was afraid that he was going to kill her. She'd been afraid to go home, afraid to go anywhere, and so she had begun living from place to place.

My heart was pounding at the telling of her story. "You could tell the authorities the truth!" I said.

"Mr. Stokes would just say that he was innocent and that I wanted him. Who would they believe? Me or him?"

She trembled again and added, "The only way I will testify is if the other three men who were there at the killing would testify."

"What three men?" I asked. The hair stood on the back my neck.

"The ones Rufus had with him for back-up. They hid in the bushes and when they ran, Stokes identified them. They won't testify either, because he threatened their families. Other people he's threatened have gone missing or dead, Miss Graham, you have to understand."

Wasn't it just like Rufus to go to jail rather than put anybody else in danger? "Who were they?" I asked.

"I don't know," she said and I believed her.

In the month or two that followed, I launched my own investigation, trying to discover the identities of these three men. Eventually, I realized that one of them was Edwin. He was a lifelong neighbor and friend. I begged, I pleaded with him to go to the authorities and free Rufus.

In the meantime, I settled the girl in a spare room and fed her until she started to look alive again. But as she gained more life, I noticed that my sister Blanche was losing it. She claimed everything was fine, all was well, but death had cast its shadow on her face and I knew it. There were so many things to worry about. When I look back now, I wish I had slowed down and spent more time with Blanche because it would be all the time I had.

But things progressed, no matter how much I wanted to slow them down. The girl, well, she took to making an oak basket. I had no idea if she knew what it would stand for at the time she started it. She made it for her baby, a place for it to sleep, but I think even then it was supposed to be more than that and she knew it.

She soaked the splints in water first, and created her two hoops, one for the handle and one for the rim. Then she made the bond lashing at the juncture of the handle and the hoop. The Eye of God, is what that part of the basket is called. Then she wove the splints over and under, around the rim and back down again *until the basket was finished. With each weaving of over and under she sang a song; "Speed, bonnie boat, like a bird on the wing, Onward! the sailors cry;* Carry the lad that's born to be King over the sea to Skye. Loud the winds howl, loud the waves roar. Thunderclaps rend the air; Baffled, our foes stand by the shore. Follow they will not dare."

Her voice was clear and concise, almost piercing in its purity.

I've never seen a finer basket. Uniform weave length and a tiny weave of thin splints. She must have been taught by a master.

Two days later the baby was born, howling into the night air, and her mother screaming right along with her. Blanche and I held the girl's hands, wiped her brow and caught her tears, while Stella delivered the baby. I still say Stella missed her calling. She should have been a midwife.

That girl carried her baby, whom she'd named Stella Mildred Blanche, after the three of us, in the basket she'd made. She went everywhere with her. Baby Stella was the most content, sweet, blue-eyed, blonde-haired baby I'd ever seen. Things seemed good. I thought she was going to stay at the boarding house and just go to work for me, but one day she said that her father was sick and she had to return home.

Rhea gave her a dress trimmed with ivory bows and an old pair of shoes to wear. We all gave her what change we could spare. I'd bought the baby a new gown and Blanche had given the girl one of her amazing hats. It was one of the last kind acts that Blanche would do before leaving this earth. But Blanche's story is for another time.

We thought everything was fine, but in the middle of the night the girl left and did not take Baby Stella with her. She'd left a note saying that she could not return home, seventeen, unmarried with a baby, but that she promised to return. "Please take care of her, Mildred. I know you will be the best."

And that's why I had Baby Stella with me on that horrible day.

Word came that Rufus was to be released. Edwin had come through for me. He and the other witnesses went to the authorities with their statements. They realized they had no evidence against Rufus. He couldn't return home to the Bend house, though, because he had to stay in Charleston and meet with lawyers and such. And Stokes knew that his days were numbered and put his plan into motion.

You know the rest, it was in the papers. I took Owen and Baby Stella to meet Rufus for lunch. Rufus had only seen Owen through bars on a prison cell, from a distance, but had never been allowed to touch or hold him. On the ride there I could barely breathe I was so excited. Owen was such a good boy and on that day, he sat in the front seat and played with the baby who was nestled in her basket. He counted her toes and he played peek-a-boo. And Stella would laugh.

"Mommy, she's pretty," he said and I agreed. My fingers tingled as they gripped the steering wheel. My beautiful black-haired boy would finally get to be with his father, and I with my love.

I've thought about what came next at least a thousand times. How could two human beings do what they did on that day? How? When the shooting started...you can imagine... the horror. I was senseless with fear, knees so weak that I could barely stand, but then I saw Owen climbing the mound, screaming and running as fast as his legs could take him. One of the men raised his gun toward Owen and I plowed into him, knocking him to the ground, and then I ran.

Without thinking, I ran toward Owen. If I could only reach him, I could throw myself on him and save him from any bullets until help could arrive. At least that's what I imagined doing. I was too scared to actually formulate a thought or a plan, it was just this primal drive to run after him and protect him.

By the time I reached him, the men had gone, but a gathering of people had begun to pool together under the tree and around Rufus's dead body, as one might expect.

As the shock began to wear off, I realized that I didn't hear Baby Stella crying. I pushed my way through the crowd, Owen latched to my hip, trampling over the blanket and the picnic lunch and Rufus' bullet riddled body. Owen clung to me now, wailing loudly, clawing at my skin like he was trying to climb inside me. I pushed and shoved some more, people stared at me, some asked if I needed help, but I ignored them all. I shoved my entire body to get people out of the way and then I saw it. A few yards away, lying on its side was the oak basket.

When I reached it, I heaved with panic. Baby Stella was not in the basket. She was gone.

The authorities arrived quickly and Edwin followed shortly thereafter. My grief was replaced by the horror of knowing that Baby Stella was missing and that there had been a death warrant issued for my son and me. I didn't have time to grieve. I only had time to be scared.

I couldn't help but play the events over and over in my mind. If Rufus had stayed in prison he'd still be alive. Baby Stella would be safe at the Bend house.

The girl who'd shown up on my doorstep half-starved and shoeless had unwittingly set everything in motion. All because she had wanted justice. And why wouldn't she? She hadn't asked for any of this to happen. None of it. She had wanted a world where she would have been loved by the man who first took her and where people didn't kill each other over a black rock buried deep under a mountain.

But still, if Rufus had stayed in jail, he would have been released eight years ago, long after Stokes had relinquished his power, and I could have kept my boy.

So that's the long and short of it. Baby Stella was never found. Some say that the gunmen took her and gave her to Stokes, who did God only knows what with her. He had figured out that the girl was staying with us at the Bend house and that the baby was his and that the girl had planned to testify against him with the other three men. It would have been the end of him. Some say an opportunistic person saw an abandoned baby and in the middle of the chaos snatched it for themselves. There were rumors of wolves and coyotes and panthers, but nobody really believed any of them. Most people believed that whatever happened to her, it was at the hands of Stokes.

On that day that Rufus was killed, I picked up the empty basket that the girl had so lovingly made and took it home. Some speculated that she had never had any plans to return for her baby. She had made the basket as a vessel for her to be safely delivered into the hands of somebody else. Mine. She, had, in effect, handed her over to the people she'd thought she'd be the safest with.

I buried Rufus at a lovely hillside cemetery halfway between here and Charleston. I'd had a line from The Song of Hiawatha engraved on his tombstone. "For they both were solitary, she on earth and he in heaven." So many people showed up. So many miners. His death was having a profound effect on people. There was much unrest among the miners and their families. Owen and I seemed to be the point with which they rallied.

Edwin came to me a few days later and told me that Owen and I would never be safe. He was hysterical and crying. "You must go. Get out of town. Don't come back for a very long time."

"Why? Rufus is dead. His testimony can't hurt Stokes now."

But Edwin insisted. "Vengeance is all that fuels him now. Nothing more. He won't rest until he sees you both dead."

And so I made up my mind. My child would not be used as a pawn. He would not be sacrificed for another man's greed, agenda, hatred. I put him in the car and I drove and drove, and the first major city I came to, I stopped and found the orphanage.

Maybe if I had waited a few weeks, things may have ended differently. Maybe Owen and I might have both ended up dead. I'll never know. But I can't help but think, what if Stokes had changed his mind? I could have returned *home with Owen and lived out our days in the valley in the shadow of the mountains. But I didn't wait. I was hysterical, in shock, trembling. I honestly cannot believe I made the drive. I remember nothing of the trip, that's how insane I'd become.*

Maybe if I hadn't witnessed so many boys sacrificed to Europe, I wouldn't have felt so strongly. I wouldn't have been so sick with fear and disgust at my gorgeous boy being slaughtered to satiate somebody else's hate. Maybe. Maybe. Maybe.

But the point was, I had witnessed it. I had made a vow never to let it happen to mine. And I didn't wait.

As I pulled up to the orphanage, I was struck immobile with grief. All I could see was Rufus's dead and opened eyes staring at the sky. I could run, but for how long? I could hide, but what if they found me? I realized then that I didn't much care if they found me. It was Owen I was worried about.

Would he ever be safe?

What life could I offer him?

I could offer him love. Unconditional love, but it would do no good if he was dead.

It's hard to imagine how much power Stokes and others like him had. They were sort of a mountain version of the mafia. And if he wanted us dead, we'd be dead. I had no doubt.

And so I opened the car door and handed Owen off to a new life. I'd seen all those soldiers' faces while sitting in that car. All of the ones that had passed through my tent. They had been sacrificed to a machine much larger than them. But if given the chance, would their mothers have sent them away to save them?

Owen often stayed with my sisters, so he didn't cry when I handed him over. He simply gazed back at me with a confused expression. I said, "Night-night. Be a good boy."

For days I wanted to die. I drove to the ocean and wanted it to carry me out to sea and smother me in a deep, dark, blanket of water. Resting on the ocean floor with so many others, I'd be oblivious to the world. I didn't eat. I didn't sleep. I simply wandered waiting for the angel of death to come and usher me into the beyond. But it never happened.

After a few days I drove to D.C. where I survived for almost two years. I had not stepped foot in West Virginia or my home town. I had not looked upon the faces of my family for months and months.

And when I finally returned, I found that I could not look at Edwin. I blamed him somehow. If he'd testified in the first place, the tragedy could have all been avoided. But he hadn't. He'd been a coward. And no matter how the logical side of my brain tried to reason with the emotional side—Edwin had been scared, he'd eventually done the right thing—I still could not bring myself to even speak to him. Of course, he had been on the run himself and had only just returned the week before I had.

And the reason we'd returned? Stokes had been killed in another mine related incident in 1928. Of course, it had been too late by then. My boy was somewhere safe with his new life and his new parents who surely adored him, for how could they not?

But it was not lost on me how, if I could have found a way to hold on just for a year or two, my problems would have been over. I can't begin to share what all I did to stay alive for those two years. There were times that I ate lard because there was nothing else to eat. And the only thing that kept me from imploding into a pile of guilt and grief-riddled dust, was the fact that Stokes had never stopped looking for me. On two occasions I had escaped with my life by minutes. I knew I had made the right decision for Owen. But there was no way to let him know that.

I met my husband John about two years after that. We married and had an uneventful life. We helped to raise Blanche's children and I kept right on working at the Bend house. There were times I'd go to Charleston to work at the hospital for a few months, just to earn some extra money, but I always returned to the Bend. I think on some level, I thought, just maybe, Owen would remember the place, and just maybe, he'd come looking for me.

For the record, nobody spoke of him again, except Rosie. She would ask me what happened to him and I'd tell her that he had died. And she would always say, "I loved him so much, Aunt Mildred. As much as a brother." After a few years she finally stopped asking.

The young girl returned and never truly recovered from the loss of Baby Stella. She then married the first man who'd asked her because she was used goods and thought there would be no other offers. And what was to become of her if she wasn't to be somebody's wife? I felt so sorry for her. While my troubles were just as large, I had at least known love. I knew what it was like to have somebody wrap himself around me, hold me like a treasured object. She had never known that. Certainly not with Stokes and not with the man she married.

You could see her sort of fade from that day—the day I'd lost her baby. She retreated farther into herself, carrying that basket with her everywhere, clutching it, stroking it, singing to it, as if that baby was still in there. And of everybody—Rufus who'd given his life, me who'd lost a man and a son, and my son who'd been raised away from his family and spent his whole life looking for us—it was the girl who'd suffered the most. Her guilt over having caused all of it has eaten her alive.

I know how she feels, though. To this day, I still hear Owen cry in the middle of the night.

And then, he showed up in Greenhaven and bought the Renshaw house. Jeb, it would seem, had come full circle. And I now had to answer for my actions. But, he did not hate me, he did not blame me, he did not mistrust me or accuse me. He'd simply opened his arms and forgave me.

And I knew he was truly his father's son.

My Heavy Heart

When my Aunt Mildred had finished talking, my mother was sobbing again, and my cheeks were wet with tears. She had loved her son so much that she would rather he be raised by a total stranger than to even chance that he would be harmed. The fact that within two years he would have been perfectly safe with her seemed to just rub salt in the wound. She'd given up her whole life with him for the sanctuary of two years. But it had kept him alive.

Nobody said anything for the longest time. Even Gunnar seemed to be physically moved, almost stricken. He cleared his throat, finally. "When did Jeb confess to you who he was?"

"I had suspected who he was from the moment I laid eyes on him. He has...had, his father's green eyes and my dark hair. He stopped by one day to speak to Olivia and mentioned his birthday, and I knew for sure it was him. It took everything I had to keep my composure. Finally, I'd turned to walk back to the house and before I reached the porch, the tears were flowing. I locked myself in the house and cried the whole night. He knocked on my door the next morning, offered to help me with something. I don't remember. I brought him in, gave him some coffee and a piece of pie. Before I could tell him that I knew who he was, he said, 'I'm your son.' Simple as that. Three words."

"Did he let on like anything was wrong?" Gunnar asked.

Mildred shook her head.

"Any enemies? Anybody have a grievance against him?"

She hesitated for a second and then said, "Not around here. His ex-wife wasn't too keen on him."

"So, nothing? Everything in his life was wonderful?"

"In fact, yes. He had come home. He'd answered all his questions and faced his demons. He had found the places and faces that had haunted his dreams for so long," she said. Then she looked at me. "And he was looking forward to a life here, getting to know his other family. He loved Olivia almost immediately."

I buried my face in my hands to try and hide the tears, but it didn't work very well.

I wiped my eyes and tried to act as though I was all right. But I seriously doubted that I was ever going to be all right. I understood Jeb's last words to me now, *"Tell her I understand and I forgive."* Gunnar looked over at me and shrugged his shoulders. It had all been for nothing. We'd learned a lot about what had brought Jeb here, but nothing about his murder. But at least that part of the puzzle had been solved.

"I have a few questions," I said. My mother looked dutifully appalled.

"I knew you would," Aunt Mildred said.

"Did the rest of the family know about Jeb? Or just Blanche and Aunt Stella? What about your dad and everybody back here in Greenhaven?"

The Bend was about thirty minutes away from here in a modern car. Back in the day, it could have been a few hours. Nobody had ever spoken of Jeb in my presence, so it made me wonder who knew what.

"Everybody knew," she said. "Although my father had asked that I not come back to Greenhaven until I was married. I was the talk of the town, as you might imagine."

"Did you know who he was when you sent me up there with that chicken?"

She shook her head. "No. When you reported to us that he was from Baltimore, that raised the alarm for me, but I told myself I was being silly. What were the odds? What were the chances he would remember any of it? Enough to track me down? I was just being a silly old lady who wanted to lay eyes on her son one more time before she died. But when I went to church, that first Sunday that he showed up, that's when I first suspected. Once I saw him."

I thought back to that day and realized that she hadn't come up to meet him or introduce herself to him like Runa and Dotie had. I thought nothing of it then, but now it made sense. She was most likely watching from a distance, in a slight panic, thinking, *Could that be him?*

Gunnar seemed defeated. All of this, and he still had no more answers. Just then Edwin came in the back door. "Mildred?" he called out. Gunnar stood then. I assumed he wanted to save Mildred the embarrassment of having to explain why we were there. After all, Edwin knew about Owen, but he didn't know about Jeb. My mother dabbed her eyes and straightened her skirt, ready to leave.

But I had one more question. "Aunt Mildred," I said. "Quickly. Who was the girl? Who was Baby Stella's mother?"

Her eyes flicked over to Gunnar and she said, "Now dear, that's not for me to say."

Something passed between them, and then Gunnar said, "My mother. My mother is Baby Stella's mother. And she was my half-sister," he said. "Is that right, Mildred?"

Mildred nodded, just as Edwin came into the living room. His smiled dropped when he saw all of us. One look would tell you that we weren't a happy lot. "What's going on?" Edwin said.

"Oh," Mildred said. "Rosie and Olivia were going into town and wanted to know if I needed anything. Gunnar just came by to ask me a few questions about Jeb McDowell."

"Why?" Edwin asked, genuinely curious.

"Routine," Gunnar said. "I'm off to talk to Stella and Runa next."

And then he tipped his hat, walked out the door, and left me in total shock. The girl in the story had been his mother!

Letter to Olivia from Aunt Viola

Olivia VanBibber
Greenhaven, West Virginia
16 December 1958

Dearest Olivia,

I've since spoken to Mildred Anne and know that you know the whole story. I was out of the country at the time Rufus entered her life, and then I was off to Ohio with Eckhard shortly thereafter. Your mother was not the only one who was told that Owen had died. That's the story Mildred gave our father and most everybody in Greenhaven. Only her sisters knew the real story, and we kept it secret. None of us ever actually thought they would be reunited. And if he'd not nurtured his imagination and his dreams, they probably wouldn't have been. It was the Bend House and the Criel Mound that did it. Those were his markers. Once he'd found those the rest fell into place.

You mustn't think badly of Mildred, Olivia. She was in an impossible situation. Stokes was a vicious and cruel man, who would have thought nothing of killing her and Jeb both.

I'll not lecture you about snooping into one's private business since Jeb so obviously wanted you to know. On that note, have you finished his book?

My dear, lovely child, my heart aches for you. He meant so much to you and you to him. My heart aches for my sister to lose her son only to find him and lose him again. She'd only just found him! But it's over now. I don't think that you will ever be the same. Obviously not, you will soon be a librarian because of him! But, beyond that, he's touched you forever. But you must move on.

I think that you are a wonderful, bright, and intelligent girl.

I think that Jeb McDowell was an exceptional man trapped in self-doubt, driven to find his origins.

I think that my sister loved her son more than she loved anything else.

I think that you will make a fine librarian.

I think that you should name the library after Jeb.

And I think that you should bake a cake in honor of the estimable Jane Austen's birthday, which is today, which I'm sure you already knew.

Goodnight, my love.

Forever,

Your Aunt Viola

JEB

The first time I laid eyes on the mountains, I nearly wept. They were so green that at times they appeared almost blue. Lush trees and fauna, teaming with wildlife and cold streams and springs meshed together in a harmony so perfect that it nearly stopped me cold. But only for a second. And then a transformation occurred. Mere mountains morphed into mystical, consecrated, hallowed ground, and I was no longer a human being looking at the geological and terrestrial record of Mother Earth. I was somehow enveloped into the fold. Eternal arms wrapped around me and whispered, "You have come home."

And then the mountains breathed. And I stood transfixed. And there were no moments before this one and none that would come after that ever brought me so close to the knowing of it all.

How frightening it was. How frightening and glorious and exciting it was and must have been all those years ago to the first settlers. And how my ancestors must have quaked at the vastness of this frontier. For in between those mountains there were narrow hollows that severed the hills, allowing just enough land for people to make their homes. Intimate channels and grooves of colonies spotted the landscape. Hamlets of people, some who'd never ventured more than fifty miles from where they were born, fighting to survive in this world, and yet, basking in the bounty of those eternal ridges.

The mountains took life. The mountains gave life. The mountains were life.

And in one of those hamlets, bisecting across the land lived my mother.

I knew it now, and I knew her name. I had no idea how she would react to me and so my plan was to just live among my people for a while and test the waters, so to speak. I would be content to admire her from afar. I'd be content to be a part of her life and all of their lives as a misguided stranger on a quest to find the perfect writing sanctuary. My evacuation of the real world for the development of the imaginative one would take place on Sassafras Mountain, anonymously among them. If it took years to confess to her, so be it. If I never confronted her, so be it. I would just be.

But I had to wonder how much I looked like my father. Would she recognize me? I'd found a photograph of him in a few newspapers but they were always fuzzy, distant pictures and I couldn't really get an idea of what he looked like. The most I could make out was that I did have his chin. Would she recognize me by a chin alone? I didn't think so and didn't care.

To my surprise, the family came to me, almost immediately. I'd underestimated the mountain folk's mistrust of strangers, and so they sent a scout to ferret out just what I was doing among their community that had been mostly unchanged, except for a few television and radio antennas, for a hundred years. She was the perfect ambassador. A girl of eighteen with large eyes so dark that no light escaped them. She was intelligent, calm, watchful, defensive, loyal to her people, self-aware, opinionated, and in love with the written word. She was also completely unaware of her own qualities, as she'd been told for years what would be her life. She'd taken the attitude of what was the point in cultivating anything aside from that? She was also a cripple, struck down with polio at a tender age. But make no mistake, her experiences in the hospital were what made her unique. That was where she learned to be a consummate marksman with a bow and arrow. That's where she fell in love with literature. That's where she learned to survive and to give her opinions freely. That's where life came into focus.

Some people spent their whole life never coming into focus. But not her.

She was the first relative that I would meet, my first cousin once removed. I would learn much later that her mother, my first cousin, was one of the few relatives that I'd had daily contact with as a toddler. I suppose what I'm trying to say is if it were not for that girl ambassador, I may never have confronted my mother. I may never have gained acceptance to an otherwise closed community. But, make no mistake, she knew that I was not who I was, and I deceived her. She saw through me, but loved me anyway.

A Small Confession

Having read through most of the night, I put the book down. It was impossible to read through tears, anyway, and I figured I should turn off the light since Bessie had a towel wrapped around her head because my lamp was keeping her awake. Wolfe and Ernest both sleeping next to my bed, raised their heads when I changed positions. They were just checking to make sure I was all right and didn't need them. I realized why I didn't want to finish Jeb's book. It wasn't just because our long conversation would be over, it was because I had been apprehensive about learning who his mother was and how their story ended. Apprehensive is too light of a word. In truth, I'd been terrified. Terrified more of whether or not the reconciliation had gone well, more than who she turned out to be, because the thoughts of Jeb being rejected was more than I could take. But Aunt Mildred had already told me her story, and I now knew that he was not rejected, so I thought that finishing the book would be easier.

But then, all those kind words about me. To think I meant that much to him. I suppose I could take offense at the "opinionated" and "defensive" remarks, but I wouldn't, because they were true.

I wondered if Bessie would accidently strangle herself in the middle of the night if I didn't wake her up to remove the towel around her head. But then realized she'd be fighting mad if I woke her up, even if it was to save her life, so decided against it. I turned off the light and drifted off to dreamless sleep.

Gunnar Ryan
Colton County Sheriff's Department

Gunnar had finally found Andrew and Mosie. The two had been living on the run pretty much since Jeb had been murdered. It was not uncommon for Mosie to go off into the woods and not be seen for months, but for Andrew to disappear was a bit more suspicious. Especially since his wife was pregnant, though it wasn't as if history was devoid of jerks who abandoned pregnant women.

Apparently, Andrew had returned home and, while he was sleeping, his wife had tiptoed to a neighbor's house and told them to call the sheriff's department. An honest woman. Something hadn't felt right to her and she acted on it. She had set aside all thoughts of herself to do the right thing. What would she do without a husband? Without his income? She could be in serious trouble if Andrew went to jail for any length of time. But, she'd made the call anyway. It made Gunnar want to kiss her.

He had been spending most of his spare time trying to find Andrew and Mosie. He'd turned over every squatter's camp, trampled through every abandoned home in the county, but to no avail. He'd realized that they had most likely been holed up in another county without the help of others. Because it was always the "others" that screwed up an otherwise perfect plan.

His hands shook and his fingers tingled as he made his way through the department to the interrogation room. He would start with Mosie first. He wasn't sure why his hands shook, other than he was strung tighter than rope. The incident with his father still had him jumping at all sudden moves and loud noises. And the ordeal with Mildred had been emotionally exhausting. What she'd been through was devastating, and the ripples were still being felt...It boggled his mind.

And then of course, there'd been the revelation of the girl in the story and just what that basket had represented to his mother. What had happened to his half-sister?

He couldn't think of that because it made him want to hurt somebody. Specifically his father, but that ship had sailed already. James Ryan couldn't even get out of bed from the damage Gunnar had done to him. Gunnar had tried to take him to the hospital in Charleston, but his father had refused. When Gunnar thought of his father breaking that basket, the expression on his mother's face...well, he was better off not thinking about it.

Mosie Gibbons was not nearly as ancient as he looked. When Gunnar entered the room, Mosie looked up and quickly glanced away. "Hello, Mosie," Gunnar said. "You may not remember me, but I'm Deputy Gunnar Ryan of the Colton County Sheriff's Department."

Mosie said nothing. His face was deeply marked with the passage of time, the whites of his eyes yellowed and his lips cracked and dry from lack of proper hydration and nutrition. His hands seemed overly large for his body, but Gunnar attributed that to the fact that he was fairly thin. He had thick nail beds with cracked skin along the curves of his fingers, and the pink of his palms was unnaturally bright compared to the black of his skin.

"You are Mosie Gibbons, right?" Gunnar asked, even though he knew who he was. He just wanted Mosie to acknowledge it.

"Yessa." His voice was deep, multi-timbered.

"Now, I know all about the money you took from Mr. McDowell."

Mosie shook his head negative. "No suh, not me."

"Yes sir, it was you. I was the one hiding in the tree that night and saw you and Andrew Holbrook taking the money from the outhouse and running into the woods."

Silence.

"Not to mention I've got several people who have made statements that it was you and Andrew. Harvey Grose, Humpy VanBibber."

Still nothing.

"I'll tell you what, Mosie. This type of crime, well, it can carry a really high price. Lots of jail time."

With that Mosie's eyes flickered to Gunnar's. Mosie didn't care if prison offered three meals a day and a roof over his head. He was too wild to be kept enclosed. He'd go crazy. He'd rather fight for his survival and be free.

"I could get that reduced if you'd help me."

"Wif what?"

"With who murdered Mr. McDowell. Because, you know, a jury just might think it was you who killed him. He came outside, interrupted your thievery and all."

"No. Wasn't me. I didn't kill him."

Gunnar shrugged. "I don't necessarily think that you did, but others do. A jury might. You know what a jury is, Mosie?"

He shook his head.

"That's who passes judgment on you. You get arrested. Then you go to trial."

"I didn't kill him."

"Do you know who did?"

Nothing. Not even a blink of his eyes.

Gunnar knew Mosie didn't kill Jeb. He didn't have it in him. Gunnar had his suspicions as to who killed Jeb. For the first time in two months he actually felt like he knew exactly who killed Jeb. He just had no idea why. And the not knowing why made him doubt his suspicions. He was looking for any shred of evidence that would say, *Yes, you're right. You do know what you're doing.*

"Was it Andrew?"

He shrugged. "Not while I's around, he didn't."

"You guys spend a lot of time together over the last two months?"

"Always. Drew's not the smartest," he said. This made Gunnar laugh. "But he ain't mean. He never talked about killing nobody. Not to me."

"Humpy? You know Humpy?"

He nodded his head, yes, he knew him.

"He talk about killing Jeb?"

"Not dat I knowed of."

"Harvey Grose?"

He nodded his head again. Then shrugged. "How's I supposed to know what these men capable of?"

Gunnar thought about his question and realized that most people wouldn't know if a casual acquaintance was capable of murder. "Okay, the night Jeb was killed. Were you out that night?"

"What night was that?"

Gunnar doubted that Mosie had a calendar and knew what any given day was. "The night of the storm. Took out that willow tree."

"Yeah, I's out dat night."

"And what did you see?"

His gazed darted down to his hands quickly.

"Mosie, this is important."

"Humpy, goin' into the outhouse. I gots a camp up there on the top of the mountain, behind where dat feller moved in. Couldn't go to it too much, cause I's afraid you be watching it."

Which was true. Gunnar had been watching it, but he was only one man and couldn't watch it around the clock. "But this night was different?"

"I knowed it was supposed to storm and I wanted to get my things. Drew and I had a couple hidin' places and the one had a roof. He told me he drive me over there, but he wasn't goin' up the mountain with his car. He didn't want to wake Jeb. So, he parked down at the road and I ran up to get my stuff. I gots tools, ya know. On my way back I saw Humpy goin' in the outhouse."

"That's it? Did he go into the house?"

"No."

"And the dogs?"

He shrugged. "Didn't see or heared them."

"Nobody else?"

He shook his head.

"Did you mention seeing Humpy to Andrew?"

"No."

"Why?" Gunnar asked.

He shrugged. "Didn't seem important. Humpy do strange things sometimes, ya know?"

Gunnar looked at Mosie long and hard. He saw no deception there, but that didn't mean anything. Interesting, though, that he'd seen Humpy that night because Humpy had seen somebody, too. Had he seen Mosie? Had they seen each other? That was a depressing thought, because he'd really been hoping that one of them had seen the killer coming and going.

"So?" Mosie asked.

"So, what?"

"I answered your questions. Truthful like. What happens to me?"

"Well, I've got to talk to Andrew first. See what his side of things are. I'm gonna let you rest in lock up for a while."

Gunnar realized then that their tiny jail had three cells and all three prisoners had stolen money from Jeb. Humpy was in one, Andrew in one and Mosie in the other.

"Can I aks you a question?"

"Of course," Gunnar said.

"Why dat man keep all dat money in the outhouse?"

Gunnar smiled. "It wasn't his. He came upon it accidentally and he was afraid to keep it in his house, because he didn't want to get caught with it. He was just trying to figure out what to do with it, Mosie. But, he had a book to finish writing. After he finished his book, then he didn't care if he went off to jail for a while. He was just keeping it until he could finish his book. Then he would have turned it in. I'm sure of it."

Mosie Gibbons shook his head. "He was a right unusual fella."

"Yes," Gunnar said. "Yes, he was."

After he escorted Mosie out of the interrogation room, he had Boland bring in Andrew Holbrook and deposit him in the chair that Mosie had just vacated.

Andrew Holbrook was a skinny, wiry sort, with brown hair that stuck out in every direction, even when he had a comb. He wore newer clothes, a plaid shirt and some denim pants, but his shoes were still scruffy and holey. He had a five o'clock shadow and he fidgeted. A lot. But he met Gunnar's gaze with a defiance that said he wasn't quite scared enough.

Gunnar studied him for a minute, rocking back and forth in his chair. He pointed his fingers like a steeple and peered over them, trying to make Andrew look away. Eventually, it worked. Now Gunnar could start asking questions.

"I know you took Mr. McDowell's money," he said. Andrew started to protest and Gunnar held up a hand. "I get it. Your wife's expecting. You're only working half the time. Still, it wasn't yours to take. So, I'm prepared to testify for you at your hearing that you're an otherwise good man and you were just trying to provide for your wife and baby. That's right? Isn't it?"

He nodded. "Absolutely. I bought the baby a crib and a blanket. Got my wife some new shoes. She ain't had no new shoes in years. I bought her two pair!"

Gunnar was pretty sure a lot of that money went right into the Charity of Andrew Holbrook, but he wasn't going to make him defensive by suggesting it. "That must have felt good to buy your wife new shoes."

"Yes."

"So, the night of the storm, the night Jeb McDowell was murdered…"

"I didn't kill him!" Andrew interrupted. "Neither did Mosie, so you just go be gettin' that outta yer head."

"Well, see, I got a big problem here, Andrew. I need some information from you if I'm to speak well at your trial. I've got a man brutally murdered. I've got you at the base of the mountain, Mosie up on top of the mountain and Humpy in the outhouse, and not a one of you saw a thing except each other."

Andrew was silent.

"There was a lot of traffic on that mountain that night."

"Cause that damn fool put that money in the outhouse. 'Course he did try moving it around on us. He was getting suspicious. But then he put it back in the outhouse. Made me think he was tellin' us to take what we wanted."

Gunnar thought about that for a moment and wouldn't put it past Jeb. He could almost hear Jeb saying how much more the people in the valley needed that money than him or Clarence Ford. Maybe that's what he was doing. He complained of a prowler at first, then stopped. Why? Was it because he'd seen the poverty in the valley and just decided to let Andrew and Mosie have their fill until it was time to turn it over to Clarence? Maybe he was willing to just tell Clarence that the money had been stolen again. With Jeb, any scenario would hold weight.

"I need you to think, Andrew. While you were waiting in the truck for Mosie to come down off the mountain, did you see anybody? A car? Anything."

Andrew fidgeted some more and then closed his eyes and took a deep breath. "It was a frightful storm. Rainin' all over the place. Lightnin' and thunderin' to beat the band. One of those last big hurrahs that happen before winter sets in. I was pulled off the side of the road with the lights out. There were a few cars that went by. I found that strange, bein' it was the middle of the night and stormin'. One of them was Arnie Pickins. I recognized the car. He probably had to stay late repairin' somebody else's car. He does that now and again. The other one I didn't know. Mosie went up the mountain and a little bit later somebody come walking down it."

Gunnar sat forward. "Who was it?"

Andrew shrugged his shoulders. "It was raining and it was dark."

"Was it Humpy VanBibber?"

"No," he said.

"Was it a male or a female?"

"Male."

"Old? Young?"

"Couldn't tell."

"Were they drunk? Stumbling around?"

"No. I done told you it wasn't Humpy."

So there was another person. Humpy had seen somebody that wasn't Andrew or Mosie and Mosie had seen somebody who wasn't Humpy, and now...Andrew backed that up. A fourth person. A fourth male.

"They was limping, though."

Gunnar sat stony-faced and frozen to his chair.

"Limping?"

"Yeah, I remember they was limping. They headed off toward Wellston."

And Gunnar knew he had been right.

***

Gunnar braced himself as he took the last step on Mildred McCutcheon's front porch. He noticed with trepidation that Olivia's quiver and bow were next to the step which meant she was here. Gunnar didn't want to do this in front of Olivia. But maybe it was just as well.

He knocked, hat in hand, head down. Olivia answered the door. Her face lit up when she saw him and then her expression fell almost immediately. Instinctively, she knew he was not there for her, or for a friendly visit. "Olivia, is your Aunt Mildred home?"

Olivia's brow furrowed and there was a slight nod of her head. Then she backed up and let him in.

Mildred came in from the kitchen, wiping her wet hands on her apron. Flour from whatever she was baking was smeared on her elbows and chin. "What can I do for you, Deputy?" She was curt, which he'd expected. Old-timers didn't like to air their dirty laundry in front of others and she'd most likely be formal and awkward with him for some time.

"I'm looking for Edwin."

She glanced at Olivia.

"What for?" she asked.

"I need to speak to him and he's not at home. Neighbors say he hasn't been home in a day or two."

"Well, whatever do you need him for that it can't wait until he comes back?"

"I just need to speak to him."

Olivia glanced between the two of them. Her hair was down long, as if she'd just been brushing it. In fact, the rubber band that once held her thick head of dark hair was cutting into her wrist. He'd interrupted a casual moment in their lives and it was something they'd remember forever. What were you doing when Gunnar knocked on the door? *Aunt Mildred was baking a pie and I was brushing my hair,* he imagined she would say.

"I...uh..." Olivia said. "I just came down to kill some rabbit for Aunt Mildred. I should probably go."

That explained her quiver on the front porch. "No, you should stay," Gunnar said.

"No, I really think I should go," Olivia said.

Why? Why would she be so quick to leave? If she sensed that this was official business, surely she'd stay to be with her elderly aunt. The only thing he could think of was that there was something she didn't want to be a part of. She was either insisting on leaving because she wanted to warn him that there was something wrong, or because she truly wanted no part of what was getting ready to happen. It was most likely a combination of both.

"Mildred," he said.

She didn't move. She stood stock-still with only the pulse in her throat to betray any stress.

"Is Edwin here?" he asked.

"Why? What do you need him for?"

And then Olivia burst out, "Yes, he's here."

Gunnar instinctively raised his right hand to hover over his gun that was snuggled on his hip.

"Get out!" Mildred said. "You've got no right! Out of my house!"

"Aunt Mildred!" Olivia cried. "He's an officer of the law. You can't speak to him like that."

"Don't tell me what to do!" Mildred shrieked. "He has no idea what's he's doing!"

"Aunt Mildred, calm down," Olivia said.

Gunnar could barely hear what they were saying now, because all he could do was focus on the fact that Edwin was there. *Where* exactly was Edwin? Was he hiding? Was he on the back porch? Was he high-tailing it down the meadow at this very moment?

He pulled his gun then, and began looking in the rooms leading off of the living room.

"Get out of my house!" Mildred screamed at him. "I'm calling the sheriff."

"Great, you do that," Gunnar said.

Bedroom number one was all clear.

Just as he came back into the living room, Clive came through the front door saying, "Livvy, Mom sent me down to pick you up. You wanna grab a burger in town? I'm starving."

And then he stopped dead in his tracks as he took in the scene of Gunnar, weapon drawn, looking behind doors and under sofas, Mildred in a state of hysterics and Olivia trying desperately to stay calm. "What in the hell?" Clive asked.

"Gunnar's looking for Edwin," Olivia said.

"What for?" Clive asked.

There was a silence so loud that it made Gunnar's ears roar. Olivia leveled a gaze at Clive. "He's looking for Edwin. For a reason," she said. Even she couldn't say it out loud, it would seem. She could not seem to say, "Gunnar is here to arrest Edwin for the murder of Jeb McDowell," even though Gunnar knew she knew.

Understanding dawned on Clive as his mouth made a perfect "o" and his eyebrows shot up.

That was the last thing Gunnar really noticed because at that moment, Edwin shot out of the pantry in the kitchen and out the backdoor. Gunnar followed tripping over the legs on the kitchen chair and knocking over the trash can, and chased Edwin onto the back porch. He should have known that Edwin would do something sneaky. He was an old man with a bum knee. There was no way he could outrun Gunnar, and Edwin was well aware of it. And so when Gunnar stepped out onto the porch, a broom handle whacked across the front of his ankles and Gunnar went down with a thud.

Searing pain flowered across his shin bones and the last thing he remembered was looking up, and seeing Edwin's half-crazed face and the bottom end of a flower pot just as it smashed into his forehead.

Confrontation

My heart was in my throat. What was going on? Gunnar thought that Edwin had murdered Jeb? What motive could Edwin possibly have? How...? Why...? No matter how hard I tried, my mind could not wrap around the accusation. It simply made no sense.

Until Edwin jumped out of the pantry and took off running. Nothing made a person look guiltier than running away!

Aunt Mildred stood in the living room with her hands raised to her face. I glanced over at Clive who was moving toward me. "Where are you going?"

"To see if Gunnar needs any help!" Clive answered.

"Don't you leave me here!" I cried. But he was already gone.

I pushed myself past Mildred into the kitchen and shoved the chair out of the way. I wheeled over the trash that had been strewn across the floor and headed to the back porch. Gunnar lay on his back, broken pot in pieces, dirt all over his face and uniform and a giant knot forming on his forehead. I glanced up the valley and saw Edwin, running along the bank of the creek as best he could.

"Clive, get me off of this porch and then go around front and get my quiver and bow."

"What?"

"Just do it!"

Clive turned me around, got me onto the lawn and then ran back through the house, reappearing in a matter of moments. Aunt Mildred had followed him out this time, screaming. "Where are you going with that bow, Clive?"

Clive handed it to me and I said, "Push as fast you can until I tell you to stop."

Edwin had thirty yards on us at least, and we weren't going to gain much speed considering my chair magnified every dip, hole and bump. But Clive pushed and I held on. "Edwin!" I called out. "Edwin stop! Don't make me shoot you!"

"Olivia," Clive said. "You can't shoot him! He's running away! You cannot shoot a man in the back."

"Why not? Doesn't that mean he's a coward?"

"This is crazy! You cannot shoot a man just because he's a coward!"

"Let go of my chair."

"What?"

"Let go!" I yelled.

I had no intentions of killing Edwin. But I also had no intentions of letting him get away. If he really did kill Jeb, he was going to pay for his crime.

"You don't even know if he's guilty!" Clive cried out.

"This way, we'll get to find out."

I raised my bow, nocked my arrow, focused. *Breathe, Olivia. Breathe. Steady.* I let the arrow fly, felt the whoosh of it as it flew past my hand and hit Edwin in the calf of his left leg. That was exactly where I had been aiming. He fell to the ground immediately. I started to push myself over to him, then felt Clive pushing. "This is insane," he said. "I cannot believe what you just did. Can't believe it. Oh. My. God."

When we arrived by Edwin's side, he was rolling around on the ground moaning and screaming in pain. My arrow was still sticking out of his leg. "Did you kill him?" I asked. I didn't even recognize my own voice. It was cold and steely. I didn't want it to be true, but I was pretty sure it was. If it wasn't true, I was going to be in a heap of trouble, and still might be even if it were. "Did you kill him?"

"You shot me, you...crazy..."

I pulled my bow up and nocked another arrow. This time I aimed for his head. "Did you do it?"

His hands flew up instinctively. "Yes! All right, yes, all right, I killed him."

"Oh, shit," Clive said from behind me.

I raised my head to the sky and cried out. The scream tore from me so hard, ripping my throat until I could taste blood. I felt Clive's hands take my bow and arrow from me, which was probably a smart move. Now my head hung, hair whipping my face in the wind. Tears dripped from the end of my nose and ran off my chin. All I could see was Jeb's face and all the blood and him gasping for his last breaths, and tried to make sense of the fact that Edwin, somebody I'd known all my life, friendly Edwin, had killed him. "You...why, Edwin?" I said sobbing. *"Why?"*

"B...because he knew."

"Knew what? That Mildred was his mother? You killed him for *that?*"

He was trembling now and anger boiled in me. He didn't have the right to feel sorry for himself. He didn't have the right to be scared. "I'm the reason Rufus Peebles is dead. I sold him out. I wanted him dead because...because..."

"Because I loved him," Mildred said from behind me. I didn't know how much she heard or when she had arrived, but she stood utterly still.

"Yes," Edwin said. "I loved you so much, Mildred. I have loved you since the day I met you. I told Stokes where Rufus was staying. I told him how you were meeting him that day in the park. I gave evidence to get him out of jail, just so Stokes could kill him. It wasn't 'cause I found a conscience."

Mildred began to sob and then her whole body seemed to collapse like an accordion, and she fell to the ground.

"Somehow, Jeb knew," Edwin said. "Oh, Mildred, don't cry. Please."

"How did Jeb know?" I asked.

"I don't know," he said. "But he said he'd been investigatin' the murder for a long time. He told me he knew I sold his father out. He told me I should do right by Mildred and leave her be. The gall of him telling me what to do!"

Mildred's cries became more and more out of control, more guttural, more animal. Clive went to her, down on his knees, and cradled her in his arms. "Shh," he said. "Aunt Mildred, shh. It'll be all right."

"You bastard," I said to Edwin. "She gave up her son because Rufus had been murdered. Her son!"

Edwin began to cry then. "I didn't mean for that to happen. That was never part of it. I thought she'd just hide for a while and then we'd get together. I'd raise Owen as my own. I never thought..."

My chest hurt so badly I sounded like a wounded elk trying to breathe. I glanced over at Aunt Mildred being rocked by my brother and I thought, *she'll die. This will kill her. She will never recover.* Jeb was gone because Edwin had been a selfish rat. Even at sixty-eight, he could not live with the shadow of my Aunt Mildred's one true love, Rufus.

Just then I heard Gunnar running up behind us. "Olivia?" he said skittering to a halt beside me and holding his head. "Are you all right?"

"I suppose," I said.

"Are you or aren't you?"

"I'm fine," I said. "I'm perfectly fine."

It looked like a ghost had flittered across Gunnar's face when I said those words. It occurred to me that he wasn't unscathed by Edwin's actions either. Baby Stella, his half-sister, had been abducted or murdered on that horrible day. That day that would have never happened if Edwin could have just been a man instead of a child.

"He admitted he killed Jeb. Jeb knew that Edwin plotted Rufus' murder."

Gunnar just stood there for a second, staring down at Edwin and his injured leg. "You shot him?"

"Well, you were taking a nap," I said. "Didn't want him to get away."

Gunnar leaned down and put handcuffs on Edwin, while Aunt Mildred had dissolved into hiccups and shock.

"How did you know it was him?" I asked.

"The marks in the blood next to Jeb's body. Edwin's leg brace had made an imprint in it from where he'd kneeled to stab him. A witness said he'd seen a man limping away from Sassafras Mountain the night Jeb was murdered. Those two things combined with his close connection to Mildred...I just knew. I just didn't know why."

"Isn't that sort of backward? Don't police usually figure out the why and then the who?"

"There's not always a script, Livvy," he said. He hauled Edwin up onto his feet and led him back toward Mildred's house, limping with both legs now and bleeding from one.

"Clive," I said. "Would you take Mildred back to the house and call my mother. Wait until my mom gets here, then come back and get me?"

"Of course," he said. He stood then and raised Aunt Mildred with him, and I was struck by how they both looked like frail little birds. One beyond wounded at the turn of events, the other traumatized by seeing his aunt so distraught.

I sat alone in the cold with the bare trees and the icy water babbling across the rocks. I was as numb and as cold as that stream. I looked up at the mountains on the other side of the creek, brown and gray with winter's leaden filter. That was one more family tragedy they'd witnessed. One more.

I glanced back up the valley at my Aunt Mildred's house and Aunt Runa's just across the way. They would never look the same to me again. Nothing would ever look the same to me again. Jeb had changed all of it in one way or another. He'd brought color and brazen joy to our little hamlet. And now with his murder, it seemed dark and bleak. In some odd way, I felt as though his whole existence had been accidental. Like he was not supposed to be, but was, and so he wreaked absolute divine madness on all our lives. The boy who was surrendered. The boy who was found. The boy who dissolved into memory.

JEB

All of my trespasses I have made out of stupidity. I am not a mean person, nor a vindictive person. But there are days that I wonder how I survived on so little wits. This collection of words that I've put together is nothing more than a very long confession. A confession to myself, both mothers, my son, and my ambassador.

I've lived through the murder of my father, the abandonment of my mother, the strange and often alien world of my childhood, war, and women. And none of those are as bad as my own stupidity. All of those things seem to pile onto each other, like the layers of the quilt, each individually a thing, but put together a whole different and new thing. And my stupidity is the thread that binds them all together.

At times I think that stupidity is really nothing more than the deliberate decision to not know. I know what people are capable of. I choose not to see it. Not to worry about it. If I choose to believe the good in them, maybe the good will worm its way out. If bad things come to me because I believe this way, so be it. At least I won't be an accomplice to hate.

And the first time I laid eyes on my mother, not a photograph, but in the flesh—my heart all but stopped. She'd been at church that very first day. And afterward she'd been talking at the end of the porch. I heard somebody call her name and I looked up to search for her face. This was the moment I'd waited for my whole life. Here, standing on the porch of the white clapboard country church that my mother had been baptized in as a baby, was the culmination of all my searching. She looked at me and held my gaze, not the least bit shy or awkward or fearful. She held my gaze and seemed to say, "I see you. Do you see me?" And I knew at that moment it didn't matter if we ever spoke. I was content to just be in her presence.

I'd gone back to my conversation feeling whole and centered. A convergence of then and now swam throughout my body. I could finally answer the big question: Who Am I?

Well, I am a man who used to be a boy who was loved so much by his mother that she'd given him to another to be loved. And that boy loved his new mother and his new family and it was their love for him that allowed him to be safe in his existence. They were the water in which he floated, waiting to be plucked by self-awareness onto the rocky shores of the real world. I am a man who took solace in books and words, always hoping to create himself from the shadowy recesses of his memory. And I am the man who succeeded at just that.

I am me. And I no longer need to know.

Unfinished Business

Christmas came with a dark nebula of grief centered over our valley. My mother went about her business, baking and preparing for our Christmas meal, but I did not participate. Clive and I were both despondent, to say the least, and so we exchanged small gifts—Clive pretended very much to love his blue twirly scarf that I made him—but decided our day would be better spent helping others. For the past two weeks, we'd collected money outside of the courthouse. At Christmas, we bought a ton of food and hopped in the car to take it to the squatter's camp on Dutch Bottom.

Both of us were in a state of shock, more or less, over Edwin's confession, as were all of my aunts. It was almost as bad as the week that Jeb had died. Aunt Stella couldn't even speak when she'd heard the news about Edwin. She and Aunt Runa and Aunt Dotie had all rallied around my Aunt Mildred, offering comfort and warmth and safety, but not one of them said anything. They all just sat with her for days. My mother cried for a week.

It seemed as though everybody had trouble finding words. Like grief had just sucked them up before we could even think them. Clive and I would just sit in quiet, which is why the fundraising had been such a good idea. It got our minds off of things for a while. Gunnar had not been by since he made the arrest that day. Part of me was angry because I thought we were friends now. Part of me said I shouldn't be angry. I shouldn't have expected anything else from him.

As Clive and I drove down the road a ways we came to the fork in the road that led up Sassafras Mountain. We would never be able to pass this road without slowing down, looking, thinking of what could have been. And as we came around the bend we saw something we weren't expecting. It was Gunnar. He had cut up the debris from the willow tree and was digging a hole.

"What's he doing?" I asked.

"Looks like he's going to plant something," Clive said.

"In the winter?"

Clive shrugged. "Maybe he's just getting it ready for the spring."

As Clive drove on, I could not look away. Gunnar glanced up, waved a hand and I just stared until we made the turn and I could no longer see him.

I got my answer as to what he was doing a few hours later.

Clive and I had returned home from the squatter's camp and were enjoying a cup of cocoa to warm us up. There was one piece of pecan pie that had not been eaten. "One piece of pie," I said and smiled at Clive.

He made some motion like he didn't really want it, but I knew he did. I turned the pan around and pushed it toward him. "You can have it." He smiled and began eating. In the other room I heard my brother making some noise about not being able to find his favorite shirt. He'd come home after a few weeks in jail. He had played a part in Jeb's death, after all, only unwittingly. Edwin had given him twenty dollars and told him to pick a fight with Jeb, which Humpy had done without question. The fact that Jeb was so beat-up was part of what helped Edwin to overcome him. Humpy had been unable to meet my eyes and that made me happy. It showed that he knew what he'd done and it meant that he was ashamed of it. That was a beginning.

There was a knock at the door and my mother went to get it. Immediately she bristled. It was Gunnar. I think my family was going to have that reaction to him for a while. "Is Olivia here?" he asked.

My mother hesitated and then, "Livvy!"

I rolled into the living room to find Gunnar, red cheeked from the cold, standing in the doorway in a Norwegian-type sweater. His mother had probably made it for him, as it looked an awful lot like the one she'd been making for her other son, Kevin. "I was wondering if you'd like to go for a drive?" he asked.

I was somewhat taken aback. I hadn't seen or heard from him in two weeks. "Uh..."

"Well, if you're busy," he said and turned to leave.

"She'd love to," Clive said from behind me.

Gunnar looked over at Clive and then to me.

"She'd love to go, wouldn't you Livvy?" Clive said again.

"Well, okay," I said.

"Wear something warm," Gunnar said.

I quickly added some layers while Clive entertained Gunnar with the stories of Christmas giving to the poor. As I came back into the room, I heard him say, "One lady, she cried and cried because we gave her a pound of oats. Gets you right here."

"Okay," I said. "I'm ready."

Once we were in the car I realized how much I wished that Clive had come along, because my tongue seemed to be tied and my hands could not find a comfortable position to rest. "Where are we going?"

"I want to show you two things," he said.

I just loved those answers that weren't really answers.

"What were you doing with the willow tree this morning?"

"Cleaning up the mess. Dug a hole. I'm going to plant a willow tree there this spring."

"Why? It's...it's not even your property."

"As long as the dead one litters the area, we'll always think of Jeb's death. I don't want to think of Jeb's death. I want to think of his life. So, I'm going to plant a tree there."

"Oh," I said, moved by his thoughtfulness.

"And I have it on good authority that it was a favorite tree of a lot of the residents around here."

I glanced over at him, but his gaze never left the road.

We drove in silence for a minute. Then we came to Wellston. He made a turn and a few more turns and finally he came to a stone building that was for sale. He parked, got my wheel chair out of the back and then took me up the stairs. "I talked to Jeb's lawyer," he said. "There's a board of bigwigs that are going to oversee a lot of the library stuff."

I giggled.

"You like my legal jargon, do you?" he said, smiling. "But you have the power to veto anything. They want to buy this building for the library, Olivia. I think it's a good choice. It's big inside, with tall ceilings. They can always hire work to be done on it, you know, building shelves and offices and what not."

I wasn't sure what the old building had been used for. But it was all one story with big windows in the front. It had been empty as long as I could remember. Gunnar pushed my chair around the back. "The best part is this right here."

"What is it?"

"This was the old sheriff's building. Right back here, there's this area that can be turned into an apartment. For you. Because how else are you going to get to work every day if you live out there on that mountain?"

I hadn't thought of that. I studied the building. It was sound and large and not unattractive. "I'm going to call it the Peebles-McDowell library."

"So, you like it?"

"I love it. Can I get a quote carved into the side?"

"You can do pretty much anything you want with it," he said, smiling down at me. "What do you want to have inscribed?"

"When a little Girl, I had a friend, who taught me Immortality—but venturing too near, himself—he never returned."

He looked at me for a second and then had to glance away. "That's perfect," he said. "Who said it?"

"It's Emily Dickinson."

"Well," he said with a sigh. "I think you should get the ball rolling on Monday."

"I will," I said. "Now that...all of it's over. I can really focus on this."

"You're going to make a wonderful librarian."

"Thanks. So, what's the other thing you want to show me?"

About thirty minutes later, Gunnar pulled off the road on top of a mountain. "We can't go any further by car," he said.

"Well, then...how...?"

"Don't be angry."

"You do realize that anytime anybody starts a sentence with 'don't be angry' there's usually a reason to be angry," I said.

"I talked to Clive and, well..." He reached into the backseat and pulled out the papoose contraption that Willie Gene used to carry me into the woods when we went hunting. "I know it's awfully presumptuous of me and terribly forward. But I really want to show you something. Before I have to show it to everybody else. And I don't know of any other way to do it, unless I just carried you the whole way, which could be a little tricky because then I couldn't use my hands."

I was silent for a second. My mind raced and yet it didn't seem to form a coherent thought at all. What was he doing? Clearly he wanted me to see this. Witness something. But why? Why me? I was just a girl with broken legs, the future librarian...

Tear down those walls, I heard Jeb say.

"I, well, I understand," Gunnar said. "It was just a thought. I...I should have asked you first, I guess."

"Yes," I said.

"W-what?"

"Sure, show me whatever it is you want to show me."

"Are you sure?" he said. A smile played across his face, and pink crept into his cheeks.

"Yes," I said. "Just don't drop me."

"I won't drop you. But, how do I work this thing?" he asked.

"You have to let me get into it first. Then you pull it up on your back and fasten it around you."

"Okay," he said.

"It's not easy," I said.

"I'm strong," he assured me. "And you're little. And we're not going far."

We got out of the car and within about ten or fifteen minutes, Gunnar had me safely secured on his back. And then he trekked into the woods. About another fifteen minutes later we came to an overlook and he turned around so that I could see the view. "My Grandpa used to bring me up here when I was a boy."

"It's beautiful," I said.

"You should see it in the spring."

Then he kept on moving, his feet never once slipping or darting. He knew exactly where he was going, which went a long way toward alleviating some of my anxiety. By the time he reached his destination, he was huffing and puffing and the straps were starting to hurt my groin. On one hand I was terrified he was going to lose his balance and tumble down the mountain with me. On the other hand, I was far too excited to see what he wanted to show me to let my fear win.

There was a cliff facing with a lot of growth all over it. "In the summer," he said. "It's impossible to see this, unless you know it's here. In the winter, it's a little easier."

I heard him moving brush and branches and dead ivy vines. "Okay, I'm going to turn around so you can see it."

"Wait," I said. "You need a rest. Get me off your back and set me down for a minute."

"No, I'm good," he said. "Going down will be much easier. Besides, there's really nowhere to set you."

He turned around then and I saw, carved on the rock facing, a figure. A stick figure of a man, a figure of what was an elk or a deer, and the weeping eye motif. It was a petroglyph made by the ancient peoples who used to live here centuries ago.

"Do you see it?" he asked.

"Yes," I said. "Who made it?"

"Adena culture, possibly? I'm not sure. As far as I know, nobody knows about it. Nobody except me and now you."

I stared at the petroglyph for longest time. Thousands of years had passed since this was carved. At that distant point in the past, somebody had stood right here, in this spot, and felt the need to express himself. He'd felt the need to leave a record of his thoughts on that day. I guess in some ways, that's what we all do. We try to leave a record. We try to say, hey, we were here and this is what we loved.

Later, after we'd come down the mountain and driven back to my house, Gunnar took me up the stairs on my porch. All the way home he'd talked about the ancient peoples and the ancient ways and the significance of the petroglyphs and how he knew he had to tell somebody about them eventually. We didn't talk about murder. Or Jeb or suspects and clues. Or Humpy. We simply talked like normal people. And that gave me hope. Because if we could talk when there wasn't something forcing us to talk, then we really could be friends. A new addition to my realm of human beings.

"Thank you, Gunnar," I said. "For sharing that with me."

"Thanks for trusting me enough to get you up there and back."

"I won't lie. There were moments I was afraid for my life," I said, laughing.

We were quiet a moment and he began walking away, down the steps, and then he turned back toward me. "And thanks for the other night. Here on the porch."

I nodded. Then he got into his car and drove away, down into the valley where my aunties lived. Into the folds of the mountains.

About the Author

Rett MacPherson is the author of eleven Torie O'Shea books, pioneering the popular sub-genre of genealogical mysteries. In addition to writing, Rett is a bead and fabric artist and loves all kinds of fabric, laces, buttons, and beads. She loves to be outdoors and she likes to run, even though she's slow and has to ice her knees afterward. In addition to reading—sometimes reading as many as fifty books a year—she also loves genealogy and is descended from a long line of English lords, Irish rascals, Scottish highlanders, Viking marauders, and French vintners and horse breeders. If time-travel were possible, she'd like to visit all of her direct ancestors. She's obsessed with British television and loves almost all music. She lives in St. Louis with her family, where she can often be found practicing yoga...unless she's at the winery.

Word Posse Fun Fact

My first significant writing experience, aside from making up fake news reports and then dragging the TV tray into the living room and reading the "news" to whomever would listen, would have to have been when I was twelve years old and had gone to see *Star Wars*. I came home wanting to play in that universe, so I decided to write a sequel. I suppose you'd call that fan-fiction, but I did add some new characters (primarily a little sister for Princess Leia who just happened to be twelve), and new planets, and it was significantly different from *The Empire Strikes Back*. Princess Leia's little sister, Lana, destroyed Darth Vader, but not before delivering one of the best "you are scum" speeches ever written. I loved having control of the ending and to this day have difficulty watching a television series if I think it's going to end differently from how I think it should end. After all that time invested, I want a decent resolution.

Made in the USA
San Bernardino, CA
20 January 2015